Praise for the Kris Longknife novels

"A whopping good read . . . Fast-paced, exciting, nicely detailed, with some innovative touches."
—Elizabeth Moon, author of *Engaging the Enemy*

"A fast-paced adventure." —*Booklist*

"Enthralling . . . fast-paced . . . A well-crafted space opera with an engaging hero . . . I'd like to read more." —*SFRevu*

"Everyone who has read *Kris Longknife* will hope for further adventures starring this brave, independent, and intrepid heroine. Mike Shepherd has written an action-packed, exciting space opera that starts at light speed and just keeps getting better. This is outer space military science fiction at its adventurous best." —*Midwest Book Review*

"I'm looking forward to her next adventure."
—*Philadelphia Press Review*

"[Shepherd] has a good sense of pace . . . Very neatly handled and served with a twist of wry. A surprisingly talented read from a very underrated author." —*Bewildering Stories*

"Shepherd does a really good job with this book. If you're looking for an entertaining space opera with some colorful characters, this is your book. Shepherd grew up Navy and he does an excellent job of showing the complex demands and duties of an officer. I look forward to the next in the series." —*Books 'n' Bytes*

"You don't have to be a military sci-fi enthusiast to appreciate the thrill-a-minute plot and engaging characterization."
—*Romantic Times*

P9-DNE-385

Kris Longknife
RESOLUTE

Mike Shepherd

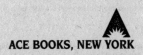

ACE BOOKS, NEW YORK

THE BERKLEY PUBLISHING GROUP
Published by the Penguin Group
Penguin Group (USA) Inc.
375 Hudson Street, New York, New York 10014, USA
Penguin Group (Canada), 90 Eglinton Avenue East, Suite 700, Toronto, Ontario M4P 2Y3, Canada
(a division of Pearson Penguin Canada Inc.)
Penguin Books Ltd., 80 Strand, London WC2R 0RL, England
Penguin Group Ireland, 25 St. Stephen's Green, Dublin 2, Ireland
(a division of Penguin Books Ltd.)
Penguin Group (Australia), 250 Camberwell Road, Camberwell, Victoria 3124, Australia
(a division of Pearson Australia Group Pty. Ltd.)
Penguin Books India Pvt. Ltd., 11 Community Centre, Panchsheel Park, New Delhi—110 017, India
Penguin Group (NZ), Cnr. Airborne and Rosedale Roads, Albany, Auckland 1310, New Zealand
(a division of Pearson New Zealand Ltd.)
Penguin Books (South Africa) (Pty.) Ltd., 24 Sturdee Avenue, Rosebank, Johannesburg 2196,
South Africa

Penguin Books Ltd., Registered Offices: 80 Strand, London WC2R 0RL, England

This is a work of fiction. Names, characters, places, and incidents either are the product of the author's imagination or are used fictitiously, and any resemblance to actual persons, living or dead, business establishments, events, or locales is entirely coincidental. The publisher does not have any control over and does not assume any responsibility for author or third-party websites or their content.

KRIS LONGKNIFE: RESOLUTE

An Ace Book / published by arrangement with the author

PRINTING HISTORY
Ace mass-market edition / November 2006

Copyright © 2006 by Mike Moscoe.
Cover art by Scott Grimando.
Cover design by Rita Frangie.
Interior text design by Kristin del Rosario

ISBN: 0-441-01453-4

ACE
Ace Books are published by The Berkley Publishing Group,
a division of Penguin Group (USA) Inc.,
375 Hudson Street, New York, New York 10014.
ACE and the "A" design are trademarks belonging to Penguin Group (USA) Inc.

PRINTED IN THE UNITED STATES OF AMERICA

10 9 8 7 6 5 4 3 2 1

Lieutenant Kris Longknife's footsteps echoed off the walls of the space station. Kris had expected High Chance to be bustling with business. Instead it looked like a tin can, rinsed and ready to be dumped in the nearest recycle bin.

There was no sign of a welcoming committee from her new command . . . Naval District 41. No sign of anything . . . alive.

"They told me it was an independent command," Kris half whispered to herself.

"Did they mention it was solitary?" came from behind her.

Kris turned. Lieutenant Penny Pasley-Lien had been very quiet on the trip out to Chance. Penny was recently a bride and only slightly more recently a widow. Kris measured Penny's words for joke or serious, and found them balanced on a knife edge.

"At least there's no sign of an attack," said First Lieutenant Jack Montoya, in full battle armor—and paranoia mode. Now of the Royal United Sentient Marines, Jack formally had been in Wardhaven's Secret Service. The exact circumstances of his change in service were something Kris did not want to think about.

His uniformed presence at her elbow served as a too-present reminder that even though Great-grampa Trouble was well over a hundred years old, he was still very much trouble. Jack's M-6 assault rifle tracked his eyes as he surveyed the empty station. "No sign of anything," the suddenly-a-Marine concluded.

Kris had had enough of this blind man's . . . or woman's . . . bluff. "Nelly, *please* access the station's security system."

Nelly was Kris's pet computer. A half kilo of self-organizing circuits wrapped around Kris's shoulders. Since the last upgrade, Nelly was plugged daintily and directly into Kris's brain. She was also worth about half of what this station cost. Maybe more, since this station looked much worse for its lack of occupation.

"Kris, I can't," came back, almost plaintively.

"And why can't you?" Kris demanded.

"'Cause somebody turned this station off at the switch," Chief Beni answered as Nelly got out a more accurate explanation that boiled down to the same. Nelly actually sounded huffy as she finished well after Beni.

This confirmed a growing suspicion that Kris's electronic tech whiz Beni and electronic tech miracle Nelly were developing a sibling rivalry. *Just what I need.*

But she'd needed Beni's technical wizardry for the last three months during her Training Command assignments. And she'd need him even more at Naval District 41. From the looks of things . . . or lack of things . . . she couldn't afford to lose anyone.

And life without Nelly was unthinkable.

As Kris was learning to do of late, she sidestepped the thornier problem and faced the immediate one. "So where is this switch?"

"That way," both the chief and Nelly said. The chief was a bit slow to point since Jack had him in full space armor. Nelly flashed a light at the alley beside The Dragon Queen's Chinese Take Out among the midstation shops.

Like everything else, it was boarded up.

Kris led her crew from the station's Deck 1 with its usual gray carpets and unusual decorations. Just about every square inch of wall was a painting. The station looked like an art museum. Or maybe art studio. The paintings ran the full breadth of art history from primitive to Impressionistic. Kris's mother might have bought some.

Even the dim alley Kris led her three associates into looked like an artist's day at the zoo.

It was hard to think of Jack as her subordinate for reasons that were becoming clearer every time the Marine first lieutenant gave *her* an order. And she'd learned at OCS *never* to consider a chief as anything less than God. Beni had weakened his case for divinity by failing to locate that bomb on Tristan and just barely spotting the one on Kaylia in time. Still, Kris was none the worse for the two assassination attempts, but she was definitely persona non grata in Training Command.

Hopefully, Naval District 41 would go better.

The elevator was in a blandly gray space that still stank of garbage. Jack looked like he wanted to test-ride it, but Kris got to the button first, punched it open, and led right in. She took position at the back, daring Jack to haul her out.

Jack eyed her for a second like he wanted to toss her over his shoulder and lug her back to *Pride of St. Petersburg*. He apparently thought better of it as Beni punched Three. Nelly announced the command deck was on three. They took off, Penny standing quietly in her own corner, seeming so much smaller than the beaming woman who said "I do" to Tommy such a short time ago.

The ride progressed in fits and starts, with I-told-you-so glares from one Royal marine. Kris stared at the ceiling, something she was getting very good at, until the elevator bumped to a stop.

The doors hung up halfway open.

Kris leaned over to peer around two male heads eyeballing a large open space dimly lit by one flickering light. Passageways headed off in various directions, some poorly lit. Others dark. Everything was painted a standard Navy gray.

Except for a splotch on the far wall.

"Looks like blood," the Marine lieutenant snapped. "Beni, why don't you have your weapon out?"

"Yes, sir," the chief said, drawing his service automatic.

"You Navy types keep back," Jack said to the senior officers present who were craning to get a look over his shoulder.

"Beni, cover me," and the Marine slipped through the door in full-assault mode.

Since his OCS had been abbreviated to just a Gunny Sergeant showing him how to wear the uniform without embarrassing the rest of the Corps, the Secret Service must have included SWAT drills in Jack's earlier training. The guy did look deadly and determined.

Kris figured now might be a good time to pay attention to his concerns. She pulled an automatic from the small of her back. It looked standard Navy issue. But she was one-of-those-damn-Longknifes. Its magazine held three times the normal load of 4-mm darts.

Penny drew her own automatic, identical to Kris's. It had been a wedding gift, one of several Kris hoped would make Penny and Tom's life around her safer if not saner. Silly Kris, she hadn't wrapped a single gift for blowing up a battleship.

Kris swallowed survivor's guilt for the forty-eleventh time.

Penny had not taken her eyes off the stain as she checked the safety on her automatic. "You sure that's not rust?"

"Navy, I told you to keep your heads down," Jack bit back as he tried to check every direction at once. His M-6 snapping from one hallway to another as he tried to check every direction at once.

Chief Beni wiggled his growing gut through the stuck door. Training Command chow had been very good to him. He did keep his automatic at the ready . . . sort of. He frowned at the wall and its mottling. Ignoring the Marine, he sauntered over to it, dipped his pinky in the offending matter, smelled it, tasted it, and then looked up.

"Yep. It's just water and some rust."

"It kind of looked like that," Penny said, her voice half-distracted. "Tommy would have been able to tell at a glance. He was good at things like that."

Kris reached over to rest a gentle hand on Penny's shoulder. "Yes, he was."

"Well, thank all the gods in space it was just a bit of poor maintenance," Jack muttered at full volume. "You can come out, Lieutenant, Your Highness, Commandership. I hope you keep not needing the Security Chief you so eminently ignore."

If Kris followed every instruction, order, or bit of advice

Jack was authorized to give her and that she was required by regulation to obey, she'd never set foot outside her bedroom at Nuu House on Wardhaven. Some Naval career that would be.

But then, both Grampa Trouble and Grampa Ray, his Royal Kingship included, had known she'd keep right on ignoring half of Jack's orders. Only now he got to nanny her through every square centimeter of space. And she'd been gulled into drafting him into his new authority over her. *Grampa Trouble, you are so trouble. And Grampa Ray, you're not much better.*

Pulling herself up to a full six feet of regal majesty, automatic still at high port, and dredging the Imperial "we" up for impact, Kris smiled. "We appreciate your concern and rest assured that you will continue to spare no effort for the safety of our high and august person."

Jack snarled, teeth showing, but he limited his response to drumming his fingers on the barrel of his weapon in silent frustration. He'd been doing a lot of that lately.

"That's the door to the Command Center," the chief and Nelly said at close enough to the same time that only a computer could have told who spoke first. Kris was not about to ask Nelly which one had.

Computers were supposed to be scrupulously honest, but Kris wouldn't bet an Earth dollar that Nelly still qualified for that virtue. Not where the chief was concerned.

As Jack took station to the left of the not airtight door, he motioned the chief to the right. With his free hand, he waved Kris and Penny to spread out. Kris gave some thought to the two bombs in the last three months and decided standing behind Jack and his wide, armored shoulders might be a good idea. She sidestepped to there; Penny stood behind the chief.

"Open it, Chief."

Beni screwed up his face in a "Why me" complaint, courage not being one of his obvious virtues, but then did it. The hinges complained but the door opened better than partway before it screeched to a stop. The room inside was dark.

Rolling his eyes to the ceiling as if he might find a reason why such valiant effort was suddenly becoming his portion in life, the electronics wizard felt around inside the door with his right hand, keeping most of his body outside. With a click, flickering illumination lit up the space.

Kris edged out from behind Jack to get a better view. There wasn't much to see: silent workstations, overhead lights struggling to come on. Some succeeded. Others gave up and settled for dark.

"No boom," Penny said, giving voice to all their thoughts.

"Chief, put those bells and whistles of yours to use for something besides paper weights," Jack snapped. "Tell me something I don't already know about that room."

Kris might be in dress whites for the change of command ceremony that seemed to be very much delayed, but she hadn't been totally lacking in survival instincts. Rigged in her hat, indeed in every hat she now owned, were antennas that should let Nelly take the measure of every electron within several miles around her more active than those in a glass of water. NELLY, TALK TO ME.

THE ONLY ACTIVES IN THERE ARE FROM SEVENTEEN OVER-HEAD LIGHTS. NO, SIXTEEN, formed in Kris's brain a full second faster than Chief Beni got the same words out. "Nothing ticking. Nothing tocking, Your Marineship," the chief added.

Beni had never been what the Navy called "spit and polish." His time in Training Command, bouncing from planet to planet with Kris and her team of hooligan Navy mosquito boats had not been a good influence on him. Clearly, Kris needed to have a counseling session with the young chief soonest. Either that or promote him to officer and have some old chief square him away.

Since the newly minted Marine officer ignored the chief's last remark and began a slow, cautious entrance into the Command Center, Kris assigned the chief's future counseling and/or promotion a low priority and returned to the problem at hand.

Where *was* her new command?

Jack and the chief did a quick search of the center. Kris and Penny, their automatics pointed at a nondescript overhead that didn't dare move, kept an eye on the wavering shadows in the several hallways leading off from the elevator. It was spooky, but the shadows stayed empty.

"I got something," the chief announced.

"What is it?" three voices asked.

"A letter."

"A letter?" Kris said.

"Yeah. On flimsy."

"Is it booby-trapped?" Jack demanded.

"No strings attached, and nothing but the minimum static charge to keep the letters on the page, sir. It's just a memo, addressed to the next CO. And it's laid out, each page, side by side, so you don't even have to pick it up to read it."

"What's it say?" Kris said, ducking her head inside.

"Ma'am, I think you better read this yourself," the chief said, sounding, if anything, bashful.

Kris raised an eyebrow to Penny. If there was a dirty joke in human space that Beni would balk at sharing in mixed company, they hadn't heard it. What would make the young man unwilling to read them this message intended for Naval District 41's next Commanding Officer?

Kris stepped into the empty command center. *Her* command center. The air was stale like the rest of the station. No low hum of blowers. No human sweat. This was supposed to be the command center for several par secs of human space. It stood vacant, defending nothing.

Maybe five years ago, when the Society of Humanity's writ still held sway in human inhabited space, a planet might take such a risk. Not now. Not in today's worlds of battleship diplomacy. Someone was taking a huge gamble with their future.

Jack wasn't gambling with Kris's personal safety. Like a good Secret Service agent, he backed into a corner that gave him a view of all three entrances to the command center. It had seemed like such a good idea when Grampa Trouble suggested maybe Kris could use a Chief of Security on her new command.

She'd readily agreed. Too readily, it seemed. Only after the paperwork was cut and a fuming Jack was decked out in dress red-and-blues and sporting a single silver bar of a first lieutenant, one very significant promotion below Kris, did he show up suddenly smiling. It seems that Grampa Trouble had taken him aside and walked him through the new regulations that came into play when a member of the royal blood was a serving member of the military.

As if there was more than one of Kris.

And suddenly Kris discovered that the chief of her security

detail, no matter what his rank, could issue *her* orders. Tell her what she *could* and *could not* do!

It had been a rough trip out. It looked to be a rough command as well.

And that was before the skipper of the *St. Pete* commed Kris and told her that High Chance was only responding with automatics. No human voice. Nothing but the basics.

Beni and Nelly's scans showed only the most fundamental activity on the station. Solar cells feed battery back-ups and not much more. No reactor on-line. Just about nothing.

The skipper of the *St. Pete* balked at docking at High Chance under those circumstances, but Kris pointed out the contract he'd signed for her transportation. He *could* dock, therefore he *would* dock or face the legal assault an angry Longknife could throw at his company. Fuming, he brought his ship alongside the station, and, to his surprise, the automatics clicked into gear and hauled it in. The last thing Kris heard as she crossed the gangplank was that the *St. Pete* was even drawing reaction mass from the stations' tanks. And being charged for it. Some things were working. Some things always worked if you paid for them.

Like BuPers. Navy personnel always got assignments. Probably not the one they wanted, but, what with the fleet growing, there were always plenty of vacancies to go around. Unless your father happened to be the Prime Minister and your Great-grandfather was the king, of sorts, of the hundred-planet association that Wardhaven tried to lead.

"And don't forget that situation on the *Typhoon*," General Mac McMorrison had reminded her at their last meeting.

Situation. What a nice ambiguous word. It avoided the more specific and nasty word . . . *mutiny*. Kris had actually taken a friend's half-joking suggestion and hired a PR firm to come up with a better word for what developed on the *Typhoon*. Several large checks later, their report had been hardly worth a laugh. Probably because Kris hadn't felt all that much like laughing after the Battle of Wardhaven and the loss of so many friends. No, the *Typhoon* and mutiny were going to be tied closely with her first year in the Navy.

"Still having problems finding skippers willing to take me?"

"Afraid so. Commodore Mandanti put in a good word after

your service in Squadron 8, but most of his friends are retired, like he was. And even his good word kind of leaves skippers wondering when you'll decide you've had enough of being a good subordinate and head off for points unknown."

Kris shrugged. "Training Command was working so well."

"But no planet small enough to need Fast Patrol boats for its defense can afford the kind of security you need. And no one wants to be the planet that has to explain to Ray Longknife . . . or Billy . . . that you got killed on their watch. Sorry, Your Highness, but once again, we need to find work for you."

"What's Sandy Santiago doing?" Kris said, with hope.

"You mean Captain Santiago," Mac corrected her. "I've got her straightening up some of the mess left behind by that little visit those six pirate battleships did on us."

"Pirate battleships my eye," Kris spat.

"You want to attack the Greenfeld Confederacy?"

"No," Kris admitted. Wardhaven's United Sentients and Greenfeld's Confederacy were too evenly matched; open war between them would lead to all kinds of horrors. Which was why Greenfeld dearly wanted Wardhaven in a fight with someone while Greenfeld added this or that additional star to its black and red flag. Meanwhile, they skirmished around the edges.

"So Captain Santiago doesn't have a ship command at the moment," Kris said. As a very junior lieutenant, Kris very much wanted to stay in the fleet, not get tagged as a staff weenie.

Mac shuffled flimsies, one of which was Kris's resignation. They never had one of these counseling sessions without him having her resignation handy. "You adamant about a ship assignment? What would you think of an independent command?"

"Didn't you tell me during an earlier one of these chats that lieutenants don't get independent commands?"

"I may have been mistaken. It happens occasionally, even to folks with stars on their shoulders. Ask your gramps."

This was after Grampa Trouble pulled his "draft Jack" stunt and Kris wasn't talking to either one of her grampas just then. She kept her face blank and said, "What kind of independent command can a lieutenant have?"

"How about a Naval District?"

Kris frowned at the joke. "Aren't those slots all Rear Admirals?" Kris struggled to keep her voice even. Lieutenants do not chide four stars. Even when the lieutenant is a princess. Especially when the lieutenant is a princess.

"That's what I'd have said a week ago. But BuPers got this retirement chit from a lieutenant commanding Naval District 41."

Kris didn't know which to react to first. Lieutenant. Commanding. Naval District 41. She'd never heard of any such Naval District. She settled her face to bland and let Mac play this one the way he wanted to. After all, he did wear four stars. He ought to have some fun sometimes.

"It seems we inherited 41 when Society broke up. Earth hadn't been paying much attention to it, except to cut its budget every year. I don't think they've had anything but local reservists on the staff, except for this lieutenant commanding."

"How did a lieutenant get command of a Naval district?" Kris couldn't sit on that question any longer.

"Actually, he was temporary acting. A captain assigned to Naval District 41 died in transit." Mac shuffled his flimsies. "Next one wrangled a better assignment. They never got around to assigning anyone else, so this fellow put in his twenty and filed for retirement." Mac looked up. "With us."

"Retiring at twenty as a lieutenant?" Kris whispered.

"Says here he wants to run a chicken farm full-time."

"You're thinking of sticking me out there for my twenty?"

Mac shuffled her resignation to the top of his stack again.

"Cut my orders," Kris said.

"Besides First Lieutenant Montoya, do you want anyone else?"

"Lieutenant Pasley-Lien on Intel."

"She's still not fully recovered from her wounds," the general said, raising an eyebrow. The physical wounds were healing. The mental pay for being alive at the cost of her bridegroom's life would be a long time balancing.

"She did fine in Training Command. She needs work more than anything else." And Longknifes take care of those they break.

The general nodded.

"Does Captain Santiago want Beni back?"

"Actually, she was hoping you could make a sailor out of him. Any progress there?"

"Not much, but he is due for his chief's hat."

"A bit early, isn't it," the general said, and danged if he didn't have another flimsy to check.

"Deep selection, but he deserves it."

And so Kris found herself hundreds of light-years away from home, clicking the safety back on her automatic before she holstered it and staring down at a set of flimsies written to her by a man she'd never met but whose fate in life she might repeat.

To: Prospective Commanding Officer, Naval District 41
From: Commanding Officer, Naval District 41, retiring.
Subject: Change of Command Ceremony

There ain't going to be one.

Sorry about that, but I had to do what I had to do while I could still do it. The reservists have served with me for a whole lot more hours than any of them ever expected to. They deserve the retirements I signed them in to.

And they don't deserve to be dragged all over space to fit into whatever plans you Longknifes may have for them now that you've noticed that they're here. Wardhaven and Earth ignored us for as long as it suited you. So now that you noticed us after I applied for my retirement, I figured I better look after my own. Bet nobody expected me, a mere lieutenant to exercise the full authority of a Naval District Commander? Got you there.

NELLY, CAN I APPROVE THE REQUEST FOR RESERVISTS TO RETIRE?

PER EXISTING REGULATIONS, YOU MAY APPROVE RETIREMENT REQUESTS FOR ANY ENLISTED RESERVE PERSONNEL WHO HAVE MET THE STATUTORY REQUIREMENTS. AT LEAST, A NAVAL DISTRICT COMMANDER CAN, Nelly added.

But who'd have expected a lieutenant to do that. Well, you leave a lieutenant in an admiral's job for fifteen years and he's bound to notice options the usual JO wouldn't.

AND HE IS RETIRED NOW. IT IS NOT LIKE WE CAN DO SOMETHING TO HIM.

There were snickers from behind Kris. Chief Beni and Penny were looking over her shoulder. Jack looked about to bust a gut wondering what the message said that was causing such humor, but he manfully stood his watch.

"There won't be a change of command," Kris said for Jack's benefit. "Seems the last CO also retired all his reservists."

"No active duty?" Jack said, frowning.

"Not a one," the chief chortled.

"At ease," Kris growled.

Jack blinked, taking it all in, then shook his head. "You can't command if there's no one to command," he said with much the same absoluteness that a child might say, "One and one is two."

"I am the commander of Naval District 41," Kris said, letting that Longknife determination salt the words.

"It may get a bit lonely," Penny said, glancing around, then settling into a chair at the table.

Kris wasn't going to wait for any more nay saying. "Chief, activate this station. Let's see what we have here."

"All of it? I don't think the solar arrays can."

"If the chief will throw that main switch," Nelly said, "I have developed a plan to activate the security system and other key subsets so we can determine if the station is safe."

With a scowl at Kris's neckline, Chief Beni went where Nelly said, threw a switch, punched some buttons, and started doing his own version of waking up the station.

"Don't activate the central power station," Nelly said.

"We have to," Beni shot back.

"Nelly, Chief, you two take it over there and argue among yourselves," Kris ordered. "Penny, Jack, verify that we are alone on this station and it is safe and stable."

"I have verified that you should be getting right back on that ship that brought you and leaving this station," Jack snapped. "We are what, two, three jumps from Peterwald space since they took down the government on Brenner Pass. Kris, this is not a safe station for you. Not like this."

But Penny backed her chair away from the table, spun in it

and started initializing a workstation, bringing it up as a security monitor. It gave her a quick report of ALL CLEAR. She then took it through a slower and more specific survey, ending with her eyeballing several locations around the station. "Everything looks as good as a place can be that's been powered down for the last, ah, three weeks, at least."

Jack looked over Penny's shoulder for a minute, doing his own check, lips going tighter as the moments passed. "Yes, yes, if you aren't bothered by a security system that doesn't ask you for any password when you wake it up," he growled, then turned to Kris. "So, it doesn't look like there are some hungry cannibals hiding out, waiting to roast you for dinner. Still, Kris, ah, Princess, you can't mean to leave yourself hanging out here for any passing ship to take a shot at."

Jack had a point. A good one, as his usually were. But like most of his good points, it was not what Kris wanted to hear.

She gave him her best optimist smile. "Isn't there an old Navy tradition that says 'Don't give up the ship?' "

"This is a space station," Chief Beni said, helpfully, from where he and Nelly were still arguing how much juice they could pull. "Maybe it doesn't count."

Kris eyed the young chief. His lower chin . . . and middle one, too . . . was quivering. He'd proven he could be plenty courageous when all hell was busting loose. He just didn't believe in going there if he could avoid it.

Kris settled into a chair at the table. Nice simulated wood. Solid. Wide. Jack couldn't get at her without giving plenty of warning. She let the silence fill up. Penny was the first to notice it. She spun her chair around and returned to the table. Chief Beni and Nelly reached some sort of accord, and fell silent. The chief came to the table. Kris actually felt a more concentrated presence of Nelly in her head and on her shoulders. Jack finally double-checked the safety on his assault rifle, laid it on the table, and settled into a chair beside Penny.

"Well, Your Highness, it appears that you want to hold a staff meeting," he said. "Is it to seek advice or, as usual, to let us know what mess you're getting us into next?"

"The usual," Kris said with the best perky smile she could manufacture at the moment. Jack didn't look fooled. He kept drumming his fingers on his rifle.

"Look, we've got a Naval District to defend," Kris said.

"Does it need defending?" Penny asked.

That gave Kris pause. "Of course. How can you say that?"

"Well, just look at it," Penny said, slowly turning her chair from one side to the other. The Intel officer was mostly quiet these days. Withdrawn. But she wasn't any dumber than she'd been when she said yes to Tommy's proposal. "The place has been sitting here unattended and getting along fine. It's been ignored by Earth and Wardhaven since forever, and no one bothered it." Penny shrugged. "I mean, Kris, if you want to have the command, I'm all for sticking with you, but, defend this place. Aren't you getting a little carried away?"

Kris sat back in her chair. No, Penny wasn't dumb . . . and she'd seen straight to where Kris lived. But she hadn't totally read Kris's mind.

Or Nelly's. JUST LET US FIND OUT WHAT LIES BEHIND MY NEW JUMP POINTS, the computer said, AND WE SHALL SEE WHO IS INTERESTED IN CHANCE.

YES, GIRL, BUT WE CAN'T GO CHECKING OUT ALIENS RIGHT NOW.

YES MA'AM, Nelly said obediently. Sort of.

Kris made sure her conversation with Nelly didn't reach her face. Slowly she eyed Jack and Chief Beni. They looked pretty much in agreement with Penny. That was the problem when you worked with people you let become close friends. They knew when you were pulling the wool over your own eyes even before you did.

Kris really did want her own command. Even if it was just quiet Naval District 41. She let her breath out in a sigh. "Okay, let's start over. Naval District 41 doesn't look like much, but it's mine, see. All mine. I'd like to see what I can do with it. That honest enough?"

"And if a half dozen Iteeche destroyers come loping through the local jump point . . . ?" Jack said.

"We head dirtside, rouse the locals to guerrilla warfare, and hide in the deepest caves we can find," Kris said.

"I can drink to that," the chief said, raising an imaginary mug of brew.

Jack shook his head. "I don't like it, Kris," he said for the millionth time.

"You're not paid to like it, Jack," Kris answered for the millionth and first time.

"So we're going to just sit here and play target?"

"No," Kris cut in, letting her Longknife grin out to play. "I have no intention of just sitting anywhere. We've got buoys to tend, places to explore."

YOU BET, Nelly said with as much of a playful grin as a computer was allowed. I WANT TO SEE WHERE THOSE NEW JUMP POINTS LEAD.

DOWN, GIRL. ALL IN DUE TIME.

"You don't have a ship, Kris," Penny pointed out. "Not really. You don't intend to use that cruiser for anything but show, do you?"

Kris had gotten a good look at the *Patton*, an Iteeche Wars era light cruiser, tied up to the station when the *St. Pete* was on approach. Her orders were not to commission the ship except for a major emergency. Her orders didn't define what was a major emergency, but after a quick glance at the report on the old cruiser, Kris was pretty sure she'd have to be very desperate to even try to get the reactors going for that old bucket of bolts. The contractors who brought it out had slept in space suits . . . something about not trusting the ship to keep its pressure up. They'd been only too glad to be quit of the ship. They'd spent the trip out identifying discrepancies, not looking for them, just listing the ones that slapped them in the face. Kris ran the list and quit when it went past four hundred thousand.

Some brilliant type at headquarters had come up with the idea that the people on planets might feel safer in these uncertain times if they had a warship in their sky. Maybe other planets got something better, but clearly Chance had drawn the bottom of the barrel. No, the *Patton* was not a likely means of transportation for Kris.

Besides, Kris didn't need a full-fledged cruiser to check the Jump Point buoys and do the looking around she had in mind. No, something much smaller would fit her needs very nicely.

"We need a buoy tender. Nice little one."

Penny shook her head. "I don't think Naval District 41 is funded for a buoy tender, even part-time. My record check showed it hasn't had one pass through for the last five years, then I quit looking. No way will the Navy assign one to us."

Kris grinned at Penny. "So we don't ask the Navy for one. Ever leased a boat before?"

The Intel officer relaxed into her chair. "That's a relief. For a moment, I was afraid you wanted me to hijack one."

"She'd never do that," Jack said, face dead serious. "If there's a ship to be stolen, she'll do it herself."

Kris shot Jack a glare but he just grinned back at her. Kris returned her attention to the Navy lieutenant. "All we need is a small merchant vessel with a hold large enough for a half dozen spare buoys. Obviously, it needs to be jump capable. Bigger than our PFs, smaller than a corvette like the *Typhoon.*"

Penny was nodding, but a frown was growing. "And you want me to lease it. With what?"

"Nelly, arrange a line of credit on my account."

Penny shook her head. "Kris, didn't you learn anything from all the flack you got from the Navy for using your personal computer for official business. Just because they've given up telling you that you can't have Nelly do this or that . . ."

"I should hope so," Nelly cut in.

"But renting your own ship for Navy business . . ."

"So we don't tell them and it won't bother them."

"What they don't know won't hurt us," Jack sighed.

"You're catching on," Kris said.

"*Lorna Do* is the next port of call for the *St. Pete*?" Penny said, getting lost in thought. "I guess I could rent something."

"A six-month wet lease," Kris advised. "Include a crew. From the looks of things, we're going to need one."

"For buoy tending," Penny said.

"And other duties as I may assign," Kris added.

"Don't tell them a Longknife is involved or no one will take the contract," Jack added dryly.

"You really think so," Penny said, then seemed to think better of it and nodded. "Yeah, you're right. I don't think I'll mention who I'm working with."

"You going to send her alone," Jack said, softly.

Kris didn't need the hint. Left all on her own, Kris wasn't sure Penny would survive a long trip. "I'll send Abby along to make sure no one hassles you," Kris said. "I won't need her to gussy me up for balls. Things ought to be pretty quiet here."

"Things *are* pretty quiet here," the chief pointed out.

"Wonder how long that will last?" Penny said.

"At least five or ten minutes," Jack said.

"Folks, this is a backwater. Nothing ever happens at Chance. That's why they gave me Naval District 41."

"Yeah. Right," came from Kris's three nominal subordinates.

Kris watched on the station's screen as the *Pride of St. Petersburg* boosted out of orbit. Abby had been hired by Kris's mother to be a personal maid but she hadn't complained about being sent off with Penny. Kris was no longer surprised by anything Abby did. Or didn't do.

"I wonder how many steamer trunks she's got with her this trip?" Jack asked no one in particular.

"She brought twelve aboard," Kris said. "I was looking forward to seeing how many she rolled off the *St. Pete*." For some strange reason, Abby always had a better idea of how much trouble Kris was headed into. The number of steamer trunks following Abby rather regularly . . . and accurately . . . foretold how many rabbits Kris would need to pull out of hats to get free of whatever mess she ended up in.

Kris kept telling herself she needed to have a talk with Abby, but somehow the time was never quite right for such a sit-down. Maybe, if Naval District 41 was as quiet as claimed, she and Abby could finally have that heart-to-heart girl talk.

Kris turned away from the screen, rubbed her hands together, and smiled, an optimistic little thing that she rarely got to use. "Let's see what we have here."

Six hours later, she kind of wished she hadn't.

She started with the *Patton*. Or those parts of the ship not closed off with doors marked Do Not Open. Low Pressure Beyond. That eliminated a major chunk of the ship from review.

On the bridge, Kris could only shake her head. "I was very glad to see the *Patton* and the rest of Scout Squadron 54 show up at Paris when they did. The reserve crew's work to get her moving must have been nothing short of heroic."

"The *Patton* helped you?" Jack was one of the few people cleared to know exactly what happened when the Wardhaven and Earth fleets gathered at the Paris system to sign the de-evolution agreement that formally dissolved the Society of Humanity . . . and why they didn't go to war over it. Kris's part in that was still much debated by those in the know.

"Yep, it turned out Grampa Trouble served on the *Patton*, a long time ago. He and Great-grandma Ruth honeymooned on it."

Jack raised an eyebrow. "Must have been in better shape."

"Not as Grampa tells it. They were attacked by pirates once. The skipper ordered a broadside and the ship did loop the loops instead. A system board had been installed backward."

Jack shook his head. "Well, it doesn't look any better now. Your orders frock you up to commander if you commission her." He arched an eyebrow.

Does he really think I'm that rank happy?

"I think I'll live longer if I stay a lieutenant."

"Finally, something we can agree on."

Nelly wanted Kris to power up the sensors on the boat, see if Kris could locate the putative extra jump point out of the system that the data on Nelly's bit of rock from the Santa Maria mountains seemed to show. Most of the navigation instruments had red flags draped on them. Out of Order.

GUESS WE'LL HAVE TO TAKE THAT LOOK ANOTHER TIME.

Nelly wasn't buying that answer. BUT DOES IT MEAN OUT OF ORDER OR JUST THAT THEY WERE PICKING UP MY JUMP POINT AND DIDN'T KNOW HOW TO READ IT?

DOWN, GIRL. THE SHIP HAS NO POWER. THE STATION'S BARELY ON. YOUR TIME IS COMING. PATIENCE MY DEAR.

PATIENCE MY NONEXISTENT ASS! Was Nelly's unladylike response.

Kris found herself biting her lip to control a laugh.

"Want to let me in on the joke?" Jack asked.

"No, just me and my insubordinate computer. Nelly is not behaving." Jack accepted the explanation with visible doubt.

The rest of the station was shipshape and empty. Kris checked an auto gun. It was locked down locally, ammunition belts removed. If she wanted to defend this station, she'd need them reactivated. And people to monitor their fire. The station had close-in defense lasers. Kris didn't have the juice to power any of them up. So long as the station was on solar cells, it could operate. To become a going concern, it needed its fusion reactor on-line. Three people could not run a reactor even if they were trained to do it. Kris's weren't.

"I could run it if you want me to," Nelly offered. Jack and Beni both looked relieved when Kris declined the offer.

Kris found her quarters as Commander, Naval District 41. Somehow in the quick turnaround of the *St. Pete*, Abby had slipped one of her steamer trunks up to Kris's room. Just one, and it held only Kris's uniforms and personal effects.

Jack found a trunk in his quarters, or at least the quarters for the District's never-used Deputy Commander across the hall from Kris's. His trunk also had Beni's duffel bag on top of it. The chief settled into the room next to Jack's, a nice one officially designated for VIP guests. Jack and Beni arranged enough security along the corridor to satisfy themselves that neither needed to maintain a watch through the night.

Kris left them to worry about that, set Nelly on watch, and slept the night through.

She awoke early the next morning to find that the station had continued its routine journey around Chance, there was still air to breath and no cannibals had nibbled her toes. Finding a set of fresh khakis in the trunk, Kris showered, dressed, and went looking for something to eat. That last lunch on the *St. Pete*, while nicely cruise-ship huge, was a distant memory.

She found a mess large enough to seat a hundred, a kitchen fit to feed a similar mob, and a pile of combat meals gathering dust. One had been opened. Apparently the chief, quick to point out he was a growing boy, had done a bit of culinary exploring yesterday. Kris got a small coffeepot going, and soon found Jack at her elbow. Showered, shaved, and in undress green slacks, khaki shirt, and field scarf, he frowned at Kris's food choices.

"No one ever died from field rations," Kris reminded him, less he invoke some security regulation to leave her famished.

"Yes, but no one ever called them food, either," he said, filling a coffee mug from Kris's first handiwork. "Hmm, Your Highness, you can boil water."

"Suborn crews, steal armed vessels, and boil water. Not a bad résumé."

"Between just us, just how long will you keep this up?"

An honest question deserved an honest answer. She decided the scrambled eggs could warm without her attention, took her own mug, and settled across the table from her Security Chief. Keeping a table between them was getting to be a habit. At the moment, if Jack decided to throw her over his shoulder and carry her off to someplace safe . . . there really wasn't anyplace safe to go. Still, it was a good habit, and Kris maintained it.

"I don't know, Jack. Believe it or not, yesterday took me by surprise."

Jack nodded. "So you were making it up as you went along."

"Who'd have thought . . ." But Kris stopped herself before she rehashed their yesterday. Today looked to be a bigger problem . . . and they were going to have to face it.

Jack seemed to be doing a good job of mind reading. Or maybe he'd been around her enough to know her usual pattern of problem solving. "So, what do we do today?"

"Eat first, I hope," Chief Beni said from the door. He hadn't shaved and was still in a worn sweat suit proclaiming Go Navy. "If you can call that eating. Remember, Your Princessness, I joined the Navy cause they ate better." He scowled at the meal warming. "So why are we eating grunt food?"

"Cause it's all that's available," Kris pointed out.

Beni drew his own cup of coffee, and sat down. "This station has twelve different restaurants. Everything from New Chicago Pizza to Retro Cantonese."

"All closed," Jack reminded him.

"Yeah. How do we fix that?" Kris asked.

"If you feed them, they will come?" the chief asked.

"More like if we have work for them, they will come, and then they have to eat," Jack corrected.

"So why ain't there nobody working here?"

"If I knew the answer to that," Kris said, getting up when Nelly suggested her eggs might be done. "I'd be a whole lot happier commander." They ate, dumped the leavings in a trash bin that would need emptying soon, and were no closer to a solution to their problem.

"Well," Kris finally said, "if there's no one here to answer our questions, I say we go where someone is. Three hundred klicks down there's plenty of folks. Must be someone willing to talk to us. Tell us the local score."

"There's a bit of a problem, boss," the chief said.

"There's a shuttle. Nelly checked before I marooned us here."

"Yes, ma'am, there's a shuttle for us, maybe a dozen."

"We've got reaction mass," Jack said.

"Yes, sir. *St. Pete* quit fueling when they got a look at the price. Said they'd fill up at Lorna Do."

"So."

"There's just enough antimatter in the shuttle's motor to boil the reaction mass we need to land." The chief grinned. "Unless we can fill up dirtside, if we go down, we stay down."

Kris took a moment to absorb that before turning to Jack. "I *really* want to meet this Lieutenant Steve Kovar. I have *got* to thank him for the wonderful condition of the command he's turned over to me."

2

An hour later, they boarded a small Boeing shuttle. It was in standby mode drawing from the station's power to keep juice flowing to the antimatter containment pod. Kris had just enough power to break out of orbit and glide to the port outside Last Chance. She set those coordinates into the nav computer and let herself grin. "Landing this will be no strain."

"Assuming we don't run into traffic on the way down," Jack said, slipping into the copilot's seat and bringing up a report on traffic into and out of Last Chance.

"Looks like they're coming up on a solid hour of no business," Kris said.

"Assuming there's no one else dropping in unannounced," Beni said, standing between the two of them. "My old man would whap me horrid if I flew into some place with no flight plan."

"Yes," Kris agreed, "but where's the fun of telling them we're coming. They might bake a cake."

"Order out the antiaircraft defenses," Jack muttered. "You're really going to surprise them?"

Kris knew the rules, but she was tired of being on the receiving end of all the surprises this trip. If there was going to be another, she would do it. Besides, with all her skiff racing, no question she could put this puppy down just fine. A glance at Last Chance's airport showed plenty of fields around it. Kris measured the risk she was taking, found it low enough for her, if not for Jack, and checked the rest of her board. Everything showed green. "Strap in, Chief, we're headed down."

"Is it too late for me to get out and walk?"

"It was already too late when you said, yes, you'd work for this woman," Jack said, cinching his seat belt in tight.

Fifteen minutes later, Kris had the shuttle on final approach. No one at the port had called her, but she decided she'd better check in. "Last Chance Space, this is Navy shuttle 41, I'm on final approach for a dead-stick landing on runway 090. Is there any traffic I should be aware of?"

"Navy shuttle 41, you got power for a go around?"

"Negative on that."

"Then I guess we better not have any traffic in your way. You're lucky we're in an after lunch slump in business. Give me a minute while I redirect a freighter."

"Thank you, Last Chance Space."

Exactly one minute later, the tower came back on, and gave Kris wind, temperature, and barometric pressures.

"Ah, that's not what your automatic station is broadcasting," Kris said, adjusting her instruments.

"Everyone local knows that station is off, and makes their own adjustments. You being Navy, I figured you might not know."

Beside Kris, Jack studied the heavens as if they might hold some hidden wisdom. What Beni was muttering wasn't fit for a princess's ears. But an experienced Navy princess found it rather mild compared to what she wanted to say.

"Thank you for the update. We're two minutes out."

"We'll get a tow for you. Have your credit card handy."

Now Kris did say a very unprincess-like word.

She set the shuttle down smoothly; the brakes were uneven, but they slowed to a stop just past a bright yellow tug. Halted, Kris opened the window and waved the tug in. It came, but stopped in front of the shuttle and did nothing. Kris waited for a minute to be hooked up to power and a tow. Then another minute. Outside, nothing happened.

"Ah, I think they're waiting to be paid," Beni stuttered.

Kris snapped off her seat belt and headed for the hatch, aft. Jack followed, whether concerned for her safety . . . or the tug crew . . . he didn't say. Kicking the hatch open almost made Kris feel better. She quick marched into a dazzling sunny afternoon. The two fellows lounging in the tug's front seat seemed to be enjoying it. "You planning on parking me right here in the middle of the runway?" she demanded.

The younger of the two, a long, tall drink of water with an unruly shock of blue hair and sporting worn coveralls, looked about ready to run. The other fellow, bald, scruffy white beard, and more substantial if not downright round, held on to the steering wheel of his tug and fired right back. "We don't move you until we run your credit card. Navy credit's no good. Operations Chief says she's got enough unpaid chits from the Navy."

"Just how much has the Navy been ignoring this place?" Jack muttered softly. Which gave Kris pause enough to eye the well-worn tug, overdue for a paint job. She scuffed the concrete runway. It was solid, but in need of recovering. *This is Naval District 41's territory. Not Wardhaven, Lieutenant Longknife*, she reminded herself.

Reassessment over, Kris reached for her wallet, went past the official Naval District 41 charge card she'd been required to oh so formally sign for and pulled out her own. When Kris signed for the District card, she'd asked what her limit was. The procurement agent 3/c said that depended on the appropriations approved for her District. All effort by Kris or Nelly to find out what that magic number might be had failed.

Kris offered her personal ID and credit chit to the tug driver. He fed it into a remote on his rig without even looking at it. At least he didn't until the remote beeped happily and approved the charge. Once the card popped back out, the driver did give it a solid look. "You this Kris Longknife?" he asked.

"Usually. On my good days," Kris answered.

"Boss, you know who she is. Don't you ever watch any vids but racing and football?"

"Nothing else worth watching," the boss said and elbowed the kid out of his seat. "We don't have all day. Let's get this thing off the duty runway."

"But she's . . . She's . . ." The tall fellow seemed to have developed a stutter.

"Just another flyguy."

With the shuttle hooked to the tug, the two piled back into their seats. "Is there a crew truck coming for us?" Kris asked.

"Nope."

"Can we ride in with you?"

"Nope, seats are full."

"Can an old chief hitch a ride in on your back bumper?" Beni asked, not interested in a long hike to the facilities.

"Suit yourself, Chief," the driver said. "If you're not too proud, the rest of you can share the bumper. Or walk."

Jack offered Kris a hand up, not that her six feet needed all that much of an up. Still, it was nice of him. It also reminded her that she was a princess and serving Commander of Naval District 41 and it would be undignified to screech at a tug driver. And might upset the locals if she killed him.

The drive to a tie-down slot was sedate. Their shuttle was exiled to one well away from the terminal. After making sure it was secure, the driver offered them a ride to the operations center, a dilapidated building with a very threatening windsock hanging limply in the center of a patch of brown grass.

"You better settle up your bill with the port manager," the driver warned as he dropped them off. Inside Kris found flies, a desultory ceiling fan, and a middle-aged woman behind a counter. Kris approached, then cooled her heels while the woman finished a game of solitaire on her old-fashioned computer.

"So they did send us a Longknife," she said, not looking up.

"Just a young one," Kris countered.

"A Longknife is a Longknife. The old ones are doing you. The young ones are dreaming of when they'll be big enough to do you. Which one are you?" she said, looking Kris's way. The eyes held Kris. Whether the frumpy outer show was real or fake, the eyes were a piercing blue that cut deep. There was ice around them, too. They took Kris in, weighed her to the last milligram and found her . . . worth keeping an eye on. She leaned back from her computer and kept those eyes locked on Kris.

"I'm Kris Longknife," the Navy lieutenant said. "I commanded at Wardhaven."

"You are that one," the woman nodded slowly in agreement. She let that hang in the warm, summer-filled air for a moment before posing her next question. "And I am Marta Torn. What brings you to our neck of the backwoods?"

Kris had a dozen answers to that, but none got past the woman's eyes. "They didn't have any other job for me. I think they're hoping I'll hang around here, get bored, and resign."

The woman snorted. "I think you just told me the truth. But it will serve as good as any lie. Nobody'll believe that."

Kris shrugged. "None of them ever crossed Billy Longknife."

"That's the fate of every kid hatched, honey. Mommy, Poppy are never happy with you. Happy the parent who finally realizes the kids are their own best judge of what's good for them. God help the kid who gives in and lets Mommy and Poppy rule."

"Any chance you could talk to my mother, father about that?"

The woman laughed, a big one that started low in her chest and reached all the way to her eyes. "If they ain't listened to you, what makes you think they'll listen to me?"

"Speaking of listening . . . or talking where talking's not all that wanted, I'm kind of the new commander of Naval District 41 and it's going rather strange. You wouldn't happen to know where I could find Steve Kovar and have a little talk with him?"

The woman tapped her computer. "He should have been here by now. It's Tuesday afternoon, so he's driving a cab."

"I thought he'd be running a chicken ranch?"

"He does, and cabbies, too. You can ask him about that. I think I just heard the cab pull up."

The front door of Ops opened and a short fellow in jeans and a flannel shirt walked in. His red hair was long and his beard shaggy. "You got any baggage?" was his only question.

"Only a one-day hop, down and back," Kris said. "You will see that my shuttle is refueled," Kris said back to Marta.

"I guess your card is good for it," the Ops manager agreed. Steve gave the woman a raised eyebrow. "She's using her own card. No Navy IOU from her."

Steve shook his head ruefully and turned for the door; the Navy had to hurry to catch up. The cab had four doors in front. About halfway to the rear, it turned into a pick-up. Well, this was the Rim; everybody worked.

Kris settled in the front seat beside Steve; Jack and Beni shared the back. The former commander of Naval District 41 took off, spieling a monologue about the crops in view. "We export the most prized, single-malt whiskeys this side of Old Scotland. Or the new one. And our wines are highly prized as well. We also grow several modified crops for feedstock to the pharmacy industry. Chance is proud of its trade balance. We import only the critical items needed for our growing industry. Fifteen of our twenty largest cities have their own fusion reactors. The others are making use of our natural waterpower."

"I got that briefing on the way out," Kris said.

"Yes, but no briefing gives you the smell of the thing. The pride in the workmanship," the man pointed out. "Look around."

Kris did; they were coming over a slight rise. Behind stretched fields of grain. Almost lost in them were the tower and two long runways. Ahead, in a shallow bowl, was the city of Last Chance, stretching along both sides of the wide An'Ki River. There were tall buildings, none as tall as those on Wardhaven, but still, the city compared with several of the smaller metropolitan centers back home.

"Looks nice," Kris said. "Why name it Last Chance?"

"It was intentional. Place like Greenland back on Earth, Greenfeld with the Peterwalds, are intended to fake people into thinking they're headed for a great place to live. Folks that settled Last Chance didn't want those kind. They wanted folks looking for a challenge. Willing to fight a planet for their future. Our population's over a hundred million. We've got no unemployment to speak of. We like it here."

That hadn't been in Kris's briefing. Oh, the raw numbers, yes. But the attitude. Hmm. Something to think about.

"How do you like my station?" That question still showed pride of ownership even if he wasn't interested in taking Kris for a change-of-command tour.

"Very clean. Very shipshape. Very empty."

Steve laughed. "Yes, I imagine it is very empty."

"You know, anyone could have come along and grabbed it. You're just two jumps from Peterwald space now that the Greenfeld Confederacy pressured Brenner's Pass into joining them."

"Yes, but no one did until you came along and took it."

"It's a Wardhaven command."

"Is it? Ask Marta Torn back there how long it took her to get payment from Wardhaven for my chits. Ask any merchants I wrangled supplies from." There was raw anger behind those words.

Kris chose to watch the road. It had widened into four lanes as they passed through a residential area, and needed the extra lanes for the amount of traffic sharing the road with them.

"Where we going?" she finally asked.

"I figured on dropping you on the mayor's doorstep. Ron Torn, you met his mom back at the port. Let him handle you. We don't have a planetary government. Each city has a mayor and takes care of itself. Kind of like the classical Greeks."

Kris recognized the reference. "Those city-states didn't do so well when the Persian Empire took an interest in them."

"But they did fine up until then. And seeing how small we are, and how much we've been ignored by all the Empire builders, we kind of figure we can keep on keeping on. At least we did until we found ourselves entertaining a Longknife brat." He softened that with a wry smile. A very small smile.

"If I understand your defense posture," Jack said from the back seat. "It's to make like roadkill in the ditch and hope no vulture takes an interest in you."

Steve glanced over his shoulder. "I should have expected a Marine to put it that delicately. But yes. You got it in one."

"It won't work," Kris said.

"Says you. Tell it to the mayor. You'll like him. He's even less likely to buy what you're selling than his mom."

While Kris absorbed those twists, Steve pulled out of traffic to an unloading zone in front of a tall building of concrete and gleaming glass. Waiting for her was a tall fellow in slacks, a long sleeve white shirt, and sweater vest. He studied her with his mother's blue eyes and looked uninterested in buying anything she was selling . . . the standard face of an opposition politician. He let her open her own door. Once she and her team were on their own feet, he offered her his hand.

"Hi, I'm Ron Torn, Mayor of Last Chance."

Kris did the introductions for her own crew.

"You hungry," the mayor asked.

"You bet," the chief cut in. "All we had for breakfast was those ration boxes someone left out. And for supper, too."

Steve joined the group. "Any of you know how to cook?"

"Peanut butter on toast," Beni said. Jack shook his head.

"Jack says I boil water very nicely," Kris offered.

Steve looked hurt at the skill level of his replacements. "I guess I'll take the chief over to The Old Camp Store. They've got travel chow that is a step or three above Army issue."

"I'm yours," Beni said, arms open wide.

"Get some fresh eggs," Jack said. "It can't be all that hard to scramble a few."

"And fresh coffee," Kris added. "And bread and cold cuts. I can make a sandwich." Beni started looking very poor as the list lengthened. "Nelly, give the chief a credit voucher" got a happy smile from him. Steve rolled his eyes. But no one made any nasty comments about a helpless damsel in distress. Maybe she'd outrun her Princess label.

Kris and Jack followed Ron into the office building. "Nice city hall," she told him in the spacious foyer, cool in black marble floors, gray granite walls.

"We only rent space here. Not even a whole floor. Chance is death on big government. Keep the beast small and out of the way. 'Nothing important is ever done by government.' "

"You don't look like the type to settle for something that doesn't do anything," Kris said as they entered the elevator.

"My family curse. Great-grampa was central to raising Chance's troops for the last campaigns of the Iteeche Wars. Folks just kind of expect a Torn to go into government. I think they leave it to us." Kris didn't see an opening there to talk defense and decided to put it off for a while. Going hard from the start hadn't gotten her anywhere with the lieutenant. Maybe polite chitchat would show her a better opening.

The mayor's office was on the thirteenth floor. "We get a discount for taking that unlucky number."

"Why didn't they skip it?"

"I think they liked the idea of our address starting with thirteen," Ron said, opening the door for Kris. The small waiting room held a woman at a computer, some chairs and a table covered with readers. The mayor led Kris and Jack into his own office.

The view from Ron's corner office was spectacular. As he offered Kris a chair she said, "I'm surprised a government that has so little respect gets such a grand view."

Ron waved Jack toward a chair. "I think the business folks want me to see what they're doing. Admire it. Be intimidated by it. Which do you think?" Again those blue eyes were on her, now with a hint of a smile at the edges. Was it for her, or the sardonic twist of their conversation? Hard to say.

"You must have some tax base," she said, turning the topic to something Billy Longknife's daughter would. Something neutral they could talk about. She wanted to keep him talking about his world. Not her issues. Not for a while.

"Yes, there's a small tax on imports. Not exports, mind you. But if we buy something off-planet, I get my milligram of flesh. Tells you how much we want to be self-sufficient."

"It can't be enough for essential services," Kris said, taking in the view and measuring it against what she knew of the cost it took to support a place this size.

"Fire department is mostly volunteer, with a few full-time folks to hold it together for the rest. Same for the police, though we don't have much crime. What with near-full employment, most everyone is too busy to bother with stealing from their neighbor. Again, I do have a few full-time members of the constabulary. Most are older folks, the kind of grandma or grandpa types who can settle disturbances with a stern glare and a few reasonable words." Ron's eyes broke from Kris to sweep the vista of his city. "It may look big, but we are pretty small town in our attitudes. It's embarrassing if your kid gets in trouble, more trouble than Grandmama expects," he said, with a wink for Kris. Then he shrugged.

"There's a lot to like about Chance. Wear out a pair of shoes here, and you'll never leave."

Kris glanced down at her nearly new shoes. "That what happened to Lieutenant Kovar?"

"Didn't he tell you his story?"

"It didn't come up. We were discussing other things."

Ron raised an eyebrow at that. The crinkle around his eyes got thoughtful. "Maybe I shouldn't tell his story. Then again, maybe my mom knows his story better than he does." There was a pause. Kris let the silence hang.

"Mom says he was a real hard charger when he came out here. Not bothered at all to find that he was the only officer here besides the captain. When that captain retired and left before his replacement got here, Mom says he was really tickled to be acting commander of his very own Naval District."

Ron must have read the question in Kris's eyes. "No, not strutting around making a big thing of it. Steve's too serious to let rank go to his head. No. But serious as a heart attack about doing a good job of it. Because that was what the next Commander suffered on the last leg of his trip out here. They brought him off the boat on a stretcher, and then wheeled him right back on board. Question about when he'd recover kind of left the command up in the air for, oh, six, nine months. Then they appointed a new boss for 41. Who wrangled new orders while in transit. I think the Jonah curse was already pretty plain to see. At least for anyone not here on Chance. Somehow, Earth got busy with other things and never did bother appointing a new commander. Glitch in the computer. Who knows?"

"And Lieutenant Kovar just sat here and did nothing?" Kris could understand a year or three. But fifteen?

"Well, there was a lass. Lovely girl. My mom's youngest sister. She seemed to make his exile quite survivable."

Those blue eyes smiled at Kris. Edges nicely crinkled. Lips full. Was he offering to soften her exile. Did she really want to keep knocking her head against all the stone walls people put in the way of her Navy career? That was not a question she needed to answer today. Time was something she had plenty of. But no reason not to answer one question. NELLY, IS RON MARRIED?

CHANCE CENTRAL RECORDS SHOWS HIM UNMARRIED, KRIS. BUT I SHOULD POINT OUT THAT MY REVIEW OF THE FILES SHOWS THAT THE LAST MARRIAGE ENTRY IS DATED OVER A YEAR AGO. BIRTHS AND DEATHS ENTRIES ARE UP TO DATE AS OF YESTERDAY, BUT OTHER DATA IS BATCH ENTERED AT SPORADIC INTERVALS.

Right. Whenever they can get a volunteer to do it.

Kris realized she was letting the conversation sag, and not on a note that she wanted to emphasize. She grabbed for something and her mouth opened on, "And he wasn't bothered by the lack of active duty personnel assigned to District 41?"

"Maybe the Chief should answer that one. Chief," he yelled.

The door opened in a moment; the woman who'd been occupied with the computer asked, "What you bellowing about, Mr. Torn."

"The Navy here wondered how it came to pass that all Steve was honchoing were reservists. You, being the Chief of Personnel up there for so long, I thought you might give her your take on why he put up with all your lip and back talk."

The woman, only slightly shorter than Kris, and with middle age helping to fill out her curves, shook her head. "The real question is why I put up with *your* lip," she said, but she came in. Jack leapt to his feet to give her a seat, which she took with full nobility, leaving the Marine to hold up a wall.

The chief put one leg up on the desk, then crossed the other pants-suited one over the first and leaned back comfortably. When Ron did the same, Kris made to imitate them, and almost went over backward in her chair.

"Oops. Sorry," Ron said. "You got the bad chair."

Kris got herself balanced upright, back to prim and princess. And made a note of just who rated comfortable chairs from Ron . . . and who didn't.

"I don't think the lieutenant noticed what BuPers was doing to him, not for a while. A couple of permanent parties shipped in after him. Other folks shipped out. Then more shipped out and no one came. And the budget would come through with more in the reserve account for active days and less in the active-duty account. Come second year, when we were down to just four permanent and him, he and I had a long talk about what we saw going on. I told him you can't make a silk purse out of a sow's ear, especially when no one's offering you a sow to de-ear."

"What did the lieutenant say?" Kris asked.

"Something about how did they expect him to defend a whole sector of space with nothing but part-timers." That was a sentiment Kris could agree with. But it sure didn't sound like Steve the Taxi Guy that she'd talked to this morning. Then again, ten years can change anyone. Or wear them down.

"What did you do?"

"The rest of us part-timers ratcheted up our ball game. Had to when all four of the active duty types shipped out together. The real bitc—ah problem was that they didn't allow for us to recruit any new reservists. Leastwise, not to start with. Fill the hours, but do it with the same old hands. Something about saving on training. We did what we could. And some of us had kid sisters, little brothers that maybe tagged along and took up some of the slack. You know, you can learn a whole lot about operating a 6-inch laser in makie-learnie fashion."

Kris wasn't sure she'd like to trust her defenses to someone who'd picked up their laser training as monkey see, monkey do. Then, no one was offering her anyone with any kind of training.

"You said 'at first.' That changed?"

"Yeah, right about the time you and Earth split the sheets, they let us know that anyone who wanted to join up was only too welcome. By that time we old hands were kind of sour on all things blue, and we also noticed that things were more than a little bit hot in this place or that. You must have noticed. News stories tended to mention that you were there."

Kris nodded as innocently as facts allowed.

"So I told my kid sister that if she wanted to join and get paid for what she'd been doing, I'd tear her arm off and beat her over the head with the bloody stump." The chief eyed the ceiling. "I recall my objections to my sister were the gentlest of several we all made. Anyway, I called everyone's attention as to how all of us were coming up on retirement about the same time."

"And you all went out together," Kris said.

"Most of us joined together. During that long peace we sure as blazes didn't join to fight anyone. No, we joined for the friendship, and we quit as friends."

"And the volunteers just did it for the friendship, too?" Kris said. Just how altruistic was everyone here?

The chief and Ron exchanged glances, the kind thieves do late at night over beers. "Friendship, helping out big sis, and Steve did manage to pay them a bit under the table," Ron said.

The chief was grinning from ear to ear. "Every morning down on Chance, the lieutenant would fill the shuttle's tank with reaction mass. Up at High Chance, he'd unload all but what he needed to get home that night. We all did it. And sold the reaction mass at a premium to ships going through. The proceeds paid a stipend to our volunteers. Worked great."

"No accountants ever noticed," Kris said dryly.

"Nobody from any headquarters ever came by to check the books," the chief grumbled.

"Ah, this might not be the best approach for you, Your Highness," Ron said. There it was, the princess thing was back on the table. "I understand that you recently had trouble about using your own money on a relief mission. This informal staffing solution definitely wouldn't pass anyone's idea of a smell test."

"I'm glad we agree on that."

"However, my mother said to tell you your shuttle is topped off on reaction mass. Please unload the extra mass to the station's tanks to the account of High Chance Welfare and Aid Fund, a certified charity here on Chance."

"And you think that is legal?" Kris paused before asking Nelly for her opinion.

"Defense personnel are authorized to render aid to certified charities, per 18 U.S.C. 8525. I am prepared to stand up and swear in any court of law that this is such, my mother serving on the board of said charity," Ron said, the crinkle back around those blue eyes. No question, the crinkle was for the game.

NELLY, IS RON A LAWYER?

HIS LAW DEGREE IS FROM THE PUBLIC NET. Public net degrees didn't get a lot of respect. Still, they were recognized before the bar as equal to anything from Earth's near-mythical Harvard. She might not hire Ron to present her case, but she'd definitely be glad for his testimony.

"Nelly, do everything you can to set up legal barriers between me, my command and the High Chance Welfare and Aid Fund."

"Doing that, Kris."

"So that's the other head you sport," Ron said.

"Very helpful on things like this."

"Well, tell me, are you as hungry as your chief?"

"Breakfast was abbreviated."

"At least the part we risked," Jack said.

Everyone stood. "Well, I know a great place for a steak dinner. Maybe a bit more. And our local civic theater is doing a revival of Gilbert and Sullivan, I think this month's feature is *HMS Pinafore*. The reviews say the humor has aged well. Would both of you care to join me? I have three tickets."

For someone who had not filed a flight plan, Kris had the very strong suspicion she was very much expected.

Dinner proved that Chance's beef industry was easily the equal of any, certainly Wardhaven's. Ron ordered one of the local wines, but made nothing of Kris sticking to water. Jack praised the vintage lavishly enough for both of them. Dinner was down to the bones well before time for the local theater, even if it did have an early curtain, "So all could be early to bed and early to rise."

But there was a live band and a full dance floor even at this hour. "Folks with desk jobs have to get their exercise somehow," Ron offered as he stood and reached for Kris's hand. She humored him, but found no reason to regret the move; Ron was a fine dancer. He, unlike so many "official" partners Kris had survived, did not endanger her toes. After two dances, Ron handed Kris off to Jack with a smooth motion that came so suddenly and seemed so natural that Kris found herself dancing with the Marine.

"I guess it's not fraternizing," she said as they went into the second dance.

"It's quite public and certainly above board," Jack said. "And so much more modest than the last time."

Kris frowned at the reference, then remembered the rescue mission on Turantic that involved passing herself off as a working lady of the night and Jack as her trick. Of several possible replies, Kris chose, "All in a day's work."

"If you work around Longknifes," Jack agreed.

"What are you two talking about?" Ron asked as he cut in near the end of that dance.

"Top secret stuff," Kris said darkly.

"Right," Ron agreed, taking Kris into his arms. "If you told me, you'd have to kill me."

"No, draft you," she said, laughing.

"As a citizen of Last Chance, a sovereign polis of Chance, I am not subject to your laws be they drafty or otherwise."

"But you are subject to current events, Ron."

"Every day we get out of bed, Longknife, we take a risk," he said, twirling her out to arms length. Then he pulled her back close. "Your idea of my risks and mine are seen from different perspectives. What do you say we avoid this argument tonight?"

They did for another dance, and then he passed her back to Jack. "Should I ask what you two were talking about, or is it top secret? And remember, you already drafted me."

Kris accidentally stepped on his toe, marring his Marine-perfect shoeshine. After that, they just danced. Kris spent the better part of half an hour on the floor, being passed between the local man and her official protector. When Ron called time for the theater, her feet didn't even hurt.

The local theater was pure amateur. Still, the sets were well done, several of the leads had good voices and they seemed to have a clear eye for what they wanted to do with the ancient comedy. Kris was not surprised when she was gently nudged in the ribs at the reference to making Admiral by polishing up the handle on the front door. She elbowed Ron right back.

To her surprise, she didn't even get a raised eyebrow at the line about the junior partnership being the only ship she ever did see. Apparently Ron had done his homework. That was good for him, because she'd planned to do major damage to his kneecap if he didn't respect her ship time.

But Kris didn't make any defense when Ron added his own emphasis to the stage's reference to never thinking of thinking for herself at all. Her hard-won independence from the Longknife shadow, and the voluntary surrender she had finally chosen to make to her name and the legends attached to it was not something she could explain in a whisper during a libretto.

Intermission came with Kris wondering at the fate of women who had to struggle against arranged marriages, and doing her own measuring of the difference between her mother and the Captain's leaning on his daughter. No wonder the humor stayed with us. Some things hadn't changed nearly enough for one girl.

Ron suggested they get something to drink at intermission. Jack maintained his careful two steps behind her, and 360 degrees of concern. The two of them were the only ones in uniform and, though the khakis might have blended in with dust, they didn't blend well with the suits and dresses tonight. Ron had failed to mention that theater was an occasion for showing yourself in style.

The refreshment line was an ambush, but not one Jack could protect her from. They joined the back of the line, and were immediately mugged by three elderly folks leaning on canes and proudly displaying lapel buttons earned for valor in the Iteeche Wars. Kris spotted them as they closed on her at a fast hobble. Of late, her father had been using her to meet with the veteran wing of his party, a portion of his constituency that, until the present troubles, had never been his strong suit.

Kris smiled, and froze that smile as the white-haired woman on the right said, "What you going to do with that wreck they got swinging around our space station?"

"Now Mabel, that's no way to talk to the woman," the bald man on the left said, spruced up in a suit two sizes too large for his sparse form. "Not if we want anything out of her."

A more substantial man, hobbling on two canes between the two, now showed that he could manage without either. He elbowed both of them. "You two hush." He squinted at Kris, now leaning on his canes. "Lieutenant, isn't it?"

"Yes," Kris agreed.

"We hear that you have an old Iteeche War General class cruiser docked at High Chance." He paused, but his watering eyes fixed on Kris and held her.

"Yes," Kris said. "The *Patton* is a veteran of all three of the Iteeche Wars, as well as the Unity War. I understand she helped put down the pirate outbreak after the Unity War."

"Good ship," the woman muttered.

"Bad ship. She can't even hold air," the left man snapped.

"Oh, I've been aboard her. She holds air. At least part of her does," Kris made quick to point out.

"But does she smell like a fighting ship?" two canes asked.

That was about the last question Kris had expected. She paused for a moment to reflect on the smell of the *Patton*, then to compare it to the blend of ozone, air conditioning, motor oil, and human sweat that Kris had come to expect of a working man-of-war. She shook her head.

"That's what I expected. She's dead. Lost her soul," the left man said sadly.

"Well, she hasn't had any people to loan her their souls since we were kids," the woman pointed out.

"There's no chance you're planning on fighting her are you?" the man with two canes asked.

Ron had deserted Kris, moving ahead with the line toward the order counter. Jack was still at Kris's rear, guarding her from the wrong dangers it seemed tonight, snickering softly at the question. Kris apparently let the question hang there too long, because the white-haired woman took a stab at answering it.

"There is no way this young woman could fight that ship. The second reactor is deader than my late husband, and the main propulsion system has two engines bad out of seven. No doubt the laser capacitors won't hold a charge. And she's got no crew."

So much for the brilliant idea of some desk-bound commando back at Main Navy that putting a ship in orbit around every planet would make its people feel protected. "We were kind of hoping to keep that a secret," Kris whispered.

"Maybe from someone born yesterday," the man leaning on two canes snorted. "Not from us old maintainers of warships."

"It's been a long peace," Kris said as her only contribution to a conversation that was headed she knew not where.

"That's what bothers us. Kids aren't learning anything about our wars in school," the woman snapped.

"Don't know what they're teaching them these days," the man on the left added.

"We aren't going to be around forever," the man in the middle added softly. "We have great-grandkids we'd like to show what it was like to fight an Iteeche Death Sun, to close with a Burning Star knowing half your squadron wouldn't be coming back."

"Not like they see in those vids they make nowadays."

"All kissing and boom boom shoot'em up," the woman finished.

"I certainly agree with you," Kris said.

"Good, then you won't mind us doing some work on that cruiser of yours." "Not like we could do it any harm." "Any worse than it is already." The three shot at Kris in rapid succession.

"We have grandkids that need to put in civic-duty hours to graduate from high school. Why not have them do them with us. Listening to our stories."

"We could show them how to get a ship into fighting shape."

"My grandson has a couple of his buddies working on their engineering degree in power systems. They'd love to fix up the reactors on that bucket. It would look great on their résumés."

"Or so Mabel keeps telling him."

"I bet we could get that old tub in good enough shape for a trip out to the moon and back. We could."

Kris held up her hand, to slow the machine-gun-fast patter. These old vets wanted to fix up *her* warship for some pleasure cruises. No. "You want to turn the *Patton* into a museum!"

"Yep." "Pretty much." "You got it, Lieutenant," came back.

"It's not like you ever planned on commissioning her and taking her out for a fight," Jack whispered softly behind her.

"That was supposed to be a secret between the two of us," Kris whispered back. The three oldsters in front of Kris grinned from ear to ear.

"It's not just us that want to work on your ship," two canes offered, careful to use the "your" where the ship was concerned. "There's fifty, sixty of us old farts chomping to get our hands on that bit of history, scrap of our youth, if you don't mind me putting it that way. It's not just our kin alone that will be working on it. There're several high schools, and not just those around Last Chance. We could do it up nice."

"And put some fight back in the old girl," the woman added with a faraway smile. "Just cause she's old don't mean she don't still have some fight in her."

"Mabel, don't scare the lieutenant. Ma'am," two canes added quickly, "we're old, but we ain't fools. We just want to fix up the old boat. Nothing more."

Kris nodded, not risking words. Kris had been finding humor in the idea of these old folks painting the *Patton* and maybe putting some of the circuits back in working order. But Mabel's words had struck an echo, a reminder of enthusiastic volunteers Kris had led out against battleships. Those wonderful optimists had fought and, too often, died.

No, Kris was not interested in a bunch of superannuated vets and their adoring great-grandkids turning the wreck of a ship into a false facade that would crumble on them when put to the test. Well, there was one quick way to squelch this: "Nelly, as the Commanding Officer of Naval District 41, am I authorized to accept the donation of labor and equipment in the performance of my official duties?" A quick no should end this.

"Your Highness, you are," Nelly said simply.

"What!" NELLY, THAT'S NOT THE ANSWER I WANTED.

SORRY ABOUT THAT. YOU ASKED ME. YOU SHOULD HAVE ASKED ME BEFORE YOU DRAFTED JACK, BUT YOU WOULD NOT EVEN LET ME GET A WORD IN EDGEWISE. "Your Highness, as a member of the Royal Family, you are authorized to accept donations of labor and products for the defense of the realm and for historical purposes. It is not for me to say which covers the offer these fine people are making, but it does fit into one of these options in 10 U.S.C. 21215."

"Let me guess," Jack said from behind Kris. "A new reg."

"Promulgated after the attack on Wardhaven," Nelly added. "It seems that several of the donations of equipment, even the ones that were intentional, were not legal." Was Nelly sassing Kris for some of the more piratical ship acquisitions she'd made in her three days of sweating before that battle?

Ron returned with sodas for Kris, himself, and Jack. His timing was perfect for catching the final offer of the vets . . . and Nelly's take on current events. The crinkle around his eyes and lips looked potentially terminal. He handed Kris her drink. "I'd heard of the famous Nelly, but I hadn't really believed the stories. Is that what we all have to look forward to in a couple of more years?"

"Not if I have Aunt Trudy reboot her," Kris scowled.

"She is always threatening that," Nelly said primly. "She never does. And I personally think Aunt Tru and her own computer are enjoying me too much to ever let Kris harm me."

"Some day I'm going to let Tru wear you for a week. Then we'll see what you're sounding like."

"You could not survive a day without me."

"I don't mean to interrupt," Ron said, "but there is a motion on the table to let these fine people donate supplies, and work for the repair and maintenance of a warship in Chance orbit.

Considering how concerned Lieutenant Longknife is about Chance's defense, I should think she would jump at the chance to improve them. What say you, ma'am. We need a decision."

"Ron, the *Patton* is not a warship. It's a wreck looking to happen. It is not contributing anything to your defense."

"Then let us turn it into a museum," two canes shot back.

"You want our people to be more aware that the universe out there is a dangerous place," Ron pointed out so reasonably. "What better way than to have these old veterans passing along to our young the true stories of what they faced."

Kris did not like being manipulated. Father did it. Mother did it. And Grampa Trouble had just done a superb job of it. She wanted to take this bunch and tell them to stuff their idea where the sun didn't shine.

"And if we're working on the *Patton* up on the station," two canes added, "we'll need food, things like that. Tony Chang has agreed to reopen his New Chicago Pizza and the Chinese Waffle House for us. I understand you're living on tight rations."

Kris glared at Ron. "I didn't tell them," he insisted.

"I ran into your chief at The Old Camp Store," the white-haired woman said. Surrender did not come easy to a Longknife. But clearly, this was one of those times when surrender was an option, and best done quickly.

"We," Kris was careful to use the royal pronoun, "are glad to graciously accept your donation toward the common education of the youth of your planet." Education. Not defense. Never would Kris let that ship sail into combat.

After intermission the rest of the play went quickly. The guy got the girl, or maybe it was the other way around. Ron drove Kris and Jack to the port late that night. He turned on the runway lights and did not try to kiss Kris good night but he did surprise her.

"Hank Peterwald never would have let those people mess with a ship of his. But then, I'd never expect to see him out here with just a hulk."

"You know Hank?" Kris got out.

"I had a scholarship to Peterwald University on Greenfeld. Took classes with him. You are not at all what I expected."

NELLY?

YOU DIDN'T ASK AND YOU WERE BUSY AND HOW WAS I TO GET A WORD IN?

Kris got the shuttle back to orbit and safely docked. She left the men to put away the groceries and got to her room before the shakes started. *I spent the day with a buddy of Hank's.* What was the real story of this planet? And where was a ship when she needed it?

3

Kris woke next morning to the smell of bacon and eggs. She showered and dressed quickly and went in search of the source of that wonderful aroma. Jack had a small corner of the huge kitchen working; a griddle sizzled with the source of Kris's aromatic joy. "I thought you said you couldn't cook," she said, filling a mug with coffee.

"I asked my computer how to scramble eggs and fry bacon and, surprise, surprise, those instructions were in memory."

"Of course," Nelly sniffed. "Every computer knows how to cook basic items. I kept wondering why none of you asked for instructions. I assumed you doubted you could follow them."

"You really do want a session with Aunt Tru, don't you?" Kris muttered.

"You're looking awfully chipper this morning," a bleary-eyed Chief Beni said from the mess door. In bathrobe and flip-flops, he looked like he'd had a rough night.

"You didn't sleep well?" Kris asked, sipping her coffee.

"She really did sleep through it," Jack said. As Kris would have expected, he was showered, shaved, and impeccably uniformed, the damage to his shoeshine repaired. But closer observation showed dark edges under his eyes.

"Sleep through what?"

"The arrival of our first contingent of museum techs at two this morning, station time. You didn't hear the defense alarms."

"No. Nelly?"

"I was aware we had a shuttle approaching. I backtracked it to its launch site, checked the video of it loading, and verified the IDs of all the passengers. They were all part of the Historical Society, of which the three veterans Kris talked to are charter members. So I concluded the shuttle was no threat. I tried to tell the station's security system of my conclusion, but it refused my input. It insisted only you two could make a determination. Since Kris authorized me to make a security determination for her, I let her sleep. Maybe you should let me do the same for you," Nelly added.

"Do you want to trust her computer?" Beni said to Jack.

"If it lets me get a good night's sleep," the First Lieutenant said, ladling eggs from the griddle onto three plates. "It looks like we're going to have traffic from the surface at all hours. You want to stand a twenty-four/seven watch?"

"No," the chief said.

"The jump points are another matter," Jack said setting loaded breakfast plates down for all of them.

"Both the one from Lorna Do and the one from Peterwald space are over two days out at one g. Nelly, wake us up if something comes through those jumps," Kris said as Beni attacked his eggs.

"Of course," Nelly said.

"Then it's settled," Kris said. "Nelly is now part of our security team and will stand a twenty-four/seven watch for the station."

"Access to our rooms will be much tighter," Jack said, waving a momentarily empty fork Kris's, or Nelly's, way.

"Of course. I do not want to be stolen."

Kris grinned at Nelly's developing sense of self-interest.

As they finished breakfast Jack said, "I need to refine the security situation on the station. Kris, could you have Nelly hitch into my computer and work with me."

"Nelly, please do." Kris went on thoughtfully. "I'll spend the day reviewing our bunch of willing workers on the *Patton*.

See how much of a danger they are to the ship . . . and to themselves. Chief, you want to come with me?"

Beni scratched under his bathrobe and nodded. "Give me time to clean up and I'm yours for the day."

The tour of the work effort on the *Patton* was interesting. No one was actually in charge among the Proud Old Farts, or POFs as they called themselves, but no one seemed to need to be. They had divided the work up and were in the assessment stage.

"It is bad," one old gal in coveralls told Kris. "I read the report, but you have to see it to believe it. Kid, this tub ain't nearly as old as me and she's in a whole lot worse shape."

"She never got the loving you got," the codger next to her put in, which set the tone for the day. Kris was neither lieutenant nor princess to these folk. No, she was *The Kid*. Either that or General Ray's Brat to those who'd served with him, usually with an aside about how hard it was to believe the old bastard lived long enough to have such a lovely great-granddaughter. Kris was used to not getting much respect, but this paternalism, or maybe maternalism, that ended just short of pinching her cheek, was totally new. She weighed her options, considered invoking her rank . . . and dropped the idea without further reflection. It was clear, even to a blind man, that around here the status she'd earned with the Navy counted for nothing. Less than nothing. She could accept these folks on their terms or be ignored.

Kris decided she didn't much care, their presence got New Chicago Pizza running by lunchtime. For that heavenly gain, they could call her The Kid and maybe even pinch a cheek. Watching Beni demolish a large pepperoni, she suspected if she loused up this deal, he'd mutiny. And might take Jack with him.

Before she left, she introduced herself to Tony and asked how he'd powered the ovens. "Oh, we service folks have an auxiliary power source. Antimatter powered. I just unplug the pod from my shuttle, move it inside, then unplug it later and take it back to the shuttle. Recharge it down below. No problem."

"Mind if we use it when you're not using it?"

"I think, if you check, Steve had one installed as a backup for the station's reactor."

That was news to Kris. "Chief," she called to the growing boy who wasn't finished with his lunch yet.

"Yeah, boss."

"Call your good friend Steve the Taxi Man and ask him about the station's antimatter backup power."

"We got backup power?" Beni said, mouth gaping open, pizza slice in a holding pattern.

"Mr. Chang, here, says we do. Please find out more."

The day before, Kris just called up the station plans, and made no in-depth check on what they showed. Now Nelly checked for all plans and found one updated last just three weeks before Kris arrived.

"Call up the standard plans for an A-class station when built. Compare the two," Kris ordered.

Nelly whistled. "Big difference, boss." Apparently the sibling rivalry between her and the chief didn't extend to shunning his language. Well, Kris couldn't protect Nelly forever from the bad influences of the universe.

Nelly overlaid the two plans. Kris concentrated on the important points . . . at first. The automatic machine guns she'd checked out the first day were, for the most part, not where the original plans had them. "Nelly, show me the 4-inch lasers."

They'd been moved, too.

Central Net was now a machine shop. The network was located next door to the command center. "Interesting mods," Kris said.

"Looks that way to me," Beni agreed, between the last bites of his pizza.

"You look into that auxiliary power supply. I'll check on how things are going on the *Patton*." The afternoon shift was reporting. Whereas the morning crew was white-haired, gray, or bald, this bunch was tall, gangly, and noisy, with hair of many hues and voices that cracked at the most embarrassing times.

"Did we get signed agreements to not hold the Navy responsible if they hurt themselves?" Kris asked several of the elders who seemed to be more in charge than usual.

"Your computer gave us a form. We signed copies before we came aboard and sent copies down to their parents. Parental consents are all recorded with your computer."

I DID NOT JUST MAKE SURE THEY WERE HARMLESS WHEN I SAW THEM COMING. I MADE SURE THEY CROSSED THE LEGAL T'S AND DOTTED THE CORRECT I'S.

NELLY, YOU ARE A JEWEL. *Frequently.*

I HEARD THAT.

GOOD. "I'm glad we have all those necessary legal matters covered," Kris said and set about looking over everyone's shoulders, which seemed to be a good junior officer's job. But she found little need to offer advice. Each of the work details was balanced, two or three youngsters in green shipsuits to an elder in blue. And if Kris found the paternalism of the POF irritating, the blatant hero worship and awe of the teenagers was just as hard to handle. Behind her she'd hear "Battleships" or "Mucho Grandest battle." But let her turn face on to them and the kids got terminally silent or attacked by stutters.

Course, as she left that group, there'd be some older voice pointing out, "She puts her pants on same as you. Don't you let her fool you." Which wasn't fair. Kris wasn't fooling anyone. It was their own delusion, their part in the Longknife legend.

Chief Beni got the backup power going, and that helped with the power needs of both the work on the *Patton* and the station. Kris powered up a laser; it took the charge. But about drained her antimatter pod. Four days after her first trip to Last Chance, she filed a flight plan for a second trip. She needed antimatter, eggs, bacon, milk, coffee, fuses, peanut butter, and a few other things. Jack strapped in beside her, though Beni was only too happy to stay with "his" crews on "his" ship.

Ron was a natural on her list of people to see. A lawyer, she wanted his official view on Nelly's Hold Harmless agreement.

"No question, that will hold up before any court here," Ron assured her. "You'd be just as safe if you'd had them sign something like, 'We're doing this 'cause we want to. If we get hurt, it's our own damn-fool fault.' Kris, this isn't Wardhaven. This is the Rim. We don't let the lawyers tie us up in knots."

"Strange." Kris smiled. "I've heard the same spiel from my father. Wardhaven is the Rim, you know."

Ron's eyes and lips were fully engaged in a smile. Or was it a budding laugh. "Yes, but there is rim and there is *the* Rim. To us on the real Rim, Wardhaven is as hide-bound as Earth."

Kris chose to dodge the barb. "So I'm not risking the entire

Wardhaven defense budget to a lawsuit. Now, can you tell me, or should I talk to Steve the Taxi Man about how someone totally redid the station. I thought with his limited crew he couldn't move the lasers."

"He couldn't have, if it was just him and his reservists. Chief, you want to tell the tale?"

"Wouldn't miss it for the world," the former Personnel Chief for Naval District 41 said, coming into Ron's office. Kris had left the good chair empty, expecting this development. Jack was already holding up his wall.

"You have to realize, to you Wardhaven types, this is just Naval District 41, one of many. But to us, this is *our* Naval District." The chief leaned back, put her legs up on the desk and made herself comfortable. "Now, it took me and my folks all of five minutes to figure out we were in trouble. Anyone with a set of plans for your standard class-A station could come along and scoop it up and we'd just be smears on the wall. Not the way I wanted this fine figure to end its days, I assure you."

Kris nodded as the woman laughed at her own joke.

"But we were way too few to even move the machine guns. So, what do you do?"

Kris raised an eyebrow at the rhetorical question.

"Down on Chance, we had high-school kids that needed to do volunteer civic hours and had good grades in their shop and mechanics classes. We offered the best kids a chance to work on reorganizing the station's automatic defenses. They and their teachers got free rides to orbit, a real fun project and free pizza. It also looked good on their first job applications."

"So that's how my guns and computer got moved."

"Among other things, ma'am. Look your plans over carefully, there're lots of surprises in them."

"And we didn't just do this for the hard science students," Ron said, jumping in. "The station's walls provided all sorts of blank space for the art classes to cover."

"So the budding artists got a ride to orbit and a chance to see their planet from a whole new perspective," Jack said.

"Our local galleries have some really spectacular results of those trips to space," Ron said proudly.

"And the entire planet views that station as *our* station," the chief finished.

"So how did the planet take to having a Longknife move into your station?" Kris asked. The long empty pause that came told her all she needed to know. "I begin to see the problem I am. I have. We are all in."

"Kind of like that," the chief said, standing.

Ron eyed Kris. "I note that you scheduled your trip down for late in the afternoon. May I interest you and Mr. Montoya in dinner and a play. Our Little Theater has changed its playbill."

"You willing to be seen in public with me?" Kris was none too sure how she felt being this close to a buddy of Hank's.

"Public opinions on you are still out. Me, I try to keep an open mind."

"What's the new play?" Jack asked.

The Pirates of Penzance." Why was Kris not surprised.

The dinner was delicious. The dancing was equally . . . pleasant. Jack really knew how to maneuver a woman around the dance floor. There was no reason why the ability to maneuver a woman out of tight and dangerous places should make that skill more or less likely. Still, it was nice to find.

And Ron was not bad at all.

The play was also pleasant. When the modern Major General finished his breathless boasting, Ron nudged Kris. "Kind of fits a modern Navy Lieutenant, don't you think. Except you'd have to add twenty or more stanzas."

Not sure how to take it, Kris insisted, "Thirty-seven, at least, and no one would have the breath for it."

Kris spent much of intermission listening to couples' happy reports that "their station" was keeping grandma off the streets, giving a son or daughter their first real work experience.

Kris nudged Ron. "It's still 'our station,' not that damn Longknife's, huh?"

Ron's "You think so" sounded evasive.

One old gal took Kris aside to say it was good to have the kids working on a warship, "They need to see things aren't always as nice and quiet as they have recently been around here." That took Kris by surprise; the woman wasn't wearing a veteran's pin.

The woman leaned closer. "I lost my first husband in the war. He died fighting with your Great-grandfather Trouble on Muy V. Good man. Thank God I found one almost as good or

I'd have gone crazy." Kris gave the woman the hug she seemed to want.

The ending of *Pirates* was just as Kris remembered it . . . contrived. "Problems aren't settled that easily. Not if it's real pirates or other nasties gunning for you."

"I won't argue, Longknife," Ron said. "But that still begs the question, why would anyone bother us? It's been fourscore years since anyone tried to score. Why not fourscore more? Hank thought so."

Kris ignored that Hank reference. "Wardhaven wasn't scored on for years. We were fighting for our lives four months ago."

"Point taken. Still, Lieutenant, don't you think you and your father and the rest of your family were making yourselves more of a target than little old us?" Around them, a knot of people, more interested in the conversation than in leaving the theater, had gathered. Heads nodded at Ron's point.

Kris played her final card. "Some folks on Wardhaven considered our planet too sacred for anyone to attack. When the attack came, we were scrambling to defend ourselves. We barely managed to lash up enough of a ragtag-and-bobtail force to hold the line. I know. I commanded. And I attended the funerals of all those men and women who stood with me, and weren't as lucky." Kris looked around the ring of people watching, her lips gone thin. "When you are in desperate need, it's no time to start looking to your defense."

There were nods for her, too. Agreement with Ron. Agreement with her. No movement to action. Kris swallowed a scream that would accomplish nothing and put her hand on Ron's offered arm.

"We should continue this thought," someone said in the back. Kris didn't see who. The crowd around them broke up into murmuring groups and made for the no longer crowded exits.

"Kris, you see what you're up against," Ron said. "The vast majority of these folks are just starting to think about what you've been living with for what, the last two, three years. How long did it take you to switch your head out of the long peace?"

"About five seconds, listening to an old woman tell how she'd been beat and raped, her husband murdered before her eyes."

Ron blanched . . . but he said nothing.

Kris sighed, remembering. "But then my second in command didn't buy in nearly as fast. It took him until later in the day to see that we needed to get serious about shooting back."

"What's he doing now?"

"He died at the Battle of Wardhaven."

"I'm sorry."

Kris let out a shudder. "So am I. I miss him very much."

"You want me to drop you back at your shuttle?"

"Could we stop by a grocery store on the way. Jack, do you have the list?" Nelly, of course, did, along with several addendums, involving candy desired by some of the kids working with Beni. Or so he claimed. They were back at the station before eleven with two extra antimatter pods. There was still someone working on the *Patton*, or maybe that was a shift from a town on the other side of Chance. Kris went to bed.

She spent the next two days checking out the changes to her station, and began to wonder what was taking Penny so long to rent a boat. Penny must have had the same feeling, because when Jump Point Alpha spat out a ship, it sent out a quick message, "I'm back," and took off at one and a half g's for the station.

Kris and Jack were at the pier when the good ship *Resolute* docked. It wasn't much to look at. Maybe three thousand tons built around an internal hold, crew and ship facilities, and tie-downs on the outside of the hull for containers. It was in need of paint. Scars showed where the ship had met the pier not nearly as smoothly as it did this time.

Kris rode the escalator down the several hundred feet to the dock area, and ran into Abby leading ten steamer trunks toward the elevator. Kris watched Jack count them, and frown as he came up with the expected number. Maybe Kris truly was in for a quiet tour. Or Abby's wonderful crystal ball was not in the know. Then again, Kris had been neck deep in plenty of pain when the count on Abby's trunks was only twelve.

"I'll put these away," Abby said as she passed Kris.

"I reserved the room next to me for you."

Penny showed up a few minutes later with Captain Bret Drago. A bit theatrical in gray slacks, a red silk shirt open at the throat, and a drooping mustache, he walked his ship like he knew every weld and chip in it and smiled confidently as

Penny introduced the commander of Naval District 41 as his new client.

The smile died. "You look familiar. Have we met before?"

"I doubt it."

"I never forget a lovely face and you are surely one of the loveliest I have gazed upon. Tell me, when you are not a young lieutenant commanding a Naval District, what name do you go by."

Jack rolled his eyes; Kris glanced at Penny. She shrugged. "Nelly gave me a credit chit on a holding company. Didn't have a name. I think Nelly wanted to make it hard to trace."

"You got that right," came from above Kris's collar bone.

"And you have two voices. I must confess, I prefer the one with lips attached."

"Ever met Lieutenant Kris Longknife?" Jack said dryly.

"You aren't one of *those* Longknifes, are you?" The mustache took an extra droop. So did the bushy eyebrows.

Kris came to attention, clicked her heels together, and smiled. "Her Highness Kristine Anne Longknife, Lieutenant, U.S. Navy, at your service, Captain."

Alarm sparked in two dark eyes as Captain Drago turned to Penny. "You said this was a simple contract. Just jump buoys, transportation. You didn't say anything about fighting."

"And we won't be doing any fighting," Kris assured him as they walked to the escalator. "I need to check out some buoys, recharge or replace them. I want to do some scouting around this system. Nothing at all dangerous."

"Says a Longknife," Captain Drago said gnawing his mustache.

"That's what I said."

"And everyone knows a Longknife's word can be taken to the bank," Jack said, following right behind them.

"Word on money. Yes. But if problems arise?" Drago asked.

"We'll blow up that bridge when we come to it. I find it only makes things more difficult when you blow them up before you come to them, don't you," Kris said.

"Mother warned me there would be contracts like this."

New Chicago did take-out, so Kris ordered it in to the wardroom. They were enjoying Greek salads while Abby finished unpacking, and Kris debriefed Penny on the ship.

"The *Resolute* was in port and available. I ran a background check on the crew. They passed."

"I'm glad you did," Kris said. "If you hadn't, Jack would not let me set foot on the boat until he did one."

"I'll need to run my own," the Marine pointed out.

"I'm not staying cooped up in this station five minutes longer than I have to," Kris shot back. "They're going out to tend buoys and I'm going with them. I need to feel a ship under my feet, Jack. I need space time."

"I need to check these guys out."

"Check out the background Penny got, then tell me why it's not good enough. And you better have a good reason."

Penny shot Jack the report; he spent the rest of the dinner with his nose in his reader. Kris brought Penny up to date on the vets turning the *Patton* into a museum ship and the extent that the station was customized, which brought up the general situation. Penny shook her head after that part of the debrief. "They are the original ostriches with their heads in the sand."

"And they've gotten away with it for three, four generations. And it's not as if they haven't been encouraged to be that way," Kris said, surprised she was defending them.

"Just how cute is this Ron fellow?"

"He does dance nicely. I'll have to take you down to meet him. Maybe Jack will let me go down without him if you agree to watch over me. Huh, Jack?"

"Not until we settle his Peterwald connection," the Marine said without looking up from the background checks.

Later he did look up. "I guess you could get some space time with this crew. You're going spacey hanging around here."

Kris exchanged a demure glance with Penny. The woman was working hard at swallowing a smile. Clearly, the female was the smarter of the species.

4

The *Resolute* had a spacious hold that could be pressurized to work in. Kris found a dozen ancient jump buoys in storage near the hub. The *Resolute*'s crew made easy work of getting half of them aboard. They were away from the station, leaving Penny in charge, well before noon.

Jack insisted on going. For some reason Abby did, too . . . which did not cause Jack to smile. Chief Beni slipped aboard at the last moment. "Someone needs to help with reloading the software, checking the old code." He may also have heard of the reputed culinary prowess of the *Resolute*'s cook.

That left Kris and a very inquisitive Nelly on the bridge as the *Resolute* headed for Jump Point Beta. The buoy there was not responding to radio checks, and, since this jump point led, via just two more jumps, to Peterwald's new holding on Brenner Pass, it was Kris's first concern.

But not Nelly's. Kris's computer was all eyes, ears, and whatever a computer could be checking on the navigation readouts. I SEE IT! MY JUMP POINT IS THERE! I THINK IT MAY BE ORBITING THAT GAS GIANT. COULD THAT BE WHY NO ONE NOTICED IT BEFORE?

Kris eyed the navigator's board. She had to in order to keep her concentration. Having an excited computer dancing around inside her skull was . . . difficult. It reminded her of little brother Eddy. He got so excited at his sixth birthday party. Kris wasn't joking when she said she could tie a string to his toe and fly him as a kite. Poor, dear dead Eddy.

Kris put Eddy aside. Once he'd been the only death she mourned. Now, he was one of so many. What did Grampa Trouble say—"If you live, they add up. If you don't. Well, you join them. They'll wait for you. Trust me girl. They'll wait."

Kris concentrated on keeping her head on while one excited computer did her best to blow it off. YES, NELLY, I CAN SEE . . . WHATEVER IT IS.

IT HAS TO BE MY JUMP POINT.

IT DOESN'T LOOK LIKE A JUMP POINT.

YES, IT IS DIFFERENT. BUT IT *IS* A JUMP POINT.

Kris tried not to be too obvious eyeing the nav computer. The *Resolute*'s navigator was to the captain's left. Sulwan Kann was a dark-haired, petite woman almost to the point of being miniature. After getting a good look at the possible third jump point out of the Chance system, Kris backed away and divided her time between nav and the rest of the bridge. The controls were laid out to a standard format. Navigator, captain, helmsman. No need for weapons or defense. The *Resolute* was a standardly built ship, nothing as expensive as smart metal here. No ice to ward off lasers. *Right, Kris, she is a merchant ship.*

The crew of eighteen gave the ship just enough personnel to stand three watches, and Captain Drago set his course for Jump Point Beta at a brisk 1.5 g's. "We'll get your work done quickly and get this contract over, if we're lucky, before anything violent comes your way, Lieutenant."

"I thought my lieutenant signed you up for six months."

"Right, she did. But if we get all your work done in less, maybe you'll decide to save money and cut our contract short?"

"Strange behavior from a merchant captain," Kris said.

"Yes, no question about it," Captain Drago readily agreed. "But working for a Longknife is bound to bring out strangeness."

"All too true," the navigator agreed. Kris noticed, however that her eyes, while staying attentive to Jump Point Beta, did have a tendency to stray briefly, again and again, to the gas giant with the strange, tiny fuzzy presence in its orbit.

SHE SEES MY JUMP POINT!

YES. PROBABLY. BUT, NELLY, SHE'S NOT TALKING ABOUT IT. WHAT SAY WE DON'T TALK ABOUT IT, EITHER. THIS IS ONE SECRET I WANT TO KEEP BETWEEN US GIRLS.

BUT SOONER OR LATER WE HAVE TO TALK TO SOMEONE IF WE *ARE TO GO* EXPLORING.

YES, GIRL. BUT LET'S NOT TALK TO ANYONE UNTIL WE *ARE GOING* EXPLORING.

YES, MA'AM, YOUR PRINCESSSHIP, SLAVEDRIVERNESS.

NELLY, *BOSS* WOULD DO JUST FINE.

The long day at heavy g went slowly; Kris set out to get to know Drago and his officers better. They were ready talkers . . . about anything but their recent work. Jack flashed Kris a scowl after he tried to turn the lunch conversation toward what their Bid For Contract said was their latest work at Lorna Do. That effort was cut short by Abby introducing the need for Kris to expand her wardrobe to more informal wear that would fit Chance better.

"When we get back, could I have a modiste visit?"

"That shouldn't be a problem," Kris agreed, and found that Captain Drago had left the dinning room.

Fifteen hours after leaving the station, the *Resolute* came to a standstill beside the jump buoy. It was nowhere close to the jump point; they would not have found it except for the flashing beacon. Its radio was silent as death.

Two sailors captured it and maneuvered it into the hold. A quick survey showed it was in sad shape. One of the merchant sailors put her finger into the hole in the fuel tank. "Goes in here and right through to the second tank. Got both."

Jack studied it up close. "I guess it was a meteorite. Don't see any evidence of a laser. We can check the tanks better once we get them back to the station."

"You might as well take the whole buoy back," Chief Beni put in. "The batteries won't take a charge and half the solar cells are gone. We were lucky that it had power for the light."

"Pull out a replacement," Kris ordered. Twice. The first one came up dead. The second one came up alive . . . once they swapped out the solar cells from the first one.

Two hours later, they placed the buoy on its own and put it

to work, passing through the jump point with orders to send the one from the other side through to verify that there was no ship waiting there to come through. It came back.

"I guess no other buoy," Captain Drago said. He edged the *Resolute* through carefully, at only a few kilometers a second and rock-solid steady on its lateral stabilizers. Ships that went through at high accelerations tended to end up at jump points they didn't intend to. Ships that were spinning could end up lost. The navigator of the *Resolute* was a very careful woman.

"No beacon," the captain reported, to no one's surprise. "I'll have my crew get another spare buoy up and running."

"But what happened to the assigned one?" Kris asked.

Drago shrugged. His toothy smile didn't make Kris any more satisfied with her ignorance.

"Beni, report to the bridge. Captain, what search sensors does this ship have?"

"You've seen them."

"I want to search for something maybe blown down to atoms."

"You sure it didn't just wander away?" Sulwan asked. "If it lost all its solar cells, it wouldn't even show a light."

"Possibly, but humor my paranoid side for a while. Okay?"

Beni and the Comm Chief got to work boosting the *Resolute*'s sensor suite. By the time they launched a replacement buoy, Beni was frowning over reports. "This chunk of space isn't nearly as empty as it ought to be. And the mixture of atoms is about what you might expect if someone blew a buoy to atoms."

"How recently?" Jack asked.

"Say a month ago."

"Too recent. Let's go home," Jack said.

"Long enough ago that the ship should be long gone," Kris countered.

"*Could* be long gone."

"Is there any ship in this system?" Kris asked Sulwan.

Lips pursed, she studied her sensors. "Doesn't look like anything's here but us chickens . . . and one vaporized buoy."

"We need something more substantial than this to change minds on Chance." Kris turned to Captain Drago. "Your board shows no buoy at this system's Jump Point Beta. That's only two jumps away from Brenner Pass. We need to replace it. How quickly can you get us over there?"

"We can maybe make two g's," the Captain admitted.

"And if we get into any trouble, what kind of hold-out guns are you carrying?"

Captain Drago looked pained. "Ma'am, I'm just a simple merchant captain. The *Resolute* is no kind of a warship."

"Yes, and I commanded a dozen friendly-looking merchant skippers and their ships at Wardhaven, all just as deadly as they needed to be. What have you got if things get terminal?"

The captain studied the overhead of his bridge for a long moment, then glanced Sulwan's way. She shrugged. "She's a Longknife. You knew she was going to ask," the navigator said.

"Yes, but I was hoping for much, much later." He paused for a moment longer, then said quickly. "We have two fourteen-inch pulse lasers and capacitors that can normally be recharged in five minutes, assuming everything else is running smoothly and our reactor hasn't been shot to Swiss cheese."

"Good, Captain. That didn't hurt. Who's your gunner?"

"Three ex-Navy types who know the lasers from soup to nuts."

"That's nice to know. Now then, Captain, let us get to the next jump point as quickly as we may. Chief Beni, make sure the software on this buoy will have it go through the jump to report to Chance anytime the other buoy is activated."

"Already did, ma'am. It's standard software after that mess up at Wardhaven."

"Glad to know someone learned something from that."

"Madame client," Captain Drago began most formally, "Our high g stations are not nearly so fancy as those on Navy ships. In fact, you may find the plumbing rather crude. May I suggest that you and your maid use your room. The men use their own room while we make Godspeed for where you want us."

"Thank you, Captain. Jack, Beni, with me."

"If you think I'm going to leave you all alone when that puffed-up pirate has just told me to leave you all alone," Jack started as soon as they were alone in the passageway.

"You wouldn't be half the man I take you for," Kris said to cut off a long lecture that she already knew by heart. And one, at least today, she agreed with.

"Jack, Beni, get your high g stations. Give Abby and me about ten minutes to get ourselves modestly arranged in our own, then you join us in my room."

"What about *my* modesty?" the chief asked.

"Trust me, I'll close my eyes," Kris answered.

"Abby probably will, too," Jack added.

Fifteen minutes later, they were ready for a day-long trip at high g. Jack had his station facing the door of Kris's stateroom, automatic at hand. Kris had a similar field of fire. Abby had set up a game hologram between the four of them. She started off with chess, but quickly beat all of them soundly. Even Jack. Abby suggested they try their hand at poker, but neither Kris nor Jack were one of those born optimists that ever answered yes to that question. And they refused to let Abby play Beni for a sucker. They settled on bridge at a penny a point.

By midafternoon, they were down to a quarter penny a point and Beni owed Abby his next two paychecks. "Aren't cards supposed to make this a game of chance. The way she plays, you'd think she was reading my hand. Or my mind."

When it came rest time, Kris had them rotate sleeping, first the boys, then the girls. "Keep that door covered at all times," Jack warned as Kris dimmed the lights and he closed his eyes.

NELLY, CAN YOU HEAR ANY TRAFFIC IN THE PASSAGEWAY OUT THERE?

I HAVE BEEN LISTENING SINCE YOU SETTLED IN. ONE PERSON MANAGED TO STALK BY. NO ONE ELSE.

WAKE ME IF YOU HEAR ANYONE COMING.

Jack ended up waking Kris. "You have that computer of yours covering for you?"

"Yes. Nelly, did anyone come by here while we were asleep?"

"No, Kris, it was just you sleeping beauties," Nelly said.

Kris tapped the commlink. "Captain Drago, when will we reach Jump Point Beta?"

"We'll kill the engine in five minutes. You need the time to freshen up?"

"I think I'll wait until we're in zero g," Kris said.

Ten minutes later, Chief Beni was hunting for any evidence there ever had been a buoy at this jump point. He found it, but only at the cooling atomic level. But not that cool. "It was burned, but not too long ago. Not long ago at all."

"Captain, would you mind nudging us through the jump point," Kris said, ever so properly for her status as client aboard.

"Shouldn't we post a buoy? Have it look before we jump?"

"Captain," Kris repeated less properly.

"Captain speaking," Drago announced to all hands. "Stand by for a jump we hopefully will all live to regret. You ex-Navy types, I'm not moving until you tell me the board is green on those long-legged ladies we don't have."

Kris pulled herself down to a jump seat next to the helmsman and strapped herself in. Jack settled in a spare seat next to the captain. Beni got close to the navigator and her sensors. Then three separate voices verified that the lasers that weren't aboard were all go.

It took only a moment to glide through the jump, another to recover from the disorientation. "No buoy," Sulwan said.

"Hot, very hot plasma here," Beni added.

"And I may know who's been eating our porridge," Kris said, "And breaking our chairs. Look what I see."

Not fifty klicks out hovered a ship. Nice and shiny and new. And easily twice the size of the *Resolute*. What kind of weapons hid under its bright work was anybody's guess.

"Howdy folks," came on guard channel in an oh-so-chummy voice. "What brings you to this part of space?"

Kris took it all in: blasted buoys, a ship too close to the fastest route between Chance and Peterwald space, and the tenor of that hail. Without being able to explain how she got from point A to point Dead, that was where she went. Someone would die in the next few minutes. It wouldn't be her or hers.

None to gently, Kris nudged the helmsman's hand. The *Resolute* rolled right and pushed everyone back in their seats with a sudden burst of acceleration. But just a burst. In a moment, the ship was back to drifting slowly, but in a roll.

"Helm, what's wrong," Captain Drago demanded, his hand still on the open mike. *Good. He's a quick study.*

"I don't know," Kris answered before the helmsman could get out a squeak. "It's that same old problem. It's back again."

Kris tapped the helmsman's hand again and the ship did

another jump and roll. "Captain, we got a serious problem with our lateral stabilizer this time," Kris added.

"Well, tie it down," Captain Drago snapped.

"Trying," Kris said, and made sure the ship did another dodge and weave.

"Looks like you folks could use some help," came from the other ship. "You go into a jump with a bad stabilizer and the Great Goo only knows where you'll come out."

Bret chewed his drooping mustache, and a bit of his lower lip as well. Then he scowled at Kris, a multifunctional thing. Finally, he looked into the commlink as honest as anyone born yesterday and said. "This is Captain Bret Drago of the merchant ship *Resolute* out of Lorna Do. Our best mechanic can't do a thing with the problem. You have anyone good with stabilizers? Maybe thrusters. Could just be the computer."

"I'm Captain Arnando Jinks of the good ship *Wild Goose*. I got people good for what ails you," the other answered with a wide, friendly smile. "What do you say that you close down all your power systems and we'll come over?"

"Captain, I think I can dampen the spin, and leave us dead in space," Kris said, mouthing "Do it" silently to the helm. He did. "Maybe it would be easier if they just matched hatches to us and came aboard. Save time on hauling tools back and forth."

Captain Drago's tapping toes looked like they were about to blow a fuse, but he turned a bland face to the other captain. "We do seem to be stable. I think we can hold it. I'll pop out our airlock tunnel. Think you can match with it?"

"It would be a lot easier on my repair crew. Wouldn't have to wait for our locks to cycle. And some of my best techs get space sick if you get them outside a solid hull."

"Good. I've powered down. You match. Captain Drago out." He killed his commlink; watched it switch from green to red standby. Then he mashed a button and the red light went out. He waved at Sulwan who flipped a switch on her board.

"We are as silent as a tomb," she reported.

"And maybe about to become one. Longknife, what have you gotten me and my fine ship and its very thin-skinned crew into?"

"That helpful Hannibal is likely the fellow who's been blasting our buoys. You want to have a shoot-out with him?"

"No." Captain Drago agreed, though his expression said he'd rather swallow a dead fish than agree with Kris just now.

"You can't tell me that this fine ship and its resourceful crew have never been boarded before. Boarded when you didn't want to be. Where's your weapons' locker. You must have a goodly supply of Pfizer's best sleepy darts?"

"And if we do?"

"We shoot first and ask questions later," Kris said.

"What do you take me for, a pirate?"

"Actually, we were hoping you were," Jack said. "Our pirates. Not their pirates. Our gal here gets along right well with pirates. When she's not stealing their ships."

"Well, she's doing nasty things with mine. And without my permission." Kris considered that charge, evaluated whether or not he was most upset about what she was doing or that she was doing it without first consulting him. She concluded that his main complaint was with the process, not the proceedings.

"I'm sorry, Captain, but there wasn't time to staff out our options. I didn't see a lot of good things happening if we tried to fight. You know what hold-out laser he's hiding?"

"Not the faintest," Drago spat.

"And, if we do this right, we'll be hustling through his open hatch to take his bridge well before he can take yours."

Drago snorted, seemed to warm to the idea, but still wagged a finger Kris's way. "Not bad. But next time, young lady, you warn me before you go getting me in a mess like this."

"I will," Kris promised, trying to sound contrite.

Jack shook his head. "Not a chance. I'd never bet money on that. Congenitally impossible to her whole family."

Kris watched Jack and the captain exchange glances, one of those male-bonding moments that would make them friends for life. Why were those moments so often at the expense of some poor woman? Oh well, she had things going the way she wanted. With luck, she'd take that ship with nothing more painful than a few headaches for the *Wild Goose*'s crew. With luck.

"You plan on welcoming them aboard in that Navy uniform," Abby drawled, her head just ducking inside the bridge hatch.

Kris hit the release on her seat and propelled herself for that same hatch. "Captain, if you will distribute inconspicuous weapons to your crew, we should be in a position to take down our assistants before they can become our assailants."

"Sulwan, see to that," the captain said, not budging from his command chair.

Jack followed Kris off the bridge; he needed to be out of uniform, too. "Beni," he shouted. "I want you in my room five minutes ago."

Abby had shed her prim skirt and blouse for a tank top and very cutoffs. Any not-dead male, faced with her long legs and full breasts, would be too locked in indecision as to what to lust after to notice minor things like Abby shooting him.

Kris ended up in a bulky sweater and oversize sweat-pants . . . that hid the spidersilk undies and ceramic armor plates that Abby put her in. "And there's five minutes of emergency air in that pack between your shoulder blades. If somebody doses the atmosphere, that ought to give us a chance to rescue you . . . again. The undies will help if we go to zero pressure."

"Thank you," Kris said, and then again to Sulwan when she came by with a nasty-looking, but tiny weapon. "Sleepy darts?"

"Low power for close quarters. What's *your* hold-out gun?"

Kris produced her service automatic from the small of her back. "I'm not using Pfizer's best with it."

"Well, power it down or you'll be punching holes in Bret's ship. He doesn't like that, and it kind of makes it hard for the rest of us to breathe."

Kris held the weapon up for Sulwan to see that she already had it dialed back to the smallest squirt of propellant for each fléchette. "Don't want to make holes in my station."

"Should have known I wouldn't have to teach a Longknife how to kill folks. Or not—if she wanted."

The knocking of tubing against tubing had echoed through the hull as Kris changed. Now her conversation with Sulwan was punctuated by the solid thunk of the attachment being made. Then came the whooshing sound of the tube pressurizing. "We better get back to work," Sulwan said as she did a racing turn and pushed off for the hold to greet their kind assistants. Kris followed, with Jack close behind. He had switched into battle dress bottoms and boots, but a red tank top that showed off nice pecs.

Beni came up the rear in a rumpled set of khakis with the chief's anchors gone. And a sandwich in one hand covering an electronic monitoring station.

Kris brought them to a halt, then towed her three into a crewman's quarters on one side of the hold. With the door partially closed, she watched as six "helping hands" from the other ship followed Sulwan toward the bridge. One of them looked to be the captain of the reputedly good ship *Wild Goose*.

Ducking her head out, Kris checked the passageway, then waved her team toward the hold. There they paused for Jack to move to the head of the line. He pushed himself off first, gliding unsteadily into the hold and made an awkward grab for the busted buoy, pulling himself to a halt on it.

Kris allowed herself to show more grace as she jumped for one of the new ones, Abby right behind her. The chief held back, out of sight, content to let the three of them go in harm's way.

Lounging free beside the open airlock were three from the other ship. Eyeing them as they floated in were two men in shorts and T-shirts, and a redhead in full body armor. *Ouch!*

"Hi." Kris waved. "Captain wants us to get a replacement buoy up and running." Kris flipped open the maintenance hatch on her buoy and did her best to appear busy.

The armored woman eyed Kris narrowly. "You do that."

The two fellows seemed to lose interest in everything but Abby's rear once she expertly bent over the open buoy service hatch and waved it their way. Jack fumbled to a second buoy and managed to get it open. Kris had hoped the woman in armor would concentrate on Jack, but she gave all three an eagle's attentive eye. And her hand kept going to the small of her back. She was packing and looked eager to use it. Kris took a deep breath and sentenced the woman to surrender or die.

Humming to herself, Kris passed behind the buoy, pulled out her service automatic, switched the power up and the safety off with one sweep of her thumb, and came back in view of the three strangers with her automatic sighting on the woman's head.

"We got a problem in the hold," Kris called on net, switched off, and said, "Don't go for the gun."

Two soft pops of sleepy darts from Abby and Jack and the men floated like jellyfish. The woman sneered at Kris—and reached for her gun. Kris shook her head and fired. The woman's head disappeared in a red smear before she even reached the gun.

"Did you have to do that," Beni asked from the safety of the passageway?

"She was armed and going for it," Jack snapped as he moved to the sleeping beauties, checked for a pulse, then put another dart into each butt to make sure they took a nice long nap. Then he frisked them. All three yielded ugly knives and pistols of various flavors. All lethal. No sleepy darts here.

"We surrendered or else," Abby drawled softly.

Captain Drago shot into the hold, deflected himself off a buoy and aimed himself for the open airlock and tube between the ships. "Did you have to start shooting so soon?"

Jack waved at the captured horde of weapons.

"Yes. Yes, I know," Drago said, grabbing the airlock and propelling himself down the tube. "But we barely were in position on the bridge." Four beefy sailors followed in their captain's wake.

"Yes," Kris agreed. "But that also means they were just getting in position, too." The captain was too far up the rabbit hole for Kris to hear any reply. She shoved off to follow.

"Don't you think we ought to wait?" Jack said.

"We've still got air. Let's go," Kris shouted, putting her service automatic between her teeth. She flew past Jack; he scowled. She grabbed for a handhold on the airlock and pulled herself hand over hand into the void between ships.

Jack shouted, "Beni, get over here," and made to follow.

Abby shot in ahead of him. "You could break a nail on these handles. Way too awkward," she muttered.

Kris concentrated on grabbing hold and pushing along fast. The tube was clear, though the moisture of their breath was making it fog. Beyond, the dark cold of space loomed, speckled by unblinking, forever-distant lights. Kris had seen this view before, from a racing skiff. She'd always had a well-tested pressure suit hugging her at those moments. She paddled faster.

The air took on the smell of fried fish and dirty laundry, overpowering even the taste of the weapon in Kris's mouth.

Flashing out into a wide space at the other end of the tube, Kris found two sleepers drifting. Before Kris touched down on the far wall, she had both guns out, covering the passageways up and down in the ship. No head came in view. No nothing.

There was noise forward and Kris turned to go there as Abby and Jack glided in to do their own check.

"Hold it," came from the chief as he wiggled in behind Jack. One hand held his electronic gizmo; his eyes studied its flashing colors. "Something strange going on aft. In Engineering."

Kris did a flip and headed that way, Jack right behind her, Abby took station with two guns out, ready to hold the tube against all comers. Beni followed Kris, bouncing from one side of the passageway to the other but his eyes never left the electronic monitoring station in his left hand.

Kris paused at the open hatch to Engineering. Inside, two men were anchored by their feet to impromptu holds. One held a huge wrench, the other an automatic pistol. He fired off a burst at Kris but couldn't control the weapon. Rounds went high, then higher, ricocheting inside. Kris shot for the dead center of his chest; he flipped over. He went one way, the pistol the other.

Kris swung her weapon toward the guy with the wrench. But he'd vanished aft into a maze of machinery. Now the guy in stained khakis strapped into the Engineering command station drew Kris's attention. He was hunched over a button, knuckles white as he pressed it down hard. Beads of perspiration glistened on his face to form globules and float free into the air around him.

"You going to shoot me?" he asked, not looking up. Kris saw herself reflected in the instruments of that station.

"Wasn't planning to," Kris said, glancing around for the wrench fellow. Jack followed her in and started doing his own check. Beni held station outside the hatch, but the look he gave the engineer rapidly turned to raw terror.

"Kind of wish you would shoot me," the man said. His hand was trembling. "It would solve all my problems. All yours, too."

Kris's father hadn't raised dumb kids. "That what I take it for?"

"Probably. The bridge activated the self-destruct sequence. My job is to finish it by letting go of this switch. That's what they pay me the big bucks for. I let go and the reactor's containment just goes away. Then we do."

"But the folks who put that in your contract aren't the ones standing here just now," Jack said.

"You got that one right."

"Somebody really doesn't want any evidence, do they. And don't much care who pays the cost for what they want," Kris said softly. Her knees were starting to shake, making her glad to be in zero g. Floating, waiting to be blown to atoms was a whole lot more nerve-racking than throwing herself into a shoot-out.

"I'm too old for this shit," the engineer said. "And I kind of wanted to get older." He shook his head. "They can't pay a man enough for this."

"Any way to safety the destruct sequence?" Kris asked.

"You can't do that," came the half scream, half screech. "We swore a mercenary's oath." The missing fellow launched himself from behind something big and gray. He had his wrench out ahead of him and was aiming straight for the guy holding back the reactor blowout.

Kris stitched him with a three round burst of sleepy darts.

Jack launched himself at the suicide, caught him in midair. The two of them crashed into the Engineering station just at the elbow of the fellow with his finger in a most lethal dike.

"You still have the situation well in hand?" Kris asked.

"If I didn't, you wouldn't be asking," the guy said with a soft snort. "Listen, my hand is getting a mite tired. You see that blue switch there, just out of my reach if I tried for it?"

"Yes," Kris said, gliding softly to the point of interest, but trying to touch nothing.

"And that red button about half a meter away from it?"

Kris looked for it. And pointed at one.

"No, not that red one, the smaller one below it."

Kris pointed to the right one.

"You throw the blue switch. Then you have five seconds to push the red one down and hold it down until you feel it click solidly in place. You got it?"

"And if I mess up?"

"You really don't need me to tell you, do you?"

Kris wrapped a leg around a stanchion for the work station, stabilized herself, and reached out. For once, she was glad of all of her six feet and the reach that came with it. She had the blue switch under her right hand and wasn't even stretching to reach the red. "Flip one, then push down hard on the other."

"Until it clicks."

The switch flipped easily. The button went down. And did nothing. "I'm not getting a click, here," Kris said.

"You better before five seconds is up."

Kris leaned hard, wishing maybe there was more of her to lean on that button, but they were in zero g and even if she weighed a thousand pounds it wouldn't matter.

"Can this thing be turned off," Kris muttered, as she wrapped both of her legs around the support and bent herself to get more leverage behind her fingers.

The button sank deeper, but still no click. Kris grabbed for the edge of the work station to get more purchase.

Beside her, the engineer was muttering, "One hundred thousand and four. One hundred thousand and . . ."

The button gave a gentle click. "Will it stay down now?"

The engineer eyed his board. "I think you did it. Keep pushing down on that thing. I'm gonna let go." He did. Kris counted to twenty. And found she was still here.

"I think you can let go of that," the engineer said.

"You don't sound nearly as sure as I want you to sound."

"Ain't run this procedure all that many times."

"How many times have you run it?" Jack asked.

"This is the first time I've heard of."

Kris's knuckles were white and several, no, most of her muscles were screaming. "I need to let go?"

"Try it. If we don't blow up, you did things just fine."

Kris considered her options and found that standing here for the rest of her life might interfere with too many things she wanted to do. Like going dancing with Ron and Jack again. She let up and counted to twenty.

"No boom," Beni said from the hatch.

"No boom is good boom," Kris agreed and offered the Engineering officer her hand. "I'm Lieutenant Kris Longknife of Naval District 41."

"Nur Chim, Chief Engineer of the *Royal Flush*."

"Not the *Wild Goose*?" Jack said.

"Oh, were we using that set of papers today?"

"How many sets of papers does this ship have?" Kris asked.

The engineer shrugged. "Ma'am, I'm paid to run a reactor. The fewer questions I ask, the happier the skipper is."

"Why don't you help us corral that young fellow that's watched too many mercenary vids. Grampa Trouble always told me the only true oath one of them took was to get a paycheck on a regular basis or walk."

The engineer produced wire and helped Jack lash the two together. "Grampa Trouble. You one of *those* Longknifes?"

"Yep."

"Just my luck. Any chance I can talk you into keeping me separate from the rest of this bunch. I don't think they're going to be too happy to discover I didn't blow the ship."

"I think that can be arranged."

Back on the *Resolute*, the crew was storing sleepers in three large lockers. Kris might have found their presence a surprise on a merchant ship under other circumstances. She flashed a smile Abby's way and said. "Glad they have these."

"Nice of them isn't it."

The engineer suggested five guys he wouldn't mind sharing quarters with. Captain Jinks and the hard cases got another cell. The others filled up the center one. "Now let's see what we've captured."

Captain Drago was on the other ship's bridge. He'd found four sets of papers, each for a different ship of the same description, each from a different port. All ports, however, were in Peterwald space.

"Haven't I heard somewhere that there's bad blood between you Longknifes and the Peterwalds?" Drago asked.

"Do you believe everything you hear in the media?"

"No, but if I hear something often enough, it kind of makes me shy when I get hit on the nose with something that smells of real proof."

Kris changed the subject. "Nelly, can you access this ship's network?"

"No. It's solid-wire access only, no hot spots for remote."

"Kind of makes you wonder if someone wasn't paranoid about their privacy," Kris said, then shouted, "Chief."

"I'm here. I'm here. What'cha want, boss?"

"I want to plug Nelly directly into this network. You got an adapter?" It took the chief a minute and three tries, but he finally found one that worked. "Nelly, will you be safe wandering around in this thing?"

"Of course, Kris."

A moment later Nelly muttered, "Ouch. That was not polite."

"What?" came from all four humans in earshot.

"Well, everything on this system is encrypted. Heavily. Several different codes. You are right, Kris, your fake friends like their privacy."

"You've handled codes before."

"Yes, but this nasty idiot sister of mine is loaded with bombs. I go hunting for something, and she sends unpleasant little things right back at me."

"Get out, Nelly. Now!"

"I am out, now, Kris, but there is nothing to worry about. Do you remember that triple-buffer system Aunt Tru gave me to use when I was looking for data on the rock chip from Santa Maria?"

"Yes."

"I am using it to buffer me from bombs in this nasty network. None of them have gotten by the first buffer. Kris, I am safe. Now may I continue?"

Kris gnawed her lower lip. Why was Nelly so confident about rushing in where mere humans feared to tread? Did the computer really have the situation in hand or was she just a teenager blind to her risks. "Continue, Nelly. But if any bomb gets into your second level of buffers, stop and bring it to my attention."

"Yes, Kris, I will most certainly do that."

"Think she can handle it?" the captain asked.

Kris considered letting him in on just what Nelly had handled so far, then decided against it . . . for now. "She'll do just fine. You finding anything interesting?"

"Not much hardware I dare touch," he said. "There's a lot of workstations on this bridge. Too many for an honest merchant ship. But with them all dead, there's no way I can tell what they might be used for."

Kris eyed them: helm, command, navigation. And two more. Weapons and defense she would have named them on the *Typhoon*.

"That's interesting," Nelly said.

"What's interesting?" Kris asked.

"This merchant ship packs four twenty-four-inch pulse lasers."

"Four twenty-four-inch pulse lasers! My first ship, the corvette *Typhoon*, carried that armament. Nelly, keep searching."

"Kris, I think this ship has Smart Metal." Nelly said.

"Smart Metal? Beni, what do you show?"

The chief's face screwed up in puzzlement as he studied his black box. He glided over to rest it in contact with the steel of the hatch. "No, it's standard metal, same as any caveman used. But I am getting something. This is weird."

"Kris, I think it would be best if I activated the defensive station," Nelly said. "You will need to see what they are doing to get a full understanding of it. It is very unexpected."

"Do it," Kris said.

The station next to the helm lit up. On the screen appeared a replica of the ship. Most of it was red. One patch was green. The green section covered the side of the ship broadside to the *Resolute*. "They sheathed the ship in Smart Metal," Nelly said.

"I thought you couldn't mix smart metal and regular steel?" Jack said.

"That's what the techs at Nuu Enterprises said. When you made a hull half smart, half steel, the new stuff migrates and mixes under unusual circumstances. Like when you're hit."

"Someone has put a film of Smart Metal over the regular hull, then shifts it around," Captain Drago said. "You put this where you're likely to get hit, and it ablates the laser heat."

"Glad you didn't get in a shoot-out with it," Kris said.

Drago cringed.

"You think someone came up with a smarter way to use this stuff than the folks at NuuE?" Jack said.

"Looks that way. Though I wonder how this stuff does if you get a burn-through. Can it patch a hull breach?" Kris asked.

"Don't know," Captain Drago said. "But if it keeps my hull intact through a few hits, I'll not look a gift horse under the arm pits."

Kris didn't like the idea of someone building on Nuu Enterprise's patents. Or fighting ships like this one. And she liked even less that the idea had come from someone other than Grampa Al's crew. "Nelly, find the nav and ship control routines and get them working."

"I am hunting for them, Kris. This is not easy sledding."

There were muffled laughs from the humans around Kris. "Keep up the good work, Nelly. Let us know when you think the ship is safe to move."

"You planning on putting a crew aboard?" Drago asked.

"If you will loan me a full watch. Can't leave this hulk drifting out here. No telling who might steal it."

"Good point," Drago agreed with a grin that would have fit well on any pirate from the proverbial seven seas of Earth.

5

Three days later the *Resolute* docked at High Chance. The ship of many names docilely followed in its wake. Kris spent the time in transit composing a full report of what had happened for General Mac, and a shorter version on developments for Grampa Al. "Your brain trust isn't being very brainy," Kris began. Kris composed a request for permission to visit New Bern, the nearest colony to Chance. Normally, she'd just visit a place, but being Commander, Navy District 41, and a princess . . . and a Longknife, New Bern might want to know she was coming before she showed up.

Kris watched the docking from the bridge of the *Resolute*. When she stood to leave, Sulwan stood as well. "Ah, Your Highness, the crew has asked me to pose a question to you?"

Very formal. Even a tiny ducking of her head for a bow. "Yes," Kris answered, trying to quickly slip into Noble when all she'd been thinking was Navy.

"About that ship out there. Is it a prize?"

Oh, right. Prize money. How could I have missed that? Kris did some quick thinking. "It certainly looks like a prize to me, but as to whether or not we can keep it, or sell it under the ancient prize rules is a question I don't know how to answer. Tell the crew I'll try to have an answer in a day or so."

The bridge crew seemed content with that answer.

NELLY, LOOK INTO HOW WE CAN MAKE A SHIP APPEAR. PAPERS AS SOLID AS FALSE ONES CAN BE. AND NOT TRACEABLE TO MY HOLDING COMPANY THAT PUTS THE MONEY OUT.

I HAVE BEEN WORKING ON THAT. WHAT DO YOU WANT TO NAME THE SHIP?

Kris had had enough of being all sugar-and-spice nice. THE *WASP*. CROSS IT AND IT WILL STING YOU.

Penny waited at the gangway, Ron at her elbow. Kris raised an inquiring eyebrow. "A Longknife goes out with one ship and a second follows her home. I figured you'd want to keep it and needed an adult to ask if you could," the mayor said.

"Depends on what legal niceties Chance will let me pull over some eyes, Mayor."

Kris filled in both on the vanishing jump buoys and her little discovery of why. Captain Drago wandered up and stood by listening, apparently ready to provide a non-Longknife viewpoint.

"So you blasted the ship blasting your buoys," Ron said.

"Hardly," Kris answered. "If there had been a fight, we would have been the one blasted. That ship is as heavily armed as a Kamikaze-class corvette."

"A *Typhoon* in sheep's clothing," Penny whistled.

"Yes, yes," Captain Drago cut in. "This young Longknife did very well. She had my ship fake steering problems and we *invited* the other ship over to help us. Thank heaven for that."

"We put most of the crew asleep with drug darts," Jack said, quickly gliding past the "most." "Upon interrogation, several admitted they boarded us with the intent of seizing the ship and taking us captive. Only the captain knows what he intended to do with us once we were prisoners. He's not talking."

"So you did unto them before they could do unto you," Ron said in summary.

"By about half a second," Captain Drago said.

"Why was the ship destroying the buoys?" Ron asked.

"Your guess is as good as mine," Kris said carefully. "There was nothing in their records and those who know aren't talking. I replaced all the buoys. They'll tell us if any ships head this way from Brenner Pass."

Ron looked at Kris like she was crazy paranoid, but didn't say it. "Where is this ship registered?"

"About four different places, depending on which of its four sets of papers you're looking at," Captain Drago said. "All in Greenfeld territory."

Ron's next glance at Kris said she was less paranoid than before. "I want you, Captain, to come with me. There're some folks dirtside that will need your testimony."

"Not mine?" Kris said.

"I don't think you could help this matter," Ron said.

"You don't trust me because of what Hank told you."

"I don't trust either of you any further than I can throw that space station of yours. Kris, until my people can make up their own minds, the less they see of you, the better."

"We have twenty members of that ship's crew in custody," Kris said. "They appear to have been involved in crimes ranging from destruction of government property and endangering the spaceways to conspiracy to commit piracy and maybe murder. I'm not prepared to try them. Can I turn them over to Chance?"

"Judge Maydell is working on that wreck of a ship of yours along with Judges Billie and Ardnet. They should be able to convene a court. Try them. Half a dozen of those old farts have tried or defended cases. It'll be good for the kids to see justice in action."

"And the final disposal of the ship?" Kris asked.

"Forfeiture of property involved in a crime is not an unusual penalty here on Chance," Ron said. "Now, Kris, if you will excuse me and the Captain, we need to leave." And he did.

Kris waited until the mayor was out of earshot, weighed several dozen nasty things to say, and found that all she wanted to do was ask Penny how things were going. Penny's brief boiled down to fine. "Everything okay with the *Patton* Museum?" Kris asked. "No kids hurt?"

"Nothing a bandage couldn't handle." Penny studied the new ship through the ports. "She got a name?"

"Several. If I can swing buying her, she'll be the *Wasp*."

Penny considered that for a moment. "Nice name. I think I like it. Armed like the *Typhoon*, you say?"

"And protected by a Smart Metal cladding. Chief Beni can explain it to you." Penny's commlink began flashing.

"That was fast. Judge Maydell wants to borrow our court facilities. Do we have any?"

"If they say we do. Let them have anything they want."

Kris was surprised, considering how long she'd been left hanging when charged with misappropriation of government property on Wardhaven, to find that the court would convene at noon the next day. She was not surprised to find that the court-assigned lawyers divided up the accused pretty much the way the *Resolute*'s brig had them. Those with Engineer Chim pleaded guilty to lesser charges, threw themselves on the mercy of the court . . . and turned state's evidence.

The seven in the middle cells were found innocent of most charges by right of youth and ignorance. They were found guilty of being something that boiled down, at least to Kris, to being stupid and sentenced to probation and community service.

The last six were the hard cases. They denied that the court had any jurisdiction over them, seeing how the actions they were accused of were committed closer to Brenner than Chance, and demanded that they be sent there. They entered that plea on their own after declining the provided legal assistance.

Judge Maydell made short work of that. "You're here in my court, and I don't pass off my problems to others lightly. The property you destroyed was from High Chance. The ship you boarded was chartered to High Chance." Her gavel came down hard. "Prosecution, present your case."

Kris was the first witness. Again, she recounted the story of how the *Resolute* and ship of many names came to cross paths.

"You caused the *Resolute* to appear to malfunction?" Judge Billie, a short, white-haired woman, asked.

"Yes, Your Honor. It was my professional judgment that in a shoot-out, the *Resolute* would not survive."

"And what did you find on that ship?" the prosecutor asked.

"It was heavily armed." Kris described both the ship's hidden armament and the weapons taken from the boarding party. "And when we boarded, the first officer threw a destruct switch. Only the action of the engineer saved all aboard from death."

Cross-examination did not go nearly as well. "She murdered my girlfriend in cold blood," was former Captain Jinks' opening statement. "She should be here, not us."

An objection was followed quickly by, "Overruled."

"I imagine there's a question in there somewhere for the witness," said Judge Maydell. "Did you kill anyone?"

Kris swallowed hard and described switching to lethal ammunition to take down the woman in armor.

"See," Jinks spat. "Cold blood. They say we were armed. Of course we were. There're crazy people out there in between the stars. Crazy people like this Longknife girl."

The gavel came down for silence. "Your point is made. Do any of the defense lawyers have anything to add to this matter?"

"Not at this time."

There was a pause while the judges studied the ceiling, and Kris began to wonder where she could hire a good lawyer.

Judge Billie was the first to speak. "You say this was a judgment call on your part, Ms. Longknife."

"It was my professional judgment that the woman was armed and dangerous and that the *Resolute* was in severe danger. I ordered her not to go for her weapon. She did. I shot her."

"And you based that professional judgment on . . ."

"Combat experience, Your Honor."

The prosecutor stood. "May I lay the witness's military record before the court?"

"Please do."

The prosecutor entered into evidence his exhibit, a three-page listing of Kris's Navy experience. First copy went to the court reporter, then to the defense, then one each for the judges. Their reading was interrupted by a whistle from Ardnet. "You've seen a lot of action, young lady."

"The prosecution understands that this is not a complete record of her service, but only what is in the public domain."

"There's more?" Judge Maydell said, eyeing Kris over reading glasses.

"Yes, ma'am."

"She should have to give it all up," Jinks demanded.

"This is a full list of your awards and decorations?" Judge Billie asked. Kris nodded.

"Nothing spectacular there," Judge Ardnet said.

"Clearly you never served, Ardy," Billie said. "The Wounded Lion is dated right after the Devolution ceremonies on Paris.

I notice that you've got a V for combat valor added to your Devolution Medal. Is that a mistake? There's no official report of any combat taking place while we and the Society of Humanity were arranging that whopper of a divorce."

"You are correct," Kris said.

"That there was no fighting, or that you got a V for valor in combat there?"

Kris said nothing.

"She has to answer the court," Jinks half screamed.

"Not if the court chooses to withdraw the question," Judge Maydell said. "Judge Wilhelmina?"

"I withdraw the question. I can wait for the memoirs," the woman said. "But it is clear to me that this young woman has seen combat far beyond what we have come to expect recently of one so young. I find her professional judgment is something this court should respect. What say you, Madame Senior Justice."

Judge Maydell eyed Ardent. He nodded. "This court finds that no one should have to wait until they are dead to prove that they are in harm's way. We find that the witness exercised legitimate professional judgment in this matter and shot first. The court will withhold final judgment in this matter until all testimony has been heard. Now, shall we get back to the case at hand." And the gavel rapped down.

The prosecution rested its case at three o'clock. The court adjourned to let the defense think on its case that night. It didn't help. The next day's presentation by Jinks was strident and hardly helped him. By noon the judges had ruled; ten years incarceration to be arranged at salt mines up the coast from Inside Strait, and forfeiture of the ship involved in the crimes, "to pay court costs and replacement costs of the lost property. All other benefits from the sale of said ship to accrue to Chance's general fund with a strong recommendation from this court that they be used for the common defense, and spent quickly." And Judge Maydell gaveled the proceedings to a close.

Almost.

Once Jinks and the hard cases had been removed, Judge Maydell brought her gavel down again. "The court will now entertain proposals for the disposal of that ship. We understand Lieutenant Longknife would like to buy it."

"I would, Your Honor," Kris said from where she'd been sitting in the back row of seats, surrounded by kids taking a break from working on the *Patton*.

"Andy, you have any idea what a proper price is?" Judge Ardnet asked the lawyer who a moment ago had been Mr. Prosecutor.

"When the court ordered the ship forfeited, I had my assistant start a search on recent sales of similar ships on Lorna Do and in the Helvetica Confederacy. That's all we have in our database. However, the armament and the smart-metal defense are hard to place a value on."

"I might be able to offer some assistance on that," Kris said. "I worked on a project involving the modification of the Kamikaze class, so I have the present value of Smart Metal. Nelly, feed that to the court."

DONE, but the real verification was Ardnet's whistle.

"That stuff doesn't come cheap."

"Nor do four twenty-four-inch pulse lasers," Kris said, and added what Nuu Enterprises charged for arming a Kamikaze.

"We couldn't charge that much for this ship on the open market," Andy muttered.

"I'm not sure we'd want to sell all that to just anyone," Judge Maydell said.

"I'm willing to pay that price," Kris said, "for the ship in that configuration."

"And what would you do with the ship?" Judge Maydell asked.

"Keep it here at High Chance. Initially," Kris said, then shrugged. "For how long? That would depend on . . ." She considered several ways to end the sentence. Whatever she said would be on the news in an hour. She left the sentence dangling.

"I can think of a dozen reasons the young lady might have to move on," Judge Billie said. "None of them good for Chance. But at least some of us Proud Old Vets are happy to have you."

Kris appreciated the sentiments, but she did have a problem. "Your Honor, if it pleases the court, there is a problem with the sale of the ship and disposal of the funds you generate." Kris filled them in on the hope by the crew of the *Resolute* that there might be some prize money in it for them.

"That doesn't please the court," Judge Maydell said. "But we should not bind the mouths of the kin that tread the grain. Clearly, they earned something at the risk of their very lives."

"If I may offer an alternative," Andy said, "the actual cost of the ship, verses the value of the weapons and Smart Metal added might serve as a good basis for splitting the sale. We take the value of the basic ship. They get the premium Her Highness is paying for the military aspects."

"We'd be better off taking the other," Ardnet muttered.

"But it was the lasers that they were betting their lives against." Judge Maydell's gavel was up. "This court holds that the crew gets the value of the warship part. Chance gets the value of the ship. Court is adjourned. Your Highness, we will take a check." And the gavel came down.

Kris had Nelly draw up a credit voucher for the clerk of the court. He reminded her not to remove said property "until said voucher cleared." It felt strange to have a voucher in her name questioned. But this was a rather large one, and Chance was out at the end of nowhere.

Navigator Sulwan Kann just happened to duck her head in the courtroom. "You done here?" she asked.

Wondering how rapidly news traveled on her station, Kris motioned Sulwan over and told her how much of the ship's sales price would be available to divide up among the crew of the *Resolute*. Sulwan raised an eyebrow at the amount. "Good thing we already agreed on who got what part of it. Captain Drago found something in the Ancient History section of the net and we all bought in. He included a portion for you, the ship owner."

"Not for me. I'm buying the ship and it wouldn't feel right to get part of the prize money back for having taken it."

"Do we get a part of the pot?" Chief Beni asked as he and Abby just happened to walk in. Kris made a mental note never to count on privacy in her station.

"Yep, same as any crew member."

"Well, Princess, when's payday?" Abby asked.

So Kris was escorted over to the *Resolute*. The entire crew just happened to be aboard, and quickly lined up for pay. Nelly produced credit vouchers as required for each and every hand . . . including Jack. "You risked your neck," Kris said.

"That's part of my job."

"Yes, but according to the ancient laws of the sea, today you get paid for it."

Gingerly, Jack took the check. "More than a year's pay."

"Don't spend it all in one place," Abby said with a laugh.

"I hope you won't need my ship for a few days," Captain Drago said with a broad smile directed at his crew. Several nodded enthusiastic agreement.

"Actually, I was thinking I might," Kris said. "Could I talk privately to you and Sulwan for a moment."

"In my cabin," the captain said with a grin.

"Jack, can we have a moment?"

What to do next had been eating at Kris. The powers that be on Chance wanted her gone. Where was the question. Kris would have headed for New Bern, to check out that flank. But she was getting negative replies back from the messages she'd sent out the day she got back. Some were no surprise.

The reply under General McMorrison's signature read as if the Prime Minister had dictated it. "Problems like disappearing buoys are to be expected in unsettled times like these" she could almost hear Father say. "So good of you to catch those responsible. Be sure to turn them over to authorities on Chance for prosecution. Please remember not to use your own funds to circumvent the policy established by my, no, *the* official budget. Now be a good little girl and behave yourself."

Grampa Al did not sound all that grateful that Kris had found a new use for Smart Metal. Indeed, he seemed offended that she had discovered what his own R & D staff hadn't. Or maybe they had discovered it but, since it cut into potential profits, kept mum about it. There were times when Kris found it easier to understand why some serving officers had so little taste for businessmen. This was one of them.

Grampa Trouble's short reply had been a balm. "Wow, gal! Getting them to board you so you'd have an easier time capturing them! Sounds like something Ray or I might have thought up in our younger days. Good going, kid!"

The real surprise was the quick and blunt reply from New Bern. Verbal only, the unidentified sender did not mince words.

"We do not know what you are doing here in our sector of space, but a visit now would complicate matters. People would meet you, and when next you stuck your neck out and were about to have it chopped off, we might feel pressure to ride to your rescue. You can understand our reluctance to have footage sympathetic to you in our media archives. Please stay away."

Maybe Kris should have given more thought to her reply, but she shot back her first version.

"As you probably know by now, somebody blew all the jump buoys between us and Brenner Pass. Unless you fancy having Peterwald space getting as close to you as Chance, you might want to start paying more attention to this end of space. While you can tell me not to come, and I will respect your views, you may find that Peterwald battleships are a bit harder to talk to."

Kris would have preferred to say that in person, more delicately, but swapping messages left little room for finesse.

But with New Bern off her travel plans, Kris was left with time on her hands and a need to go. Why not give Nelly a treat?

WEE! Nelly shouted in the back of Kris's skull. WE'RE GO-ING TO GO EXPLORING. WE'RE GOING TO GO EXPLORING.

NOT IF YOU GIVE ME A HEADACHE.

On the way to the captain's cabin, Kris took Jack aside and brought the Marine in on the "other" reason Kris had jumped at command of Naval District 41.

Jack shook his head. "So that's what this is all about."

"I'll give you a full briefing when I bring the captain and navigator in on the secret. My question to you is security. Do you feel safe spending weeks with this crew while we look at what Nelly thinks may be very unique alien finds?"

"What do you think we'll discover?"

"Your guess is as good as mine."

"It could be valuable."

"Or it could be dust. Most likely it will be somewhere in the middle. And most of what we see we won't understand."

"Why do this all by yourself? And why not give us poor working folks some warning about what we're headed for?"

"I'm Great-grampa Ray's little girl. Maybe exploring is in our blood. I don't know. It's out there and I want to be first to see it."

"Me too," Nelly added.

"They don't pay me enough for this job," Jack moaned as he followed Kris into the captain's cabin. A moment later, Captain Drago and his navigator filed into the room, sat down across from Kris, and said nothing.

Kris eyed Sulwan. "I was wondering whether Navigation Officer Kann noticed some strange objects in the Chance and neighboring systems?"

The navigator glanced at her captain before answering. "You mean those fuzzy things on my screen."

YES!

DOWN, GIRL, WE DO THIS MY WAY, SO BE QUIET OR FORGET ABOUT US GOING EXPLORING.

YOU ARE MEAN TO ME AND A SLAVE DRIVER AND I WILL BE QUIET.

"Yes," Kris said to the navigator, trying to keep two conversations straight. "What do you take them for?"

"I don't know," Sulwan said.

"What fuzzy things?" the captain asked.

"There's one in the Chance system," his navigator answered. "Another one in the next. They show up on our scans just like jump points, but not. A jump point is a solid gravitational expression on my nav board. Every jump point I've ever seen looks the same. A point. These two aren't. Not exactly. I don't know how to say it, but they seem kind of fuzzy."

"You didn't tell me about them?" Drago frowned.

"They're not on the charts. The last thing you need is a navigator who's seeing things that aren't there."

Drago's raised eyebrow showed agreement with that. "So how come you, Most Princess of Longknifes, are asking about what my Sulwan doesn't want to talk about?"

"Last year, when my job was kind of boring . . ." Kris started.

"You in a boring job," Sulwan said, failing to suppress her feigned shock.

"It only lasted a few seconds," Jack said, dryly. "Less than a minute."

"May I go on?" Kris asked. They nodded. "My old friend, Trudy Seyd, retired Chief of Wardhaven's Info Warfare, asked if I'd help with an experiment. She slipped a piece of rock from Santa Maria into my personal computer's self-organizing matrix, and added software to protect her while she tested this rock."

"Rock?" Captain Drago said.

"It was from the Northern Range of Santa Maria. The ones Grampa Ray blew away. Anyway, the folks doing research on Santa Maria thought those mountains had been nanotech-modified for data storage by the computer the Three put in charge of that planet."

"We don't hear much about the Three species who some say built the jump points a couple of million years ago and then went away," Sulwan said. "Unless we stop at Santa Maria. They've got festival days there about the Three. I was there once."

"I still think the jump points are natural," Captain Drago said. "I don't like the idea of trusting my ship to some high-way other species built while we were still throwing rocks."

"Lots of people share your view," Kris agreed, and let it hang there.

"But?" Drago went on.

"Nelly has been finagling that rock, and she thinks she has found star charts. Charts with more jump points on them than my Great-grampa Ray saw when he was still able to see stuff on Santa Maria and drew up the star charts we use today."

"You bet I have. And you have seen them, too, in your dreams, Kris."

"Yes, I have, Nelly," Kris agreed. The others were staring at Kris's collar bone, where Nelly rested comfortably.

"Are you sure these are jump points?" Captain Drago asked.

"They appear to be. The charts seem to show stars we've identified and connections between them. At least one connection for each point."

"But why do these look different?" Drago asked, his bushy brows coming down, nuzzling each other like two caterpillars that couldn't decide whether to fight or be friends.

"Your guess is as good as mine," Kris said. "Possibly, they built most of the jump point net, the part we know about, us-ing one technology. Maybe these points used a new technol-ogy and were built after Santa Maria U was closed down."

"And you want me to risk my ship on those 'maybe's'?"

"You got it in one," Jack said. "Don't you love working for this young optimist?"

"Maybe, maybe not," Drago said, rubbing his chin.

"It would be interesting, giving those jump points a look," Sulwan said. "And we have the jump buoys already aboard. We could send one through first. Us later."

"You want to do this!"

"Why not, Skipper? How often does anyone get a chance to open up a chunk of sky? Who knows? Maybe this is the hole the Three crawled in and pulled the road up behind them."

Jack shook his head. "And Kris, here, wants to stick her head in the lion's mouth and count its teeth."

Captain Drago raised an eyebrow, then seemed to make a decision. "I'll need to bring aboard more food and supplies. Nine tomorrow morning soon enough?"

"Sounds fine, Captain." That would leave Kris time to explain to Penny why she again had Kris's command. Kris told her over salads at the New Chicago Pizza Place.

"I wondered what you'd do about Ron asking you to make yourself scarce," Penny said, biting into a small tomato. "I learned you were leaving from Chief Beni when he came back, waving a check fit to choke a horse. Remind me to go out with you next time you go hunting."

"We captured the ship. I paid fair market value and . . ." Kris said, unsure if she should tell Penny where she was off to.

"If that admiral at Wardhaven had surrendered his ship, would we have sold it and split the profits?" Penny asked, her voice distant.

"The engineer was supposed to blow up the *Wasp*. I think the battleships had the same orders. It was really a waste of time for me to offer them a chance to haul down their colors."

"And while you talked, that SOB targeted the 109," Penny said in a barely audible whisper.

And Tommy died under that fire.

There. It was out. Kris had tried for something that wasn't even there, and it had cost her best friend his life. Or it would have cost Penny her life if Tommy hadn't knocked her out of the way . . . and died for it.

Their eyes locked. But today Penny didn't flee the room. There wasn't even a tear tracing its way down her cheek. *I guess she's getting better. Maybe I should be, too*, Kris thought.

Three of the old vets came in, waved at Penny, saw who she was with and took another table. Penny waved back. She did use the napkin to daub at her left eye. "You know, Kris, you ought to hang around here a bit. These are good people. I've been working on the *Patton* with a whole batch of them. End up eating most of my meals with them."

"They talk a lot?"

"They listen a lot. Really good listeners. Most of them lost buddies, lovers in the war. Eighty years later, they still remember them. They still hurt, but the pain's scarred over. I'm starting to think there's hope for me."

Kris glanced out at the crowd in the place. It was filling up, but they had a quiet corner in the back and, though everyone who came in seemed to have a smile and a wave for Penny, none moved into their private space.

"I hear you've taken to shooting first even if you can't ask questions later," Penny said, then filled her mouth and leaned forward to chew . . . and listen.

"That word all over the place?"

"Judge Maydell was working with me this afternoon. She says it looks like you made the hard call for the right reason, but she's wondering if it was only for the right reasons. She thinks your combat vita is way too full for someone our age."

"She have any idea how I avoid getting shot at next time?"

Penny shook her head, and kept chewing.

Kris gazed up at the ceiling. "If I got a sleepy dart into her cheek, would it have done the job? Or would the dart have just broken her jaw on the way into her brain? If I hit her eye, she'd be just as dead as she ended up. And if I planted a few darts in her scalp, would they have put her to sleep or just aggravated her?" Penny nodded along.

"They were armed and dangerous. She wouldn't freeze, but went for her gun. The ones we captured said they intended to take over the *Resolute*. I *was* reading the situation correctly."

"But," Penny said.

Kris tried to ignore the "but." Still, it hung in the air.

"I enjoyed shooting her," Kris finally admitted. "I never got a chance to blow the head off that admiral on the *Revenge* who gutted the 109. Was I shooting at her, or at him." Kris paused to let the question bounce around in her head for the forty millionth time. "I just don't know."

"You need a break," Penny said.

"I thought Training Command was supposed to be a break."

"Maybe for me, but you ended up dodging a couple of bombs. Did you ever relax? *Do* you ever relax?"

"You're starting to sound like that police officer on Turantic. What did he say? 'Each time you pull the trigger, it gets easier to pull it the next time.'"

"And you get more and more different from the person you started out being," Penny added.

They both munched a few forkfuls of salad on that thought.

"And I thought I'd have dinner with you and counsel you a bit," Kris finally said.

"You *are* counseling me. You're making *me* feel great. I'm getting better a whole lot faster than you. I can't tell you how good that makes me feel," Penny said, sticking her tongue out.

Kris threw a cucumber slice at her.

"More of your aggression," Penny said, shaking her head in mock despair. "You know what we need to do?"

"I can think of several hundred good ideas, but which one are you interested in particularly tonight?"

"We need to get drunk."

"You know I can't afford that."

"I'm sure we can get several Proud Old Vets to make sure you get to your ship on time tomorrow. They've told me enough tales of rolling buddies into the liberty launch in the nick of time. They'd cover for us if I asked." Penny was looking over the crowd, as if already picking out their shepherds.

"Penny, if I start drinking, there's no guarantee that I'll be sober by the time we get where we're going."

"Were you that bad a drunk?"

Kris nodded. "But, in college, I found I could get quite high on good friendship and a large bottle of ginger ale."

"Well, I'll just have to provide the friendship, and, Barkeep," Penny shouted. "A bottle of your finest ginger ale."

They polished off several bottles of ginger ale. And they didn't do it alone. Penny's new friends dropped in, to swap tales of battles lost and won, friends who survived, and those who didn't. There was no method to the stories. No moral or lesson. They were just where life had taken these people. Life that, over the years, they had learned they could live with.

This wasn't like her talking to Grampa Ray or Trouble. There, too often she sat as understudy, trying to find out how they did the family business and lived through it. How to be a Longknife and survive the experience.

Here she was listening to people whose biographies would never fill shelves in libraries. But they'd lived just as long. And maybe some of them had lived just as well or even better. Kris listened to them, and later in the evening, she learned she could cry with them. And later on, they showed they could cry with her. The place closed, and Tommy Chang joined them. His story wasn't of war, but of man's inhumanity to man. And of the rugged nature of a new planet that could snatch away the life it seemed to offer. Not all courage wore a uniform.

It was very late, or rather, early, when Penny escorted Kris to her room. "Feel better?" she asked.

"Are they always like that?"

"Sometimes. Usually it's not so intense. Like all things Longknife, I think you ratcheted up the demands on them. And they came through. They're beautiful, aren't they?"

"I've never felt so surrounded by friends."

"Yes," Penny said.

6

The *Resolute* hovered a kilometer from the gravity anomaly that loomed with the unknown. "We ready to send a buoy through?" Kris asked. Actually, urged.

"We've rigged it with a camera so we can see what it sees once it comes back," Sulwan said.

"Assuming it comes back," the helmsman muttered.

"Let's be optimists," Captain Drago said. "We're working for one." He punctuated that with a glance Kris's way. Those dark eyebrows hinted at thoughts quite different from his words.

"Buoy is headed out," Sulwan said. "Buoy is gone. Should be back in one minute," she added quickly.

It was a very long minute. Nelly counted off every second in the back of Kris's skull. If Kris herself hadn't been so antsy, she might have shushed her computer.

Nelly hit sixty and nothing happened.

The bridge stayed quiet. Very quiet. Not even the sound of someone breathing. No surprise. Kris wasn't breathing, either. She listened as Nelly counted. At sixty-three, the errant buoy reappeared and the main screen came to life.

"That's a whole different set of stars," Sulwan whispered.

"Can you match it to anything in our charts?" Drago asked.

"Not enough coverage."

"Well, Your Highness, what are your orders?" the captain said, eyes still on the screen.

"Would you please slip your ship through this jump? We don't want to end up in Iteeche space," Kris said, trying to keep the proper petitioner's tone of voice that one should have when riding in another's ship. Not the flaming eager voice that was in her throat.

"Send the buoy through, then follow, Navigator, *pianissimo*."

The buoy vanished. Sulwan nudged the *Resolute* forward.

It seemed to take forever to reach the jump point.

"I wonder if maybe the reason these jump points look so different might be 'cause they're cargo jumps. Not meant for something alive," Jack said.

"Shut up," Kris said, along with most of the bridge crew. Not Sulwan. She had her eyes on her board.

They made the jump, shook off the effects of it, and stared at that strange star pattern they'd seen from the buoy report.

"Tell me where we are," Captain Drago called softly.

"Just a moment, sir," Sulwan said, her eyes on her board, her fingers flying over it. Then she smiled and looked up.

"We're about fifteen light-years outside human space, in unclaimed territory," the navigator reported. The main screen now showed a familiar star chart. A new point flashed red in an area that was dark with inaccessible stars.

"Doesn't look like much of a system," the helmsman reported. "A couple of rocks close to the star. One of them huge. Several gas giants way out. Nothing in the potential zone of life."

Kris looked over the helmsman's shoulder. A more thorough study might take a day. And likely would tell them little more.

"This a dead end?" she asked Sulwan.

"No. There's a jump point not more than an hour away."

"Head for it," Captain Drago said, too eager to ask Kris.

"Leave the buoy here," Kris said.

"I'm glad to see Your Highness has some sense of self-preservation," Jack said, leaning close to her ear.

"I do know how to leave bread crumbs."

Abby and Chief Beni picked that moment to step onto the

Resolute's bridge. Jack had serious questions about taking leave to accompany Kris's expedition. "Anytime I'm within five light-years of you, Princess, I'm working. Or dodging incoming."

Beni had no such questions. "You bet I want to be in on whatever you're up to. It pays good."

Kris had said nothing to Abby. She'd actually planned on leaving the maid behind. But Abby had shown up waving a fur bikini. "You'll need this if you have to make a formal appearance as a Barbarian Princess to these folks."

"Just how secret is this little shindig?" Jack remarked.

Kris shrugged . . . and remembered the steamer trunks trailing Abby aboard the *Resolute*. All twelve. None got left behind.

Jack raised an eyebrow as if to say "You sure you want to do this? Even Abby's magic Ouija board is saying it's dangerous."

Abby didn't trail any trunks onto the bridge just now.

"Anything interesting?" Beni asked, chomping on an apple left over from lunch.

"Doesn't look like it, just another jump," Kris said.

"I've only got two more cameras to mount on the buoys," the chief said.

"We've only got three buoys," Captain Drago pointed out. "I do wish you'd let me order some drones. It might mean a delay, but we'd be better prepared."

"And why would the *Resolute* be ordering a batch of remotes," Kris said, shaking her head. "We don't want questions raised. Don't worry. It's all taken care of."

The look the captain gave Kris didn't look persuaded.

The second buoy's exploratory trip through the next jump brought back more strange stars . . . and something recorded in the radio bandwidth.

"Can you make anything of it, Chief?" Kris asked.

"It's more static than anything else. It's just that it's static in the wrong place and static with too much organization in it to be ignored."

"Go through?" Sulwan asked.

Captain Drago raised an eyebrow to Kris.

"You see anything in the buoy's report that says we'd be in danger if we went?"

"Can't say that I do," Beni said, almost making it sound like he wanted to.

"If you would, Captain," Kris said, and the *Resolute* followed its buoy through the jump.

This time they found themselves deep in a system's inhabitable zone, orbiting a distant moon of a planet that had several more closer in. A planet beautifully blue and green.

"That's where the noise is coming from. Right down around the equator," Beni reported.

"Do we go down there?" Captain Drago asked.

"Just a moment. Nelly, do you have design instructions for remote deep-space probes in your gizzard."

"I have such designs in my memory banks, Your Highness," Nelly answered formally. Very formally. *Did I hurt her feelings*, Kris wondered. *No, not possible.*

She must have thought it too solidly, because Nelly answered. I DO NOT LIKE IT WHEN YOU MAKE FUN OF ME IN FRONT OF YOUR FRIENDS. I WANT RESPECT.

OKAY, GIRL, I'LL REMEMBER THAT.

"Abby, I have three ten-kilo bars of Smart Metal in my trunks."

"Of course, ma'am."

"And some extra self-organizing computer goo, don't I?"

"You know you do."

"After Turantic, I never leave home without the stuff," Kris said, giving Jack and Captain Drago a big smile. "Abby, please get one bar and a vial of the goo and meet me in Engineering. Let's get ourselves some outriders before we go anywhere. Who knows what might be in our way."

An hour later, Kris and Nelly had conjured up a dozen remote probes and fueled them with antimatter and reaction mass from the *Resolute*'s power plant. Captain Drago was much more enthusiastic about shifting his ship to a lower orbit, now that he was following behind a scout force that verified it was safe.

They settled smoothly into a comfortably low orbit and turned on all the cameras and sensors Kris had snuck aboard her leased ship. After two orbits of the planet, Kris was smiling from ear to ear. Oceans covered 65 percent of this blue-green world. Ice caps glistened at the poles. Two large continents had grass plains and forests spread over their temperate zones. The tropics were either desert or jungle with a really lovely area of green savanna. What looked like a major tropical storm system was swirling its way north from just above the equator.

"Kind of reminds you of Earth before we got done with it," Abby said.

"What do you make of these?" Kris asked Beni, highlighting several large mounds. Some were in huge meadows amid forests. Others were scattered widely among the grassy plains.

"I'm more interested in this one," he said, pointing at a section where the high canopy of the tropical rain forest made way for lower mounds and one tall spire. "This is where that radio noise is coming from."

"Nelly, make us up some small drop scouts to send down to look that place over closely."

"They will be ready for the next pass over that site."

"Call it Site One."

"What about these?" Jack said, pointing to one of the savanna pictures. A herd of something on eight legs was racing along. "Looks like they're running from something!"

"Or someone said 'last one in the river is a rotten egg'," Abby said.

"Animals don't waste their metabolic economy on frivolous things like that," Jack growled.

"Unless the fastest girl gets the fastest guy," Kris said. "Let's launch the probes and get a closer picture."

Three hours later, and two more orbits completed, they were no nearer to any solid answers. "They got big animals and little animals," Abby said.

"They got animals dining on plants, and others that dine on them," Beni pointed out.

"I say those are ruins," Jack said, pointing to what looked very much like ruins . . . or large rock outcroppings in the middle of plains and forests.

"And none of the animals we're looking at look at all like any of the Three species that built the jump points," Kris said.

"Assuming anyone built them," Captain Drago put in.

"And assuming the pictures your Great-Grampa Ray saw on Santa Maria really were of the Three," Sulwan added.

"Questions, assumptions, everywhere and not a drop of data to hang a hat on," Nelly finished.

"So let's go down and see some of this up close," Kris said.

And ducked at the onslaught of "not now," "we're not ready," and "you can't be that crazy" that followed.

"Okay, okay," she said, raising a hand. "I want to go down there, so we are going down there. What do you bunch of nannies insist on us doing before we go?"

Actually, Kris wasn't at all surprised at the safety burden laid on her. If they'd given her a minute of peace, she would probably have outlined everything they said. Still, it must have made Jack, Captain Drago, and even Abby feel good to tell her what to do. So she let them.

Kris brought the shuttle down in a spray of water, waited until she'd bled off most of her speed, then swung the shuttle around gently to head it for the bank of the river. With no sandy beach to aim for, she settled for the foot of a trail that seemed to be where most of the locals came down to drink. The shuttle lost the last of its momentum among what looked like reeds and planted its nose gently onto the muddy bank.

"Not bad," Jack said. "Now to get out of here as easy."

Kris held up her arm, encased in a fully armored space suit. "I won't drink the water. I won't breathe the air. What more do you want, my loyal security officer."

"A nice safe chair by a crackling fire . . . at home," Jack said. He'd been so happy to find that the *Resolute*'s storage included full battle armor for this trip that he hadn't even asked just how it came to pass that a simple merchant ship happened to come so equipped.

Kris had. "I bought them surplus. Armored suits were cheaper than the usual spacewear. I was saving money," Captain Drago insisted. Leaving Kris to wonder if Captain Drago and Maid Abby shopped the same sales.

Jack helped Kris on with her gauntlets and helmet, then Kris did the same for him. Chief Beni was paired with the *Resolute*'s communications officer, the same tech who'd upped the gain on their sensors last cruise.

Captain Drago had offered four strong backs to do the

fetching and carrying. Abby had suggested that she might fill one of those slots. Kris had considered her options and decided she'd rather have her group made up of four knowns to balance the unknown loyalty of the ship's personnel.

"That assumes anyone knows where Abby's loyalties lie," Jack muttered darkly, but since he made no stronger objections, Kris waved Abby aboard.

With everyone suited and checked out, Kris had them crack the shuttle's hatch. The air that came in was breathable, but laden with a wide selection of pollen, bugs, and the likes, enough to make Jack remark: "Now ain't you glad you're breathing canned air?"

Kris shrugged—a comment lost in full armor—and stepped into water up to her knees. She waded through muck and vegetation to the beach. All ashore, she closed up the ship and looked around.

The place was green. Green of leaf and branch. Even most of what passed for tree trunks were green. Some were brown, a few appeared purple. Strange sounds came from the mikes mounted to the outside of their suits. Within their sight, nothing larger than a small fly moved. While two ship's crew tied the shuttle to solid-looking trees, Kris sent probes down the path they intended to take to Site One. When they reported back nothing that seemed worth worrying about, Kris led off.

"Who did that?" came on net.

"What?" Kris asked.

"I just got hit by a rock. Anyone throw it?" No one had.

"Let's go, crew, but take your time. Head's up." Two of the crew carried low-power lasers for clearing path. Abby and another crewwoman had M-6 weapons at the ready. Kris had two automatics strapped to her suit, but was more interested in looking than shooting. "Nelly, use audio and visuals to examine our situation. I want to know immediately if you see anything that looks intelligent or hostile."

"Or both," Nelly added. "I am at least as interested as you are, Kris. And so far I see bushes moving in the wind. I see small animals that shouldn't be able to throw a rock. I don't see anything else."

Something on six legs that reached about to Kris's knees turned the path's corner and trotted toward them. It took a half dozen steps, froze, and raised a snout with four curling tusks. Kris stared into two small eyes that stared back at her.

"Nelly, some noise please. All the speakers will take."

There was a loud screech. All around them, winged things took to the air. In front of Kris, the situation didn't change. As Kris slowly reached for her automatic, Abby came on net.

"Let me try this," she said, and a large stone arched over Kris's shoulder to land in front of the critter. It bounced once, and would have hit the thing, but it made a noise all its own and bolted into the green shrub beside the trail.

"I figured it might not know about an M-6," Abby drawled. "But if someone was throwing rocks, that might do the trick."

Kris stooped to pick up some rocks. Soon, anyone who didn't have his hands full with black-box gizmos had a couple of rocks. Two crewmen talked about a slingshot and how they might make one out of what they had on hand. Since most of it involved cannibalizing their suits, slingshots remained just talk.

The path split in two, but the place Kris wanted was straight ahead. The laser cutters took over, making trail. They took another rock as they left the trees.

"Nelly?"

"I only saw the latter part of the rock's trajectory. Who- or whatever threw it was in the trees."

They stood for a long minute, eyeing the tree line they'd have to cross to get back to the shuttle, but nothing moved out of what they had already determined was "the ordinary."

They crossed the six-foot-high grass as quickly as they could. Ahead, the gray spire gave them something to aim for. What it may once have been was impossible to say, but it was tall, and thin, and looked very well worn. Yet it stood.

They broke out of the grass to find themselves walking over broken stones or maybe shattered concrete. Cracks allowed for tiny invasions of growth."

"A million years old and it looks this good," someone said.

"The road between the stars wasn't the only road the Three made," Kris said.

And a rock bounced across her path.

"I saw that!" Abby said.

"What was it?"

"It looked like a string of oversize jelly beans on centipede legs. Only the first two legs were throwing things. It disappeared into that pile of rocks," Abby said, waving her rifle's snout to the left of the column.

"Let's not shoot anything we don't have to," Kris said.

"It didn't look like anything a big-game hunter would want to mount on her mantelpiece, anyway," Abby said. "Leastwise none of the hunters I worked for."

"I just don't want them mounting *my* head on *their* mantelpiece," Beni said.

"Let's keep all 360 degrees covered," Jack said. "You two at the tail. You're the back door."

Kris turned to find that the rear of the column was already walking backward, rifle or pistol up, covering the rear. Nice to find field craft like that among merchant sailors.

YEAH, RIGHT, Nelly muttered in Kris's brain. I CAN ADD TWO AND TWO AS WELL AS ANY HUMAN.

DOWN GIRL. DON'T LOOK A GIFT HORSE UNDER THE ARMPIT AS OUR CAPTAIN SAYS.

YES, BUT I HOPE YOU WILL DO A BETTER JOB OF CHECKING THE HOOVES OF ANY GREEK GIFT HORSES WE NOW STUMBLE AMONG.

THAT'S A GOOD ONE, NELLY. NOW CONCENTRATE ON THE PRESENT PROBLEM. WE CAN'T AFFORD TO BURN MORE THAN ONE BRIDGE AT A TIME.

"There's one," Nelly said, and Kris got a fleeting look at what was tossing things their way. And sidestepped the latest rock to come at them.

It did and didn't look like one of the Three. Grampa Ray's "download" from Santa Maria of some of the records from the Three showed three distinct species. One, the strangest, was a segmented species that started as one section of tubing, then added more as it grew. It didn't grow them, but attached other singletons. Adults might have five or as many as seven segments, though there did appear to be one picture of an eight. For obvious reasons, they'd become known as the Caterpillar People.

Beyond that, people didn't agree on much about this weird species. "You sure we aren't trying to figure them out from say, a Donald Duck cartoon. How much about humans would a classical Road Runner and Coyote snippet tell you?" was a question Kris found funny when she was a kid.

Now, looking at something that didn't fit the expected, she had to wonder just how much she knew . . . or needed to unlearn.

"Keep your eyes peeled," she ordered. "Let me know if you see one of those things with more than three segments."

"You think we've found one of the Three?" Jack asked.

"Or what it looks like after a million more years of evolution," Kris answered.

"Evolution?" Abby said, "or de-evolution? This place don't look like the place I'd want my great-to-the-nth-degree-grandkids to be living in." Abby had a point. That point was emphasized when Kris spotted one of the critters in question defecate, pick up the droppings, and hurl them at her crew. That one missed, but not the next one.

"You know, Princess," Chief Beni said, trying to scrape the muck off the leg of his battle suit with a large green leaf, "I don't think they much like us."

"Kind of looks that way," Abby agreed.

They reached the edge of the greensward. Ahead lay a series of rock piles. On closer look, they turned out to be less of a jumble. Kris could make out the underlying walls, many of them cracked but still standing. Inside you could see open spaces, shaded by only a few stunted trees or shrubs that had found footing.

"They look man made," one of the sailors said.

"At least intelligently made," Kris agreed.

Underfoot was more of the paving. It showed different textures and hints of different colors. Here and there it was broken by growth, but the handiwork of some engineer was fighting a long, slow retreat. Kris considered what on Wardhaven might still show that humans had been there in, say, a million years. She doubted anything would be left in a hundred thousand.

"Chief, are we still headed for the source of the signal?"

"Yes, Lieutenant. It looks to be coming from that tower. Don't know if the signal is originating from way up there or from someplace down around its base."

"That's what we are here to find out."

That turned out to be no easy walk. Rocks and muck were bouncing off them regularly now. That didn't impede them, but the work of the builders here did not always hold up as well. They had to cut their way through a thousand yards of grass, that or take a long walk around. There were also some pretty tall trees rising above the grass, and some nasty thorn bushes.

"Now aren't you glad we're in this armor," Jack said.

"You don't remember getting an argument from me, do you?"

"She was kind of unusually pliant, as I recall," Abby said.

Jack might have shrugged, but the battle suit absorbed most of it. Kris decided to credit him with a shrug, because he said nothing to Abby's defense of her.

There were more of the critters here in the trees. Kris spotted what might be a family or clan. Anyway it had several of the triple segments, as well as several double segments and a few singles running around under what Kris took for close supervision. The rocks, sticks, and muck came mostly from the triples. A few of the doubles did try their "hands" at throwing, but theirs seemed almost comical in their poor aim. Were they teenagers imitating their elders?

"Would be nice to take a sample of those home with me," the sailor Captain Drago had identified as Doc said.

"Crew, if we don't have to kill anything here, I sure would like to leave here with no blood on my hands."

"You assume they have blood," Beni said.

"Let's give these things the full benefit of the doubt."

"And if they start throwing hand grenades?" Abby said.

"Then you can give them the full benefit of your rifle."

"Amen to that" came from somewhere in the rear.

They were still a good thousand meters away when they got their first partial view of the structure at the foot of the spire. "That place looks huge," Beni said.

The satellite pictures and feedback from the scouts had not prepared Kris for what she saw. The building, she mentally tagged it "noise central," was already too big for them to get a full view of it. What she could see showed multiple sides, a slight corner every hundred meters, no telling how many sides there was to this one.

Beside Kris, the city, if she dare call it that, was in less ruin. No way to tell if that was because it was better built or just protected by its surroundings. Still, while most of the roof might be intact, there would be some holes, made evident by a tree poking its leafy head through. Or a wall would be cracked, letting grass and shrubs into the shadows.

Kris called a pause to let suit radiators catch up with the heat. They were only edging into the yellow, but Kris didn't intend to get into anything today without plenty of reserves. Abby and one of the sailors, claiming that their suits were already in the green, took it upon themselves to laser down some shrubs and take a good look inside one of the buildings. The Doc provided a lookout or, in their case a look in, at the hole in the wall while they did some rummaging around inside.

And returned empty handed.

"It don't look any different inside than it does outside," Abby said, the helmet on her suit turning back and forth in as much of a rueful shake as it could.

Satisfied with the color showing on her team's readouts, Kris ordered them forward. The wind had been blowing softly as they made their way through the city. It fell calm as they reached the base of the spire. The jungle sounds also went suddenly missing. No rocks were tossed their way.

Kris eyed the base of the silvery spire. No cracks in this wall; no grass grew on its smooth sides. There was hardly any pitting in the shiny blue-black facade it presented her.

"About this time in all the vids don't the intrepid explorers decide to split up?" Abby muttered.

"And half of them vanish," Jack added dryly, "into something truly vile and revolting. No thanks."

"The photos say," Nelly said, "there are three identical indentations in the building that might be entrances. They are equally spaced around it. The nearest is about five hundred meters away to your left, Kris."

"Thank you, Nelly," Kris said. "What say we skip the vile and stupid mistakes some fiction weavers resort to and do this smart." Kris turned to the left and took a step.

Her second step sank deep into goo.

"Where'd that come from?" Kris muttered. "Folks, watch your footing. Some of this paving didn't wear as long as the contractor promised."

That got a laugh. But Jack noticed Kris's limp. "How bad?"

"More embarrassing than hurt. I think I can walk it off."

And even if she couldn't, she wasn't going to admit it. It was hard to tell in armor, but the shape of Jack's shoulders seemed to say he didn't buy her claim. She kept walking.

"Whoever built this took pride in his or her . . . or its . . . workmanship. Look at how this shines after all these years," Beni said after a few minutes of walking around the wall.

Maybe it was the armored suit, or the familiar canned air, but Kris didn't feel any of the shivers that she did around the old houses on Wardhaven, or some of the really ancient sites— three or four thousand years old—that she'd seen her one trip to Earth.

Or maybe it was just that it looked too good. She'd marveled at Stonehenge on Earth. It "felt" old. This . . . just seemed too modern.

Or maybe too alien.

They arrived at what might be a door . . . or not. Here was a longer side some two hundred meters between turns. Only this one had an alcove cut two hundred meters into it.

"Looks like a murder hole," Abby said, then had to explain. "Ancient castles or forts let you get at their gates, but only by walking into a space like this where they could shoot at you from all sides. You see any gun ports along there?"

A search of the walls showed no holes for guns, arrows, or fire of any sort. From the ground to as far as they could see, the wall was just blue-black, seamless, and shiny.

But then, in front of them there also was no evidence of a door, gate, portal, or any other way in.

"Maybe it's not a murder hole," Kris said. "Maybe it's just a place to sit and smell the flowers."

"I don't see no flower," Beni observed. "And I don't see anyplace to sit."

"In a million years, those things could get lost," Kris said. "Nelly, could you modify our nano-scouts to go over this place with a fine-tooth comb, see if they can find any cracks that we can't."

"Doing it, Kris," Nelly said. "Done."

"Have them start there," Kris said, pointing at the middle wall where a human architect would have put a door.

Ten minutes later Nelly reported, "No luck. That wall is solid down to the quantum level. Very solid."

"Maybe that's not where these folks would put a door?" Jack said.

"Yeah, maybe the door has to face east or west," Beni said. "Aren't there some ancient cultures that were like that?"

"Yes," Abby agreed. "But they usually oriented the entire building that way."

"But this building is just one big, round half sphere. If these people were made in six or seven segments, and could bend themselves around?" Kris said slowly, not at all sure where she was going with this thought.

"Or are we bending our logic into a pretzel?" Abby asked.

"I am sending the nanos to scout the other sides of this U," Nelly said.

"Maybe we need to look at the paving," Beni said. "Maybe they liked to walk downhill into a place."

"We didn't see any basements in the buildings that are open," Abby pointed out.

Kris let the chatter wash over her, something she'd react to if and when she needed to. The building itself was having its own effect on her. It towered, but it also leaned back, away from her, hiding its upper limits from her eye. What impact had the original architect sought on his public. No columns here. No towering straight walls.

Totally alien.

"Kris, we seem to have found a break in the wall that is linear," Nelly reported.

Kris led an avalanche of "Where?"

"I will try to have the nanos mark the separation. It hardly qualifies as a crack. The nanos cannot penetrate it."

"That really is small!" Kris said. It took several tries to mark the outline of the potential door. The first two efforts at marking it resulted in slight puffs of dye marker drifting away on the tiny updrafts rising in the heat of the building.

The third try succeeded in leaving a thin yellow mark. Slowly a pattern formed. It started about five meters away at the bottom where the building met the pavement. Then it rose in an arch, widening. "They were round centipedes," Kris said.

The circling pattern met at the top. No flourishes, nothing that Mother called gingerbread. Just a circle cut off at the bottom by the flat line of the pavement.

"I guess that qualifies as a door," Jack said.

"Only if we can open it," Kris reminded them. "Nelly, have your nanos look for something like a keypad or door lock. Anything that might open it."

"I have had them scouring the wall around it, as well as the wall across from it. Kris, what you see is all that we have found. This is a very blank wall."

"Thank you, Nelly," Kris said. Nelly's nonexistent feathers seemed to be a bit ruffled. Maybe some human respect would soothe. "Beni, do you have any signal that we might use for an 'open sesame'?"

"All I'm getting is the usual noise I've been hearing. Static with too much of a hint at some organization."

"Anyone want to try explosives?" Abby said.

"You really think anything we've got will mar something that's withstood a million years?" Jack said.

"Nothing beats a try but a failure," the maid answered.

"Let's start with the lasers," Kris ordered. The lasers had been very low-powered to cut brush. Now the sailors dialed one up and applied it to a section of wall.

To no noticeable effect.

"Kris, feel that?" Nelly said a full minute later.

"It ought to be white hot."

"Yes, but my nanos report that it is no warmer than the surrounding wall."

"Where's the heat going?" the sailor with the laser said, putting it down.

Kris reached slowly for the place he'd been working on. No heat came back at her. She touched it. Her gauntleted hands transmitted no warmth. "Whatever this stuff is, I want it on the hide of my next ship." Murmurs of agreement filled the net.

"Kris, I may have spotted something in the static," Nelly said, interrupting them all standing around looking dumb.

"What do you think you have?"

"Among the signals I found on the stone chip I have been analyzing are a whole series of sequences that seem to make no sense at all. They are just in this one place on the chip with no reference to anything."

"And," Kris said.

"One of the sequences coming from the spire is the first half of one of those sequences from Santa Maria."

"An entrance code?"

"Your guess is as good as mine," Nelly answered. Kris could almost hear a laugh run through the humans on net. Almost. Maybe they turned their mikes off.

"Well, let's see how good your guess is, Nelly. Play the sequence back," Kris said.

There was a pause. The door, if that was what it was, stayed closed. "I just played it," Nelly said.

"Do we need to hunt for a different frequency to reply?" Beni asked.

"That could put us here forever," Comm Boss at his elbow sighed, but he seemed to have intercepted Nelly's signal and was already working his own black box.

"Or maybe we didn't send it right?" Abby said.

"Your thoughts," Kris said.

"Nelly, you sent it the whole sequence, right."

"Yes."

"But was it sending out the whole sequence, or just part of it?"

"It was sending only the first part."

"Send only the second part," Kris said.

And in front of them, the entire door moved up and out of their way. "Very, very good, Nelly," Kris said as the doorway reached full open.

Ahead of Kris spanned a large, empty space. The only light came from the open door. By it she saw the building's ribbed outer wall rising up. The floor inside had a series of designs laid into its speckled-green stone that formed no pattern Kris could comprehend. NELLY, YOU WORKING ON IT?

I AM STORING IT FOR LATER STUDY, KRIS, WHEN I HAVE MORE OF IT AVAILABLE.

RIGHT. "Are the nanos inside?"

"Yes, Kris. They report nothing dangerous. However, they

do appear to be gaining weight. They are having to use extra fuel to stay aloft."

"What's making them heavy?" Jack asked.

"I do not know. I would have to bring them out to evaluate the problem fully."

"Bring a couple out and let's have a look," Kris ordered.

A minute later, several nano-scouts were out. "Ah, Kris, they are no longer overweight. I can find nothing on them," Nelly said, sounding rather puzzled for a computer.

"Interesting," Jack said. Kris could almost hear his eyebrows going up behind the mirror of his faceplate.

"So, a million years ago some clean freak designed gear to keep this place spotless. And they're still at it. Too bad we can't tell her how good she was."

"Maybe so, but how will it effect our suits?" Jack asked.

"I intend to find out," Kris said.

"I'm glad you got your itty bitty buddies out in front," Abby said, coming back from across the street twirling a stick as tall as she was. "But I'm gonna trust something a bit more primitive to test out where I put my dainty feet."

"I think I'll get a stick, too," Beni said, heading for the same small copes.

"Get me one, too," Kris said after him.

"Me three," Jack added.

"I'll get one for everyone going in," a sailor with a laser answered as he followed the chief.

"How many are going in?" Jack asked.

"You, me, Abby, Beni. Doc, you willing to stay behind?"

"I really want to get a look inside. Take air samples. Why not leave our radio boss behind. He's got the antenna to net us to the *Resolute*. Him and one of the gunners."

Since Abby was one of the two gunners, that left only one. After some good ribbing about bringing back lush native girls for Comm Boss, and a hunk for the gunner, that was settled.

Beni headed back with an armful of walking staffs. "Bring me a big rock," Kris called. "Something to put in the doorjamb."

The laser wielder turned back, picked a large one that looked like it had started life as a cut slab, but been broken in half. Radio trotted over to give him a hand and the two of them lugged it in and set it upright along the right side of the door.

"Think that will stop it from closing?" Jack asked, eyeing the half meter tall block.

"Long enough for us to get out," Kris said.

"Here we are, the finest example of twenty-fourth century womanhood," Abby said, "and manhood, and we're reduced to using rocks for doorstops."

"I'm sure the next expedition will be much better prepared," Kris said. "Now, do you intend to fold this hand and leave all the fun to them, or are we going to take our own primitive step into, well, whatever."

Abby put out her walking stick, tapped the stones on the inside of the doorsill, and stepped across. "One small step for this woman, one big question mark for the rest of you."

7

Jack went next, tapping all the way with his stick. Kris
followed, letting her walking stick just slide along ahead of
her. Beni and Doc brought up the rear.

"I've got us connected to the *Resolute*," Comm Boss reported from his station at the door.

"We are delighted to see you've gotten this far," Captain
Drago reported.

"So are we," Kris answered. She wanted to trot into the
huge void in front of her, but, as she'd been trained, she
checked her back door. Comm Boss was standing in the doorway, a long pole reaching to the top of the door, ready to warn
if it suddenly decided not to be a way out. The gunner was
faced out, toward the rest of town, just the way the Marines
trained its back door. NELLY, REMIND ME TO LOOK AT THE RÉ-
SUMÉS FOR THESE FOLKS. IF THEY AREN'T ALL EX-MILITARY,
IT'S ONLY BECAUSE THEY ARE STILL MILITARY.

YOU MAY BE RIGHT, KRIS.

Satisfied that her rear was as protected as it could be, Kris
turned her attention inward. And found out why the net had
been so full of "wow" and "oh my" and "this is unbelievable."

"This place is huge," Kris added to the admiring wonder.

Kris shot a laser range-finder out. Almost two thousand meters to the silver metal spire that rose to the roof and beyond. Almost four thousand meters to the far wall.

And it wasn't nearly as dark as it had been.

"Our lights are being reflected back," Abby said, walking over to the nearest rib. There was something light beside the rib, and growing brighter as Abby's suit light got closer. "Our light is being reflected up the light beam, or whatever you want to call this thing."

"It's being intensified," Jack said. "Any chance it could burn us like moths under a magnifying glass?"

"Oh, you say the most inspiring things," Abby said. But Kris noticed that Doc and his sailor sidekick who had headed straight out onto the floor of this huge dome were now trotting for the door.

"The light in here is growing brighter," Nelly said. "However, for it to get truly dangerous to you in your suits would take several hours at this rate."

Doc and his teammate turned around again.

"Thank you, Nelly. Any other thoughts, girl."

"I would like to see more of the floor. Also, certain sections of the floor are giving me radio signals I can match against those unidentified sequences from Santa Maria."

"Think your girl found a one-size-fits-all key?" Abby asked.

"Only one way to find out. Nelly, point us at one of those sources." Nelly led them to a section of floor that didn't look all that different from the rest: speckles of sparkling gold in the dark green stone and some patterns in white and gray several centimeters in size.

"I am sending the signal," Nelly said, and suddenly, out of the floor rose a translucent block of . . . something.

Close to three meters tall, almost two wide, nearly five long, it took on their lights and turned completely clear. The sole exception to that were two light blue, six-bladed propellers that turned lazily inside the near center of the block, one at each long end about ten centimeters in.

"What is it?" Kris said.

"I have no idea," Nelly answered. "I also am no longer getting any signal from this area of the floor."

"Speaking of floor," Jack said, stooping close and struggling in armor to look up through the block. "Where's the green floor stuff that was on it?"

"Your guess is as good as mine," Nelly said.

"You're getting to like that phrase," Kris said.

"It fits too much of this place for my comfort," Nelly answered. "Kris, I agree with Jack, the full examination of this place should be left to a larger, better-equipped team."

"That was a vote I never expected to get," Jack said, standing up. "Anyone have any idea what this is?" he asked.

Doc and Chief Beni examined it with their black boxes. Slight shakes of armored helmets told Kris all she was going to get out of them for the time being.

"Well, is it likely to explode?" she asked.

"Your guess," Beni started.

"Is as good as mine," Kris ended. "Yes, I know. But a guess would be appreciated."

"I'm getting no out-gassing," Doc said. "I've rubbed the surface of the thing and gotten nothing."

"I've probed it with everything I've got that doesn't involve partial destruction of the sample," the chief said. "And I got squat."

"It's clear," Kris said, tapping her laser range-finder. The pulse she sent bounced off the end of the building and returned that measurement. "It is totally clear."

"What's the propeller for? I don't see any beanie," Abby said.

"Better question is how can it be turning in what looks like a solid," Kris said.

"Is it a solid?" Doc muttered. "Or something else we don't even have a word for?"

"I'm kind of getting the feeling of some hunter-gatherer, who's so proud of inventing the throwing spear, coming across a jet engine and not having a clue what it is," Jack said.

"Speak for yourself, Marine," Beni said. "I know what it is."

"What is it?" Kris said, in chorus with everyone else.

"It's a puzzle," the chief said, with a smile that leaked onto the net even if Kris couldn't make it out through his faceplate. "It's a puzzle we are not going to solve today."

Abby swung her walking stick at Beni's helmeted head.

"At ease, crew," Kris ordered. "And if anyone else wants to make a joke at all our expense, remember, that poor gunner back with Comm Boss would love to have your slot in here."

"Not really," someone contradicted on net.

Kris ignored the insubordination. Anything that failed to rise to the level of full mutiny struck her as just fun, all things in her past considered. She looked around. "Any more signals, Nelly?"

"I have identified forty-seven, but there are more that may qualify."

"Where's the nearest one that takes us closer to the spire?" Kris asked. And Nelly gave directions to another perfectly normal bit of floor. "Send the signal," Kris ordered.

Nothing happened. "Nelly?"

"I sent it. Nothing and now the signal is no longer there."

"Maybe that was one that was dead and didn't know it until it tried to come active," Beni guessed.

"Mark the floor with something," Kris said. Doc's escort pulled out some tape and marked an X.

Kris checked her readouts. "I show six more hours of air."

"Kris, are you having any trouble moving your joints," Jack said, rotating both arms of his suit. One moved much slower.

Kris did the same—with the same results. "One leg is moving a bit stiffer than the other, too," she admitted.

"I don't know what's causing it, but shouldn't we be heading out of here?" Jack said.

Kris ignored him and trotted toward the base of the spire. She ended up kind of limping, but the closer she got to the spire, the more excited she was. Several hundred meters out, she spotted a false ceiling or overhang around it, spreading out. Taken edge on, it was hard to tell how far it went.

A hundred meters out, they came under it.

Initially translucent, the lights from their suits caused specks to appear. "It is a star chart," Nelly whispered. "Yes, definitely a star chart as seen from here. Look, there's what Chance calls the Wild Horseman. And the Fat Lady Singing."

"There are lines between the stars," Kris pointed out.

"I think those are jump points. At least the basic ones. Chance has three jumps out from it. The system we are in is marked with a point surrounded by a circle. Do you see it?"

"I think so," Kris agreed, pointing her range-finder up and clicking it to visible red.

"That's it," Nelly said.

"That one next to it also has a circle. Those are the only two," Beni said.

"And the line between it is green. The others are kind of yellow gold, but that one is green," Jack said.

"Why the difference between two stars?" Nelly asked.

"Your guess is as good as mine," Beni said, "but my suit is getting real hard to move. Let's get out of here."

Kris joined the others limping quickly for the exit, but thinking as well. "If any guess is as good as any other, let's have a few. For starters, I'm guessing that it has to do with this spire. What if it is a faster-than-light commlink?"

"And that shows where they got a signal from," Jack said.

"If you could make jump points across space, you could send signals through those jumps," Beni agreed, pulling ahead.

"But why the low-tech radio signal we picked up?" Abby said, breathless. "That certainly isn't the interstellar commlink."

"Unless Abby's idea about the de-evolution of the species has something to do with it," Kris said, slowing to stay even with Abby. "Part of Santa Maria was left as a nature preserve. Everything else was nano-mined. What if this was a nature reserve? A place for folks that didn't want all the tech?"

"And the last interstellar message had to be radioed to the other towns?" Jack said, falling back, too. "That's a big leap."

"I'm open to other leaps," Kris said.

"When we get out of here, if we do, I'd sure like to see what that other circled star looks like," Doc said.

"So would I," Kris said, "*Resolute*, you copy this star map?"

"We've got it," Captain Drago said.

"It fits the two new jump points I've found out of this system," Sulwan added.

"How long to boost to the one we didn't come in?"

"Not too long," Sulwan answered.

"Once we're out of here, we'll see," Kris said.

"Assuming we get out," Jack said.

"Whatever this stuff is, it's sure making our suits shine," Doc said. "But I can't get any readouts off of it."

"I can tell you that it's doing something to my joints," Abby said, coming to a halt. "You go ahead. I got to rest."

Kris didn't pause, but hobbled on, each step an effort. If she remembered right, the extra weight vanished from the nanos the second they got out of the building. Jack stayed beside her.

Beni, Doc, and his helper struggled out into the daylight, their heavy breathing filling the net. Kris was throwing each stiff leg ahead of the other by swinging the suit from left to right, right to left. Jack struggled, too.

"Who'd have thought a clean freak could kill us a million years after the last white-glove inspection," Kris muttered.

"Kind of makes you wonder what a Neanderthal would think if you handed one a bar of soap," Abby drawled.

"Remind me to say something nice about you," Doc said.

"Save your breath," Jack ordered.

"You okay, Abby?" Kris asked.

"Long as my air holds, I'm just the tin man giving advice."

Outside in the sun, Doc moved the arms and legs of his suit. "It's gone. Let's see what happens," he muttered, and ran back in. He was only starting to go stiff legged when he reached Kris. He grabbed her shoulder strap, and dragged her along.

"I'm gonna hate myself if this don't work," Chief Beni said, and dashed in to help Jack.

Long minutes later, all four of them were in daylight. And the stiffness was gone. "Can't you get any readout off of this?" Kris asked Doc as she rotated her arms, bent her knees.

"Not a thing shows on any of my stuff."

"We can't leave Abby in there," Kris said.

"I was kind of hoping you'd remember me."

"Jack, you're with me," Kris said and headed back in. She and the Marine ran for Abby. The stiffness was just coming back when they reached her. The maid was locked up, stiff as a board. Kris grabbed one arm, Jack the other and they dragged her along most of the way to the shining door . . . and locked up themselves, twenty yards out.

"I'm really going to hate myself," Beni said as he, Doc, and the door guards headed back in and dragged Kris and Jack out. The two door guards, then, had no trouble going back for Abby.

"Glad that's over," Abby said.

"Look at our air supply," Kris said.

"My how time flies when you're turning to stone," Jack said.

"How do we protect this place?" Kris said, looking at the door. "If we close it, assuming we can, will it open again? If we leave it open, will we lose too much of what's inside?"

"Sure you want to save whatever that stuff was?" Abby said.

"I've got a balloon," Comm Boss said. "To raise an antenna if we needed to. We could use it to block the door."

"We'll get out-gassing off the balloon," Doc pointed out.

"It's still better than nothing."

A few minutes later, the balloon blocked the entrance and a coat of plastic glue protected the balloon from anything short of a rifle round and everyone was hurrying down the path they had taken in. Their gleaming battle armor got smeared with poop and rocks. Another large-tusked animal disputed the right-of-way with Kris, ignored the tossed rock, and had to be shot as it charged. Doc bottled hair samples of the beast but with air supply down to three hours, that was it. They arrived back at the riverbank where they'd left the shuttle. It was gone.

"It can't be far," Kris scowled, more bothered than scared. Just now, panic was not an option. Kris tossed her walking stick out into the river and watched as it drifted to her left. "If someone untied it and pushed it out, it ought to be headed that way. There's not much of a current."

Abby had waded out into the crushed rushes made by the beached shuttle. "Mind if I go upstream? Those little dickens might have thought to tow it."

"And now our intrepid heros separate into two groups," Beni muttered. "Which one will vanish, never to be seen again?"

"Stow it, Chief," Kris ordered. "It seems our jelly bean strings have a few tricks up their sleeves we didn't expect."

"Ah, Kris," Nelly said softly. "I just sent a signal to the shuttle. It is slightly west of us and moving slowly westward."

"Thank you, Nelly," Kris said, to chuckles from the other twenty-fourth-century humans as they remembered they were, after all, not cavemen.

Around a small bend in the river, the shuttle bobbed gently along, drifting broadside to the stream flow. Four waded out to capture the line floating from the shuttle's nose. The synthetic rope had not been cut. "They haven't forgotten everything they

once knew," the woman gunner said, holding the line as she and
the others dragged the spacecraft back into the shallows.

The return to space went quickly after that. Kris matched
orbit with the *Resolute*, but did not enter the shuttle bay. Crew
that had stayed behind now came out and passed them a line to
follow into an airlock. The three girls started the process of de-
contamination. In Lock 1, their battle armor was sprayed,
scrubbed, and generally scoured for anything virus size or
larger. After the lock had been vented to space and the cleaning
process run a second time and vented, the gals got to shuck
their armored duds and advance into Lock 2. There they
scrubbed themselves down, got to enjoy having the lock vented
to space down to one-tenth normal pressure, then repeated.
Stripped bare, they entered the third lock where they found
long johns to skinny into and a airlock that wouldn't open.

"Sorry Princess, but we want you to breath the air awhile,
let us test it for the creeping uglies, then we'll let you in."

Which meant Kris, Abby, and Gunner Jennifer were still
there when Jack, Beni, and Doc came through the hatch.

"Don't look," Jack growled, as he hurriedly pulled on the
same style white long johns. Kris didn't look . . . very much.

About as much as Abby didn't look . . . much.

Jennifer didn't even turn away. "I usually have to pay for a
show this good." Beni went beet red.

"Captain, I told you we wouldn't have to go through full
decon," Doc shouted at no particular speaker visible.

"Hey, be glad I'm taking you back. If one more member of
the crew had voted the other way, we were going to leave you
down there until a real expedition came along."

"You wouldn't have done that," Kris said, trying to make it
more a definite statement than a question.

"Who cast the decisive vote?" Abby asked.

"I did" came from about five voices on net.

"Well," Abby drawled, "if there'd been just one of you'all,
I might have had to be nice to you."

"Where do you want to go next?" the captain and navigator
said together.

"The planet that sent the last message to this one, or so we
think," Kris said, loosening the first button of her top and
moving along to the next one.

"You really want to go there," Captain Drago said.

"I really do," Kris said, trying to coo as she toyed with that second button. *Now, how do they do this in the movies.*

"I do, too, Princess, so that is where we're going."

"Aw, Captain, you could have at least waited to see if that second button came undone," Abby grouched.

"How am I supposed to learn to be a femme fatale if no one lets me practice on them?" Kris tried to pout.

"In case you haven't noticed, Kris," Jack drawled, "fatal is what you do."

"Fatal I don't have to work at. It's the femme fatale I need to get a handle on," Kris insisted.

Kris was still defending her right to explore other aspects of her nature when Captain Drago ended the quarantine.

The *Resolute* was already at 1.5 g's by the time Kris was back in a shipsuit and on the bridge. There was just time for chow and a general briefing on what they found before the ship hung motionless before another jump point. Again, a buoy went through first. This time it returned with no radio noise, but some decent shots of a planet, several moons, and what looked like orbital habitats. Very sophisticated.

"I think I make out ships in orbit," a laser tech with a surprising skill in photo interpretation said, highlighting several bodies in space, smaller than habitats. "Look at the size of those space elevators."

Kris whistled, along with everyone looking. "And look at the number of them. Six I can count from just this side alone!"

"Is this place active?" Jack asked, eyeing Kris like he was about to haul her back to her room and lock her away.

"No way to tell from these photos," the tech said.

"Captain Drago," Kris said. "If you please, will you take the *Resolute* through the jump at minimum speed."

"Honey," the navigator said, "you crawled faster than I'll move this tub. That is, if you say we're going, Captain."

Drago eyed Jack. The two of them seemed to be doing that male telepathic thing Kris hated. She could almost hear Jack shouting "Run, run, run for our lives" in mental silence.

Then Drago grinned. "I could never go back without seeing what we've found. Sulwan, my girl, petite steps. *Tres petite.*"

The buoy went through first. They gave it time to settle down at a comfortable distance out of their way, then Sulwan goosed the *Resolute* through, just a tad after doing the same for the five scouts Kris had out ahead of the ship.

A brief disorientation, and then they were there. Kris was out of her seat, hanging over the helmsman, eyeing his close-in scan, glancing up at the expanding picture coming back from their deeper sensors. "The buoy's there," the helmsman reported. "And all five of the scouts."

"Four," Kris said as the left one winked out of existence.

"Right a nudge," Captain Drago ordered, and it was so.

"There goes the next left one," Kris said.

"Halt the ship. Take all way off her," Drago ordered.

Kris thought they were going about as slow as they could. Still, she bumped the forward screen as the ship stopped more suddenly than she was ready for. Than Jack was ready for. He plowed into the navigator's station.

"The ship is marking time in space," the helm reported.

"Princess, do you have any more of that magic stuff for scouts. I'm not going anywhere but back through that rabbit hole until I've got lots and lots of bugs out in front of me."

"Abby, grab all our Smart Metal and goo and meet me in Engineering."

Kris paddled aft; Jack right behind her, rubbing a shoulder. "You ought to put some ice on that," she said.

"I ought to get another job," he grumbled, but did stop off in the galley and when he caught up with her in Engineering, he had a sack of ice taped to his shoulder.

"Nelly, make them plenty and dumb," Kris said. "We want a cloud of these ahead of us whenever we move. They'll tell us all we need to know when they vanish."

"And if we want to do further exploring?" Nelly asked.

"You can reform them into something bigger, smarter."

An hour later they were back on the bridge as the *Resolute* began a slow approach to what they called Alien 2.

"You have a problem with that?" Captain Drago asked. "Maybe you wanted it named Kris."

"Why not," Jack drawled as he settled into a seat. "The planet almost killed us, and Kris gets us almost killed a lot."

"You wrong me," Kris said, innocently. "What have we found out so far from visual scans?"

"Interesting planet," Captain Drago said. "Take the moons. Three of them, about equal in size. All tidal locked on the planet and each in the same orbit. Offset one third of the orbit from each other."

"Unless this is the strangest accident I've ever heard of," Jack said, "someone is moving moons around this system."

"Very likely," Sulwan said. "I'd love that power plant."

"We think we've spotted large cities on the planet," the photo tech said. "Not absolutely sure. There're no lights showing on the night side, but when we get sunlight, it sure looks like man-made structures . . . huge ones."

"But no lights?" Kris said.

"Dark is dark. Sunlit is, well, what we see."

"Infrared? Radioactive readings. Anything hot?"

"Sorry, Princess. It's as quiet as if hatched yesterday."

"Except we're missing those two probes," Jack and the captain said at the same time.

"So something is active."

"Somebody forgot to turn a few things off."

"Assuming they left."

"Seen enough, Kris? Can we go home now?" Jack said.

"No, I didn't make up all those scouts to guide us back through the jump," she said, taking a seat next to the captain. "If you will, sir, see if you can find us a closer orbit that this planet doesn't object to."

"Sulwan, take charge of the scouts our employer has so graciously allowed to us. Put half of them ahead of us. We'll use a few as a string back to the jump. I think the Marine does want to assure a line of retreat." Jack gave a sour nod. "Then send the rest exploring. See if there is any other place safe around here for us." Six hours of sweat and bad language later, they had the *Resolute* in a planetary orbit about halfway between Alien 2 and one of its moons.

"I really don't want to go any closer than this," Drago said. "We've got six layers of your bugs out around us. If something changes its mind about letting us hang here, we ought to get the first hint and have time to bug out."

Kris eyed the situation from behind the helmsman, found it good and turned to the photo tech. "How good are your sensors?"

"I've got quarter-meter resolution from here."

"I must thank Penny when we get home for hiring such a versatile crew. Or should I thank Abby now?"

"Don't know what you mean by that, Princess," the captain said, not looking her way.

"So, let's see what there is to see."

There was plenty. The moons were airless, but splotched with structures connected by what looked like a rail system. And they had large structures orbiting them that looked innocent, strange, and dangerous all at the same time. "Are those laser weapons?" Kris asked pointing at protrusions jutting from the nearest satellite.

"They don't look like anything we've got," the *Resolute*'s chief gunner answered. "God herself only knows what they are, and she quit talking to me about the time I left home."

"You see any other signs of weapons?" Captain Drago asked.

"Boss, I feel like this whole place is one big rifle range and I'm the sitting duck, sir. If you want my opinion. And I know you don't." Then she added another "sir."

"Thank you, Thong, and if you see anything new that makes you feel less safe, let me know," Kris said, before turning back to Sulwan's sensors, now ably assisted by the photo expert. "What can you tell me about the planet?"

"A lot more. A lot less, Your Highness," Sulwan said. "There are twelve space elevators evenly spaced around the planet's equator. Several of them look to be rising right out of the sea. At least three of them have what look like huge floating cities around them."

A picture appeared on the main screen. The scaling next to it said the floating structure was several hundred kilometers across. "Is it free-floating or anchored in shallows or what?"

"You make the guess, Kris. I tried with radar to ping the bottom of that ocean. No joy. Radar went out. It didn't come back. But that ocean sure looks deep to me."

Kris couldn't argue. No basis for any opinion. Kris suddenly had a suspicion she knew what a newborn felt like getting its first look around. Only this newborn was gawking at a whole world, not just the inside of a nursery. Oh, and this newborn had better not cry . . . or piss her pants.

"But there is one thing," Sulwan added. "See that, there, that elevator station." Kris watched as what looked like static electricity leaped out from the tip of the orbital station and lost itself in the blackness of space.

"What was that?"

"I have no idea, but six of the stations are doing that."

"Looks dangerous."

"Maybe. Or maybe the six stations not doing that are the dangerous ones. Pay your money and take your chances. Me, I'm betting on not going near any of them."

"Not this trip," Kris agreed. "Okay, we're learning a lot about this place we don't know. Let's see what we do know. Can anyone give me some numbers? What part of this place is city, rural, wilderness?"

Numbers came up on the screen. Someone had even added Wardhaven's stats as well as Earth's. The place had a bit more land than either Earth or Wardhaven. Much more urban than Wardhaven, but not as much as Earth. Arable land matched well. Same for wilderness.

"I don't get it," Jack said.

"Don't get what?" Kris asked.

"Santa Maria was worn down to the bedrock. What evidence of the Three that we found was mostly underground and nano in size. Alien 1 is all rubble and overgrown. What's this planet doing looking like you might find a warm supper on the table?"

The bridge fell silent in the face of that one. Kris gnawed on it for a while . . . and came up empty.

"Can I say something?" Nelly asked.

"The floor is wide open for observations, opinions, and guesses," Kris said.

"Santa Maria's moon showed no evidence of habitation," Nelly said slowly. "There was nothing left in orbit from the Three."

"Yes, Nelly, that's right," Kris said.

"Our review of what you are calling Alien 1 was cursory, but there was no evidence of any active systems in orbit."

"I think you're right about that," Sulwan said.

"Here we see orbital stations at the top of elevators," Nelly went on. "There are clearly some things still operating or we would not have lost our scouts. I notice only one major weather system on the planet, and it seems to be limited to one of the wilderness areas. There are other weather systems, but they are providing very gentle rains to the arable lands and urban areas. May I venture a guess that the weather control system is still protecting this planet from violent change. Anything that could move moons into this planet's orbit might also be able to arrange it so that tectonic plate activity also was negated. I do not know any of this. But they do seem to be reasonable assumptions."

"They most certainly are," Kris agreed. "Nelly, you have drawn some very reasonable conclusions. Tell Auntie Tru how you came to them next chance you get to send her a message."

"I will," Nelly said, almost giggling with glee.

"If what Nelly says is true," Abby said from the hatch of the bridge, "then we might be looking at the ultimate achievement of the Three. One of the last places they were at before they did whatever they did to go away."

"Yeah," Captain Drago agreed. "But I don't think the last one out remembered to turn everything off. I like the idea of leaving on the weather controls. Hell, I'd like to live where they got weather controls. But did they leave on anything like those cleaning things that almost turned you to stone?"

"Strange as this may sound, my dear Captain," Kris said with a cheerful grin, "I agree with you. Let's spend the next six hours taking pictures from a safe distance, then tiptoe our way out very carefully and make like no one was ever here."

Of course, Kris knew that was impossible. They *had* been here. Every crew member on board must be seeing dollar signs dancing in his or her head. Kris had spotted what looked like ships in free orbit around the planet as well as others tied up to the stations. Stations that were not rotating to give them something like gravity. The Three must have had artificial gravity. That would change humanity at least as much as the jump points had. That would be worth trillions.

To whoever could figure it out.

And like every other invention humanity had come up with, it would be twisted to something deadly. What would gravity waves do if you aimed them at a ship? Would ice armor be any defense against them? Questions. Questions with no answers. Who knows, Wardhaven had ships in free orbit. Maybe they didn't have controlled gravity. But High Wardhaven rotated to give Kris a feeling of up and down. No. There was something here.

And that was only what she saw at a glance.

"I'll be in my room," Kris said, kicking herself off from the helm and swimming for the hatch. Abby made way, but said nothing. She also didn't follow Kris, but edged onto the bridge to get a better view.

Kris had gotten what she wanted.

Now, what did she do about it.

8

Kris hunkered down in her stateroom while they tiptoed out of Alien 2's system and boosted direct for the next jump with Alien 1 glowing green and blue beneath them. Surprise of surprises, she was left alone. No interruptions from Jack. Kris wondered if he, too, was contemplating her leadership challenge.

At OCS, they'd handed out case studies for the future junior officers to study, analyze, and report back solutions for. None came close to what Kris now stared at. Then again, those challenges were for boot ensigns. The hairy monster Kris faced was for a Naval District Commander. One for one of those damn Longknifes. It involved a princess and a major stockholder in Nuu Enterprises. And each hat made the problem tougher.

Kris had the greatest discovery since humanity put its nose into space. An entire mature civilization's leavings lay out there for the taking. Assuming you lived through taking it.

And assuming you figured out what you had your hands on.

The material of that building on Alien 1 could make every laser weapon in human space as obsolete as the arrow. Add in the prospects of finally getting control of gravity, and weather, and moving moons around . . . Kris shivered. She held the key to a great leap into the future for all humankind.

Slight correction. She and everyone on this ship.

Let anyone on this ship blab a word of this, there'd be riots. Stocks would plummet on the off chance that this or that might be worthless tomorrow, if not sooner. And that was before every crazy dreamer with access to a starship headed for Alien 2.

And likely got themselves killed trying to be first.

Or broke something critical trying to get to something else.

Yes, Kris had a leadership problem. As Commander, Naval District 41, she could probably declare this entire trip Top Secret . . . and then some. But this crew was civilian. Well, she'd drafted Jack into the Marines. She could draft this entire ship into the Navy and slap them with the Secrets Act.

Would the crew accept their new status with a smile? Or see it as Kris Longknife, Nuu stockholder, grabbing the wealth they saw as rightfully theirs. There was a limit to how far you could push people before you ended up taking a long walk out a short airlock. Kris, of all people, understood mutiny.

Princess, trillionaire, Naval District Commander. All that power. You would think a girl could solve any problem that came her way with power like that. And if she wasn't careful, she just might find herself very dead from it.

Kris spent a long night thinking before she called the captain. "I need to talk to all hands."

"I figured so. I'll have them report for chow. It'll be a tight fit. I'll leave two on the bridge, and pipe you in."

Fifteen minutes later, Kris stood before Captain Drago, Sulwan, and most of the crew, as well as her own three . . . could she call them friends? If there was enough money involved, Kris doubted she could count much on Chief Beni. Abby was, as usual, a question mark. Jack, hmm. She'd always trusted him with her life. But Grampa Al insisted everyone had a price.

"We have a problem," Kris started. From the sour looks that came right back at her, it was clear they agreed.

"You and I," Kris said carefully, "have found a treasure of immense value." Every head nodded. "But one thing is missing."

That drew snorts. "The key," Sulwan provided.

"Right," Kris said. "We've come, we've seen, but we dared not touch. Can't risk trying to open it. That's going to take a lot of careful effort. I think most of you know that my Aunt Alnaba has spent most of her life on Santa Maria trying to crack just that part of the Three's puzzle. Eighty years of hacking at it, and most of Santa Maria is still a locked box."

That brought on a lot of nods.

"You want to get to the bottom line?" Captain Drago said.

"Anyone here not want to have their next ship made out of that material on Alien 1 that took the best our lasers had and was just as cool to the touch as when it started?"

"A ship with that wouldn't have to pay insurance against pirates," the captain observed.

"That will make someone a lot of money," Doc said softly.

"No doubt," Kris said. "But it'll take a lot of work and investment money. Anyone here have that kind of pocket change?"

There was a long silence finally broken by Abby's drawl. "You do, don't you, Kris?"

The eyes looking back at Kris were expectant, intrigued, and a few looked downright predatory. With a sigh, Kris chose to lay all her cards face up on the table. "As Princess Kris, I have access to everything King Ray can throw at this problem. I expect Aunt Alnaba will be heading here on the first ship she can hire. That ship could be the *Resolute*. You want in on a long-term contract?" That got interest.

"As Prime Minister Billy Longknife's bratty daughter, I think a few words from me will get all the support this effort needs from the not inconsequential resources of Wardhaven."

That got snorts from many, laughs from a few.

"And as a major shareholder in Nuu Enterprises, Inc. I think I can assure you that all the necessary funds will be available. My Grampa Al has his hooks in most universities' research centers out here on the Rim. Anyone who is curious and has the technical know-how will be available when we need them."

"So there's a lot in it for you," said Doc. "What's in it for us?"

"I imagine there's a lot of media outlets that will pay for your exclusive interview. At least for the first few of you to go public." That got nods. "I imagine there'd be talk-show contracts. Am I missing anything?" The crew exchanged glances. No one came up with other possible income for themselves.

"What could we get from the media?" Doc asked.

"I don't know," Kris said. "When they shove a mike in front of me, I always have to talk for free." Kris's doleful sigh actually got a chuckle from a few.

"About a million bucks," Abby said. "Those are Earth bucks, say a hundred thousand Wardhaven dollars," she added. "For the first few exclusive interviews. After those lucky ducks do their talking, the value goes down for the slow bloomers. The talk-show rounds could probably double that, but you'd have to hire you a manager, and they'd take about a third of everything."

Suddenly, maid Abby knew a whole lot about the price of information. Kris swore it was time to have that often-delayed talk with Abby on her work history.

"How come you know all this?" Someone in the back asked what Kris could not. Not right now in public.

Abby shrugged. "When my third employer got herself killed, her chief of security signed himself up for the full deal. Me," the maid shrugged. "I was young and slow. All I got was five thousand to talk about cleaning up the bloody mess."

"So you're saying," Doc said slowly, "that a few of us might make as much as one hundred and forty thousand dollars Wardhaven. And the rest of us would be sucking hind tit." There were mutters around the room at that. "Okay, Princess, what's your offer?"

This was going fast; maybe Abby's lead hadn't been a bad one. "I'll double that for each and every one of you." There were whistles at that. "I'll give you the money in either of two ways. If you want cash, now, I'll give you fourteen thousand dollars this minute. You'll get another twenty-eight thousand dollars when we dock at High Wardhaven. The rest one year from today, assuming no one talks to the press."

Several small groups among the crew took that under consideration. Kris didn't hear any complaints.

"You said there'd be two options," Sulwan said.

"The other is I give you preferred shares in Nuu Enterprises. Disbursement the same way. Value as of today."

"And if you Longknifes make a killing?" Captain Drago said.

"You're right in there killing with us," Kris finished.

"I'll take stock," Doc said. The "me too's" were unanimous.

"Do I get in on this?" Chief Beni asked.

"I said everyone on board," Kris repeated, an eye on Abby. The maid smiled primly.

Kris turned back to the crew. "The money is for silence. If this turns into a mad rush, irreplaceable information may be lost and people killed."

"Never thought I'd hear a Longknife worried about that," someone in back said.

"There's a first time for everything," Kris said. "I also don't want Alien 1 and 2 taken apart with hacksaws. We get one chance to peel this union. We do it like a bunch of wild, ignorant gold-rush nuts, and we could lose big chunks of this technology. We do it carefully, like grown-ups, and all of us may be set for life. A life like we never dreamed of."

"I think we can all see the mutual benefits of doing this the calm way rather than the hurry up and mess up way," Captain Drago said, turning to his crew. "Any of you have an uncontrolled urge to gab to the first newsie you meet?"

Head shakes answered him.

"Miss Longknife, you have just hired a crew. If you'll have your computer print out a confidentiality and nondisclosure statement, you've got a bunch of friendly folks ready to sign."

"Nelly and I will work out the fine print and be back with you before we dock at High Chance."

"You want us to put on more g's?"

"No, thank you. One and a half is all I care for. I think I'm getting too old for this charging around the universe, changing everything." That drew a laugh.

"Jack, if you and Abby will accompany me to my stateroom."

A moment later, Jack carefully closed . . . and locked . . . Kris's door. That left Kris free to turn on Abby with full fury.

"How do you happen to know so much about what the media is paying for hot dope on people?"

Abby looked at Kris like she had just crawled out from under a rock . . . on some airless moon. "Doesn't everyone know what the newsies pay. My word, Princess, back on Earth a kindergartner knows one juicy story can make you set for life."

Behind Abby, Jack's face went from someone who was about to bite into a juicy apple, to a guy who'd bitten and found a worm.

"Everyone knows?" Kris went on. "I never heard it."

"Kid," Abby went on, "don't you watch anything but what the media is doing to dis your old man. Okay, you are the folks we folks want to get the story on, so maybe it ain't all that big. Just as well. I hiked up the price. How was I to know that you'd double it. I figured you'd haggle us down. How you gonna stay so rich if you do things like that?"

"I was more worried about staying alive," Kris said. "Jack, you ever heard what the going rate was for juicy news stories?"

"Come to think of it, I think Abby's spurred my memory." He didn't look like he'd much enjoyed the spurring.

Kris settled down at her desk. "Okay, we'll forget that for the time being. I need to come up with some contracts. You two want to hang around. You might have some comments on what Nelly and I propose," Kris said eyeing Abby. "Seeing how you folks are the ones that know how the folks that want the money live."

"Always glad to be of service," Abby said, settling into the only spare chair in the room like the hawk that laid the golden egg.

And she'd again dodged the question. Oh, Kris's maid had answered the question asked: How she knew what she did know. But the question Kris really wanted answered had been shuffled to the bottom of the deck. *Just who are you?*

Once more, Kris was no closer to getting to the bottom of who Abby was than she'd been before. Once again, that answer had eluded her. And she had other things biting at her ankles and would have to tend to them and ignore the question . . . again.

"I can't hire people for Nuu Inc.," Kris said before Nelly had a chance to remind her. "So, Nelly, let's set up our own corporation, to be funded with some of my stocks from Nuu. I want 51 percent of the voting stock, the others to be distributed evenly among those here." Jack raised an eyebrow.

"Yes, Jack, you're included. You earned it."

"He earned it," Abby said. "He's just worried about a conflict of interests."

"Anyone gets close to Kris, the interests start getting conflicted," Jack sighed.

So Nelly drew up the papers of incorporation for BDQ, Inc., which Kris defined as Burrow, Dig, and Question. Abby suggested Better Do it Quick. Jack shook his head. "Better Done Quietly."

What BDQ actually meant was not defined in the documents.

All the *i*'s were dotted and the *t*'s crossed before they docked at High Chance. And, unlike Kris's last leave, she was actually back a day early. Given enough time, Kris was sure she could become the very model of a modern Naval Officer.

Kris was almost prancing up the *Resolute*'s gangway, when Penny charged out of the elevator.

"You'll never guess what we've found," Kris beamed.

"You'll never guess the trouble that just came through Jump Point Alpha," Penny interrupted, her face business deadly.

Kris stopped, shook her head, and tried to change gears from her planned "I've got a wonderful secret" bit of girl talk with her best friend, to whatever was coming at her. "Trouble?"

"Yeah, six Greenfeld light cruisers."

"Six!" Kris said, mind going down the Naval assets she had just now. It was a short list. Nil. Nothing. Nada.

"The good news is they aren't demanding our surrender."

That *was* good news. "And the bad?" Kris asked, hoping Penny was just using a figure of speech. Six cruisers were bad enough.

"Oh, that depends on if you mind that their commanding officer is an old buddy of yours?"

Kris blinked. "I don't know any Greenfeld Naval officers."

"You do now. Henry Smythe-Peterwald the thirteenth is a commodore in the Greenfeld Navy." Penny was wearing khakis, but she held up her arm as if pointing to the rank insignia strip on a blues uniform. "No thin ensign stripe for our Hank. Nope, one thick-and-wide commodore stripe for Harry's little boy. Oh, and his flagship, it's the *Incredible*."

Kris said a very bad word a princess shouldn't use. But she'd heard it enough from Navy types, and this was Navy business.

"Oh," Penny said, falling in step with Kris as she quick timed for the elevator to the main station level. "You said something about what you found. I was curious when you disappeared into that anomaly. Was it a real jump point?"

"Yeah, though that's a secret," Kris said, going up the escalator with Jack on her heels. "But what we found will have to wait."

9

Kris headed for the shuttle bay. "When did you spot Hank?"

"I was on the *Patton*'s bridge when one of the kids noticed a ship come through the jump. We stood around gawking. Most of them had never seen a ship's sensor suite up and working. When the number hit six and held, I figured you'd want to know."

Which explained why Sulwan hadn't told Kris. In just two minutes they'd gone from the greatest secret in human history to *Oh my God, look who's coming for dinner*.

Dinner or conquest? Was there a difference when the Peterwalds were involved? Kris almost missed a step. A month ago, the loss of Chance to the Peterwalds would be embarrassing for King Ray's alliance, but you win a few, you lose a few.

Lose Chance now and . . . Kris cut off that thought. It was her command and loss was not an option.

And exactly how do you intend to avoid that, your Princesshood, Commandership, Longknifeness? She asked herself.

Kris sighed; she didn't even have twelve mosquito boats to defend Chance. Just the two officers walking with her. And a chief. And Abby. And the contents of twelve steamer trunks.

Did that include the *Resolute*? Hmm. "Nelly, tell Beni to guard all channels. If the cruisers talk, I want to know immediately."

"He heard about the ship situation from the Comm Boss on *Resolute* and already has set up the watch. He assumes you will not want your name used on net."

"Good," Kris said as they reached the shuttle.

"Where are you going?" Penny asked.

"I need some face time dirtside. I'll need both of you. You *are* my entire command, in case you haven't noticed."

Kris grounded at Last Chance thirty minutes later. The boys were out with the tug beside a yellow cab with Steve and Mamma Torn. Kris and crew piled into the backseat, leaving the ground crew to find a place to park the shuttle on a ramp already growing crowded. The cab laid rubber gunning off the runway.

"I take it you've noticed your system is kind of full of warships," Kris said.

"It did not escape our attention," Marta said. Steve just scowled. "My son wants to talk to you. Steve suggested you do the talking face to face."

"The lieutenant knows security," Kris said.

Steve snorted at Kris's use of his old Navy rank. He might be a long-haired chicken farmer and taxi driver but he'd spent twenty years in blues. Even as he flew the cab low toward town, it looked like his mind was back in uniform. Good.

They pulled to a halt before a sports arena with a crowded parking lot. Ron hurried from it as Kris got out.

"We don't have much time," Ron said. "We're getting close to a quorum in there. I don't know everything we'll do but I have a pretty good idea what we'll deliver for you and Steve. I want you to start on it now, not later. Kris, what's your biggest problem?"

"Mayor Torn," Kris began formally. "I'd prefer not to have the Marines and armed Naval detachments on six Greenfeld cruisers just a quick rush from seizing control of High Chance. But by right and custom, those six cruisers have a claim on High Chance for docking privileges. Absent a pressing need, like all our docks being full, we should offer them the opportunity to dock. We can charge them for it, but money won't defend us."

Ron turned to Steve. "She's talking about what you told us." The retired officer nodded. "I'll move to incorporate the Chance Security, Entertainment and Tourist Society just like you said.

"Entertainment and Tourist Society?" Kris said.

"What does any sailor on leave want?" Steve answered. "A drink and some fun. Our local pubs will provide the drink. Entertainment may take some work. So, this society will provide for both our common defense . . . and the sailors' liberty and pursuit of happiness. Not bad, huh?"

"Maybe to protect a planet, but . . ." and Kris let them in on the secret she'd discovered. "Lots of traffic will be passing through Chance in the near future. You're going to be big."

Ron rubbed his eyes with both hands. "The only thing worse than a Longknife bearing bad news is one with good news."

"I'd like to keep this discovery a secret until we can go at it logically, rationally."

"Thank you for showing some common sense," Ron drawled and turned to Steve. "Go with her. Set our defenses up as best you can. I'm still not willing to call out the militia. Can you do it with the Society?"

"So long as Peterwald doesn't know anything, nothing's changed," Steve said.

"Let's keep it that way." Ron turned to go his way. Steve and Kris turned to go theirs.

Kris flew the shuttle back up with Steve Kovar beside her. Chief Beni was waiting for them when they docked. "Nothing from the ships. They're still quiet as a tomb." Then he spotted Steve and snapped him a salute.

"You don't salute us old farts," Steve said with a laugh.

"I do when there are six warships headed my way."

"Good idea," Kris said. "But not formal policy."

Steve introduced the woman at his side. "Chief Ramirez was my personnel honcho. I stretched her into just about everything that didn't involve the actual hands-on killing of something."

She offered her fellow chief a hand to shake. "Took all the fun out of a Navy career, dang it."

"Don't know about you, but I'm kind of glad to have a specialty that don't involve getting killed," said one of the few survivors of the gallant *Halsey*.

Kris frowned. "I've heard it said that you had a few volunteers working around the station. Wouldn't let them join the reserve. Are these the folks you're sending up?"

"Nope," Steve said. "No militia. They did their time. Besides, if I'm not careful, those enthusiasts might start saluting you. Obeying your orders. No, these are just simple workers, used to giving the foreman back talk when he deserves it. Maybe filing a grievance or two if things get too rough."

Kris schooled her face to neutral, but that might not have been the best approach. Steve went on. "And if you start bossing people around like a tin-horn god, you can expect them to down tools and walk, maybe take your entire shift with them."

"Tell me," Jack said. "Assuming Kris treats these employees as contractors, who does she talk to, maybe suggest things, occasionally plead for help when things get desperate around here, as they so often do around her."

"Thank you for that question, Jack," Kris growled. "But just now I want you and Beni to hustle over to the Comm Center. I don't want anything going out of here that talks about anything we are doing. Check the buffer on the jump buoy and erase anything that looks suspicious. You understand?"

Jack did. He and Beni trotted off.

Kris turned back to Steve. "How do we make this work?"

"I'm your main contact point, Lieutenant. I'll honcho one shift myself. The chief here will take another. I've got two other chiefs that will stand in for the last shifts. We'll be the cushion between you and the worker bees. That acceptable?"

"Will be when they get started," Kris said.

"Ramirez, is the first crew on their way?"

"The reactor start-up team should dock in fifteen minutes. They added a tiger team of reactor repair crafts in case the reactor gets balky coming on-line after all this cold time."

"Good," Steve said. "I'd expect initiative from that crew."

Which turned out to be just the ticket they needed as things slowly went down hill.

The reactor failed to light on the first try. And second. When the third time failed, a reinforced crew was requested from the power companies running Chance's reactors. The crew that was due to bring up the automatic weapons and security net were given a pass. And Kris began to wonder if her station might fall by default to a team of Peterwald Girl Scouts selling cookies.

"A watched teapot never boils," the reactor engineer said, making shooing motions. "This kettle ain't gonna boil any faster with you two looking over my shoulder. There's got to be something insignificant somewhere you can micromanage."

Steve and Kris backed out of his domain. "Old Walt is someone you have to know for a while to appreciate."

"And after I know him for a while, will I appreciate him?"

"More or less," Steve said with a shrug.

Kris spent all of a second prioritizing the thousand things she needed to do, came up with a "not yet" on all of them, and headed for the forward end of the station.

"I'll dock the Greenfeld ships far forward," she told Steve. "Care to walk around what they'll be looking at?"

They walked along Deck 1, the station curving away to their right and left, the stars visible through the window in the forward bulkhead of the station. Kris wanted to better know her informal deputy; she started with a soft pitch. "Is there any way we can get the locals to get our ranks right? I mean, it's nice to be breveted up to commander, but I've *earned* these lieutenant bars on my collar."

"What makes you think *they're* promoting *you*?"

Kris eyed Steve for a second . . . and stayed puzzled.

He chuckled. "I mean, who says it reflects anything on us. It's their district. How do you think they feel with a lowly lieutenant. They rate an admiral. A captain at least. What do they get. Me." He grinned. "You, at least, are one of those Longknifes, so that's something. But you're still a lieutenant. So they call us commanders. Get used to it." He shrugged.

"That's not something I thought much about," Kris said.

"Well, it took them a year or two, and quite a bit of grousing, to start calling me commander. I tried not to take it personal. Then I married one of them and it all made sense."

Kris doubted she had the years, or the prospects of a husband, so she'd just have to adapt on her own.

"Besides," Steve went on, "don't you have papers to commission that hunk of tin we got parked aft. Commission her and you brevet to captain, don't you?"

"Just commander, and I will not commission the *Patton*."

"Why not? From what I hear, she can actually hold air now," Steve said with a wide grin. "They've got a trickle feed on the reactor. She's making her own power. What with six Peterwald ships in the system, why not commission our own little cruiser?"

Kris whirled on Steve, her face warm with an anger she didn't understand. "I will not commission that ship. Not with that bunch of optimists and dreamers that are crawling around her. They asked to make her into a museum. I'll let them have their museum, but they will not sail that collection of spit and glue and bailing wire anywhere, for any reason."

Kris shivered, both startled . . . and shocked at herself. She spun on her heels and quick-marched for the bow. Steve had to hurry to catch up with her.

"Hey, young woman, I don't know what I just set off, but I want you to know that I was not fishing for what I hauled in."

Kris slowed. She needed this fellow if she was going to get anything done here. "I don't blame you," she said as he rejoined her. "I won't blame anyone. With luck, I won't blame myself."

He raised two questioning eyebrows.

"I don't know what you heard about the recent disagreement on who controlled the space above Wardhaven," she started slowly.

"I followed it in the media. Not sure it made a lot of sense from a professional's viewpoint. I figured I'd wait until the Naval Institute published something on it."

They walked a bit in quiet. "We needed everything we could lay our hands on. Good people volunteered. Optimists. Clubs. Gamblers. Whole families." Kris remembered faces. "And I let them. We fought. And they died. Tugs with no guns charged battlewagons and died. System runabouts were out there trying to get a hit. Not one did." Kris closed her eyes, willed down the tears. "Every one of them was wiped out."

"You had to win. And you did," Steve said softly.

"And I spent two weeks attending funerals," Kris said.

Steve attempted no answer to that.

Kris let out two deep breaths. "The *Patton* is forty years obsolete and I will not allow her to get anywhere near so much as a harsh word much less a fight with that collection of old farts and kids on board. Do we understand each other, Steve?"

"Perfectly," the retired lieutenant said.

Kris came to a halt, looked around, and worried her lower lip. "So how do we present a firm but friendly face to our visiting flag wavers," she said, eyeing the escalators down to Pier 1's landing several hundred feet below them.

"You going to park the flagship there?"

"Logical assignment if she's leading in her squadron and no commodore ever hatched has been able to skip playing boats right, boats left, follow in my wake."

The two junior officers exchanged knowing grins.

Steve turned around. "Well, we've got those security points." He pointed at four small half globes with mirror finish on the ceiling some hundred feet above them. "Cameras and auto guns in each should be able to stop anything as gross as an armed charge." He led Kris a third of the way around the station's concourse to where Pier 2's landing area was. "Four there as well. Four at Pier 3, unless they got up and walked away since I did." He laughed.

"Humor me," Kris said, and they finished their walk around Deck 1 of the station. Yep, there were four more covering Pier 3. They walked back the way they'd come, to find Pier 13, then hiked around to Piers 12 and 11. All had good auto gun coverage.

"Assuming they come up when we get power," Kris said.

"When we have power," Steve went on. "We'll have maintenance crews crawling all over Deck 1A, making sure everything we left is in just as good an order as we left it in."

Kris nodded. Deck 1A was an area that didn't show up on the public schematics of the station. A work area between Deck 1 and 2, it handled the lighting, ventilation, heating, and stuff the average tourist ignored. Kris had not taken the average tour of the Turantic Station, and had made good use of those invisible decks. "What are the access controls to Deck 1A?" Kris asked.

Steve's smile was predatory. "Not what the official manufacturer's specs say. Nowhere near that easy. I'll show you. Didn't I hear something about you and Turantic's Station?"

Kris drew herself up as primly as Abby and sniffed. "Insurance claims about what happened there are still before a court, and I have been advised by counsel not to comment on every bit of media supposition that floats by," Kris said, then smiled Steve's way. "However, I may have some ideas for improving security and keeping the riffraff and other undesirables away from delicate equipment they could 'accidentally' break."

Steve eyed her. "Yeah, right."

Amidships, between the third and fourth lines of piers was the service area that had given Kris her way up into the Command Center. All those shops were still boarded up. On the elevator, Steve used a key that just happened to be on his chain and the elevator admitted there were several additional floors above.

"You kept those?"

Steve glanced at them. "For fifteen years they were a part of me. I just couldn't turn them in. I told Ramirez I lost them. She already had the papers for me to sign about losing government property." Kris had never been around anyone long enough to have them read her mind that well. Well, Jack did, but he wasn't reading her mind so much as figuring two steps ahead of the next trouble she'd get them into. Not the same.

Painted gray, and smelling of oil and ozone, Deck 1A's air ducts and power lines stood out in loud primary colors. The auto guns were arranged in large housings above the deck/ceiling. Steve took off the cover of one. "The security cameras are out there to cover the station. But if things ever get terminal, the gun shield slides over all of the hole except for the gun's snout. These puppies are not going to be easy to kill."

"And target acquisition?"

"Oh, once they shoot up the globe, we switch to the other cameras." Steve grinned. "Dozens of tiny little things that you can't see from down there."

"What if they've got spy nanos buzzing around?" Kris said. "Real tiny ones?"

Kris nodded.

"Something tells me we're playing in a different league from what we expected." Steve worried his lower lip. "On this whole planet, I think we have only one college professor teaching nano security. Tonight I'll call him and suggest he and his class drop up here and have a talk with you and your Nelly."

"We may need more than eight hundred workers."

Steve laughed. "I knew that number was just a buy in. If we get by with double that I'll consider it a win." He looked around. "Want to see our Naval Defense Battery?"

"What you got?"

"Thirteen souped up 6-inchers."

"Thirteen 6-inchers. Not 4-inchers?"

"Yeah, we added two to the bow and stern to go with the nine scattered along the outer surface of the station."

"How'd you get different guns?"

"Interesting story, that. Surplus, brought out when ships were scrapped. Can you believe it, they did scrap some ships. Kind of amazing when you consider that they kept the *Patton*."

The 6-inch was a single, with no turret protection. How long it would last in a fight was anyone's guess, but there it was, with capacitors ready to be charged and a computer ready to lay it. Steve rapped his knuckles on some metal tubs with cooling lines running off them. "We planned to fill these with water and freeze them for gun shields. Better than nothing."

"If you're an optimist," Kris said.

"A desperate optimist," Steve agreed.

"If you say prayers at night, I hope you include us never having to use these."

"I'll tell my wife to expand her prayer list."

The walk back to the elevator gave Kris time to study the layout. She didn't like what she saw. "Anyone who opens that elevator door has access to everything up here."

"That door only opens to a key, and only when I'm sending the right code," Steve said.

Kris said nothing. The silence stretched, bent, bowed.

"You are paranoid, Longknife," Steve finally said.

"In my family, that's a survival trait."

"No doubt," Steve said. "I'm starting to understand why folks might, kind of, occasionally, want to kill you."

"Me," Kris said with her most innocent, wide-eyed face.

"No, your father," Steve muttered. "Let's see. If we use twenty millimeter deck steel, we could encase this place," he said, turning around in front of the elevator. "Arrange a desk there, give it a view in the elevator, and add a human eyeball to the security."

"And put at least one human with whatever kind of weapons you have handy as a lookout from behind the wall, just in case."

Steve was shaking his head. "I wanted to bring this thing in at sixteen hundred live bodies. That'll drive it way high. How about all elevators to go to three and be eyeballed before they go anyplace else?" They got off at three in the lobby leading to the Command Post. Kris made a face at the door leading directly into that holy of holies.

"We'll weld that shut," Steve said. "Put in a major security post here, and install a wall and locked door to all those corridors."

"Need a gunner behind armor," Kris said.

"I'm glad you're having this little talk with me and not my entire crew," Steve muttered.

"But I'm having so much fun doing it to you," Kris said.

Steve walked into his former Command Post, picked up a phone, and told it he wanted to talk to Ramirez. A moment later she was on-line. "I need to talk to you about some changes."

Kris heard, "No surprise, you're talking to that Longknife girl, aren't you?"

Steve eyed Kris. "Self same."

"Where do you want to talk?"

"I'm headed for the *Patton*. Meet me there."

Five minutes later, the three of them were going over a full schematic of the station, Steve pointing out where Kris wanted improved security.

"We can do that," she agreed. "We've got some kids working on the harvest. They'd be glad for a sit-down job once a week."

"Youngsters?" Kris asked.

"High school and college kids," Ramirez agreed.

"Rotating in for one day a week?" Kris said.

The chief glanced at Steve, then nodded at Kris.

"These folks are going to be the ones who make the call to pull the triggers if things get out of hand," Steve said slowly.

The chief sucked on her lower lip. "And you wonder if kids fresh off the farm could make that call if they are only looking at it one day a week?"

"Kind of like that. Killing someone ain't easy, even if you don't know what an M-6's going to do when you pull the trigger."

"How about we have them call for help at the first sign of trouble. We could get some adult supervision into the loop."

Kris shook her head. "You're assuming that they can call. Strange thing happened to me awhile back. I was being frog walked off my ship by a couple of nasty-looking MPs and I asked Nelly what might be the cause of my unpleasant experience. Nelly couldn't answer. She was being jammed from the net."

Steve looked at Kris wide-eyed.

"Your pet computer couldn't reach the net?"

"Yes," Nelly said from Kris's neck. "It was most unpleasant and I still do not know what happened."

"Which leads me to suspect that Greenfeld has a new jammer we haven't figured out," Kris added. "Short ranged but just the thing for putting a couple of green kids out on their own."

Ramirez spat a nasty word in a language Kris didn't know. "And they'll send their fanciest to our little coming-out party. Okay, I'll see what I can do. Steve, you get some good comm honchos up here, too. Tell the owners we need their best."

"That I will. Now, Your Highness, there's been a lot of work on the *Patton* since you last saw it. Why don't you wander around, get the guided tour while the chief and I talk."

"About me, behind my back."

Steve shrugged. Ramirez looked quite interested in what was coming next. Kris shook her head and took the escalator down to the first landing. A young man and woman were pulling sheets of plastic from a pile and walking them up the gangplank. Kris offered them a hand, was accepted, and so boarded her potential command lugging a sheet of white plastic as tall as she was and very wide. There was no ceremony on the *Patton*'s quarterdeck. The place was a madhouse of power saws, drills, and printers.

"Put the sheet down there next to the saw," an old fellow said, then took a better look at Kris over his reading glasses. "Hey, you're not Amy."

"No, I'm Amy," the girl behind Kris said with a laugh, and put her sheet down next to Kris's. "I don't know who she is, but she offered to lug plastic so I put her to work."

"Amy, this is the commander of the station," the old fellow said, looking like he might have swallowed his plug.

"Well, thanks for the help," Amy said, and headed back out for more, not at all impressed.

"Youngsters these days. What are they teaching 'em in school?" he muttered, but smiled as he watched the girl go.

"The same thing I think they've always taught," Kris said, looking around. "Who's kind of in charge?"

"That would be Ananda. Heaven knows where you'll find her but the bridge would be a good place to start."

On the bridge, Kris was directed to the forward 5-inch batteries. She was about to be sent aft to the other 5-inchers when the woman in question did indeed walk in. The single braid swaying down her back showed very little gray on the dark-skinned woman who barely came up to Kris's chest. "You looking for me?"

"I figured I should check in with you," Kris said. "I'm told there's been a lot of work done since I was last aboard."

"You bet'cha there has been, young lady," the woman said, dark eyes lighting up. "Just look at this battery. These twin 5-inchers can train as fast as they did the day they were first put aboard. And look at the plaque, there," she said, pointing.

Kris did, and saw the use for that white plastic she'd brought aboard. Beneath a quick explanation of what secondary armament was good for on a cruiser, and another short one on how the 5-inch lasers worked, was an additional annotation.

This battery was manned by the Marines of
First Lieutenant Terrence Tordon detachment during
the suppression of pirates during the inter-war
years. He went on to be known as General Trouble
to both friends and enemies.

And big trouble to his great-granddaughter, Kris didn't add. "Thank you," she said to the youngsters looking on. "Grampa would be proud that his guns are being so well cared for."

That got happy smiles. When Kris left after getting a

demonstration of how fast the 5-inchers could move, Ananda followed. "Thank you," she said, once out of sight of the kids.

"Thank me? For what?"

"For not pointing out that the *Patton*'s secondary battery during the Unity War and the Pirate Affairs were 4-inch lasers. These 5-inchers only came aboard during the Iteeche Wars."

"Couldn't fight off Puff Balls with 4-inchers," Kris said.

"So my mother told me," Ananda said ruefully. "Still, there is something special for the youth, working on a laser that your Grampa may once have touched. It adds something special."

Kris smiled. "Your mom fought such a gun?"

The woman beamed proudly.

"That ought to be enough for anyone, but yes, keep letting them think Grampa Trouble worked that laser, and I'll keep not telling them stories about my Grampa that just might ruin everything for them." They shared a laugh.

Kris considered the long list of things to do before Hank and his minions showed up, found it very long and, worse, not a single thing she could do just now, and sighed.

"Kris, Penny wants to talk to you," Nelly said.

"What's happening?" Kris said.

"Your old lover boy is calling."

"He was never my lover boy," Kris spat.

"Well, that's how he introduced himself to Jack and Beni just now. Did he do anything you don't know about?"

"Only in his dreams," Kris said. "Put him on."

"Hi Kris," he said in an all-too-familiar voice. "Too bad you don't have a visual. I wanted to show you the latest in blues."

Kris was glad she didn't have a visual. She could see perfectly well his perfectly sculptured face, one well-manicured hand waving at a sleeve with a very wide commodore's strip.

"To my eternal regret," Kris said, returning the sarcasm.

"My flag navigator tells me we'll be docking at High Chance at noon tomorrow. My sensor crew reports that you don't have your fusion reactor on-line. Will you be able to provide conventional housekeeping services to my squadron?"

"I don't see a problem," Kris said, praying she was right.

"We'll also want to give our crews shore leave, get down, get our land legs back, meet the locals. Maybe paint an orphanage or poor house. You must know the drill."

Kris's experience with port visits had been limited to saving a kidnapped kid and stopping six battleships from paying such a call on Wardhaven. A normal old-fashioned fleet visit was quite beyond her short experience in the Navy. "I think the locals are planning quite a show," she said.

"And I think we can return the favor. Just make sure you're ready to render services, Longknife, and that there's plenty of beer dirtside. Don't want things to get out of hand, do we."

"I'll look into that myself," Kris said, and found she was talking to thin air.

"Penny, where can I meet up with you?" Kris asked, assuming that anything she said on net was being listened in on.

"I need to do some stuff at Pier 62. Can I meet you there?"

That being next to the *Patton*, Kris had no trouble being back up on Deck 1 when Penny sprinted down from the Command Center area to stop at Pier 62 where the *Wasp* was refitting.

"How's the *Wasp* coming along?" Kris asked.

"Beautifully," Penny said. "We've erased all its software right down to the stuff that was in firmware for permanent load. We've copied most of what we want from the *Resolute*'s basic load. That boat has quite an interesting collection of software."

"No doubt. Just how much did Abby help you in hiring it?"

Penny frowned in thought. "I didn't think she did all that much. I was looking at a couple of other ships, but Abby pointed out their weaknesses. *Resolute* was strong in all areas. Even had a formerly military crew. I liked that. And the Doc almost was a doctor, not your usual first-aid type. Why, Kris?"

"Nothing. You know she's packing a pair of 14-inch lasers."

"Yes. Now. I needed that software for the *Wasp*, so I'm glad it had it. Kris, are you concerned about something?"

"Just my usual question as to where Abby really comes from? What she's up to? You know."

Penny shrugged and changed the topic. "You called for me?"

"Yeah, I need to drop down to Chance. Among other things, Hank hinted if the beer runs out, his sailors might get rowdy. I need to talk to Ron where I can't be listened to."

Penny nodded, then focused on something behind Kris. Kris turned to watch a wiry young woman race up the escalator three steps at a time. She arrived not even out of breath.

"You Miss Longknife?" she asked. Kris admitted she was. "We've got the *Patton*'s sensors fully on-line and were watching the approaching ships. Kind of training, you know?" Kris admitted that she did. "Anyway, the chief said you might want to know that the ships have upped their acceleration to 1.5 g's. They'll be here well before noon tomorrow."

"It's nice to have eager guests," Penny muttered.

"Penny, you've got the watch. I'll be dirtside," Kris said.

A yellow cab waited for Kris, driven by a kid that looked a lot like Steve but not nearly old enough to drive. At least on Wardhaven. But then, the kid didn't exactly drive, it was more like flying low in a racing skiff. Kris tightened her seat belt and managed to say nothing.

Ron was still at the sports arena. There were small rooms under the stadium, all now filled with tables, computers, and people doing things intensely. Ron came out to greet her.

Inside, Marta Torn and two men stood around a table with a map spread across it. Marta looked up and grinned. "I hear you've heard from your lover boy."

"News travels fast when some idiot uses an open net, and may I point out you only heard his side. We went to lunch once and dinner once. Not much loving. And my office was rocketed during the lunch and there was a bombing halfway through our dinner. Didn't even get to dance."

"I hadn't heard about the lunch date," Ron said. "But you left out how you ended up on his yacht late one night."

"That doesn't count as a date," Kris snapped. "I was looking to steal the fastest boat available. I didn't even know it was his."

"Someday you must write a book about your love life," Ron said, grinning. Similar grins grew on the other faces in the room. Even his mother's. "Me, I'm hoping to have a nice long chapter devoted to me. Lovingly," he added.

"You can hope for anything," Kris said, not really minding Ron's ribbing. Or was it a proposition. Certainly it didn't rise to the level of a proposal. They joined the group involved in the map exercise. "What's happening?"

"We picked up your conversation with Hank," Ron said. "The Beergartens along Hamburg Street will turn the whole five blocks into an Oktoberfest. They have plenty of practice and plenty of beer, right, Hans."

"Bismark Park will be set up with arcade games, penny pitch, good fun stuff," said a round fellow with just a hint of an old German accent adding interest to his words. "We garten owners have plenty of good beer, but only the prizes left over from last year. Our new production run isn't done yet."

"Then we better have something lined up in case we run out," Ron said with a worried frown.

"The Highland Games are held here at the college," Marta said, pointing to a large area two blocks off of Hamburg Street. "They do a caber toss, rock toss, and races. The prizes are just ribbons. I think we can stretch that out through a lot of match contests before we get to the prize rounds."

"Gasçon is our Chief of the Peace. Can you handle it?"

A tall, lanky fellow a bit older than Ron shook his head. "Mayor, I won't know until I see what I get. You going to staff me for a riot, or for a quiet night?"

"If we staff you up, we look like we're looking for a riot," Ron said slowly.

"And who's going to pour my beer," Hans said. "We can't throw a party if you put everyone in an arm band, Gassy."

The Chief of the Peace nodded. "Ain't you glad you didn't lose that last Mayor race?" Ron made a rude noise.

"You need enough folks pulling beer to keep it flowing fast," Kris said slowly. "And enough safety and security people walking the streets to see that any problems are handled quickly, in the early stages before they grow into something ugly."

"I know," Ron said. "I've seen enough news to know how the Peterwald work this scam. We throw their sailors in jail, 'on trumped-up charges,' they come down to liberate them from terrorists, and somehow, in the process, a government falls and another planet ends up in Peterwald's hip pocket," he growled at Kris, but the others around him nodded along.

Kris was glad to hear that from Ron. Apparently those years on Greenfeld hadn't blinded the mayor to what his bene-factors did. But then Kris knew a Peterwald and wasn't in bed with him.

"You know," she said softly. "Those ships are going to ar-rive at my station well before noon tomorrow."

"No," echoed back at her.

"Yeah, the Greenfeld squadron has hiked up its g's."

"Will they be down here earlier?" Gasçon asked.

"No way of telling," Kris said.

"So they'll have more time to wander around your station," Ron said, rubbing his chin.

"A station that still doesn't have a working reactor," Marta pointed out before Kris did.

"This is not good," Hans said. "Not good at all. Those auto guns need to be tested. My boy Alex is supposed to be up there checking them out before the ships get here. If he's up there, he won't be pulling beers down here."

"We need power to test those guns," Ron said.

"How many back-up generators do you have?" Marta asked.

"Two," Kris said. "One for the aft set of shops that's going now, and one that we aren't using for the midship set."

"So you could double what you have," Ron said, running his hands through his hair.

"The *Patton*'s not taking any power from the station, or so my kid brother says," put in the Chief of the Peace. "Could it kind of donate power?"

"I'll check on that," Kris said slowly. "If we managed our power carefully, we might bring up some of the gun stations a few at a time for testing, then close them down."

"I'll see that you get extra antimatter," Marta said.

Kris eyed the map with its Oktoberfest and games. "I take it this is your answer to the last part of Hank's transmission to me, the part about his boys getting rambunctious if they don't get shown a good time."

"Yeah," the Chief of the Peace said. "Normally they say

visitors are like fish, they smell after three days. This guy ain't even here yet and I'm detecting an unpleasant aroma."

"Watch it, Gassy," Hans said softly. "We don't want feelings like those showing through."

"I know, I know," Gascon said, eyeing Marta. "We don't hold against this bunch what we may have heard through the news. But can I hold against them what I'm seeing right now?"

"The plan is to smile, smile, smile," Marta said. "It's harder to invade a planet that's smiling at you. Don't give them an excuse to do something we'll all regret."

The others around the table nodded along with Marta's words, which Kris suspected by now must be an oft-repeated mantra. She'd been taught in OCS that hope was not a plan. She weighed Chance's plan and found it loaded with a whole lot of hope. It was clear that one Longknife was going to have to provide the iron to counterbalance all that hope.

"If you've got the party well in hand, and I've got some power options to look at, I'll head back upstairs."

"Kris," Ron said as she turned away. "You did bring your dancing shoes and a couple of nice party dresses, didn't you?"

"And if I did," Kris answered noncommittal.

"We figure the officers won't be all that interested in seeing how much beer they can guzzle and still toss a caber. We're planning some social events that will equal the best you ever saw on Wardhaven. Thought you might want to give your maid advanced warning to get the swirly stuff ready. I've heard a lot about your maid. Abby's her name, isn't it?"

"Yep, and I'll tell Abby to get ready to do that princess thing she does so well. That is unless you think I should leave the tiara in the box."

"Oh no." Marta grinned. "That'll be half the fun. Seeing who fawns all over a bit of royalty, and who doesn't."

"I've used the princess card for a lot of things," Kris sighed. "This sounds like it will be a whole new gig."

"I get the first dance," Ron said as Kris headed out.

Kris didn't look back. "You and Hank can arm wrestle."

"Well, at least that Marine won't be ahead of me in line," Ron called after her. Almost, Kris turned back to see the look on Ron's face. Was he joking? Or actually glad to be considered ahead of Jack on Kris's dance card.

A lot was going to be revealed come tomorrow night.

Steve Jr. was waiting outside to take Kris back. And he did get her back safely to the shuttle, if a bit worse for the experience. Strange how a battle-hardened vet could find riding with a teenaged driver a terrifying experience. Course then, enemy fire and a spun-out car left you just as dead.

The shuttle had extra antimatter, as promised, and a couple of passengers. Most looked like craftsmen and -women to go with the toolboxes stored in the proper bins. One was older, grayer, and carrying a nicely sized potbelly. And though he wore a plaid flannel shirt and jeans, Kris greeted him with "Hi, Chief."

"You're not supposed to know. What gave me away?"

"Well, you're wearing an old Navy-issue belt."

"Lot's of folks do. They're cheap."

"Yeah, but others don't have a razor sharp gig line."

The old chief sucked in his gut and looked down. Shirt, edge of buckle, and fly were so straight, they could have been done by a theodolite. He hitched his belt around, disrupting the perfection of habit. "You won't tell the commander, will you."

"Mum's the word. What part of my station are you going to look at." Kris didn't emphasis the "my" in station, but she got it out there in clear sight.

"The auto guns. That's what all of us are here for."

"News travels fast," Kris said.

"This is Chance, ma'am. Everybody knows everything."

Kris delivered them smoothly to her station, arranged with Tony Chang to have two of his boys get the other auxiliary power station up and running just as soon as the lunch rush was over, and headed for Engineering aboard the *Patton*.

"Was expecting you," a woman said as Kris entered the other holy of holies aboard a ship.

"Everybody on Chance knows everything," Kris said.

"Glad you're getting the hang of the place," the gal said with a grin. "The second reactor is dead, but the first is running solid, and I'm expanding the racetrack to give us more power and feeding it up the line to the station's capacitors." Electricity to run the ship and power the lasers came from sending plasma through a magnetic field. When the ship was doing 1 g in space, there was plenty of juice. When the ship wasn't under way, there was a, usually small, racetrack they ran a trickle of plasma around. Kris hadn't heard of anyone expanding the track, but she was glad this woman could.

"The capacitors should be full in a few hours," the woman went on, "but there's enough for Chief Tando to bring up guns. If the station needs more power, we'll give it."

Kris didn't want to ask the wrong question, but if everyone knew everything . . . "Do you know how things are going with the station's reactor?"

The engineer shook her head. "They had a major failure last time they tried to bring it up. This station was in need of major work when they shut it down. They've ordered some parts, but they'll have to be machined from scratch. I'd expect the reactor to be on-line by noon tomorrow."

So everyone didn't know everything. "The ships are arriving before noon."

"I'll pass that along. We'll need to speed things up."

Kris did her best to suppress the anger rising in her as she walked slowly from Engineering. This was *her* station. *She* should not have to play silly games like this to find out what she needed to know . . . and to see that people who should be her subordinates knew what she needed them to know and did what she wanted them to do.

"Nelly, find out who's in charge of the contractors on this station right now and tell him or her to see me at Pier 61."

"Kris, Steve will be arriving on the next shuttle and he requests that he be the one to talk to you."

"You tell Steve he better get out and push that shuttle cause I want to have this talk soonest."

"He says he will be at the shuttle landing in thirty minutes and that he will be out pushing."

Thirty minutes later, Kris was at the shuttle dock when it came in. Steve wasn't exactly outside pushing, but he was the first off. "We need to talk," Kris snapped at him.

"Yes, ma'am, but please not here," he said, taking her elbow and leading her along with him, ahead of a small tide of workers moving purposefully out of the shuttle and off to assignments with hardly a word spoken.

Kris kept her mad up, but she couldn't help glance over her

shoulder at the crew behind her. There were no more perfect gig lines, no one was visibly ex-Navy. Still, she would take them on board any command. A look at their determination said Grampa Trouble would take them, too. Kris found herself edged out of that driven tide and seated at a table in the back of Chang's New Chicago Pizza and Chinese Waffle House with a deftness that seemed to show planning on Steve's part.

Once seated, she repeated her opener. "We've got to talk."

He eyed his watch. "One day. Damn, we all lose the pool."

Kris's curiosity won out over her anger. "What pool?"

"We figured we'd keep you buffaloed for at least two days, some figured three or four. No one bet on you calling our bluff in less than twenty-four hours."

Kris leaned back in her seat and took a deep breath. Maybe anger wasn't the best way to handle this situation. If it was, she could always pull her mad back out and slap Steve around with it a couple of times. But if it wasn't, well, there was no way to take it back. "What is going on here?" Kris demanded.

"When you took command of that fast patrol boat of yours, PF-109 was it, how much respect did your crew give you?"

Kris frowned in thought. "I don't know. Some. Not much. They were green as petunias. We skippers were, well, everyone knew we were problem kids. Juvenile delinquents, hooligans were some of the nicer things we were called."

"I read about you and your helmswoman landing a racing skiff on the green of some golf course." Steve laughed. "What were you trying to do?"

"Fintch scored off the charts when they used games to test her, but she'd never actually maneuvered a ship, never even been off planet in her life. I figured she deserved a go at something smaller than a PF before she started honking it around the sky." Kris shrugged. "So she missed on her first try. She was never that far off again."

"She learned she could respect herself," Steve said softly. "And the whole crew found that they could count on you to help them do their best. And respected you for it." Kris nodded.

"How long did you have to get things shipshape before things blew up in your face?"

Kris knew almost to the second how long they'd had from the moment she first came aboard the PF-109 until she'd been relieved of her command and hauled off in cuffs. But that wasn't the question Steve was asking. "A whole lot more time than you've got right now," she answered.

"All my people know is that you're one of those damn Longknifes."

"That's all one word," Kris interrupted.

"However you say it, some may hold it against you. Some may look at your grampas and think, wow. Me, I look at the package, and I worry for my friends and neighbors. Just who are you? What have you got to prove? Are you going to turn a perfectly good day into a bloody massacre because you have something to show people who are thirty light-years away? I need answers to those questions before I dare take the muzzle off you."

The former Naval person leaned back in his chair as Tony Chang settled drinks in front of them and left. "Who are you, Longknife?" Steve asked.

Kris took a long pull on her soda as he did the same. A soda, today, not a beer, for him, too. The place where everyone knew everything wanted this to be a very sober discussion.

"My father, Prime Minister that he is, figured me for the permanent campaign manager for my older brother, maybe his, too."

Steve frowned at that. "Parents often have the worst expectations for their kids."

"Mother just wanted me to marry wealthy. Give her a couple of grandkids to mess up as bad as she messed up us kids." This drew a deep scowl from the retired lieutenant.

"So you ran off and joined the Navy," he said.

"Fool me, I thought it was one place where I would be just me. Where I could be measured on my own merit." Kris turned, stared at the bulkhead. "But wherever I go, they've heard of those-damn-Longknifes, and I'm just one of them."

Steve shrugged. "Sorry, kid, but you are."

"So I've discovered. But . . ." she nailed him with her eyes. He did not look away. "Let's get a couple of things straight.

One, I want just as much for Chance to be left on its own as anyone born here. Fourth generation, or whatever. Do you hear me?"

"I think so."

"Second, I do not want a bloodbath before, during, or after this little squadron visit. I don't even want Hank to cut his little pinky. I want Hank to come, to see, and toddle right back out Jump Point Alpha, or Beta, or whatever. I don't like the idea of there being a Longknife and a Peterwald in this system any more than you do. The last thing I want is for us to come to blows. You hear me?"

"I hear you, but, I'm kind of having a hard time figuring out what I'm hearing. I mean, the Battle of Wardhaven and all. I figured you'd be gunning for him."

Kris eyed the ceiling and said a prayer to any God willing to listen to the likes of her. She let out a long sigh and chose her words carefully. "Steve, you study much history?"

"I like to think I studied a lot of it."

"What were the longest, nastiest wars?"

He thought for a minute. "Aside from the irregular ones, those where you had a hard time finding one of the sides, I guess I'd say the ones where the two sides were evenly matched. Where neither side would win a solid victory over the other."

"And so the war dragged on year after year, campaign after campaign, with both doing a lot of hurt to the other, the people paying a higher and higher price for the war, but neither able to swing a knockout blow at the other?"

"Yep."

"What would you say about the strength of the two alliances, Peterwald verses Longknife." *Yeah, let's get personal.*

"Your Grampa Ray is ahead."

"Enough for a knockout blow?" Steve shook his head.

"My feelings exactly. Now do you see why I want to make sure this station doesn't just plop itself into Hank's lap? And why the games dirtside go smooth as they can?"

"If I didn't know you better, I'd call you a pacifist."

"Hell no," Kris spat. "Given enough time, I figure we're going to have Peterwald so beat that he'll give up without a fight, like, what were they? The Soviet Union back in the twentieth? But in the meantime, we have to keep our powder dry and never turn our back on them for a second."

"So now all I have to do is persuade folks that you will not ride roughshod over them," Steve said, pushing his chair back.

Kris stood. "When we were trying to get that collection of extraneous junk ready for the Battle of Wardhaven, I did walk-arounds to see how things were going for myself . . ."

"I was planning on doing just that. Why don't we do them together for a while?"

"Fine, the other was stand-up meetings twice a day. That way folks learned what others were doing."

"Stand-ups," Steve echoed.

"Stand-ups. So no one gets comfortable."

"I like it.

And so security was enhanced, auto guns were checked, cameras were on-line and a small horde of nano-scouts released into the station next morning. The capacitors were full and, just fifteen minutes before Hank's flag was due to hook up, the reactor came up to cheers stationwide. Oh, and Kris even got six hours' sleep.

"I guess we're about as ready for them as we'll ever be," Kris said, turning to Steve. "So, do we meet them at the pier or stay safely behind security in the Command Center?"

"Oh, didn't Ron tell you?" Steve grinned.

"All my stand-ups, all my walk-arounds, and why do I think I'm about to be slapped with a surprise?"

"Well, the Last Chance Ballet and Modern Dance Class of Mrs. Toronado will be meeting Hank's flag and giving him flowers and a basket of baked goods from the 4-H prize winners at last year's Last Chance County Fair."

"And the other ships."

"We have kids from the Highland Dance school, and German Culture Classes, the Kabuki Theater, the Desert Dances and . . . , anyway, there will be pretty little girls and boys stammering hello to all the ships and offering them baskets of goodies that won't have been totally eaten on the ride up." Steve was grinning from ear to ear.

"Drown them in kindness."

"That's the whole idea. Show them that there's a lot to like about Chance, and not a whole lot we want to change."

"Hank ain't gunna like that."

"Why don't that bother me," Steve said through a huge grin.

10

"We have unknown nano-scouts loose on our station," Beni reported fifteen seconds after Hank's flag opened its hatch.

"No surprise there," Kris sighed, and prepared to see that her station stayed *her* station.

"Our nanos are trailing them and will report on what they are interested in," Beni added.

While nanos did their tiny thing, locals that were somewhat larger, but still tiny in most perspectives, did their thing. Kris and Steve watched as each of the docking details came face-to-face with a mob of short people, doing cute to perfection while dancing their own particular version of ancient Earth folk dances. To Kris, it looked like the shortest, say four- to six-year-olds, were doing about the same thing. But they were backed up by ten- to twelve-year-olds doing a better job of telling the polka from the Highland fling.

And the adult supervisors made it clear to the grizzled chiefs of the docking details that those cute kids holding baskets almost as big as they were intended to give them up only to the captain of the ship.

Kris's Command Center struggled only moderately successfully to keep from rolling on the floor, laughing, as chiefs made hurried calls to their superiors and officers arrived, many still putting on formal dress, to receive this bit of local largess.

"Don't those dolts have any experience with a formal port visit?" Beni asked no one in particular. "Commander Santiago briefed us on what to expect on Hikila. We were all looking forward to topless babes in grass skirts. In zero g."

"What happened?" Kris asked, remembering nothing like that.

"You went dirtside and we got no show at all. No shore leave, either."

"No shore leave?"

"Yeah," Beni sighed. "She kept us locked and cocked for a rescue mission. I heard her tell you that you were on your own, but she was lying through her Navy-issued teeth. If you had so much as whispered for help, she would have had the Marines and half the crew of the *Halsey* down there in no time at all."

Which was interesting information for Kris, but only of historical value.

She kept her eyes on several rows of monitors, following the proceedings at all six ship's landing areas. On the *Incredible*'s monitor, four men in civilian clothes slipped across the brow and dodged past the greeting party.

"Mark those four," Kris ordered. "Keep your eyes peeled for similar teams," she ordered Jack, Beni and Penny at her side. Steve was talking into a headset. At the top of the escalators from Pier 1, two youths in the uniform of Last Chance Safety and Security joined the four. The uniform wasn't much, just jeans and flannel shirts, but the smiles from the young man and woman were uniformly wide.

Kris took a step back to evaluate the whole situation. "They're from Hank's flagship. Doesn't look like there are any other groups trying to make a breakout."

Heads nodded agreement, but eyes stayed on the screens. Now two more came active as the four made their way along Deck 1, not in any straight path, but meandering between different landing areas, eyeing the globes that held the auto guns. Frowning now and then and whispering to themselves or their commlink.

"Commlink," Beni said. "I'm tracking communications but I can't crack the code. Kris, can Nelly take a look at it?"

"Nelly, have at it."

"This should be fun," her computer said.

"Here comes a second team of walkers," Penny said.

"Different ship?" Kris asked.

"No, flag. I think Hank's holding it close to his chest."

"Let's see where these go," Steve said, and whispered into his link. Two kids waited for them as they topped the escalator.

"This is rather easy," Jack said.

"Well this code is not," Nelly reported. "It is totally revised from what we saw on Turantic and the six battleships at Wardhaven. I'm going to need a lot more transmissions before I can crack it."

"Monitor it, Nelly, and have fun."

Jack was still giving his monitors an unhappy frown. "If I was in charge here, I'd try something outside the station."

"We're looking for that," Steve said. "All the 6-inch batteries at the tip of the docks have cameras." So saying, he switched several monitors over to show the outside of the ships. "No activity."

"One of their nanos just tried to burn one of ours," Penny said. All sixty kilos of Kris's Smart Metal were nano-scouts.

"Wonder how many scouts Hank has," Kris said. "Penny, scout weapons release. Let's see who has the last one flying."

The battle was short and one-sided. Hank had not brought nearly enough scouts, or they weren't as heavily armed as Kris's. Since nanos offered no quarters to each other, there were no prisoners taken, none to interrogate or examine. Well, not many.

"We've identified the wreckage of several nanos, not fully burned," Jack reported shortly after Penny reported the firefight over. "I'm marking them for retrieval. If they're Smart Metal, we can examine what makes them tick, not tick."

"Ouch," Kris said, the realization dawning on her that the ability to program your own metal might offer your enemy the option to reprogram it at the worst of all possible times. "Jack, I do not like your line of thinking."

"I like you, too, Princess," he said without looking up.

"That second foursome is making straight for the amid-ships service area," Steve reported. "And I think they know where our elevator is." Four men in bulky coats piled into the elevator that a month ago first brought Kris to this Command Center.

Steve eyed his board. "They punched for two. Anyone want to bet they want 1A?"

"No bet," Kris said, her eyes roving all the boards.

As programmed, the elevator took them straight to three and opened. "Can I help you," came a cheerful voice from the desk just outside the welded-closed door of the Command Center.

The four seemed surprised by where they were, but they were good, recovered fast, and stepped forward into the closed-off foyer. Two of them leaned over the desk of a young woman intentionally chosen for her busty blond appear-ance . . . that covered an honors degree in psychology and counseling. Two men tried in several different ways to ask di-rections to different places on the station, cutting her off when she made to answer, and in general did their best to dominate her attention and confuse the situation. The other two tested the doors, found them locked, and began to pick them with both electronic and physical tools. The one working hard on the solidly welded Command Center door did not bother Kris.

The other door could be a problem.

"Jack, you're with me," Kris said. Jack, in dress blues, pis-tol, and sword, was right behind Kris as she quick-timed for the left exit from the center. Outside, she turned two corners and brought herself to a halt before a door, caught her breath and waited only to the count of two before the door opened.

The crewcut and hard muscles of the young man in front of Kris shouted Special Forces. He looked up from where he'd been jiggling the door handle, saw Kris in undress whites scowling down at him, took in Jack with his hand resting on his pistol . . . and had the good sense to close the door.

Kris opened the door, stepped through it, and gave Jack the second he needed to follow her. He shouted "Attent'hut on Deck" and the rest of the proceedings came to a roaring halt as all four of the Greenfeld men braced at attention.

Why was that not a surprise.

"Gentlemen," Kris said crisply. "As I am sure you have heard from the receptionist, you are in a restricted area. You will remove yourselves immediately. You have received the only warning you will get. Your pictures and basic biometrics have been recorded. If you violate these precincts again, you will be restricted to your ships for the remainder of this port of call. Do you understand me?"

"Yes, sir," rocketed back at Kris.

"The elevator would be a good exit, don't you think?"

The four piled in the elevator and the door quickly closed.

Jack stood there shaking his head. "Too easy."

"I agree," Kris said. "They were a throwaway gambit."

"So where's the main thrust?"

"Yet to come," Kris said, and turned to the receptionist. "You okay?"

"I'm fine, but this is not working. They blew through our locks like they were hardly there."

"So I noticed," Kris said.

"Oh, and this eye-candy gambit," the gal said, looking down at where her first two buttons were undone. "I might as well have been in a nun's habit," she said, redoing her buttons.

"I'll tell Commander Steve of your observations," Kris said.

"Better you than me," she said, and went back to her work.

In her Command Center a minute later, Kris found Steve on the commlink to the *Patton*. "We need all the machinists and mechanics you can loan us. We've got to install physical bar locks on every critical door. And we'll need your kids to stand behind them and only open them when they're told to. Yes, I know that's going to be boring, but these folks brought pick locks that go through our security like it's not there. Yep, just ask Marilyn. She's the one that couldn't keep four guys at her desk for two minutes. Yes, Marilyn. You talk to her but get me those mechanics to install the bar locks and people to unlock them."

"Sounds like your crew don't always do what you want them to do even when you're the one telling them," Kris said.

"Yeah, that was part of what I was keeping a secret. Around here, you give an order and wait to see what the vote is."

"Can you bar lock the doors?"

"I've already messaged a lockout to all the networked

locks. Every door on this tub is deaf, dumb, and making rude noises at anyone trying to get it to open. I can make a specific exception from here, but . . ."

"Talk about micromanaging," Penny grumbled through a smile.

"Talk about losing control of the situation," Kris said. "How are our four doing on their walkabout? Any more come out?"

"It looks like a new four are leaving the flag, probably to replace the four you just spanked. I'm watching them closely," Penny said. "The first four just seem to be walking from pier to pier looking the place over and going on."

"Just the six their ships are using?" Kris asked.

"No, all eighteen. At this point, they've gone past the amidships shops and are now at Pier 51.

"Probably looking for one that doesn't have as many auto guns," Jack said. "Maybe park a landing craft full of Marines outside that pier and charge up an unguarded landing area."

"They all have their allotted four guns," Steve said.

"So they will report," Kris said. "Any more nanos out?"

"Nothing new reported," Penny said.

"Keep the nanos spread out wide. They could use the shuttle bay to send some in or some other odd place. Expect anything."

What Kris didn't expect was a call from Hank.

"Hi, lover girl," he said for an opener as his perfect face came up on-screen.

"Hi, Hank, all services coming through fine to your ships?" Kris said, staying business.

"Could use a bit more electricity, but I understand your reactor just came on-line a few minutes before we docked. If you want, I can keep an extra trickle up on our reactors, lower our demand on you. Of course, we'd want a discount on our bill if we did," he said with a salesman's grin.

Kris glanced at Steve's board, the reactor was at 100 percent. She refused the urge to cut her visual; that would make her station look less than 4.0. She schooled her face and voice to friendly, something the Prime Minister's Darling Daughter had learned early, and said, "Thank you, Hank, but I think I've got that problem solved. The Chance Service District has let me know that they won't be allowing any discounts this month."

Hank's mouth moved several times as she spoke, but she managed to keep the words flowing so syrupy smooth that he failed to break in. When she finished, he seemed to boil for a moment before snapping. "It's Commodore, Lieutenant. Commodore," he repeated, waving the sleeve of his blue uniform at her.

"Fine, Hank, fine," Kris said. "Commodore. Is there a reason you called me. I'm rather busy just this moment. We seemed to have a sudden infestation of nanos. Oh, and some of your crew were wandering around and didn't read the signs about which parts of the station are public and which are secure. Do I need to resend the standard instructions on that, Hank."

"Commodore."

"Right, Commodore."

"No, no need. Everything is fine."

Which did not tell Kris anything about the state of his nanos. But then, that was not something she planned to ask.

"If everything is fine, I'll talk to you later," Kris said, and made to hang up.

"Don't hang up, Kris. I called to tell you that the locals are putting on a bash of some sort for me and my crew. But then you might have heard about it."

"I'd heard they were planning something to entertain your crewmen," Kris lied with a straight face.

"They also have arranged a ball in my honor. I'm told it will be the height of the social season." Kris made nice noises.

"Anyway, I wondered if you'd like to ride down in my barge. Bring your whole command with you."

"Why Hank, I'd be glad to."

"Commodore," he corrected.

"You can't call the Commander of Naval District 41 'Kris' and expect her not to be on a first-name basis with you, Hank. But, yes, I'm glad to accept the invitation for the ride. When should I be there?"

Hank said eight o'clock, which took him out of the game of who was what rank, and Kris rang off before he could get back to it.

"That boy is a twit," Penny said.

"Over his head," Steve agreed.

"Neither of which makes him any less dangerous," Jack muttered. "Why are you riding in his scow?"

"It saves me having to steal it this time," Kris said, her face now struggling to stay as straight for her team as she had kept it for Hank. The entire room, Jack excepted, broke up.

"I'm glad the rest of you are enjoying this, but I repeat, why are you offering yourself for a ride in the barge of a guy who would just love to lock you up and throw away the key?"

"Because he wants to and he can't," Kris said. "Face it, Jack, neither he nor I can do something that actually harms the other. A lot of people may die before this whatever-he-thinks-he's-doing is over, but the last thing I want is to harm him. And the last thing he can do is kill me."

"I seem to recall several attempts to capture you and serve you up naked for a long and deadly torture session for Hank's old man," Jack reminded Kris.

Kris shivered at the memory. "Yes, I can't seem to forget them either, but those were all done below board, by other folks that would give Henry Smythe-Peterwald the Twelfth all kinds of deniability about his fun. Sending a squadron on an official port call with his own son and heir commanding is totally up front. And everything about it has to be played that way. No, Jack, the safest place for me tonight is in Hank's barge. Trust me, any shuttle that doesn't have him and does have me is in extreme danger of developing a bad case of the sudden blowups."

As Penny listened, Kris could almost see the Intelligence Officer's brain spinning through all the options. "I think she's right, Jack. So, Kris, are you actually going to ride down on the barge or develop a last minute case of being elsewhere?"

"I probably will go along for the trip down. Steve, I may need a ride home, in case my official ride runs out of gas, turns into a pumpkin, you know how that can happen to a girl."

"I have a daughter," he growled. "I'll want to make those arrangements in person. No telling what the nanos planted on our comm lines before we scorched them."

"You do that. Oh, and Steve," she said as he headed for the door. "In my early wanderings around the station, I noticed that I command a rather full armory. Jack and I field stripped a couple of weapons and found them in good shape. Would you mind having some of your contractors do a full maintenance workup on everything in the armory?"

"Did it the first day I was back up here, Princess. I may not have been sure I trusted you with those guns, but I sure didn't want to need them and find out they aren't good to go."

"Thank you, Commander," Kris said.

"Glad to be working with you, Commander. Or should I say 'Princess'?"

"I answer to either one," Kris said. "Oh, speaking of answering, Nelly, get me Abby on the line."

"You finally remembered me, Your Absentmindedness," Kris's official maid said a second later.

"But you were never far from my thoughts," Kris said, glancing at Penny. "It seems that I will be going to a dinner and dance tonight. A simple thing, don't want to outshine all the other girls there. Since we're dancing it might be just as nice if I was in that red gown that swirls so nicely."

"You mean the simple red one that goes well with blue accessories," Abby said, seeming to catch on immediately that network communications might not be as secure as they once were.

"Yes. Just the simple stuff."

"And how much time will you give me to do your hair?"

"Not nearly enough," Kris assured her. "But I'll try to break away from here before too long."

"I'll be waiting for you."

Kris rang off, waited until Nelly assured her that all comm lines were now off, and then shrugged. "Just how much time I have will depend on how Hank reacts to that."

Whatever Hank had in mind, it didn't become apparent for a while. Into the quiet, Penny asked, "What is the uniform of the evening? You may have Abby to get you ready, but I need to think about what I can throw together."

"Dress whites for you, Penny," Kris answered quickly and easily. "Jack, what you're wearing, sidearms included."

"And you?" Penny asked.

"Not a uniform," Kris said defiantly. "Since Hank has promoted himself to commodore, I'll trump him with princess. Tiara, Order of the Wounded Lion and all."

"That boy's pride won't take kindly to that," Penny said, smiling at her board.

"Disappointment is something he's going to have to learn to live with," Kris said. "And if you ask me, he hasn't had nearly enough of it in his life."

"Oh-oh," Penny said. "I think I see where his next disappointment is coming from. Either his or yours."

"I don't need any more disappointment," Kris said, eyeing Penny's board. "I've had all a growing girl can use."

"The reactor," Jack breathed.

The new four had been meandering their way down station. Now they made a straight line for one of the two elevators among the aft shops. Kris mashed her commlink. "Engineering, are you prepared to repel boarders?"

"What?" came from the chief engineer, a grandmotherly woman who frowned at Kris, then glanced off screen, apparently at her security monitors, and then said a not very grandmotherly word.

One of Kris's monitors showed the foyer they had created to block off the passageways around the reactor. Similar to the one in front of the Command Center, this one had a six-foot plus, linebacker type standing in front of the elevator as it opened. He opened his arms wide and blocked the door. "This is a secure area. Unauthorized people are not allowed," he calmly bellowed.

That should have settled the matter.

One of the men in the elevator started a long, high-pitched spiel that Kris didn't try to follow, while the other three ducked under the big fellow's arms and headed for the doors.

"Hey, you can't do that," the linebacker shouted, turning to chase after them, but it was like four mice being chased by a lone cat . . . and the cat had been briefed not to do anything lethal to the mice. The rodents took maximum benefit of that edge.

The strapping fellow would jiggle one doorknob to disrupt the lock picking effort, only to have to trot over the next door and mess up another lock pick. And the fourth fellow was in his face all the time, talking, and his feet were as likely as not to be where the big guy put his down. It was better than most comedy routines, but this was not funny. Once they broke into the reactor room, there was no telling what they'd do. Or Hank.

"I'm getting a report of Marines on the cruiser's quarter-decks," Penny said. A glance showed Kris that the kids were still on the landings doing their cute.

"Order the kids out of there. Don't let them get mixed up in this," Kris ordered.

"Doing it."

"Engineering, you're about to be boarded," Kris repeated.

"Not on my watch, Commander," came right back at her. "Tu, Sanchez, Ladonka, grab the biggest screwdrivers you got and a hammer and get your rear ends moving for the doors."

"Screwdrivers? What're we doing with screwdrivers?"

"Didn't they teach you kids anything in school. Your heads are all full of book learning and you don't know anything practical," the grandmother type was muttering as Kris followed her fast walk from one screen to another. "I bet I'm the only one here that can hot-wire a car if I need to."

"Probably, Granny Good-Good," said Sanchez from well off screen.

Granny was at one of the doors into Engineering. "You take one honking-big screwdriver and wedge it in the doorsill next to the end with the hinges, not the doorknob, you doorknob, and you hammer it in good and hard. Nobody's opening that door.

"Here's a doorstop if you want it." A wooden wedge flew across the room to bounce off the door. The younger woman taking all the guff from Granny grabbed it, set it in place at the bottom of the door, and Granny gave it a whack, too.

"Now, if a couple of you big lugs will do your usual lazy lean up against this door, it ain't opening for no one," she said, and headed back to her main station.

Kris checked all of her monitors. The situation seemed stabilized, but she didn't trust those four. Just what did they have in their bulky coats? Explosives? What would Hank decide to authorize if he got too frustrated? Kris hoped Hank had some kind of trainer with him. Daddy usually only turned Hank loose with someone who was supposed to teach him the ropes. Was this trainer an admiral? No, more likely some captain was stuck trying to explain to Commodore Hank why his latest bit of brilliance was not a good idea.

"Steve, we've got a problem," Kris said on net.

"I know. I've got a set of plumbers from the *Patton* trotting over there to add their two cents to the conversation."

Kris cut the commlink. "Plumbers?"

"Ever see the size of the wrenches those folks use," Jack said, a grin growing on his face. "You get hit with one of those and you don't need to be hit twice."

The comedy continued in the Reactor Foyer for a minute longer. One fellow actually managed to get his door unlocked, but found that the door would not budge for him. All four of them were congregated before that door, devoting their full effort to pushing on it while the linebacker did his best to push them sideways off the door. It was a sight to behold.

And the elevator door opened on six big guys. No, four big guys and two big gals, each with a very big wrench in their hands, stepped into the foyer.

"Hi, guys," a healthy farm girl, her blond hair in twin pony tails, her right hand lifting and dropping one honking big steel wrench into her left. "You got a problem?"

Two of the Greenfeld types reached for things that were inside their coats. One of them made a grab for the linebacker who broke the hold and stepped back.

Kris mashed her commlink. "This is Commander Longknife. Do we have a problem in the Reactor Foyer that I need to bring to the attention of Commodore Peterwald?"

"No." "Nothing." "No problems here" came quickly from the four. Kris's six provided sideboy . . . or girl . . . courtesy to them on their way to the elevator, and punched button One.

"Do we want to let them off that easily?" Nelly asked.

"We don't want to hurt anyone," Kris pointed out.

"But the elevators are all designed to go straight up and through to the other side of the station, Kris. People rarely do that because it subjects them to zero g and they have to reorient themselves because the ceiling becomes the floor. However . . ."

"What do we gain if we do that?" Jack said.

"In weightlessness, on average, one out of three humans will become very ill," Nelly lectured.

"But those aren't average humans, Nelly," Jack said. "They are Peterwald Special Forces. Surely they are space trained."

"I have no data on that," Nelly answered primly.

"Would be interesting to run a verification test," Penny said. "Seeing that we do have this opportunity."

"Nelly, redirect their car up," Kris ordered.

"Doing it, Your Highness. This is fun."

"Stall it dead center of the station."

"Done."

"Do we have a visual?"

It was one of the spare cameras, so the picture was poor. But there was no missing the dismay as they lost control of the elevator, the surprise as they lost gravity, and the disgust as first one, then a second, lost his breakfast. There were several attempts to set matters straight in the car that ended with the one Kris took for the leader growling, "Are you done with us."

"Tell your commander that we may not wait for you to get in our hair before we run the next bunch who get into an elevator up to see if all of you are space qualified," Kris said. "You have a Longknife's word on that."

"I figured as much." He ended the conversation.

"Should I run them up the rest of the way?" Nelly asked.

"No," Kris said. "Let's not encourage them to see more of the station than they have." Once out of the elevator, the four headed straight back to Hank's flag.

Kris ordered lunch for the Command Center. Tony Chang was running a special on pizza. Hank was kind enough to take lunch off, too, so they got all the way through clean-up before a new bunch of four crossed the brow of Hank's flag.

"Steve, you have anyone to walk those folks around?"

"I've got eight, drawn from the Last Chance Rifle and Marksmanship Club. And, I might add, trained and led by my old Chief Master at Arms. Watch this."

The four came up the elevator and were met immediately by four folks wearing sidearms, and trailing them at a good twenty meters were four more each sporting M-6's. The older fellow in the first group exchanged words with the four; they turned around and rode the down escalator right back where they'd come from.

"How many have you got from Marksmanship Clubs?" Kris asked.

"Enough," Steve answered cryptically.

Kris waited for an hour to see what Hank came up with next, but there was no next. She eyed the clock, calculated just how much time she was willing to give Abby to obsess over her hair, added in time for a fast walkaround to view the troops, and decided it was time to leave the duty watch to Jack.

"You've got the hot potato. Call me at the first sign of French fries."

"I still think you ought to make a quick detour come twenty hundred hours and take our shuttle down. I don't trust Hank to know what's good for him."

"You've got a very good point, my security czar," Kris said, doing her best to recognize the authority he could invoke to change her plan . . . without really giving in. "However, there is more at play than just how I get where I'm going to-night. It's *how* Hank feels about it. If you don't agree tonight we've won one, Jack, I'll give you the next one, free of charge, no back talk."

Jack eyed Kris. "You've got something up your sleeve."

"And considering that my dress tonight has no sleeves and very little else north of the border, it should be very clear to you rather quickly what I'm up to."

"This I really want to see," Penny said.

"You just show up in dress whites with full medals. Oh, Jack, before you report to Hank's barge, put on your medals, too."

"I think I smell intimidation," Penny said.

"I think I just lost my bet," Jack grumbled, but the tips of his scowl were curling up. No question, Kris's crew wanted to see Hank's pride holed solidly below the waterline.

Kris did her walkaround, smiling encouragement at those working for their defense and quickly ran into Steve doing his own bit of close oversight. They turned it into a twin tour. Doors were being locked down with steel bars that had to be thrown by a human being. The reactor's access doors got two bars. The crew was happy, joking about what they'd done to their visitors. Kris joined in their happy mood, adding only a reminder that this was just the first round. There would be more.

"Well, we surprised them, they surprised us," Kris said when she turned from Steve to deliver herself to what was bound to be an impatient and bad-tempered Abby. "The game's still very much afoot, but I think we can claim to be ahead on points."

"Points that can only too quickly be trumped by the other side," Steve said, without looking back.

11

SOMEONE once said war was diplomacy continued by other means. Or maybe it was the other way around. Father was want to say it either way. Kris wondered what that someone would think of her use of socialiting as a continuation of the war between the Peterwalds and Longknifes by other means.

Once upon a time, Kris had looked upon Hank as a potential Romeo, and her as Juliet, destined to end the bitterness between two warring families. Such romantic mush was ancient history, as Kris stepped into the hall from her room and came face-to-face with Jack and Penny.

Penny wore the requested Navy-dress dinner evening ensemble. "The manual calls for miniature medals, but I don't have any. I thought you'll be just as happy with me in full-size ones."

Kris nodded. "Easier for the blind to see."

Jack was in fresh dress blues to go with his shower and shave. He showed medals in place of a single row of ribbons. He eyed Kris. "You've got the lapel pin from the Battle of the Line on the sash of the Wounded Lion. That's not regulation."

Kris looked down at her dress. The bright red of the satin

was bound to be eye-catching; the fire red hugged her waist, the one thing about her she was proud of. Below, it flounced out to sway very nicely as she walked. Above, it opened up. Abby's push-up bra might actually give eager male eyes something to catch when her top went one way and she went the other.

Abby had arranged the sash of the Wounded Lion, Earth's highest honor, to start under her right arm, and brought it along nicely so that the golden starburst of the order closed the sash nicely on her left hip. But, not content with the silent testimony of an undocumented Earth award, Kris added the lapel pin worn by civilian survivors of Wardhaven's recent defense.

Kris had no idea what medals, orders, or ribbons Hank might be sporting. Somehow she greatly doubted the long peace around Greenfeld had presented the many opportunities for bleeding and dying that Kris had faced of late. Or maybe the correct answer was that any of Greenfeld's folks that had done that shooting and dying had done so where it was best not documented.

Satisfied, Kris offered Jack her arm, he rested it on his, and they headed for the elevator. "Mind the store," Kris shouted at Chief Beni as they passed the Command Center.

"They throw a party for us poor, overworked sailors, and I get stuck with the duty. Where's the fairness in that?"

"Nobody mentioned fairness in my commissioning papers," Jack said, eyeing Kris.

"Nor mine," Kris pointed out. "But there's bound to be a party tomorrow night. I'll try to bust you loose."

"I'm going to remind you. Nelly, you remember her," Beni shouted as they opened the locked door and entered the elevator foyer. There were two big strapping boys taking delight in Marilyn's company.

"Enjoy one of those dances for me," she called as she checked the elevator, found it empty, and opened the door.

On Deck 1, Kris pointed her team at Pier 1's landing, Jack on her right, Penny on her left. "Jack, you going to try to talk me out of this one more time?"

"Nope," the Marine said. "I'm all gussied up and looking forward to the show." He patted Kris's waist at the back. "No weapon. Are you actually going unarmed tonight?"

"Abby showed me a better place for it. Don't want to be dancing with a guy and him patting my hold-out gun."

"Especially Hank," Penny said.

"Please let me know before you start shooting."

"I will, Jack. I know it's embarrassing when I get the best of the bad guys and you get left with the second string," she said through a smile.

"It's not fair to say things like that when we're coming up on our target and I have to smile," he growled through his smile.

"I'm sure you'll get even," Kris said.

They took the escalator down to the landing. Penny crossed the brow first, saluting the Officer of the Deck, then the flag painted on the left wall of the quarterdeck. Jack followed, doing the same. Kris, playing regal to the hilt, and not being in uniform, crossed the gangplank, and presented her hand to the OOD to kiss. Apparently, this was not covered in the young lieutenant's brief, but, what with Kris's hand almost smacking him in the mouth, he got the idea that maybe he should kiss it.

Shamelessly, Kris used that effort, once begun, to get him into chasing her hand lower until he was half bowing. *Nice to know that Greenfeld sailors are educable*, Kris thought through a most Noble smile.

"Your commodore offered us the benefit of his barge for a ride down to the party. Are you going to show us the way?"

"That is my honor and duty," said a calm, low voice. Kris turned to find herself facing an older Naval officer in formal blues, four strips on his sleeve. His trim mustache was gray, as were enough of the hairs at his temple to give him a most distinguished appearance. Kris offered her hand, he bowed very professionally and kissed it. "I am Captain Merv Slovo, of the *Incredible*, Commodore Smythe-Peterwald's flagship."

"Is Hank styling himself that formally these days," Kris asked, airy as any debutante.

"His father is the President of over ninety planets. Some formality does seem apropos."

Kris did not argue the planet count and introduced Penny. The woman followed Kris's lead; rather than saluting her senior, she offered her hand. Captain Slovo did it honor, but his bow brought his eyes level with the young lieutenant's medals, and Kris noticed that the captain's nostrils flared as he read the service record of the woman before him.

This was something Kris found very intriguing about the Navy Way. She'd learned early to have Nelly subscribe to *Who's Who on Wardhaven*, and then expanded it to *Who's Who in All Human Space*. Politicians, scientists, civilians in general, could be found quickly, and their stories revealed for the thoughtful application of a young girl politician-in-training.

The Navy Way was different. It was all out there on the chest to observe and mark. And, if appropriate, be warned by.

Take Captain Slovo. The Good Conduct Medal with four oak-leaf clusters on it was in his long row of miniature medals. It was proof not only of his good and faithful service but told Kris that he had completed twenty years active duty but had not been retired. His other medals included a Meritorious Service Award for his performance, likely in a staff billet. There was also a Distinguished Service Award, probably for a previous command. He sported an unusual ribbon for a Greenfeld sailor. Most of their ships stayed close to port; he wore the space-dark ribbon with the four white stars that identified one who'd made a four-month cruise. Oh, and his sharpshooter medal said he was highly qualified with five individual or crew-served weapons.

Kris double-checked that row of medals against the latest update Nelly had found on net. No, he had not been involved in any of the officially recognized Defense Campaigns that Peterwald had declared following some of his more heavy-handed acquisitions. Unless Captain Slovo was holding back on Kris, he was not a veteran of the more egregious blood and thunder bits of Greenfeld gunboat diplomacy.

While Kris was evaluating the man in front of Penny, he was doing the same to Kris's subordinate. Penny had the usual "Beer Swilling and Party Games medal" that had been awarded to all who attended the formal and final hauling down of the flag of the Society of Humanity at the Paris system. She also wore the Turantic Medical Expedition and the generic Naval Expeditionary Medal for the assistance she and others had provided Hikila during its recent terrorist outbreak. What was unusual, at least for the Turantic Medal, was that it also showed a V for valor. While others had just gone to Turantic to deliver medical supplies and reestablish communications, Penny had earned hers the hard way—in a fight.

Proudly in last place was the Wardhaven Defense Medal. There was no V authorized for that medal. No one earned it who wasn't on the line—fighting for their life.

At the other end of Penny's medals, in pride of place, was the Meritorious Service Award. She'd probably earned that for her inquisition of Kris's shipmates on the *Typhoon*, something that still irked Kris. But Tommy had asked her not to hold it against Penny. "She was only doing her job." And falling in love with Tommy . . . and Tommy with her.

So Kris forgave her that. Still, it burned Kris. All the scrapes she'd pulled herself and Wardhaven out of and all she got were the basic ribbons for being there. Being the Prime Minister's daughter and the King's great-granddaughter was not turning out to be all that the fairy tales promised.

Captain Slovo finished his assessment of Penny and turned to Jack. They exchanged salutes. Jack's "tourist" credentials were the same as Penny's, though his started at Turantic. The two men's eyes got that hard look around the edges that two men often get when they're making the determination as to who the Alpha male is in this dog run . . . and not at all sure how to call it.

They broke eye contact so close to the same time that only Nelly could have determined the winner.

"May I offer you an arm," the captain said to Kris. "The commodore's barge is this way." All so civil. All so proper. Kris took the offered arm and let him lead her. Jack and Penny trailed them. *Despite all the ancient trappings of warriors and killers, tonight we party. Who knows what we'll do to each other tomorrow. But tonight, we drink, and dance, and ignore the obvious. Like hell we do*, Kris reminded herself.

Captain Slovo led her through his ship with clear pride of ownership. In an elevator taking them down, he turned to Kris. "Is that the Earth Order of the Wounded Lion you are wearing?"

"It is," Kris agreed.

"Little girls don't often find them in a box of cracker jacks?"

"I'm not aware that any little girl ever has."

"No," he said, "No, they have not. So, there must be quite a story behind it. There always is, I'm told."

"Yes," Kris agreed, but gave no story.

The pause grew long. "You're not going to tell me."

"Certainly you've been briefed on me."

The captain adjusted the tight collar of his shirt as the elevator came to a halt. "Actually, I have no brief on you at all. We left Greenfeld space a month ago and have been paying calls on Confederacy planets since. Four, five, one loses count," he fibbed. And Kris found herself suppressing a frown. *Why are you telling me this?* Was he trying merely to pass the time, or was this his excuse for the blundering around the station? Or was he letting her know that he and his commodore were having to make this up as they went along? Hmm.

Kris reviewed the whole of his statement and chose to respond to his first remark. "Well, your commodore has surely shared *his* experiences of me with you," Kris said as they walked across the shuttle bay. Around her, files of sailors and Marines in dress uniforms were loading aboard liberty launches, but the area around the barge was clear of activity.

"He has said a few words, nothing of major import." The captain's serious face suddenly took on a puzzled smile. "He is rather definite that you and your associates are not to be allowed near the bridge of any of our ships or the controls of any of our craft. No explanation. Leaves me wondering."

"Well, if Hank considers that to be top secret, far be it from me to spill the beans," Kris said lightly.

Without orders, but in accordance with protocol, Jack and Penny boarded the launch first, then stepping aft to give Kris and Captain Slovo freedom to enter. The Captain handed Kris aboard, boarded himself and came to attention facing forward.

Henry Smythe-Peterwald the Thirteenth in full military regalia stood beside the front seat. Long formal frock coat was topped by a hat that could have been stolen from the captain of a sailing ship, gold fringed and rising high in the middle as it tapered fore and aft. On his chest was a fistful of medals, Distinguished this, Meritorious that. Kris wondered if the poor fellow who approved all of them had actually written up some fiction, or just stamped them, To KEEP THE BOSS'S BRAT HAPPY.

And why didn't anyone on Wardhaven ever worry about what might make the Prime Minister's brat a bit happier. Oh well.

Captain Slovo announced most formally, "Her Highness, Princess Kristine of the United Sentients."

Hank took one look at Kris and let his perfect face slip into a perfect pout. *Was the Commodore just a bit upset not to have a lowly lieutenant to lord it over?* Kris thought, and suppressed the grin she felt at her first victory of the night.

Hank whirled to put his back to Kris and sat down, much like a child's balloon losing air. And got entangled in the sword he wore on his left. He should have taken the right-hand seat, but that would not have given him the direct line of sight he wanted. *Oh yes, I've totally messed up his little show.*

Beside Kris, Captain Slovo coughed softly. "I believe the last seat is reserved for you, farthest from the controls."

And I believe you blew it when you announced me, but I'm glad you did. And you only walked into the trap I set for you. I'm sorry, Captain, you deserve a better master, Kris thought as she went where she was directed.

Penny took the seat beside her. Jack settled into the one ahead of her, his cake slicer out of his way and his service automatic in easy reach. Kris automatically arranged her skirt so her own automatic, now holstered above her right knee, was easily in reach. Then she relaxed. The battle tonight would not be fought with bullets. At least not at first.

Hank made his initial play and fell flat. Kris awaited his next move, which turned out to be part of his first. Five captains tromped aboard. Apparently, Hank wanted all his skippers to witness the humiliation of the Commander, Wardhaven's Naval District 41. Unfortunately, all they saw was their own boss in a huff and Kris, smiling regally from aft as they came on board.

Certainly, that had not been in Hank's Plan of the Day.

And Kris was getting a good look at the men who called the shots on his ships. Three quickly settled around their young commodore. As a group, they were young and, Kris suspected, new to their jobs. Seated amidships with the flag captain were two others, older as well. While the forward bunch quickly found themselves something to laugh about . . . or at . . . the older captains buckled themselves in, giving quick measured glances forward, and furtive ones aft. Captain Slovo leaned forward and the other two put their heads together, but only for a moment. With solemn loyalty to their superior, they frowned at Kris and settled back into their seats, their faces Navy bland.

Kris leaned over toward Penny. "Can you get me info on these ships and officers?"

"Yes, Your Highness. They're brand-new and not in my database. I sent off a priority query, but nothing's back yet."

The ride down went smoothly; Kris could not have done it better. A glance out the window showed Last Chance's airport was not as sleepy as usual. The flight line was crowded with liberty launches; people lined the perimeter fence. Lots of people had turned out for the show. The politician in Kris wondered what they expected, and if they'd be happy with what they got.

Today, the commodore's barge was quickly towed to a spot for all to see. Sailors and Marines lined up in ranks and a brass band in Greenfeld's colors played their anthem. Kris stayed seated when the hatch opened. A stairway with a top landing big enough for a stage rolled up to the door. Hank led his captains onto it, not giving Kris a glance.

For her part, Kris gave him a friendly nod. It might have been lost on Hank, but not on Captain Slovo, or the other two following in his wake. The last one actually nodded and touched his hat. *The campaign is joined and yielding some results.*

On the stage/stairway, Hank talked into a powerful mike that carried his words across the flight line to the waiting crowd. His crew was at attention, so silence was expected from them. Through the door, Kris could see a portion of the fence line. They stood quietly as Hank announced that "Space unites us all" and went on to praise the prosperity that the recent years had brought to everyone "smart enough to know which way the wind was blowing." He ended with the firm hope that the people of Chance would take every advantage that came to people who "got on the winning bandwagon early and helped it over the top."

Some chief must have dismissed the sailors from attention, because they provided their commodore with a rousing cheer.

The fence was just as quiet as it had been through the entire spiel.

Hank muttered something to his young captains. Kris could just make out his words. "They'll learn. We'll show them."

Kris did not stand until Hank and team were down the stairs and Penny reported they had boarded limos and were leaving. Protocol requires the senior to lead. And while Penny and she were both lieutenants, Penny had Kris beaten by over a year in rank. Still, with a smile, Penny deferred. Jack stepped to the door, took a long look for snipers, grenadiers, others who might ruin his yet untarnished record of keeping alive human space's most available target, and nodded Kris forward.

Kris stepped onto the landing, smiled at everyone in sight, gave a wave as she'd been taught, and started to head down the stairs, ignored by all but the last few media hounds who hadn't yet followed Hank into town.

"Hey, there's our princess," someone shouted.

And a cheer went up. Kris found herself waving at a fence line of people. Kids, women, men, waved back at her and gave her the cheers that had somehow eluded Hank's little sales pitch.

She stood there for a long minute waving back and feeling the roar wash over her. There were a few shouts for "Speech, Speech," but they never caught on . . . to Kris's relief. Hank would be an easy act to follow, but she'd rather not have to play in the muddy waters he'd left. Let the full impact of his words sink in . . . and her humble quiet and friendly smile.

The crowd was still waving and cheering when Kris made her way slowly down the steps. A limo stopped at the foot of the stairs. Surprise, surprise, Steve Jr. was driving.

"Jack, would you please inform this young Kamikaze pilot that we do not have a schedule that requires us to be anywhere anytime soon and that he can drive us slowly into town."

"Dad said to set a new record for the drive," Steve Jr. beamed.

"He did, did he?" Jack said, sliding into the front seat.

"Yep, longest time to cover the distance," the boy said. "Which is gonna be hard to do, cause Tanona is driving that kid admiral, and she's the slowest driver on this planet."

Kris waved at the crowd as Steve headed for the gate. Most were walking to their cars, but one little girl was waving hard enough that Kris feared her arm might fall off. Kris gave her a big smile and hearty wave. As they stopped briefly at the gate, the six-year-old turned, and Kris caught the eager exchange.

"Mommy, Mommy, the princess waved at me. Just at me."

"I'm sure she did," her mommy answered without looking up from strapping a younger sibling into a car seat.

"No Mommy, she really, *really* waved at me."

The mother turned, picked up her little treasure, and saw that Kris really was close. "I hope you waved back."

"I did, Mommy," the girl shouted excitedly, waving back some more, just in case Kris had forgotten her earlier effort.

Kris smiled at the two and waved. There was one vote for joining Grampa Ray's association. Of course, the whole issue would be settled long before that girl ever got to vote. And if it went the wrong way, she might never cast a vote in her life.

Kris turned to face front, and waved at others walking along the side of the road. It was all about that little girl and other little girls and boys like her. They were the reason Chance was what it was and had to remain that way. Kris gritted her teeth and swore that she would not forget little girls.

Beside her, Penny wiped a tear away. "It would have been wonderful to have a little girl like that. One that looked a bit like me and a bit like Tommy."

Kris reached across with the hand she was not waving to rest it on Penny's knee. "Yes it would have."

Penny eyed the cars ahead of them. "That son of a bitch. It's all a game of smoke and power puffs to him."

"And you and I and Tommy have made them fall flat on their faces," Kris said through her smile.

"But it wasn't any skin off their noses. They never said so much as 'ouch.' "

"Now is the time to smile and wave, Penny," Kris said as gently as she could.

Penny waved, tears running down her cheek. "Sorry, Kris, I should have stayed on the station. I didn't know it would hit me like this." Kris kicked herself. Why hadn't she thought of it.

Because you were so busy figuring out how to pop Hank's bubble that you didn't remember how badly the Peterwalds had popped Penny's life hopes. Damn it, Longknife, but you can be so focused on 'them' that you forget everything else.

"Steve, is there a service station ahead?" Kris asked.

"Yes, but it would be a bit of a detour."

"I have a sudden need to powder my nose. Take us there."

"No, Kris. No."

Steve Jr. looked over his shoulder at the two women. "I command here," Kris snapped. "Make the detour."

Steve did. No cars followed them; there was only one car in the station when they pulled in. Fortunately, the essential rooms were on the right outside wall and weren't even locked. Penny disappeared into the ladies room. Jack got out to do a thorough inspection of their surroundings leaving Kris to answer Steve's "did I do something wrong?"

"No."

Steve Jr.'s teenaged helplessness at the soft sobs coming from the ladies' room left Kris no option but to fill the broken silence with words. "Penny loved a friend of mine. They were married and, three days later, Tommy died fighting off a Peterwald invasion fleet trying to flatten my home planet."

The youngster didn't seem any more enlightened. "But that was a Peterwald talking to us. Why aren't you at war with him?"

"When the fight was over, there was no proof of where the ships came from, no survivors from the invasion fleet."

"That's not possible."

"Not accidentally," Kris agreed.

"Good lord, what a mess," the young man said with brilliance that often evaded those many times his age.

"Yes, what a mess."

A few moments later Penny emerged, her face washed but now devoid of make-up. She settled into the backseat. "I'm sorry to be such a blubberer, Kris. I didn't see this coming."

"I know," Kris said gently.

"Do you want to send me back to the station?" Penny asked.

"Not unless you want to go."

Penny considered the matter, then nodded. "I can't trust myself around Hank. I could collapse at the wrong time. Let Steve take me back to the port after he drops you off. I can catch a work shuttle back up. Hey . . ." She brightened a bit. "I could relieve the chief, let him have some fun tonight."

"Yes you could," Kris agreed. She'd wanted Penny along to show the flag. More importantly, to show battle medals without Kris having to wear a lieutenant's uniform and take the flak Hank had planned. In truth, she'd abused Penny, but in defense, neither Kris nor Penny had expected one of them to have such a visceral reaction to the sight of the boy-man.

"We'll do that," Kris agreed softly. The glance Jack threw Kris was hard to gauge. If he felt Kris was out of line toward Penny, he didn't let it show. Then again, he'd been around Longknifes so long, he might be just as coldhearted a user of people as they were. Tommy would have called Kris on that.

She missed Tommy.

The rest of the drive was quiet. Downtown, Steve pulled over. "You ready for me to drive you in?"

"Let me out here," Penny said. "Then come back for me."

Kris agreed. That would keep Penny out of the lights, keep her from questions being raised about why she stayed in the limo.

Penny got out, then held on to the door. "Kris, this is not your fault. I figured out what you were using me and Jack for. That you wanted that bunch of rear echelon commandos to see what a team of killers looked like. I wanted to spit in Hank's eye," she said, looking away. "So to speak. I had my anger to keep me strong. And it did, Kris. It did, right up until I saw that little girl waving at you. And then I lost it. For Hank I could be hard as nails. But that little girl. She's the reason we do what we do. She has to be the only reason we do these things.

"But the moment I looked into her eyes all I saw was what Tommy and I have lost, and I lost it. Don't worry, I'm not going to start bawling again," Penny said, closing the door. "You go give Hank hell and I'll free the chief to drink a couple of dozen Greenfeld chiefs under the table."

"Plan B will work just as well as Plan A," Kris assured her. Steve Jr. drove off, leaving one Navy lieutenant to pace the sidewalk until he got back. Kris wondered if Penny would be safe, then measured the set of her subordinate's jaw and decided anyone who gave that woman grief tonight was in for a whole world of hurt.

"For what it's worth, I didn't see that coming, either."

"Thanks, Jack. Strange, we're ready for our enemies and the hard-fought campaigns. But it's the love and grace that brings us to our knees in tears."

"How else could it be. You okay?"

Kris did a gut check, found it riled but willing, checked her face and found it solid. "I'm good to go."

"Then we're on," Jack said as Steve Jr. came to a stop in a covered driveway in front of a towering hotel. Jack was out of the car in a second, opening Kris's door.

She descended from the limo in the most regal of fashions. There was a crowd and newsies. Kris smiled and waved. She spotted a teenaged boy waving, and blew him a kiss. He looked ready to die from the embarrassment and was the immediate envy of all his peers who had been too cool to wave.

Kris took Jack's arm, and leaning properly on it, passed into the hotel. Inside, a man directed them to the ballroom. Kris paused long enough to have Jack check the wrap Abby had equipped her with "in case the night is cooler than advertised or you want to show less skin." Kris measured her dress against what other women were wearing and found it far from scandalous. She also noted that others were handing over invitations. The man at the metal detector turned it off as he waved them through.

"We're getting the royal treatment all the way," Jack said.

"Just means we are not getting a choice between steak, chicken, or fish. We'll get whatever they've got left over," Kris assured him from experience.

It was showtime. With a smile and a flourish, two girls in white bow ties and tails opened the tall, gold-and-glass doors into the ballroom and Kris passed within.

12

Kris paused just inside the ballroom to orient herself. The huge room was organized with dinner tables to her left, a dance floor to the right. A small orchestra played background, but looked ready for dance music later. The place smelled of pride and confidence . . . oh . . . and hard-earned money.

Kris was not announced; Chance was too egalitarian for that. Still, heads turned in a spreading wave as word raced through the hall. The campaigner in Kris put attendance at about two thousand. The blue dress uniforms of a hundred Greenfeld officers were bunched protectively in six clumps Kris suspected represented ships. Whether or not there was safety in numbers, there surely was comfort.

While she and Jack came down the steps to the main floor, Kris spotted a large congregation of locals in full dinner dress around Hank and his captains. The locals' heads joined the general turn toward her. Hank ignored her.

No doubt, he did not appreciate the drop in attention. Into the silence he said, "Greenfeld will have no truck with royalty and the tax burden it adds." It might have been better argued by someone who didn't so obviously hold his present position by birth. Maybe Kris should have worn her Navy uniform to better show the balance between hard won and easily given.

No, the reaction she was getting as a princess, from Hank, from that little girl, and from about everyone in this hall was well worth the extra weight of the tiara on her head and the delightful pleasure of satin swishing around her legs. *Yes, tonight was definitely worth putting on stockings*.

As per Father's early-taught instructions, Kris tried to circulate quickly, passing from one group to another with only a few words spoken or a quick smile. The men in black tuxes or white dinner jackets, the women in dresses as colorful and light as Kris's wouldn't let her. Many had fathers or grandmothers, younger brothers, kid sisters, or older sons and daughters of their own working on Kris's station or the *Patton*. Everyone on Chance seemed to be related or know someone working in Station Security or the Museum or something topside. Kris thanked them for the assist and that seemed enough of a toll for her to be passed on to the next small knot.

Shortly, one of the young ladies in formal tails and white bow tie appeared at Kris's elbow with a glass of soda water and a suggestion that dinner was ready to be served if "Her Majesty would kindly take the seat prepared for her." Kris saved the girl from a mortal case of embarrassment by not pointing out that only King Ray merited the "Majesty" . . . she was just a "Highness".

The room followed her move to their chairs. Hank was slow at getting the word, or maybe he intended for his six officers to be the last ones standing. Kris did note that they were eating at tables as far from hers as physically possible without knocking out a wall. Kris also noted that Ron personally escorted Hank to his table. Kris's unbidden question as to who might be Ron's date for tonight was answered as his mother took the seat next to him. Poor Ron. Then again . . . lucky Kris. Or was Marta in cahoots with her son on seeing that he had nothing on his mind but Hank? Or maybe Hank and Kris?

It would be so nice if I could read that woman's mind, Kris thought . . . and turned to her dinner partners and prepared for the usual table banter that passed for warfare by other means.

To Kris's great surprise, she was not immediately asked what Grampa Ray was up to or for the latest rumors about the ongoing Constitutional Convention still talking to itself on Pitts Hope.

No, the man next to Kris was the owner of a machine shop and foundry. "You're employing some of my best workers, don't you know, Your Highness."

"Then I much appreciate your loan," Kris said.

"I may need them back real soon. A consortium of us is bidding to build a Kawanashi plant to fabricate the larger sections for fusion reactors. We lost a similar bid with GE just a few months ago. They chose Turantic for their new Rim plant."

"Seems Turantic was considered a better bet than us, or safer," another man around the table added with a scowl.

Kris nodded, but declined to point out that Turantic had just joined Grampa Ray's United Sentients and was now recovering from a rather lengthy financial slump.

"Anyway," the first man went on, "the Rim is growing and we need fusion reactors. Chance has a highly trained and competitive workforce. We're a growing population, over a hundred million now," he said, and smiled lovingly at his wife.

She patted the swelling roundness of her stomach. "A hundred million and one next month," she told the table, and received happy, encouraging noises in return.

"Then we want to make sure that your . . ." Kris paused.

"Daughter," she provided.

"Has the same chances that her mother and father had."

Several men nodded and glanced across the ballroom to where Hank was talking loud enough to be heard above the soft roar of the room. Dinner talk continued in that local vein, them telling her why she should love Chance, her occasionally highlighting the present question before them. There was only one break from that when the woman to Jack's left spoke.

She'd been silent the entire dinner, not talking to her partner or to Jack. Her own dessert untouched when most were finished, she turned to Kris and said simply, "Why are you here?"

The question was so out of step with the rest of the evening that Kris faltered for a moment and said the first thing that came into her head. "I was invited to dinner."

"Not here tonight," the woman said, tapping the table. Her hand shot up to point a finger at the ceiling. "Here, on Chance.

Out on the Rim. Despite what Ted says, we aren't that big a market, yet. Why send a Longknife? And that's before we go into what you did on Turantic and Wardhaven's recent battle and all that other stuff. What war are you supposed to start?"

"Ginjer, that is out of line. May I apologize for my wife," the man next to her said, half rising from his seat and placing a hand on his wife's elbow to move her in the same direction.

"No, no," Kris said with a dry chuckle. "She has probably just asked the question on half the minds in this room. Wouldn't you like to hear my answer?" Ginjer's husband seemed torn between excusing himself or settling back into his seat. The other men around the table looked uniformly embarrassed.

The pregnant mother rubbed the top of her extra curve very protectively and said, "Yes, I would like to know what war you are here to start."

"Alice!"

"So would you, Theodore. Shut up and let the woman tell us something. We can decide later how close it is to the truth."

Now Kris did laugh. "Candor is something I encounter so rarely, it's a joy to run into it twice on the same night," Kris offered in explanation for her mirth. She reached for her napkin, patted her mouth, then mused out loud.

"Why am I here? What war will I start?" Kris frowned. "You know that I have only two officers, a chief and my maid with me. Kind of slim pickings for starting a good-size war."

"Weren't most of them with you on Turantic?" Theodore, who still grated at that planet's winning of the GE plant showed that he did, indeed, know a bit about what went on there.

"I went to Turantic to break a friend loose from a guy who kidnapped him. And then I found myself running for my life. The rest just kind of happened. I went to Hikila to hold the hand of one of Grampa Ray's old war buddies who was dying. Somebody kidnapped several hundred people, started killing them. By now you've probably figured out I don't like kidnappers. Some of you may know why." Around the table there were nods.

"Wardhaven? Well, like Chance is your home, Wardhaven is mine and I fought to defend it. So did a lot of other folks who had other plans that particular week." Kris knew her face was hard, but she didn't know how to talk about that battle in a soft way. She shivered at the memory of faces she'd never see again.

"You want to know why I'm here?" Kris said, turning a face as open and honest as she knew how to wear toward Ginjer. "I'm here because I've gotten in a lot of people's hair and they want me as far away from their hairdo as they can get me. This may come as a surprise to you folks born and raised here, but in the Wardhaven Navy, Chance duty is not a plum assignment."

Beside her, Jack grinned and nodded emphatic agreement.

"If you doubt me, talk to Steve Kovar. Navy officers are not supposed to retire as lieutenants. Not supposed to spend fifteen years in the same billet and never get a promotion."

The table took that in and weighed it. The eyes that looked back at Kris seemed devoid of conclusion. All but one.

"That *is* why you're here, isn't it," Alice said, once again massaging her future daughter.

"Alice, I'll warn you," Kris said. "I just told you the best of all lies." Eyebrows raised around the table at that. "I told you a truth no one will ever believe."

The table chuckled, unsure at that.

"May I put in two cents," Jack said, breaking his silence. "For as long as I have known this woman, she has never gone looking for a fight. Never set out to start a war." He paused, grinned, then said, "Though I have known her to shut a few down."

There were snickers around the table at that.

"No, this Longknife does not go looking for trouble," Jack said. "But I must also tell you. I have never known trouble to *not* find her." Jack eyed Hank's table across the room. "I have never known trouble to miss a chance to ruin her day . . . or *mine*." Those around the table grew silent, intent on digesting the rather large chunk of raw, red truth they'd been served.

Then the music started and Kris was not surprised to find Ron beside her chair. "I think you promised me the first dance."

It took Kris only a moment on the floor to remember why she enjoyed dancing with the man. He led, but not too strongly; she followed, but not too willingly. They were a good match.

"Aren't you going to ask me about our dinner conversation with Hank?"

"Was there anything more to it than 'You need to get on the bandwagon before it runs you down.' "

"He didn't exactly threaten us, but you got the gist of it."

Kris looked around the dance floor. It was filling up with couples, mostly locals. Here and there Kris spotted a young local girl in the arms of a junior Greenfeld officer . . . the most ancient form of sedition at work. Across the room, Hank and Marta had their heads together in conversation.

"And you left your poor mother to baby-sit Hank?"

"More likely to warn any available young woman that here is an available young man you don't want to get anywhere near."

"You've changed your opinion of Hank!" Kris said in perfectly feigned shock.

He scrunched up his face as if in deep thought. "Yes, I believe I have. Most definitely. I didn't much like him in college. I like even less the little twerp leading warships into my home planet's orbit."

The music ended. No one made to break in, and they went smoothly into a second dance. Something from old Earth that allowed them to stay close and talk. "You aren't upset that he was once a potential suitor for my hand, are you?"

"The hand with the gun, or the one with the hand grenade?"

Kris squinched up her face in deep thought. "I think both."

"Foolish young man," Ron said.

"Speaking of, here he comes," Kris warned through a smile.

"Mind if I cut in." Hank did not ask.

"Of course not, Commodore. This shindig is in your honor. But don't tie up all her dances. I think a line is forming."

"Strange, I didn't see anyone," Hank said, putting his arm around Kris's waist and feeling around a bit before they began to move to the music. "What, no assault rifle?"

"I escrow heavy artillery when I come the dainty princess."

"Well, I'll assume I'm safe from kidnapping when with you."

"And I feel oh so much safer from the odd and sod assassin when in your arms," Kris shot back.

"You know, it doesn't have to be this way between us."

"It doesn't?" Kris said. No need here to play the coy innocent. The two of them knew exactly the way things were.

"No. My dad is not the monster you make him out to be. Yes, he has some subordinates that got out of control. But weren't you the one that pointed out that your own grandfather was a slumlord?"

"I most certainly did."

"And did he do anything about it, but sell off the embarrassing property, no improvements made?"

"The old guy is guilty as charged."

"Well."

"You're talking about the splinters in my family's eye that I've been hollering at them about, but I have yet to hear you say a word to your old man about the I beam sticking out of his."

"There you go again, insisting that it's all our fault."

"And there you go insisting that none of it is. Want to tell me how your father arranged that attack on Wardhaven?"

"There's no proof at all my father was involved."

Kris had been doing her best to let Hank lead, but he tried to send her into a deep back bend and there was no bend in her. She took two steps back, her own back ramrod straight, and right there, on the dance floor, they came uncoupled. "Of course there's no proof. All the survivors from six honking-big battleships died."

"You shot the prisoners," Hank shouted, his voice breaking.

"Somebody jiggered their survival pods," Kris shot back, her voice low and deadly.

"Commodore, Commodore, didn't you promise me a dance?" Marta Torn was there, at Hank's left, leading him into a turn away from Kris. And Jack was at Kris's left, turning her away from the red-faced youth in the Commodore uniform.

"Well, that went well," Jack offered.

"Think he'll want another dance?"

"I think we better arrange our own ride up to the station."

"You think so?"

"I know so. You Princess. Me Chief of your security. Me making this call. Any argument is hereby ruled out of order."

Kris sighed. "I guess this is another date I end up walking home from."

"Didn't your momma tell you a gal's mettle is determined by the ones she walks home from, not the ones she rides back with?"

Kris scowled at the mention of her mother. "Nope, I think that escaped her."

"Aren't you glad you have a security chief to teach you the most basic things about being a young woman."

Kris leaned her head against Jack's shoulder. "Yes, I'm glad," she said. Unfortunately, she could never tell him just how glad she was to have him there.

Jack expertly led them to the far edge of the dance floor, Kris did not see Hank for some time, and when she did he made a point of ignoring her. Kris did notice that the woman he danced with wore a wedding ring. Part of Marta's plan?

When the next dance was new and far too frantic for Kris, she and Jack made their way back to their table. Ron was there, and the expectant mother, her feet up on the chair next to her.

Kris eyed the empty chairs. "Are they off carrying my possibly true words to the entire gathering?" Kris asked.

"I think the entire gathering tracked every word you and the commodore exchanged. What's that about you shooting prisoners?"

"We didn't," Kris said, taking her seat and draining a water glass. One of the servers appeared and immediately refilled it. "Just a rumor the Peterwalds spread that doesn't add up." Kris didn't want to shout exactly how with the music so loud. The next song came up soft and gentle; Ron was again waiting.

"Care for another dance if I pledge myself to defend possession of your delicate body with tooth and nails?"

"Be warned, I'm armed with this cake slicer," Jack said darkly adjusting his sword at his side. "Oh, and a pistol, too," he said as if just remembering his service automatic.

"If the woman says to let you cut in, I'll consider not putting up too much of a fight," Ron agreed.

Kris danced with the mayor, and with her security chief, and with several other young men from Chance who migrated to her table and asked for the privilege of risking their toes to her missteps. She did keep an eye on Hank and his blue suits, but nothing happened. The junior officers danced, as did Hank and his young captains. The three older skippers did not, but sat together, talked quietly, and sipped wine.

It was a pleasant evening, right up to the moment when Ron and Jack both cut in.

"I think we need to leave," the mayor said.

"Problems," Kris said after just one glance at their faces.

"My Chief of the Peace has a problem. Hans isn't too happy, either. I'd like a Naval officer's opinion as to what is just sailors blowing off steam and what is an assault on my city."

Kris collected her wrap and left quickly. Steve Jr. was waiting for them and, the injunction about speed having expired, headed for the Oktoberfest at only slightly below light speed.

Hans and the Chief of the Peace were waiting outside a large daub-and-beam building signed the Edelweiss. One light post down four sailors were cuffed and laid out on the ground while a dozen good-sized men looked on. All twelve sporting a red armband with a hastily sewn, gold cloth star that, apparently, identified cops tonight. This might have passed for a normal night when the fleet was in. What didn't look normal were a couple of dozen sailors standing around giving the cops dark glowers and occasional encouraging words to their buddies on the deck.

Kris could tell a riot looking for a way to happen.

She did a quick survey of the street. Cops walked in pairs or foursomes. Other locals moved up and down row upon row of tables and benches that covered the street, handing off foaming glasses to sailors shouting for them. There were a lot more sailors shouting than hands passing out beer. "I don't see any women," Kris said. "No barmaids on Chance?"

"We sent them home," Hans said. "We run family businesses. The women working here are our wives, daughters, their friends. Some of the things the sailors said to them . . ." He shook his head.

"It was better to send the women home before they started dumping more beer over sailors heads than they put on the tables in front of them. Or their sons and husbands started fights . . . and I know we don't want no fights," Hans said to Ron.

"Mayor," he continued, "we really need more guys to shell out the beer or there's going to be a riot. Half those men Gassy has wearing armbands have worked here. I need them."

Ron eyed his Chief of the Peace. "I have barely enough, Boss. And if things get any worse, I won't have anywhere near enough. These guys keep drinking and things are only going to go downhill. I know you don't want to hear this, but I think you better close down the Beergartens."

To Kris's surprise, Hans' only comeback to that was a weak "I hope you don't do nothing like that."

"Who's paying for the beer?" she asked Ron.

"The city's paying some, and Hans's friends are selling to the sailors at half price. About midnight, we're going to let them tap out the older stuff that's gone stale. What we usually make them pour down the gutter."

"Well, if you don't have a riot before midnight, I'll bet on one after that," Jack said.

"We thought they'd be too drunk to notice," the garten owner said with a shrug. "The way they're swilling my best, they can't have any taste left by then."

Kris did a second look around. Yep, most were going through their large glasses as fast as she'd come to expect of college boys—or girls, but there were no girls on a Peterwald ship. On closer study, she spotted, here and there, a fellow who looked a bit too old to be an able seaman. And those few were nursing their glasses. Come midnight, at least a few would know what was being served. And a shout would . . .

"Jack, you see what I see?"

He nodded. "There're troublemakers out there."

Gascón following where Kris looked and scowled at what he saw. "You think we're being set up, Princess?"

"That's what the Peterwalds do. I don't see any Shore Patrol. Have they checked in with you?"

"There is no Shore Patrol," the Chief of the Peace said.

"I think now would be a good time for you to call Hank," Kris said to Ron.

The mayor nodded, a deep scowl on his face. With a sigh and a shake, he turned his face to pleasantly friendly. "Oh,

Kris, you better get over there," he said, pointing to a piece of pavement well in front of him. She and Jack did.

Ron held up his wrist and said. "Ron Torn here. Connect me to Marta Torn." A moment later he was talking to his mother. "Things going well on your side?"

"No blood on the carpet. I guess that counts for success tonight. You out on the street, Mr. Mayor?"

"Yes, Mom. Is our visiting commodore close? I need to talk to him."

"I figured you would when I saw the company you left in. How many times have I told you, son, if I'm ever going to have any grandkids, you have to leave with just the girl. Not her papa, not her best friend. Find one girl, and leave with her."

Ron scratched his forehead. "You're right, Mom, I blew it again," he said, casting a not-all-that-brotherly look Kris's way. She returned it just as enthusiastically.

"I always tell guys, listen to your mother," Kris whispered.

"Here's the man you asked for, Mr. Mayor," Marta said, the mother gone, the senior manager solidly in place.

"I missed you, Ron," Hank said, effusively. "Last time I looked around for you, you were no where to be seen. I've been dancing with all your old girlfriends it seems."

Jack elbowed Kris. She tossed him a glare before turning a wide-eyed, innocent face to Ron. He was trapped by the camera on his wrist and Hank.

"Didn't know I had that many old flames," Ron said, maybe for Kris, then cut straight to the chase, "but you, Commodore, have lots of sailors. Now, I'm glad they're enjoying themselves, but quite a few of them can't seem to handle their beer. We've had fights, sailor on sailor, sailor on innocent civilian."

"Oh, I wouldn't be so sure those civilians are innocent. There're Longknife provocateurs everywhere. Longknifes throw money around like it's water when one of our ships is in port. If our sailors don't protect themselves, they'd be tied up and hauled off to some pig farm in the backwoods."

"Our judges will help you sort that out tomorrow."

"Judges?"

"Yes. From where I'm standing, a couple dozen of your boys will be sobering up courtesy of the sovereign city of

Last Chance, and talking to a Court Commissioner in the morning."

"I should hope not, Mayor," came in a voice devoid of all the Hail and Good Fellow that Hank had been projecting.

"What *would* you hope for, Commodore? My Safety people can't just leave them on the street to start another fight."

"What does the old song say, Mayor, 'roll'em up and put'em in the longboat?' Run them out to the liberty launches. We'll take them from there. I'm certain you'd provide such a courtesy to any visiting U.S. ship."

"Don't most U.S. ships have a Shore Patrol to work with the local Safety folks . . ." Ron started and trailed off.

"Sorry, son, he just turned his back on me and stomped off."

"Didn't anyone teach that man manners?" Hans muttered.

"Apparently not," Ron growled. "Gassy, it's up to you."

"What can you give me for back-up, Boss?"

"Most of what I'd normally back you up with is up there," he said, giving a thumbs-up that Kris suspected meant her station. "But I do have some reserves."

"Not the boys," Hans and Gassy said together.

Ron's hand was back up and he was talking to his wrist. "Coach, I need all the help you can give me."

"You want just the wrestlers, or should I call in the football teams as well?"

"Everything you got, college and high school level."

"You going to let high schoolers into the Oktoberfest?"

"I got Gassy right here beside me. I promise that none of your underage kids will be busted for either serving beer or waltzing through the gartens twirling a nightstick."

"Bad precedent, Ron," said the coach.

"We get through this visit and I'll visit every school and explain why I did it and tell them we'll give them unshirted hell if they do it again."

"I've got the call tree already going. My wife and kids are calling as we speak. My teams ought to start showing up in five, ten minutes." There was as chuckle. "I think some of them may be just down the street, waiting for word to come."

Ron rang off. "Wrestlers, football players?" Kris said.

"That was Randy Gomez, head coach at University of Last Chance. He's calling every kid involved in any of the

ever-popular, nasty contact sports played at our local schools."
Ron looked up the street. A pick-up with a youngster at the
wheel and more in the back rolled up to the yellow tape that
excluded traffic from the five blocks of Oktoberfest. Those
that jumped down were uniformly tall, bulky, looking eager
and mean enough to chew red-hot steel for breakfast come
morning.

"Have they been trained in police procedures?" Jack asked.

"One hour last week. I had my best deputies show riot-
control techniques to their classes," Gassy muttered. "But I'll
team five of them with two of my deputies or reservists. With
luck a drunk will take one look at their prospects and give it
up. If not, well, things may get interesting before those liberty
launches lift off."

Ron's wrist chimed, he gave it a "what now" look and
tapped it. "Please be kind to your ever-friendly mayor," he said.

"Don't know how kind this is, but we're having trouble getting the Highland Games started. Could you stop by and
maybe offer some insights into what I'm doing wrong. What
is it with sailor suits? This is always so much easier when the
guys and gals wear kilts."

So Kris, Ron and Jack turned for the college two short
blocks away. But the walk got longer because the stadium was
on the far side of the campus. And the sidewalks meandered
around trees and a fountain. "Is this supposed to isolate the
jocks from learning, or those who want to learn from anything
resembling physical exercise?" Jack asked the rising moon.

"I think it's lovely," Ron said, putting an arm around Kris.
It wasn't that cold, but his touch sent a shiver down Kris's
spine. She leaned against his shoulder and enjoyed the walk.

A shot ended that.

They'd just come around the south side of the bleachers to
the track. They spotted the source of the shot before Jack had
his Navy-issue pistol out. Unfortunately, Kris had raised her
skirt, showing a lot of leg, and the weapon hiding in her garter.

"That's where I figured it for," Jack said, but all three of
them were mesmerized by the sight of manly excellence before them as runners raced around the track . . . or whatever.

One sailor had come out of his crouch at the sound of the
gun, stumbled for two steps, and fallen on his face and was

now adding vomit to the blood that speckled the track. Others were worse. Two charged down the track, bounced off each other, and took off in directions that had nothing to do with the chalk lines drawn for the race. One seaman started fast. Stopped. Looked around at the shouting crowd . . . and turned tail. He was now racing the wrong way as fast as his legs could carry him.

Three, no, four sailors were still galloping along in the right direction at speeds that put the Interstellar Track and Field records well out of reach.

"I ask ya', is this normal?" said a thin old fellow, a few wisps of white hair combed over his sunburned scalp. The clipboard in his hand and the kilt that didn't reach to his knees identified him as someone in charge. "I mean, I heard tales of some mighty god-awful drinking at Paris when they finished up the Society, and there was mention in our newsletters of the worst sporting events in the history of the Games, but this. 'Tis . . ." he seemed at a loss for words and settled for "disgusting."

"I've heard that beer and physical excellence don't mix, but I never saw such solid proof," Jack said, covering a smile.

"I had other fun and games at Paris," Kris said vaguely.

Ron did the introductions. Douglas MacNab ran the city's annual Highland Games. "Not sure that qualifies me for this. We finally locked up the stones and hammers. I'm afear they'd do more damage to themselves and my school if I hadn'a."

"You going to Caber?" Kris asked, eyes lighting up.

"No," Jack said.

"I'm still trying," Douglas said, "but it's no easy to get these boys to even line up, much less listen to how it's done."

"What if I show them?" Kris said through a widening grin.

"What if you don't," Jack said.

"I'm not sure about this," Ron added.

"But I've always wanted to toss a caber. I can't tell you how many times I had to shake hands through a Highland Game for Father's campaign and never got to tossing one of those poles."

MacNab ran a hand through what was left of his hair. "We let the kids play at this because they do what I tell 'em, and their parents sign waivers. I don't see anyone around to sign a waiver for you, lassie."

"I'm over twenty-one," Kris said eagerly.

He eyed her over his spectacles. "And will you listen to what I tell ya."

"Of course," Kris said.

"No way," Jack said.

"I'm not too sure about this," Ron said again.

"Where's the caber toss?" Kris asked.

"On the other side of the seats," MacNab said, and led the way. Beside them, the four remaining runners were losing speed at a rapid clip. One of them shouted for a beer and took a hard right into the infield toward an honest-to-God beer wagon, complete with four beautifully groomed horses.

"Aren't those horses lovely," Kris said.

"Let's detour for an hour or two and say hi, Princess." Jack's suggestion almost reached the level of an order.

Ron's "Yes" was merely civilian-strength suggestion.

Kris kept walking; they reached the end of the seats just in time for Kris to catch something out of the corner of her eye.

She did a quick jump back. A long, thick pole slammed down in front of her, exactly where she'd been. If her oversize nose had been a hair longer, it would definitely have been shortened.

"Oops," said a sailor at the other end of the caber.

"Sorry, ma'am," said a second. A third, one of those older types Kris was spotting now and then, said nothing as he stepped back and disappeared into a milling crowd of sailors around a second beer wagon, complete with horses.

"Princess, I strongly suggest you go get acquainted with that team of horses," Jack said, undoing the flap on his holster. "Ron, Douglas, who's the head of security for this layout?"

There was a delay while Kris was introduced to Hilo Kalako, Chief Deputy, and the two men and four boys at his side. But while they talked their line of business, Kris spotted a half dozen cabers laid out and walked over to make *their* acquaintance.

"How do you lift one of these?" she asked Douglas.

"Da I not recall you saying you'd do what Ah told ya?"

"I did."

"Then stick those fine pale fingers of yours in this," he said, holding a bucket of strong smelling black stuff for Kris.

"I didn't say I wouldn't ask questions. So, what is it?"

"Tar and other stuff you'll be needing to hold on to the caber when you want to be holding on, and let it be slipping a bit when ya need that." Kris sank her hands into the goo.

"Abby would not approve," Jack said, coming up behind Kris.

"I think you're right on that," Kris agreed.

"Who's Abby?" Ron asked. "Your mother?"

"Close," Jack said. "Her maid."

Ron said nothing to that. Kris eyed the long wooden pole and frowned. "Which end of the pole do I pick up first?"

"Normally you wouldna be asking that," MacNab said. "The last one to make a toss is supposed to stand the caber up for the next. But you're first, and me old back isn't up to this kind of lifting no more."

"So I'll do it," Kris said, and stooped down, lifted one end into her lap, then stood up the rest of the way, carefully using her knees for the lift.

"Ya did that one right, lass, but ya remember ya tellin' me that you'd do what I told ya to."

"Yes."

"Well, that also means waiting for me to tell you what ta do. For now, ya just go hand over hand until ya got the caper standin' tall." She did. Soon, she found herself with her hands high over her head and her strapless gown playing an interesting game of show and tell. She managed to get the caber standing straight up with little shown and less to tell about it. A few wolf whistles soon changed into a ragged cheer as she finished. Leaning against the caber, she did the cute curtsey she'd learned at four or five . . . and the cheer grew louder.

Through a wide grin she whispered to Douglas, "What next?"

"The hard part, lassie." He quickly whispered to Kris how she was suppose to go from leaning on the caber, it's butt on the ground, to holding the bottom of the caber in both her hands, leaning it against her shoulder while she leaned her shoulder against it. "Ya got that?" Kris measured the expectant shouts from the crowd of Greenfeld sailors, males all, and her own expectation of success and found that the only future ahead for her involved either a successful caber toss or going down in flaming failure. Had that agent planned this as his fall-back plan if he didn't succeed in driving her into the turf with that falling pole? *Nah, this is just another one of my dumb stunts.*

Someone shouted, "Hey, that's Princess Longknife. How many of you want to toss a caber like her?" And a line began to form.

That cinched it, walking away was not an option.

Kris reviewed the old fellow's instructions and squatted down, thanking her mother for the ballet lessons that had kept her supple all those years. "Gee, Mother, I do owe you."

Fingers interlaced around the pole, shoulder against it, she felt the top of it begin a wild weaving pattern that threw the weight of it first right, then left, then front, then back. She held it there until it steadied for a moment, then made the lift from the knees, feet widespread. She felt all kinds of things go wrong in places she hadn't expected to feel until that undefined future day when she might give birth to some poor girl with a nose too long. Kris struggled to shuffle her legs closer together. Oh, and somehow, she also kept the caber upright enough to not get out of control and lay her and it out flat.

Douglas had called this the spider dance and said she'd understand it when she was doing it. Yes, it would have been nice to have eight legs at the moment, but she only had the two God gave her and she was busy working them like four. For a second, the caber took off on its own, but she managed to stutter jump to her left and catch the center of gravity again.

I've flown ships to orbit, standing them up on just a pillar of flame. Surely I can balance a five meter pole in my own hands. Course, the ship had an inertial guidance platform and all I have is my head. I am not gonna let a machine beat me!

The dance went on for a couple of weeks, maybe less. It was still dark and the moon was about in the same part of the sky when Kris found herself where Douglas said she should be. She stood. The butt of the caber was in the palm of her hands. She leaned against it while it leaned against her left shoulder.

Oh, and her dress had all kinds of tar streaks on it. Abby was not going to be happy.

"That's some Manual at Arms your doing, Princess," someone shouted from the back of the crowd.

"I don't see you in line to try it yourself," Jack shouted back. While Kris got her breath for what had to be an easier finish, MacNab sent the kids with armbands to form the sailors into six lines to match the six cabers they had. Since the crowd of gawkers in front of Kris got very thin, most everyone around must have gotten in line.

Kris had her breath back . . . and her arms and legs were beginning to scream at the abuse . . . when MacNab was back at her elbow. "You're going to want to let the caber begin to topple over," he pointed downfield. "Ya go along with it, picking up speed. When ya feel you're in the best spot, ya put everything ya have into lifting up the butt of it and tossing it up and out. The idea is to have the other end of the thing land first. If the butt lands first, or it just kind o' lays down lengthwise, it no been tossed and it no counts. Understand."

"I'm not doing this again."

"You'd have to wait in a long line to get another chance," Ron said, looking back where Kris didn't dare spare a glance.

Kris let the caber begin to fall. Slowly at first, then faster, she chased after it. She'd calculated ballistics since she was in middle school. She'd flown orbital skiffs by the seat of her pants. Certainly this couldn't be worse than those.

But orbital skiffs only took a flick of a finger to send them turning. This caber was dragging along her whole body, sucking every ounce of strength she had. One misstep on this grassy field, one stumble in the dark, and all she'd done would be for nothing. She'd be a joke to all these Greenfeld sailors.

Worse, she'd be a girl.

Kris found all the strength she had . . . plus an extra boost from anger . . . and hurled the caber high.

MacNab dropped a marker where Kris's foot was when she hefted it, then watched as the pole arched high and executed a perfect ballistic flight to slam down, nose first, in the grass.

"Well done. Well done, Lass," he called. "That won't be a record, but it would be a good finish in any game I've bossed in my thirty years of doing the honors."

Now there were cheers from the crowd behind Kris. She turned to them and did a formal curtsey. The cheers got louder. Ron presented Kris with a towel. She tried and failed to clean the mess off her hands as they headed back for the racetrack. The sailors opened a path for them, to shouts of "Good going," "Good shot," "Great doing, for a girl."

Before Kris could make a comeback, a sailor provided one for her. "My sister could have done just as well. We ought to let the girls have chances like that." That started an argument, that, fueled with beer, was best left to the sailors to resolve.

"We should get back to the port," Jack suggested. "We do have a shuttle to catch."

"And you don't want to be there when Hank and his mob start filling up the sky," Ron said. "I'm not sure there's a designated driver in the batch."

"Wasn't there anyone to take the drunks off your hands at the liberty launches?" Kris said.

"The first report back said the launches are deserted. No one standing guard. No pilot standing by."

Kris shook her head. "What are your security people doing with the drunks?"

" 'Rolling them up and putting them in the long boat.' "

"But," Kris started, then stopped.

"Oh Lord, but those boats are going to stink come midnight," Jack said, almost in pain at the thought of it.

"I'm sure you want to ride up in the work shuttle."

"Please, Mr. Mayor," Kris said.

They took a different way back into the Oktoberfest that put them at the opposite end of the street. With a guy on each arm, Kris looked forward to the walk. Farthest from the busses that had brought the sailors was the Heidelberg. A glance inside showed Kris several wide, smiling women working the taps . . . ensconced behind an equally wide bar.

She brought her men to a halt, ending the happy stroll. But before she could open her mouth, she spotted the difference between the Heidelberg and other Beergartens tonight. The tables, row on row, were filled with chiefs, older, maybe a bit more sober, but definitely quieter.

"So *that's* where all the NCOs are," Jack said.

"In there, not drinking with their own men. Not making any effort to keep discipline or order," Kris mused.

"I thought having a separate club for the chiefs was normal. At least that's what Hank's contact man told us," Ron said.

"Right," Kris said. "Still, you'd expect them to keep an eye on their men, hold them to a certain level of behavior. Maybe not as high as their moms and dads, but . . ."

Kris looked up the street. A fight was just being broken up by the armbands. Here and there men, hardly more than boys, emptied their stomachs into gutters, bushes, whatever. Not a view to make you proud of your fighting men.

The next beergarten, the Happy Bavarian, held the senior petty officers. That only men manned the taps showed they were only marginally better behaved than the seamen on the street.

Gassy was headed their way, a bespeckled man in a rumpled suit at his elbow. "Thought you might want to meet Pinky here."

"Harvey Pinkerton," the man said. "I own the only remote-controlled observer system in Last Chance."

"You of the Pinkerton Security Family?" Jack asked.

"Doubt it. Family story is that great-great however-many was shuffled off Earth in lieu of prison. I don't work for Gassy if there's just some enterprising young fellow involved in an exchange of property," the guy said with a grin at Gassy, who seemed to be studiously looking elsewhere. "Mostly I track wandering husband's, wives, teenagers. Not that Ron wants you to know his wonderful Chance has those oh so normal human problems."

"Pinky, show her what Gasçon told me about," Ron said dryly.

Pinky handed Kris the oversize reader he carried. It showed an aerial view of the Oktoberfest. He tapped it and it zoomed down. "Gassy told me there's some ringers circulating among these fun-loving sailor boys. Wondered if I could spot them."

"They're just sailors like the rest. But a bit older."

"There's two of them now. They usually travel in pairs."

Kris eyed the screen. White uniformed sailors filled most of the enlarged picture. But two were in gray sailor suits.

"Something go wrong in their wash?" Jack asked.

"Spider silk doesn't look at all like cotton when you catch it in the right light spectrum."

"Spider silk," Kris said with a growing frown. "Somebody's

not willing to take chances with the rest of the poor dumb sheep they're setting up for a fall."

"Looks that way," Gassy said. "Anyway, we've isolated ten pair of off-white sailors and we'll take them out of circulation come eleven thirty. We'll give them a ride to the airport in our very own paddy wagons and see that they are on the first liberty launches down the runway." He flicked his eyebrows up twice. "The smelliest ones."

"Kris, I think we better get gone."

"Jack, I agree. Ron, I want to thank you for showing a girl a great time," Kris said, giving the mayor a kiss on the cheek.

"I thought you said *I* showed you a great time," Jack said in wounded male pride.

"You did, but this is the best time I've had that didn't involve wrecking a space station."

Ron gave Kris a hug and a kiss of his own, and it wasn't on the cheek. "Someday I really want to read about your love life."

"Oh, now you've got tar on your formal duds. What are you going to tell your mom?"

"That things like that happen if she's ever to get those grandkids she keeps talking about. You two take care. Steve, don't you wrap your father's best rig around a tree or anything."

"Tough job that fellow has," Jack said as they left.

"About as tough as yours, I imagine."

"He keeps track of a city. All I have to handle is you."

Kris shrugged. "As I said. About even."

The ride up the station was a problem. The passengers sniffed the air around Kris. One pointed out, "After you toss a caber you're supposed to change clothes and take a bath before mixing in proper company." But the vote was twenty-three to twenty-two to let their princess share their ride. This really was Chance, where everyone knew everything. And someone had told Abby. She greeted Kris at the door of her quarters with a scowl.

"Do I space that dress with you in it?"

To help Abby decide, Kris started unzipping out of it. Jack had decided that Kris's safety tonight just might require him to unfasten the top hook and work the zipper down to where Kris could reach it. "What I do to keep you alive."

Out of the dress, Kris handed it to Abby. "I guess you might as well space it."

Abby made a grab for Kris's hand. "And look at these. You broke two, no three, nails and how are we ever going to get that tar out from under your fingernails."

"I'm sure you'll enjoy doing it and it will involve hurting me a whole bunch," Kris said. She slipped into a shipsuit and ducked over to the Command Center. Penny was there with Steve.

"The chief get away?"

"Yep," Penny said. "Beni went off with a couple of thirsty types from the *Resolute* to keep him company."

"May keep him out of trouble. Anything happen up here?"

"Not a thing. All ships quiet as a church," Penny said. The board showed Hank's *Incredible*, as well as *Fury*, *Dominant*, *Fearless*, *Surprise*, *Eager*. Traditional names, but in this collection, Kris wondered if they were hinting at anything.

"Wonder which ships belong to which captains?" Kris said.

"We should have had a reply to my priority search request. Don't know what's taking them so long."

"Abby didn't space you?" Steve grinned.

"I think I may be escaping a well-deserved fate."

"Throwing the caber in a silk party dress," Penny said.

"My skirt wasn't any longer than the kilt on old Douglas."

That didn't stop the heads from wagging. But it did let Kris get a good eight hours' sleep.

13

"YOU know they caught you on camera last night" was the first thing Kris heard in the Command Center next morning.

"I hope they got my right side. The left usually breaks the camera," Kris drawled.

Chief Ramirez headed the watch this morning. She nodded toward a monitor that was carrying an early news show. Yep, there she was, raising the caber over her head, the top of her strapless gown seeming to offer a most embarrassing shot any second now. Kris held her breath as the gown failed to keep its promise. The news didn't cut away until the crowd cheered as she did her curtsey. "And later, she did toss the caber," the anchorwoman said. "That's not your normal princess, but then she's a Longknife, and this is Chance. Good going gal."

"That how most people are taking it?" Kris asked, pouring coffee and waiting to see if PR damage control must precede chow.

"Yep," the old chief said. "I'm headed for breakfast at the waffle shop. Nothing's happening here. You want to come along?"

"Things that quiet?"

The chief's grin actually sparkled. "The fun was earlier.

They docked their own liberty boats, didn't go through the shuttle bay, so we didn't get to see the wreckage. Can't tell you how glad I am of that. Gassy let us watch the dirtside half of the disaster. Thank God smellies never caught on."

They arrived as the waffle shop opened. Kris entered to applause and did a redux of her curtsey. Just as she ordered a bran muffin and juice, sailors started pouring up the stairs from the two piers she had a line of sight on and forming into ranks.

"We being invaded?" someone asked.

"I thought they did that yesterday," another one said. "Can't they come up with anything but reruns today?"

NELLY, ARE THOSE SAILORS ARMED?

NO WEAPONS IN VIEW. Which didn't really answer the question.

Kris and the chief excused themselves from their waiter and stepped outside, then slowlike, moseyed upstation for a better look. "Nelly, anything change?"

"Still no weapons visible."

"What's on their feet?" Chief Ramirez asked.

"Athletic shoes," Nelly reported.

"PT this early after last night," the chief said with an evil grin. "Somebody up there is after my own heart, vicious to the core." Someone barked an order and calisthenics commenced. Soon, sailors were falling out of ranks, some heaving their guts.

"Nelly," the chief said, "have the duty watch see if they can isolate the air over the forward two docks. At least re-circulate that air. If they can't, close the fire bay doors."

"They are happy to report that they have achieved the isolation of that air section. It may take them awhile to get the odor out the air, but it will stay up there."

Chief Ramirez turned to Kris. "Well, if that nice computer of yours can keep a look on those wayward boys, why don't you and I enjoy our breakfast. I'd keep it light. We may end up down that way before too long."

Kris and the chief had finished their meal before Nelly broke in. "They are now ordering those who vomited to run laps around the station. Oh, and everyone else as well."

"I better go talk to them, see if we can limit them to the forward half of the station," Kris said, paying their check.

The chief dismissed herself to the Command Center when Kris started to jog forward. Jack connected with Kris as she passed the midship row of shops and fell in step beside her.

"You going into that lion's mouth?"

"Goes with the job," Kris said. She spotted a gunny jogging along beside ranks of Greenfeld's finest. She angled toward him. Once in step alongside, she asked, "Who's in charge, Gunny?"

He took her in, without missing a step. "I am, sir," he said in that bull voice gunnies are born with. "Each senior NCO is authorized to exercise his men independently, Lieutenant."

Kris would have to remember not to look over her shoulder every time a Greenfeld NCO "sir-ed" her. There being no women officers in their forces, "ma'am" was a nonstarter.

"Please halt your men, Sergeant."

"Yes, sir. Platoon, Forward March," he said, which took them out of double-time. "Platoon, Halt. Platoon, Left Face."

Kris conformed to the rapid-fired commands. Doing a right face for the last one brought her face-to-face with "Gunnery Sergeant Wittmann at your service, sir." Being uncovered and in PT dress, he did not salute Kris. This guy was on the ball. *Well, let's see how this goes.*

"Sergeant, I'm glad to see you up early this morning and enjoying the services of my station," Kris said. "I require a meeting with all the senior NCOs conducting these exercises. Would you please dispatch messengers to them, give them my compliments, and inform them that the Commander, Naval District 41, requires their presence here, on the double."

The sergeant had not been briefed on this possibility, but taking time to blink only twice, he shot out orders dispatching eleven of his troopers. As the runners took off in all directions, Kris did an informal about-face and ambled off a bit, Jack at her side.

"I can't watch, Jack, but tell me what's happening."

Jack took an extra step so that it looked like he was talking with Kris, his eyes downcast, but his report was wide ranging. "The runners are making fast time of it. Okay, there's one that caught up with a whole lot of whites, I'd say a boatload of Navy. The chief, or whoever's doing the run, has got someone out of ranks to keep them running and is walking this way. A gunny is joining him. They're exchanging words. Another putative chief is trotting over to them."

"So we're going to be facing a united front," Kris said.

"That would be my bet." The two of them let a few more minutes go by, then Kris turned. Oh, this bunch was good. The senior chief in charge, or maybe the flagship's chief, had the other five chiefs in a single line and they were double-timing her way. Directly behind them came four Marine sergeants, with their own honcho calling cadence. Around Deck 1, heads in formation runs turned. Kris couldn't fault the interest. What able seaman wouldn't want to see their leading chiefs jogging in ranks like them. But senior Petty officers with no sense of humor shouted them back and Kris concentrated on her own issues.

The super leading chief dropped his small Navy file into march cadence and cut a perfect corner to put them directly in front of Kris. The Marines followed right in step. Then both chief and sergeant halted, the Navy to Kris's right, the Marines to her left. Sergeant Wittmann, cutting his corners perfectly, marched into the last place in the Marine's line.

"Leading Senior Chief Meindl reporting as requested, sir."

"Gunnery Sergeant Rothenburg reporting as requested, sir."

"Thank you, gentlemen," Kris said. "This is my first opportunity to welcome you to my station. I am Lieutenant Kris Longknife, Commander, Naval District 41." Kris paused to let them get used to the idea that the commander of this Naval district was a lieutenant . . . and a woman. Oh, and a Longknife. From the looks on their faces, they'd been told this already, but it was still uncomfortable for them to come face-to-face with something that, by all that they'd been taught to hold military and holy, could not be.

"I am glad to see you using my facilities to keep your crew fit," Kris said. "That a fit sailor is a better sailor is something we can all agree on." She paused. In front of her, bland faces began to hint with smiles at the thought of a Longknife actually quoting their own regulations back to them.

"No one talked to me about your morning routine, though. I'd like you to confine your PT, as well as any drill and ceremonies to the forward bays of the station. No further aft than that line of service facilities," Kris said, pointing to where the Dragon Café was still boarded up.

"May I ask why, sir?" said the leading senior chief.

"That's a reasonable question," she said, though Kris doubted a Greenfeld chief would normally risk asking it of one of their officers. Still, this fellow would be asked to answer questions when he returned to his ship. Probably not easy ones.

"Chief, this is not a large station, and I'm not funded with a lot of housekeeping personnel." *I'm not funded with many personnel at all*, Kris did not add. "As you may have noticed, some of your sailors are a bit the worse for wear from last night and they've left a mess around the deck." Kris sniffed the air. The senior leading chief scowled. "I don't know how quickly I'll be able to get this area policed up and shipshape. I'd prefer to limit the problem to the forward bay. Unless your commodore wants to discuss the matter further, I'm so ordering."

"We will remain forward of those facilities," he said. "Unless we receive different orders from our own officers, sir. And our sailors will police up their own, ah, leavings." Then he paused and licked his lips before going on softly.

"Ma'am, is there any chance that those facilities might get opened up? We chiefs noticed a movie house, and gaming space as well as several eateries on the station plan we were issued, but a check last evening showed them all closed. Those not on shore leave only have what we've had aboard ship for the last month. It's wearing a tad thin."

Kris eyed the NCOs in ranks behind him. They were still board-straight Navy and Marines, but Kris could taste the expectation in the air. "Those are all private establishments, Chief, but I'll see what I can do about talking someone into opening them. Although the discipline of your men on shore leave last night did nothing to encourage the locals that their property and life are safe around your men, Chief."

The chief was back to ramrod straight and a face devoid of expression. Kris paused for a moment, but there was no further reaction. "Thank you gentlemen for your attention. Leading Senior Chief, dismiss your crew to their duties."

Kris turned her back as the chief and sergeant began barking orders. "That went well, I think," she told Jack.

"What was that last about?"

"I think the request for some open facilities up here was an honest chief looking after his men's needs."

"And his reaction about the shore party?"

Kris walked along for a while. "What would you do if you'd been ordered to let your men run wild and someone from the other side pointed out how unprofessional it was."

"I'd imitate a pole, just like those poor sods did."

Kris spent the morning with Tony Chang and the contacts he put her in touch with. Tony himself ordered enough food and drinks to get three of the restaurants open for lunch. "I'm only hiring guys to work those places." Kris didn't argue.

Several movie chains agreed to rearrange their schedules and get enough movies up to High Chance's theater that they could start playing later that day. The Game Emporium was tougher. "Most of the game stations are still up there, that's no problem. They were pretty old and lame. It's finding software to load on them. They are just so out of date."

"We need something and we need it by close of business today," Kris said. "The sailors that don't get shore leave need some entertainment."

"I'll have a couple of kids up there to load the software and take their nickels."

"You are going to keep the price reasonable, aren't you?"

"I was a kid once, a long way from home. We won't rook them, Commander."

After lunch, Kris had to submit to an oil-of-turpentine manicure from Abby, who dug out a small fortune in tar from under Kris's nails and took an inch off her fingers. "If you're going out tonight, I'm going to have to glue three nails on you."

"I haven't heard what they're laying on for tonight."

"Well, you find out, young woman, cause your Mama Abby ain't gonna turn you into no princess with a snap of her fingers. Not with you in the mess you're in today."

"Yes, Mama," Kris said as she escaped from her quarters.

"You know you're henpecked," Jack said as she ran into him.

"My mother ignored me for most of my life. Why is Abby making up for it with interest?"

"Why does Abby do anything?" Jack said. "I did that monitoring you asked for while Hank's ships were coming in. No

Chance messages out that didn't have a business reason for going out. I did, however, go over the communication logs from the jump point buffers. Nelly and I recovered a message sent just after we jumped into the system, heavily encrypted, and with, as it turned out, a false sender identified."

"Bad sender address? Don't those usually bounce?"

"This was a false sender with a valid sending address. You know many day cares that send priority interstellar messages?"

"No. Has Nelly cracked the code?"

"Nope," Jack said. "And she doesn't expect to. Very complex code that seems to change about every other line. Real good."

"And you think Abby sent it?"

"I don't know who sent it, but it's interesting that it went out of here right after the *St. Pete* jumped in."

"Anything like it since our last trip?"

"No. Nothing."

Kris considered that as she took the elevator down to the shops. "Could have been someone on the *Pete* messaging ahead. Since our main concern seems not to be involved, let's sit on it." Kris ran her thumb softly over her aching fingers. "Abby may be a pain every chance she gets, but she does pull things out of those steamer trunks when we need them. Haven't you enjoyed the last couple of weeks when she didn't have to."

"Best vacation I've had in years," Jack said.

Three restaurants were open, each just happened to be even with the piers in use by the ships. Italian, German, and Chinese were officially offered, but Tony said they'd cook up just about anything. The movie theater was open. Its offerings seemed dated to a girl from Wardhaven, but there were plenty of choices for the various screens that ranged from full auditorium to small home-movie suites no bigger than the one at Nuu House.

The Game Express had all its lights flashing.

"I am so glad to run into you, Lieutenant," someone said from behind Kris. She turned . . . and snapped a salute.

"Good to see you again, too, Captain Slovo," Kris said.

He returned her and Jack's honors. "May I walk with you awhile?" he asked.

"It would be my pleasure. Should I ask my security chief to find business elsewhere?"

Captain Slovo glanced at Jack. "I assure you your princess and commander is as safe with me as she is anywhere else."

"That bad," Jack said, but he saluted and detached himself.

"A good man," Captain Slovo said.

"You've gotten my briefing file."

"Him, no, just my own assessment. And yes, we did get your file. Amazingly thin. Leaves a lot to wonder about."

"You must have gotten the digest version," Kris said.

"Maybe, but I still find myself wondering about finding you here so unexpectedly."

"Luck of the draw," Kris chose to answer. "They were looking for a place to put me, and this opened up. It works the same in your Navy, doesn't it?"

"Sometimes, yes. But when last we heard, this station was unoccupied. So you can imagine my surprise when I find my ship taking active sensor sweeps from a light cruiser. We had heard that hulks were being distributed around Longknife space, mere scarecrows to make the locals feel safer. Yet I find a cruiser with its sensors up, reactors going. Full commission?"

Kris ignored that question, and the growing question as to why a Greenfeld officer was highlighting once again how surprised he was to see her. NELLY, MAKE A NOTE THAT IF I EVER GIVE CAPTAIN SLOVO A TOUR OF THE *PATTON*, ALL THE MUSEUM PLAQUES COME DOWN FIRST.

WILL DO, KRIS.

Captain Slovo let the silence stretch a bit. "You were not briefed on my commodore's cruise around the area. We were not briefed to expect you. Strange, don't you think?"

Beyond strange, Kris could agree . . . to herself. To a Greenfeld Navy Captain all she said was, "Interesting. Is there anything specific I can help you with?"

"No, I was just taking a tour of the facilities you have opened for my men. The prices are steep for the pay of my able seamen, but not gouging. No worse than we usually meet with when we visit the inflation-ravaged economies beyond our borders." He smiled at that bit of political cant.

"I am glad to be of service. Hank said this had been a long

trip. Your crewmen need something to break the monotony of staring at the bulkheads of their ships."

"There is one more thing. It seems that I need a ride down to the planet tonight. My commodore is indisposed and there is a cocktail party that he wants some of us to show the flag at."

"And you don't want to ride down in your own captain's gig?"

"I don't have a gig. None of the captains have a gig this trip. Our commodore wanted room for more liberty launches and said we could always ride in his barge. Yet tonight, his barge is not available." The captain coughed softly into his hand.

"And you really don't want to ride back up in anything like the launches were last night." He nodded.

"You could have your chiefs provide a bit of leadership."

He looked away. Kris detected just a hint of a nod.

Kris considered letting him twist on the ropes of this un-named situation that neither the captain nor the chiefs would talk about. She also wondered if the extra boat space was occupied by assault landing craft. How would this game be played out? And since it was no "game" at all, how many would die? Kris made her call.

"I'd be glad to provide a seat for you on my shuttle. What time is the party? You'll probably have to pass a metal detector, and please don't carry any packages that someone else has provided you." She did not smile.

He did, rather painfully. "I will endeavor to keep you as safe as I do my commodore. The party is at eight. We are scheduled to have dinner with some businessmen beforehand, so could we leave by six? Oh, and I require two more seats."

"Other captains coming along?"

"Yes, the two that sat with me on the barge last night."

"Ah, the ones that are trying to provide adult supervision to the kindergartners."

He made no answer to that but began to salute her most gallantly, signaling her dismissal. She got her salute up before he touched his hat. "You have no idea how close to the truth you are, my dear Princess," he whispered softly, did a smart about-face, and left her to ponder many things.

Jack joined her a moment later from where he had kept her in sight. "An interesting man," he said.

"In an interesting situation. Nelly, you better advise Abby that I will be needing my dancing slippers tonight."

"I told her. You are half an hour late to get gussied up for a night on the town, which will not involve making tar patty cakes or tossing oversize replicas of the male anatomy."

"If I'm only thirty minutes late, I can still check in with the duty watch at the Command Center," Kris said, and she and Jack quick walked toward the elevator.

Kris tried to use the time Abby spent flustering over her to think. It didn't help. Hank's intentions were ambiguous. This could be just a ship visit. So why did Kris feel she was already in a countdown to a coup? The tightness at the back of her neck that failed to soften even under one of Abby's world-class hair washings was fed by what the chief and captain left unsaid.

They had a secret they could not share. Was that secret a planetary take down? And if it was, how did Hank plan to do it? The takeover of a planet was not something you just put at the top of your Order of the Day. It took preparation. You needed an excuse to march in and throw out a government. "What are you going to try," Kris muttered, "and when? And where?"

"You saying something, Baby Ducks?"

"Yes, but I doubt you know the answer."

"You got that right. No way do I know when Hank's going to make his play to take over this here planet."

"So you've noticed our predicament?"

"Just cause I'm underpaid, Kris, don't mean I'm blind."

It also didn't mean a lot of things.

An hour later, dressed befitting a princess, despite Abby's insistence that she needed another two hours, Kris headed for the lander bay. A bright Kelly green cocktail dress with a flounced skirt swished pleasantly about her with each step. Tonight she was wearing her spider silk body stocking. If the other side felt the need for protection, she might as well give Jack what he wanted before he asked. Jack, in dinner blues and reds, fell in step with her before she got to the elevator.

"Do you have a camera in my bedroom?" she asked.

"I refuse to answer that on the grounds that I'd be giving away state secrets and might lose the best entertainment a lonely man ever had. You and Abby are better than any comedy routine this side of Earth's Las Vegas."

"Come to think of it, all the bug catchers I have come from you," Kris said. "Do you give them a blind spot?"

"Or I could just pay Abby a few bucks a month to give me a heads-up on when you're ready to leave your room."

"She is always complaining that she's underpaid. That's a story I could almost believe."

"I doubt it would be the first time a maid picked up a few bucks on the side."

"Nelly, what shape is the shuttle in?"

"I have monitored it since Captain Slovo asked you for a ride. I also reran the records on it for the last twenty-four hours. No events out of the ordinary nor has anyone gone near it that is not on the preapproved list. We should be safe."

"And I will preflight it," Kris said.

"I feel better already," Jack said dryly.

The chief maintenance mech met Kris at the door of Shuttle 41. "It checks out. I've been running a positive charge through the skin. If so much as a fly speck out there touched it, we'd have spotted the spark and any nano would have been burned."

"You're paranoid. I like that in a crew chief."

"That was the first question the boss asked me. 'Do you trust your own mother?' I said 'hell no,' and he said 'I want you working on my bird.'"

So Kris did her own check. A half hour later, she was just finishing up when there was noise aft. Kris pulled herself out of the command pilot's seat, using handles on the instrument panel she usually considered reserved for the old and feeble. Still, she turned her ankle before she was standing in the middle of the flight deck. "The working parts of a shuttle were not designed for two-inch heels," Kris grumbled.

"You might be right," Jack said, leading Kris aft.

In the shuttle bay Captain Slovo waited with the two older skippers from the Greenfeld ships. "You are here ahead of us," he said. Jack saluted, and the Greenfelders returned the honor. Kris nodded and offered Merv her hand. He kissed it as did the others as they were formally introduced. Max Göckle of the *Eager*, Georg Krätz of the *Surprise*.

"You really are a princess," Krätz noted in surprise.

"Actually, I just found the tiara," Kris said, grinning; the officers chuckled politely.

"Hold up," came a familiar voice from the escalator. Trotting toward them as fast as their overburdened condition would permit were Chief Beni, and three from the *Resolute*. "Mind if we hitch a ride down with you, Princess. There's a really nifty bistro on the south side of town we found last night, and I don't care what anyone says, spaced beer just don't taste right."

Kris waved her junior-most subordinate aboard first, as per protocol, though somehow, captains waiting for chiefs to arrive did not seem to fit what traditionalists had in mind when they set that bit of Naval lore. She also wished he hadn't shouted where he and the *Resolute*'s drinkers would be spending their evenings dirtside. Hopefully, it would go unnoticed.

Kris boarded after Jack and headed for the flight deck. The captains boarded last. The chief and his buddies buckled into the aft seats, leaving the forward compartment to the officers.

"You are going to fly the shuttle, Your Highness?" Captain Slovo said as he buckled himself in.

"We're running a bit late and any normal shuttle pilot would have to wait for the next orbit to reach Last Chance. I figure I can cut a few corners and get us there on time."

That caused a murmur among the captains.

"All ashore that are going ashore," Jack called as he slipped Kris's shoes into the pouch at the back of her seat, then closed and verified the lock on the rear hatch. Kris finished her final preflight and glanced aft before she cut them loose. Everyone was seated; no one was pounding on the hatch to get off. *How little they know. Guess they really are reading the expunged version of Peterwald's folder on me.*

Exactly thirty minutes later, having shed excess energy with several not-so-gentle S curves that were nothing like those that had won her the trophies back home on her mantelpiece, the shuttle settled to the runway with a kiss and soft caress.

A tug waited for her at the end of the runway, but today they towed her to a hanger on the far side of the field, well away from where the liberty launches would be lined up later.

Steve Jr. brought the limo up, now with a top on. Maybe one that could stop a bullet? How things had changed in one night.

Jack slipped her heels out and laid them on the floor for her. Kris had learned to do a lot in the footwear demanded of young woman. Breaking a shuttle to a stop was something done better barefoot than in heels. Captain Slovo rose to offer Kris an arm as she walked into her shoes.

"You are quite an accomplished pilot. Now I think I know why my commodore is so reluctant to let you near the controls of our crafts. You might very well show up our pilots."

Kris rewarded the thickly slathered on praise with a smile. She noted that the other two captains seemed a bit unsure of how to react to her. Clearly, they needed practice responding to female officers. The flag captain and the royal she exited the shuttle first. Steve Jr. was in formal chauffeur dress and even held the door open. "They're going to lock down this hanger as soon as we leave and have it under guard and surveillance while you're away. Dad figured you'd want to know."

He left the "you" undefined, but Kris found it good to know, and suspected the captain did, too. And if he chose to warn anyone assigned to mess with the shuttle, they'd still have to figure out how to get to it. Kris expected Chance might be harder to crack than they expected.

But Captain Slovo took the information in with no reaction.

The ride in gave time for Max Göckle, of the *Eager*, to tell Kris, or maybe Steve, all the benefits the ranchers and farmers of Chance would gain if they joined the Greenfeld Confederacy. Or maybe he was just practicing his catechism for later tonight. Neither Steve nor Kris paid him any mind.

The three skippers were dropped off at The Vault, an upscale restaurant. "You want to join us?" Captain Slovo asked.

"The mayor hopes you'll share his dinner plans," Steve said.

Kris smiled. "A gal can hardly pass up an offer from an attractive young man." That seemed to settle matters.

As they pulled away from the curve, Kris asked Steve, "Should I have gone along with the Greenfeld skippers to listen in on what they might be hatching?"

"They have more chance of hatching a rock than they have of getting anything out of the ten they're dining with," Steve said, shaking his head. "If Dad had to pick ten business guys more committed to Chance for Chance, they'd top his list. No, those fellows won't be finding much to report back on tonight."

Dinner was at Ron's favorite steak house. Kris enjoyed relaxing in the company of two fine men who knew how to entertain a woman. And talked shop only as much as she wanted to. Which was to say, way too much of the dinner.

"Folks are pretty disgusted with what came down last night," Ron said as soon as they'd ordered.

"Never had a fleet in?" Kris asked.

"Actually, we haven't. I asked one of the networks to check their archives. No Navy here for over sixty years."

"So this catch-up all at once is something of a shock to the system," Jack said dryly.

"Is there anything we can do about it?" Ron asked Kris.

Kris leaned back in her chair and watched a ceiling fan make its lazy circles. "Let's see. You could ask him to leave."

"He'd laugh in our faces."

"Insist he make his sailors behave. Tell him we want some Shore Patrol working with your police."

"I might try that soon."

"How about having an accident at the brewery," Jack said.

"No brew. No chance. Our beer comes from small breweries. They'd all have to have a problem. All at once. Now that would be grounds for invading us. Making space safe for the brew," Ron said, raising his glass.

"Here, here," Jack agreed, and clinked glasses.

Kris raised her soda water. "So what does that leave us?"

"Waiting for him to decide to leave on his own," Ron said.

"Waiting for him to drop the other shoe," Kris said. "This feels like a card game Tommy taught me at OCS. Santa Maria Hold'em. You deal every player three cards faceup. Then two cards facedown. Players can swap out three cards from either group, but no one knows which facedown cards are turned in. Then you place your bets." Kris shook her head. "We know some things about Hank's hand. More than we did yesterday. I'll get to that in a minute. But there're some things we don't know. And some things he doesn't know. Now we're waiting to see if Hank folds, or stays in the game."

The men nodded. "What do we know more about?" Ron asked.

Kris told them what Captain Slovo had told her. "So Hank's flag captain has told you twice they weren't expecting to see the station defended?" Ron said when Kris was done.

"Seems to want to make sure I got the message. Now that might explain yesterday," Kris said. "They went for the quick snatch-and-grab as planned, fell flat, and now are rethinking things. What I don't like is Hank's up there without his adult supervision. Is he just sulking or is he hatching something?"

"Adult supervision?" Ron said, and Kris shared her comment to Slovo and his whispered response.

"Whose side is this captain on?" Ron asked.

Kris shrugged. "Would you want the job of taking Hank out for a cruise and making sure that he comes home in one piece?"

"Been there, done that," Jack said. "Got the bruises to show for my failed effort. It's bad enough having to do it for the Prime Minister's bratty daughter. No way would I take it from the perspective of a captain to commodore."

Ron frowned at Kris, then Jack. "You're a first lieutenant of Marines. She's a lieutenant in the Navy. Isn't that the same one-grade difference this Greenfeld captain has?"

"Big difference," Kris assured Ron. "They make you a commodore and you're breveted god. While a mere lieutenant occasionally has to admit to error."

"Not nearly often enough," Jack pointed out.

"But I have."

"What, once in the time I've known you."

"That's still more than I suspect Hank ever will."

"She's got me there," Jack admitted to Ron.

"I would never make it in your Navy," Ron said, shaking his head. "I make four, five mistakes a day. And that's just in spelling on my reports. Wouldn't survive without Chief Ramirez to save my sorry soul. Speaking of, when do I get her back?"

"Fifteen seconds after Hank and his fleet jump out, and not a moment sooner."

"I will try to survive," Ron said sorrowfully.

Steaks arrived, and they proceeded to do honor to them. Kris was the one who broke the pleasant munching to ask Ron, "Do you have reinforcements tonight?"

"Some, not as many as we wanted. I've asked other mayors to send me some of their best to stand up with mine, leaving out the untrained volunteers. Most are sending some, but none before tomorrow. Faced with that, I put out a call for former athletes who wanted to spend a night with the kids, any Sunday-school teacher, males only, anyone who wanted to try their hand at riot control. Word has gotten around about last night. If half of the folks who phoned in come, we should have a good turnout."

"A turnout," Jack said.

"We'll have bodies. Skill level is something else. We did have a dozen cabers donated and a couple of friends of Mac-Nab will be helping him tonight. Are you going to toss another one?"

"Not if I don't want my maid to kill me." Kris held up both hands. "If she gives me another manicure like the one I suffered through today, I may need prosthetics."

"I'll kiss it and make it well," Ron offered. Kris let him. Jack looked on dolefully.

"If I did that it would be fraternizing," he grumbled. A while later he added. "If you keep that up, it will qualify as practicing medicine without a license on 212 planets."

"I'll give you three hours to stop," Kris moaned softly. She'd never realized just how sensitive her hands were to a man's lips. She swallowed hard. More than her hands were responding to this man. A lot more.

"Kris, there's a call for the mayor, but his phone seems to be off," Nelly said.

Ron leaned back into his chair. "I turned it off for a reason," he muttered, pulling a tiny phone out of his pocket and inserting it into his ear. He listened for only a moment.

"Mother, you know those grandkids you keep talking about. Well, I think you just blew a major opportunity."

"Sorry, son, but the liberty launches are due in soon and we don't have half the busses we're supposed to. I talked to Mike and he said we've got all the ones he's managed to clean up after last night. Can you get on it?"

Ron waved for the check, and signed it, then stood to go. "You'll excuse me. Jack, don't dance the feet off her."

Kris rose from her only half-eaten meal. "Where we headed?"

And so Kris ended up cleaning busses and getting them to the airport on time. In high heels and without messing her cocktail dress. Not a bad start to an evening. The upside was that Kris found an industrial-strength tar remover to send to the Highland Games that night, just in case she decided to toss a caber.

The downside was that she was still hanging around the busses when it became clear the liberty launches were coming in faster than last night and that they'd never get as many busses as they had the night before.

So Kris ended up at the port as the launches came in. "I'd prefer you sit this out in Marta's Ops center," Jack suggested.

"But you're my security chief, I can't go anywhere without you, and you have to drive a bus." Kris managed not to coo. Not really. Jack said a very bad word.

"Besides, this is what OCS calls a leadership challenge."

"You're being challenged by five hundred woman-starved sailors of a very hostile confederation."

"True, Jack, but what girl can pass up having five hundred men hanging on her every word." Jack said more very bad words.

Jack parked his bus, behind Ron's, at the end of a not very long line. Ron dismounted as Kris walked by him. "How stiff are the rules about not standing in the bus?" she asked.

"We usually won't move a bus before everyone is seated, and belts buckled. However, the decision to board a loaded bus and stand is one for the citizen to make, not the government."

"You mean if the sailors want to load onto these," Kris counted, "ten busses, all five hundred incoming can get to the Oktoberfest on time. If not, they wait to catch the next one."

"That's it."

"Shouldn't be a problem." And it wouldn't have been except for those older "able seamen." The chiefs and senior petty officers were the first off the liberty launches and first onto the busses. So much for tradition. The rest raced off, shouting and acting like kids on the last day of school. There was much pushing and shoving to get on the busses, nothing like the orderly standing in line that was featured on all movies coming out from Greenfeld space. *Ah well, they're away from home*.

Kris moved among the sailors, urging calm in that command voice she'd been taught. There was plenty of room. She was only groped once in the press. She said nothing, but replied with lethal elbows. After that, sailors made way for "The Princess."

Things seemed to be going well once they got on the busses . . . until a fist fight broke out on the second bus over who got the last seat. Strange that the able seaman involved looked rather old for his rate. "Boys, boys," Kris called as soon as she was on the bus. "That old nanny looks so tired. You don't want to make an ancient nag like her stand now, do you."

"He hit me," the younger one said. Strange how the older one didn't seem all that interested in slipping into the seat now.

"Why don't you settle it at the caber toss," Kris said. "That old grandmama hardly looks like she can beat a spry young man like you. Hey, as soon as we get this settled, we can get this bus rolling for the beer." The other sailors shouted to get moving. The older "able seaman" slunk into the seat, avoiding her eyes.

Kris eyed the chiefs and petty officers in the front rows. Their eyes were locked straight ahead as if they were at attention. Following their orders? Kris dismounted, and waved the bus off. There was a fight on the fifth one; she climbed aboard and called, "Atten-hut," and it evaporated. "If you have any more trouble," Kris told the driver in a carrying voice, "Just pull over to the side. I'll be in the last bus."

"Yes, Your Highness."

"You going to toss that pole again tonight for us?"

"Be one of those to make a winning toss and see what I give you," Kris said mysteriously.

She dismounted, scrupulously not hearing loudly muttered hopes, and waited for Jack to pull up to her. "You have any problems with this crew?" she asked Jack. He grinned and hooked a thumb over his shoulder. Six Greenfeld Marine sergeants in undress black and greens sat in the front seats. Behind them, as silently deadly as you'd want a Marine to be, were forty-five NCOs and privates. Kris nodded at the senior sergeant, who kept eyes forward and ignored her as he well could a civilian . . . and after all, his planet didn't recognize nobility. Kris kept her place, standing beside the front door. "Follow those buses, Lieutenant. If any of them pull off, please do likewise."

"Aye, aye, Your Highness," Jack said, and put the bus in gear, maybe not as smoothly as a professional, but better than at least a few.

"Ma'am," came from behind Kris. While Kris might be a civilian and unrecognized royalty, she was a woman, and Greenfeld was old-fashioned about that. The junior Gunny Sergeant present rose to give Kris his seat behind Jack.

"Thank you," she said and took it, ignoring the shuffling out behind her as a corporal gave up a seat to the sergeant, and a private ended up standing so the corporal could sit.

The drive into town went smoothly, with no stops.

14

Little Steve waited at the Beergartens to take them to the cocktail party. Kris found herself a bit of a celebrity. Being a Longknife or a princess hadn't impressed these folks. But make a caber toss that MacNab praises and suddenly, everyone wants to shake your hand.

Oh, and thank her for keeping the sailors under control.

Which only confirmed Kris's suspicion that rank wasn't something you could confer here. It had to be earned. She was glad she didn't have to do much more than toss a tree to earn these folks' respect. Of course, the younger men didn't need much encouragement to ask her for a dance. She was on her fourth or fifth when Captain Slovo gallantly cut in.

"Did you enjoy your dinner with the young man?"

"Actually, I ended up back at the airport. They had trouble getting enough clean busses out for tonight's liberty party. Your crew last night left quite a mess."

"I hope you didn't leave tonight's party cooling their heels at the port?"

Kris measured the question and found it sincere, if lacking in surprise. Did he and boy wonder upstairs discuss this possibility? "It was standing-room only, but we made it."

"You are quite a young woman."

"We Longknifes do what we have to do," she said, keeping a smile on her face, but letting the steel show around the eyes.

"Yes, yes you do. You are making quite an impression on Captain Krätz. His wife has presented him with four girls. Sadly, no boys. I think just the sight of you is inciting the poor man to treason."

"Change doesn't have to be treason," Kris said. "Sometimes it is good for you."

"Pardon me, Princess, but I believe I'm here to show our flag, not to salute yours."

"Anytime you take the boys off the farm, you run the risk they won't want to go back." They danced in silence after that.

Kris tagged along with Captain Slovo when the dance ended. At the captain's table she asked, "Captain Krätz, do you dance?"

Slovo shot her an ugly glare, but the other captain accepted Kris's hand and followed her to the dance floor.

"You know, I shouldn't be dancing with you," Georg said. "You can't be too much older than my first daughter."

"Is she done with her college education?" Kris asked.

"Our women rarely go to college, but she is in her final year at the Gymnasium. She will graduate as a certified nurse."

"Does she plan to go Navy?"

"I hear her talking to her mother about that. I hope she won't. Too often, our young men, even officers, are not fit company for a young woman."

"If a woman is smart, she can often hit them up upside the head, knock some decency into them." Kris said lightly.

"As you did last night with that pole?"

"It seemed like a good idea at the time."

"And it still does," the captain said. "I can't tell you how many times in the last few days I've found myself wondering if my daughter would not make you a very good subordinate."

"I'd be glad to have her."

"Now some might take an offer like that to be sedition. Are you asking her father to suggest to the young woman that she desert her proper place in Greenfeld society?"

"Human space is big. Many people move about, hunting for their proper place."

"Just as you have. Yes, I have seen your file. You do a lot of moving. Don't you ever find yourself wanting to settle down in one place. Raise a family?"

"Now who's trying sedition?" Kris laughed.

"Shall we call ourselves even? I see your Marine looking worried. If I nod his way, I expect he will cut in."

"You better nod."

A moment later, she was in Jack's arms and he was dancing her away from the Greenfeld contingent. "Is there trouble?"

"Big trouble," Jack said through a smile.

"I think I need to go powder my nose," Kris said.

"I'll be waiting outside with little Steve."

Kris excused herself. Those who might have intercepted her recognized the direction of her flight. It only took two wrong turns for Kris to find herself out front. Jack was holding the door open. She slipped into the limo; Jack jumped in and Steve took off. "Where are we headed, the Beergarten?"

"Nope, the college."

"College?"

"Sailors ran into a couple of coeds," Jack said, "coming back from the library. They offered money to look at their boobs. Seems there's a really bad movie making the rounds of Greenfeld stag parties about how girls in Wardhaven space earn their living by flashing."

"Ouch," Kris said.

"Girl slapped him," Steve Jr. took over. "Big girl. Small sailor. Sailor started to knock her around. The girls yelled. The girl's soccer team was just coming back from practice. They jumped in and the sailors hollered for help. Lot of sailors came running, but a whole lot of college boys did, too."

"How big a riot?" Kris asked.

"Big," Jack said.

"Very big according to my source," the young cabby said.

"Step on it," Kris said.

"You bet," Steve Jr. said. Jack cringed as, if it was possible, the drive got even wilder. They came at the college from a different street, avoiding the Oktoberfest. Steve Jr. drove up to the yellow No Entrance tape and waved at an armband who lifted it. The limo followed the flow of interested bystanders until the press grew too thick, then they got out and joined it.

It was only a short walk to the next tape. Kris ducked under it, Jack waved off a youngster who squawked at their violation of his orders, and they soon found Gassy standing over three long lines of sailors, facedown on the grass, hands string-cuffed behind them. Not a few of them had bloody noses and blackening eyes.

Off to the left, a few armbands surrounded a large, milling crowd of young men; college boys from their dress. Far off to the right, a lot more armbands walked another yellow tape keeping an angry group of maybe twice as many sailors away from their buddies on the ground. Ron trotted around a stone-faced college building across the way and headed for Kris.

Sailors quickly recognized Kris. "What kind of shit are you throwing now, Princess," someone said. She ignored the catcalls that came with it.

"Ron, you have enough people for this?"

"Kris, I don't have anywhere near enough people to keep my people from tearing these guys apart. Chance is very much a frontier world. We respect our women. This . . ." He glanced to Kris's right and now she could see a small medical station set up behind the college men. Several women were being treated for cuts to their faces; bruises on their legs and torsos. A few were holding their tops in place. They'd been ripped off. One woman was sobbing. Another fixed Kris and Ron with an icy glare.

Kris scowled. "Nelly, connect me to Hank on his flagship."

"Trying, Your Highness," Nelly said formally. "I'm having to talk to a duty officer. This may take longer than usual."

"Keep at it. Don't say why I'm calling, just that Commander, Naval District 41, requires a talk with him."

"No," Ron said. "The Mayor of Last Chance requires a conversation with him. This is my job, Kris."

Kris could recognize a jurisdictional dispute when it slapped her in the face. Complicating it was the "Me boy, you girl" thing, as well. "We'll do it your way," she said.

Almost a full minute later, Nelly brought Hank up on audio, no visual. "Mayor Torn, why are you interrupting my evening?"

"We've had a riot involving some of your sailors down here."

"Well, put them in the liberty launches to sober up. No, lay them out beside the launches. I understand they really stank the boats up last night."

"These attacked some women," Ron said.

"Well, boys will be boys. No bones broken were there?"

Ron had not looked away from the young woman's glare. Neither had Kris. "No. No broken bones."

"Then no problem. They're sailors. Only looking for a little fun. If this was a Wardhaven fleet visit, things wouldn't be any different."

Ron closed his eyes, his teeth gritted together. Silently he gave Kris a brief wave.

"If a Wardhaven ship was in port, we'd have our own Shore Patrol out making sure our sailors behaved. Where are your SPs, Hank?" Kris demanded.

"Oh, I didn't know you were there, Lieutenant. You know how it is, the fleet's scattered thin, budgets are shrinking, and citizens are complaining about high taxes. What with the expansion and us having to protect so many planets from the pressures *some* people apply on *other* people. It's a struggle. We can't afford useless specialties. We need every hand working. Work hard. Play hard." And Hank cut the line.

Ron reached for thin air like he wanted to choke the life out of it. "I always knew the guy was shallow, but this." He shook his head. "That settles it. The next drunk that won't take no from one of our women is going to jail and will face one of our commissioners tomorrow. I've had enough!"

"Hank won't like that."

"I don't like this. Time he had something not to like."

Kris turned her back on the line of sailors and lowered her voice. "This could be exactly what he's wanted all along."

That stopped Ron. "Yeah? You think this could be the basis for that putsch you've been hinting at since he got here."

Kris shrugged. "It doesn't take a crystal ball. They send six cruisers for a port call where one would do. You have to assume they've got a change of government on their agenda."

"Let me make a few calls. See just how many reinforcements I'll have here tomorrow. If I'm going to walk off this cliff I'm being shoved over, I want company."

"You'll have mine," Kris said.

"Why does that not surprise me." Ron had not broken eye contract with the injured woman the whole time he'd been talking to Hank, and then Kris. Now he walked over to the aid station. Kris followed him; he had a hard duty ahead of him. So did she.

Ron paused a few feet from the women, took a deep breath and said simply, "I'm sorry."

"Where was the Safety Patrol?" the woman demanded.

"I don't know. They had a lot of stuff to do, but I'll find out what went wrong."

"You put a bunch of drunk sailors too bloody close to our dorms," the woman shot back. Those around her nodded agreement.

"That was my mistake. We didn't spot that in our planning," Ron admitted.

"None of us did," Kris added softly.

"I didn't think you Longknifes ever made mistakes," a woman from somewhere in the back said.

"We're not permitted little ones," Kris said. "Only really bad ones like this."

"Will we get more security?" the woman asked.

"Yes," Ron said. "We're flying in more from the other cities. We've about maxed out our people here."

"You better get them here," the woman said. "When I leave the dorm tomorrow, I'll be carrying a baseball bat. Any sailor that gets in my way will be looking for his head about three hundred meters thataway." There were murmurs of agreement. Kris kept her mouth shut. There was no use telling the women that that kind of incident was exactly what these poor sailors' commodore was looking for.

Ron turned to the college boys. There were a few girls in the circle, mostly in soccer uniforms. "You all know that you should be facing a Commissioner of the Peace tomorrow morning."

That brought a lot of muttered responses. "We were only protecting the girls," said the loudest.

"I know," Ron said, raising both hands for quiet. "And I'll have to take these sailors out to their boats and dump them in a couple of minutes." The dismay at that brought silence.

"So I'm going to turn all of you loose after we get the sailors out of here. But make no mistake. I know who you are.

You do this again, and you will be talking to a commissioner, and not Momma Okaloska, either. If you want to help us keep the coeds safe, talk to Mr. Gascón about getting an armband." From the noise, it sounded like most would take that offer.

Kris turned back to the sailors on the deck. Now a couple of med techs, all male, were walking gingerly among them, looking at noses; looking for other damage. Most seemed minor.

"They're your problem, Commander," Ron said.

Now Kris was the one not surprised. "Listen up. I command Naval District 41, and I rule that station your ships are hanging on to. In a moment, my Marine Lieutenant will pass among you, getting each name and ID. If you show your face on my station, I will lock you in my brig. Don't even think about getting another liberty down here." That brought a muttering of wounded innocence, but Kris stepped down hard.

"If the locals see your face again, I won't vouch for you living long enough to see the insides of another liberty launch. Consider yourselves confined to your ships for the rest of this port stay. Lieutenant, establish a permanent record," Kris said.

As Jack went down the line, Kris turned back to Ron. "Just how many reinforcements are you calling for from out of town?"

Ron eyed Kris. "As many as they can send me. Why?"

"Because I remember Captain Slovo mentioning that all the other ships had left their captains' gigs behind. 'So they could carry more liberty launches' I think he said. But you can stack three or four light assault craft in the space of one gig."

"You think the light thingamajigs could carry enough Marines to capture a city's communication center; power plant?"

Kris glanced up and did the attack plan in her head. "Fifteen to twenty LAC's, five Marines each. Two to a town. How many of your big cities do you think could go silent and you still defend Chance?"

"You know, Princess, there is only one thing worse than having a Longknife at your elbow."

"Oh?"

"Yeah, not having a Longknife at your elbow when all hell breaks loose," he growled. No smile softened his words. But then, Kris didn't expect Ron to smile for quite a while.

"Can you handle getting these sailors out of my sight. I've got some calls to make."

"Can I coordinate with Gassy?"

"To your and his hearts' content."

Kris used four busses to move these forty sailors out to the port. She made sure that she had forty guards with them, none drawn from the new volunteers. On the flight line, four from each bus were loaded onto each liberty launch. "See if you can get a throwing-up kind on each boat," she said. The guards were happy to comply.

She called Captain Slovo to tell him he'd have to arrange his own transportation back up. When he tried to question her further, she cut the line. "Jack, let's get topside."

Kris flew the shuttle back with only Jack and headed for the Command Center. Chief Odacheke, whom she'd rarely worked with, had the watch. "Anything out of the usual here?"

"Kind of hard to figure what is usual for this bunch, ma'am," the chief drawled, taking his feet off his desk. "But we do have plenty of sailors out tonight, visiting what you opened. And we have some walkers, trench-coated guys. So far they just walk and look. Don't touch."

"That might change any minute." Kris watched the monitors and drummed her fingers on a work station. "Your people know they can use their weapons if they have to, don't they?"

"Yes, ma'am, they know that, but I don't think most of them much want to." That was the problem with folks that were used to living and letting live. Peterwald's people could change the rules around here in a second, and a minute later these poor folks would still be wondering what was going on.

"You know about the riot dirtside?"

"I watched some of the video. Ugly."

"Things may get ugly here, too. Or they may not. Would you mind if my lieutenant sat out this watch with you?"

"Not a problem. Extra eyes are always nice."

"Jack, you keep this watch. I'll relieve you at midnight."

Jack slipped into a monitoring station. "I'll call Penny and let her know she's got the four-to-eight watch," Jack said. "Don't argue. We need our sleep tonight 'cause if all hell don't pop tonight, it will tomorrow, or the next day."

"Keep your game face on, Jack. You have weapons release."

Abby went about getting Kris out of social harness as efficiently as she always did. "I done saw the pictures, gal. The fun's started."

"Lay out a uniform, and distribute spider silk undies to the team. You have any nice whiz bangs?"

"I might find a few that have fallen down in your luggage."

"Hunt them up. Tomorrow we rig grenades in the stairwells. I will not have anyone do unto me what I have done unto others."

"That sounds like a nice way of doing business."

Kris had Nelly wake her up well before Jack's call, and was showered and dressed when the phone rang. That earned her a glower as she reported twenty minutes before midnight. She slipped into a seat between the old chief, who was briefing Chief Ramirez, and listened as he basically told her, "Lots of folks wandering around the station. Not a lot of anything going on."

The old chief of Naval District 41's personnel nodded agreement and relieved Chief Odacheke a few minutes early.

"Marine, how long were you sharing Andy's watch," she asked as soon as the chief was gone.

"An hour, hour and a half."

"You kept a mighty straight face while he was talking. Andy's a good man, but a bit blind when faced with a corkscrew."

"You mean he sees what there to see, but doesn't draw any conclusions as to what might happen next," Jack said.

"What have you seen, Lieutenant?" Kris asked.

"I've noticed something about those walkers."

"I did, too," Nelly said. "I was not asleep."

Kris rolled her eyes heavenward, or in this case, toward the center of her station. "What did you notice, my fine electronic friend, while this poor body of mine was getting twenty winks?"

"They have checked out all our stairwells, just as I think you expected them to. They have also located all our air ducts and water mains."

"A water main breaks." Kris nodded. "The stations starts to flood. Everyone is chasing that. Maybe we even issue a call to the ships to send men to help. Even if we don't, people might think we had if the troops charging up the gangplank looked helpful. Behind this a few guys with guns slip into our air ducts. Maybe explosives open the most important stairwells. Great plan. For a Sophomore- or Junior-level course, it might earn a B." Kris grinned. "Not so good against folks like us who teach the postdocs."

"Let's not get too sure of ourselves," Jack said. "There's lots of ways they could kick this off besides flood—hull breach, fire. What am I not thinking of?"

"I believe your Great-Grampa Trouble once took over a station by hiring the entire computer gang," Chief Ramirez said. "Or was that someone rescuing him. Anyway, it always made me laugh and cry at the same time."

"What about our information resources?" Jack asked.

"They're on our side," the chief said. "Also I don't think any of Peterwald's folks have had much luck talking to them." She tapped her station, brought up several scenes. "Not that those walkers don't try to talk to our watch going on and going off. But no one's hung with them for long."

"I've got Abby going through my or her or whomever's steamer trunks looking for the odd grenade," Kris said. "Tomorrow, I want explosive experts to set up trip wires and booby traps."

Ramirez raised an eyebrow. "You planning on demolishing my station? Don't know how Steve will take to that. I do know how I'll feel about it."

"We have sleepy grenades, flash bangs, plenty of stuff before we have to go to fragmentation or worse," Kris said.

"Nice to know I'm not the only pacifist in uniform."

"Grampa Trouble always says the fewer bodies there are to pick up, the easier it is to make friends later," Kris said. "Assuming they'll be stopped by something less than lethal."

"That's the trick, isn't it?" Jack said.

They spent the next hour setting up their list of where to booby trap and how deadly to be. Jack dismissed himself to sleep before they finished, once he was sure that Kris was doing it to his high expectations. Kris was well along with the task when Penny came to relieve her at four a.m. The other lieutenant went over Kris's list. "I like concentrating around the central office area and the reactor. But shouldn't we do something to make sure the *Patton* and *Wasp*—even the *Resolute*—aren't hit with something for the opening fire or whatever."

"We'd like to," Kris said, glancing at the chief. "But we're just flat running out of bodies to do things. I don't dare ask Ron for any more. He's got a major headache dirtside."

"Kris, I know the folks working on the *Patton*. They're our kind of people. If I ask them to spend more time tomorrow patrolling Deck 1, the docks, and the facilities, they'd do it."

"The old farts or the kids," Kris said, not sure which was the worst idea.

Penny chuckled and rocked her hand back and forth. "A bit of both. Some kids for enthusiastic racing around, a few older folks for judgment. Don't know which will provide the nasty craft and guile, but it will be there."

"I'll let you handle that show," Kris said, and made a note to look at it . . . often and carefully. "We have to remember that Hank decides when things go wrong big time. And it may not be tomorrow. Or the next day. Hank can wait for as long as he wants and we have to stay ready." The others nodded agreement.

Actually, they were all wrong. Hank didn't get to decide when to kick off the revolution . . . a drunken sailor did.

15

"**How's** it going down there," Kris asked at twenty-three-hundred hours next evening. She'd stayed home to mind the station. No more dancing for Kris until Hank gave up and went home.

"Pretty good," Ron replied. "They've been swilling beer like they're afraid we're going dry tomorrow. If I had to make a call, I'd say we're over the hump. They're too drunk now to walk straight, much less riot."

Noise in the background caused Ron to turn off screen. There were shouts, then whistles, like the ones they'd issued to the armbands . . . and young women . . . that afternoon.

"Kris, I have to go. I don't know what this is. I hope it's less exciting than it sounds." Why did Kris think not?

She went back over what she did know from the video of the liberty launches arriving. There were five extra boats . . . say seven hundred and fifty sailors tonight, rather than last night's five hundred. There were also no sailors in gray whites.

"No agent provocateurs," Kris muttered.

"Or they're on to us being on to spider silk and dropped it," Jack said, fingering the neck of his own armored underwear. "Did you notice what else was missing? No Marines. Ungood, my Princess, when they hold the trigger pullers on a short leash."

Kris immediately did a full review of her station. With more on the ground, there were fewer being entertained up here. There were also no walkers, no one wandering outside the area dedicated to the sailors' amusement. Did that mean all the agent provocateurs were dirtside . . . or just holding up in the ships for a sudden sally? Kris ate supper in the Command Post. Chief Beni excused himself at quitting time for another trip down with his drinking buddies from the *Resolute*.

Kris studied the monitors. She'd had teams from the *Patton* add new cameras. Now she could look right onto the quarterdecks of Hank's ships. She eyed all six at once. All she saw were empty decks, JOODs and a few runners.

"What's happening dirtside?" Chief Odacheke asked. "Shouldn't we turn on the news?"

"No," Kris snapped. "Ron has his teams working and doesn't need us to juggle his elbow. We've got our job. Penny, I sure could use help eyeballing these cameras."

"I understand several of the folks working on the *Patton* declared a sleepover."

"Sleepover!" Kris said, wondering what Grampa Trouble would think of kids holding a pajama party on his old cruiser.

"Well, they want the Museum to do overnight stays for kids. They're testing it out. Anyway, let me make a call and see if I can get, oh, a dozen folks to monitor the cameras in here."

"Good, quiet camera monitors," Kris pointed out.

Fifteen minutes had gone by since Ron ran to look into trouble the sailors should have been too drunk to cause, when a half dozen older teenagers in green shipsuits and an equal number of old folks in blue marched onto the bridge. Penny put three kids and three oldsters at six monitors. "Each of these are checking a Greenfeld ship. If you see anything different, holler." She then took the other six and sat them at a row of stations covering the rest of the station. "We want to know if any sailor, or, this time of night, anyone starts hanging around an elevator, stairwell. Anything!"

The new recruits went to work as silently as Kris wanted. Kris, Penny, and Chief Odacheke quit watching monitors and started monitoring the watchers. Jack stayed at his station. He had control of the whizbangs and the guns. If things got lethal, he would make the call and do the lethal.

For a long half hour, nothing happened. No one left the ships. The quarterdecks stayed empty except for a few sailors returning early from station liberty. At the restaurants, theater, game center, sailors ate, drank, and were entertained, apparently unaware of what was going on dirtside.

At eleven thirty, Chief Ramirez arrived to relieve Odacheke. "How are things in Last Chance?" Kris asked.

"Things were fine when I left home an hour ago. Something go wrong while I was cooped up in the shuttle?"

Kris told her what they knew. The old chief whistled.

One of the teenagers raised a hand. "Ma'am, I'm from Last Chance. I live a few blocks from the university. Before I came up here, they reported a fire around the college, but I didn't know where? Could you see if there's anything more to find out?"

"We'll check," Kris said. "Everyone stay focused on the station." Ramirez sat down at a work station and quickly switched it to news. She studied its feed, hitched into Pinkerton's aerial view, rationalized it to a map, and said, "Son, what's your address?"

He gave it quickly, she typed it in. "The fire is on the other side of the campus, five blocks from your street."

"Thank you, ma'am. I hope nobody I know is in the mess."

"That's what we're all hoping," the chief said gently.

Chief Odacheke quickly filled in Chief Ramirez on the station's condition and hurried for the shuttle to find out more about things below them. Penny stopped her circling for a moment next to Kris. "Think you ought to call Ron?"

"If I had a mess on my hands do you think I'd want a call from out in left field? No, we have our set of problems. He'll handle his. The smaller we make ours, the better for Ron."

They paced around the monitoring stations. At a quarter of midnight, the restaurants started to close, the last movie let out and the gaming hall quit making change. "Think we ought to increase security around the shops?" Jack asked.

"Pull some of the guards that are backing up a couple of the latched doors. Assign them to walking the shop beat," Kris agreed. They weren't trained, but they'd look good.

At midnight the shops closed with no more than the usual lip from their last customers. The sailors walked or swayed their way back to their ships. Kris eyed the changing monitors on four stations, when Penny came up beside her.

"I almost feel guilty," she said. "They've got fire and riots on the ground, and it's as peaceful as a church up here."

Kris shook her head. "No telling why things happen the way they do. And it could change here at the drop of a hat. Chief, do we have any shuttles headed our way?"

"No, and the first ones should have lifted off by now."

"Nelly, is Ron's phone busy?"

"Yes, Kris."

"Monitor it. Tell him when he's off that I'd like to talk to him when it is convenient." Kris kept circling. Monitoring. Waiting for Hank to make a move.

A long two minutes later, Nelly said, "Ron is off his line. I've given him your message. He's got another call."

Kris waited a tense five minutes before she heard. "How are things up there?" from Ron.

"Boring. Totally dead. I mean quiet. I notice there are no shuttles inbound. What do I tell Hank if he calls?"

"You can tell that son of a bitch that he can have his sailors back—some of them—as soon as I can sort out the ones that will be seeing a Commissioner in the morning from those that were merely obnoxious and disgusting."

Kris said nothing for a long moment. "Feel better now?"

"No Kris. This is not something I'm ever going to feel better about. Maybe you Longknifes consider this all in a night's work, but this is not the way we do things on Chance."

"We've seen the fire from up here," Kris said.

"You didn't see the drunken sailors throwing beer bottles at the fire fighters."

"No. Anyone hurt?"

"None of them," Ron bit back.

"Who was hurt?"

"Kris, two of our coeds were raped tonight."

"Did you catch who did it?"

"No. Not in the act and not on a security camera. The women aren't sure who their attackers were, but they were sailors. Seven hundred and fifty sailors to pick from and they didn't get a good look at them."

"Anyone killed?"

"None, so far. Fifty, sixty of our people are in the hospital, some for the night. A couple of dozen sailors are also in the emergency room. Some may stay awhile."

Kris let that hang there for a while. "When Hank calls, what do I tell him?"

Ron started to snap out an answer, then closed his mouth and looked off screen. His own face was soot-blackened and there was a cut over his eye. Ron had not been monitoring the situation from a comfortable distance tonight. Kris suspected she knew what he'd been through; had been there herself. It was something she would have saved him from if she could.

Finally, Ron looked back at Kris. "You tell the commander of those cruisers docked at your station that he will not be getting his liberty party back on time. You tell him he won't be getting all of it back tonight, ah, this morning. You tell him to send down some lawyers because his sailors are going to need them."

Kris found herself staring into a black screen; Ron had been cut off. Before Kris could blink, the screen filled with Hank's aquiline nose and perfect mouth. Unusual for him, his cheeks were reddened by a rising temper. "Lieutenant, what's going on here? Where are my liberty launches? We sent fifteen down and the first ones are overdue to return."

"And likely to be more overdue before you see them, Hank."

"Commodore, Lieutenant."

Kris weighed several comebacks and decided the situation was way to hot for silly games. "Have you been watching the news?"

"And if I had, what would I have seen, Lieutenant."

"Your sailors started a riot tonight. Buildings are burning. Women were raped."

"Not by my men, Lieutenant. My sailors were told to be gentlemen during their liberty. They are ambassadors of Greenfeld," Hank said, quoting the usual admonishment to sailors going ashore. "Whatever may be happening on Chance, it is clearly the work of your Longknife instigators."

"They're welcome to use that defense in court tomorrow, but if I were you, I'd get some lawyers down there to help your sailors get their stories straight."

"Peterwalds do not need lawyers, Lieutenant. We make our fine legal points at the tip of a bayonet."

Kris and Hank locked eyes at that. A long minute passed. "If that's your attitude, may I suggest that you keep your sailors confined to your ships and off my station."

"That is not something that you can demand, Lieutenant."

"It is, however, something that I am within my rights to request, considering the trouble on the planet below."

"Chance has not declared martial law?"

"I don't think they have the option in their Articles."

"No martial law, your station stays open to my ship personnel, Lieutenant Longknife."

"Now who is arguing a fine point of the law. You have heard my request. Now I'll offer you some advice, free of charge. You are taking on more than you realize. Back off. Chance does not take well to strangers trying to bully them." Kris didn't add that Chance did not take well to strangers, period. "I may have only been here a bit longer than you, but I've learned they are very definite about where they owe their allegiances. And they can be very stubborn when pushed— just my advice."

"And when does a commodore listen to anything a lieutenant says. When have Peterwalds ever listened to the lies handed out by Longknifes. Don't try to scare me, Little Princess, you're out here alone. Nobody's going to come riding to your rescue this time. I've got this situation under my control and I'll do with it what I want. You can't stop me."

Again, the screen was blank in front of Kris.

"That kid has a serious problem with authority," Jack said.

"I'd hate to be a captain with my twenty in and have to tell him anything," Penny said.

"Kind of makes you feel sorry for Captain Slovo," Kris said. Then the screen lit up in front of her.

"Kris, did we finish?" Ron asked. "We got cut off and then I couldn't get back to you."

"Hank managed to override your call. I've been talking to him for the last couple of minutes."

"You give him a piece of my mind?"

"Kind of," Kris said, and paused to walk around the room, check the monitors. "I'm looking to see if he has his Marines storming my station. So far, nothing but an unbelievably quiet night. Anyone, did we make a recording of my call with Hank?"

"Got it right here," Chief Ramirez said, and began playing it. Ron's image filled a quarter of the screen before Kris. He listened to Hank and Kris's call with a deepening scowl.

"Nice to see that you got us right the first time," Ron said as the call finished. "Chief, squirt me that file if you can."

"Doing it," she said.

Kris raised her hands as if to show that she wasn't touching anything . . . or maybe in surrender. "You folks don't like being pushed. I'm not pushing."

"But that guy thinks he has this situation under control." Ron snorted. "I'm glad you took the call. If I'd been talked to like that, I might have forgotten myself and . . ." He shivered. "Forget that thought."

"How are things on the ground?"

"We've got sailors headed for the port. We've got three busloads of sailors cuffed to their seats and headed for our jail." Ron scratched his ear. "This will overfill it. I'll have to release everyone but our worst—wife beaters, check kiters."

"I'd offer my brig, but I may be filling it real soon," Kris said. "Jack, turn off the escalators to the docks."

"Already done it."

"Ron, I'm going to have to go. There's a walker I know leaving one of the ships and I think I better talk to this one."

"Take care. Will I see you down here tomorrow?"

"Don't know. And wouldn't say on a line I suspect is open."

"Kris, one thing, we haven't found evidence of Longknife provocateurs in this. Am I missing anything. Are they here?"

That was a shot to the jaw. Kris put all the sincerity she had into the reply she gave Ron. "You've seen every cent I've spent on Chance. I've bought food, energy, a ship. To the best of my knowledge, I have not bought any people."

"I think I trust you on that, Kris. Do you trust the other Longknifes not to have?"

At that question, Kris let out a dry snort. "I'm not sure I trust any Longknife as far as I could throw them."

Ron shook his head. "Strange, that was my attitude toward all Longknifes until I met you."

Ron rung off and Kris headed for the door. "Where do you think you're going?" Jack demanded.

"Down to talk to Captain Slovo," Kris said. "You stay here. If things go to hell, I trust you on the auto guns. Anyone here you trust more than you?"

Jack eyed Penny; she did not meet his eye. "You win this one. But so help me, if anything happens to you, I'm turning loose the 6-inch lasers to fillet those ships. No warning given."

"I understand. We're a second away from hell and the sulfur fumes are getting awfully thick."

Captain Slovo apparently took his time climbing the stairs out of the dock, Kris was trotting up to Pier 1 area as he started walking toward her. She saluted; he returned the honor. "Did you have to turn off the escalator? That was a long climb."

"You are not that old, and you're not in bad shape."

"Compared to those babes in arms, I am."

"You have my sincerest sympathy, trying to educate Hank."

"Yes, there is that. Well, I am supposed to prove Peterwald personnel can indeed trespass on your command. Have I done it?"

"You know there's a five-millimeter auto cannon aimed right at your heart."

"I hope you have a good man on the trigger."

"First Lieutenant Jack Montoya of the Marines."

"Good hands to have my life in."

"My life's been there many times."

"Someday I must read the full folder on you."

"Why are we having this chat?" Kris said.

"My master told me to come out here, bay like a dog, and see what happened. He didn't tell me when I could come back in. Oversight on his part, I hope."

"I've got a ship I think you'd make a very good captain of."

"Are you attempting sedition?"

"Hardly," Kris said. "You just told me you had no place to go, and I just offered you one."

The captain chuckled wryly. "We would have quite a time, but I think that I should assume that I have done my duty to Greenfeld, and can now return. Though I suspect the commodore may be disappointed that you did not shoot me down on sight, thereby opening up all sorts of new options to him."

"And without you to provide unwanted advice and wisdom."

He did not react to Kris's last words, but started to turn. Kris held him with her eyes. "Captain, this could get very bloody very fast now. Hank is not playing with toys, or paying for someone else to write a term paper for him."

"Dear God, don't I know."

Kris went on. "There are a lot of people involved here that I like . . . Hank excluded. I'll do my best to see that Hank has chances to call it quits without bloodshed. To back out even if things do get bloody. But I do not intend to let him add Chance to his daddy's holdings by walking through a pool of blood."

"I understand you very well. 'Tis a pity he does not."

The captain made his way slowly toward the stairs, evincing no eagerness for what he was returning to. Kris quick marched back to the Command Center.

"What was that all about?" Jack asked as she came in.

"Any change in our status?" Kris demanded, got head shakes, and then turned to answer Jack. "I think the good captain was set up as a sacrificial lamb. If I'd been trigger happy about my No Go Zone, he'd be dead. As it is, watch for more walkers. How many troops do we have to keep an eye on anyone who wanders out of the ships?"

"You could use us," an enthusiastic teenager with pink spiked hair said from her station at a monitor.

Kris considered that option, found it about as effective as ordering a puppy to lick burglars to death, but lacked other options. Still . . . "Maybe eager teens could carry the right message if we had them handing out flyers that said 'You wander our station at your own risk. There are auto guns zeroed in on you and we are prepared to use them.' Penny, print up a couple hundred flyers. Have some of the young folks overnighting on the *Patton* hand them out at the ship piers."

"How about we change your message to 'and our Marines are prepared to use them,'" Jack said.

"Now that's scary," Chief Ramirez said.

"I'm doing it, and I'll get them to the *Patton* in ten minutes," Penny said. "Hey, anyone seen Chief Beni? Aren't he and his drinking friends usually back by now?"

"He wasn't on the eleven thirty that brought me up," Ramirez said. "Might be hard to catch a cab down there tonight."

Kris had other worries. Hopefully, the fellow would stay out of harm's way. That was all he usually wanted to do.

Liberty boats began to climb into orbit. They docked with their ships and Kris got a quick call from Captain Slovo. "We have a bit of a problem, Your Highness. You don't want us on your station, but our liberty parties returning are a very mixed bag. Simply put, crewmen from the *Incredible* are now on three other ships. You mind if they trek back to their bunks?"

"Of course not, Captain," Kris answered in full *Noblesse Oblige*. "I assume they'll do a straight line for their ship."

"Ah, yes, Your Highness, but, there is the matter that many of them are not in the best of shape. Could you please turn on the escalators?"

"Done," Jack said, tapping his board. "Just remember whose finger is on the auto guns."

"Actually, I'd prefer not to mention the guns to them."

"Think Hank's listening to his flag captain?" Penny asked.

"I think Hank wants to have as many of his sailors ready and armed as possible for a bit of saber rattling tomorrow," Kris said. "The way things ended up tonight, they aren't, so he sends Slovo to beg."

"Should we be helping him?" Jack asked.

"There will be plenty of empty bunks on those ships tonight. No, let's let Hank do his thing. We've just got to make sure he falls flat on his face when he does it."

Kris glanced at the clock. It was well after one. Except for a brief nap, she was running on adrenaline and four hours' sleep—not a good mix for battle. She turned to Chief Ramirez, "I'm going down for the night. Wake me at six, seven if things are quiet. Jack, Penny, you split the watch tonight."

Jack nodded without taking his eyes off his board. Penny said, "Yes," as she left to get fliers for the kids on the *Patton*.

"Which one of you is going to bed now?" Kris demanded.

"I will, after I get the fliers out," Penny said.

"I can have a kid run the fliers down," the chief offered.

"I want to talk to some seniors," Penny said. "This isn't just handing out paper, it's knowing when to duck if Jack opens fire." Jack nodded.

Kris headed for bed but, tired as she was, sleep was a long time coming. What would Hank do? What should she do?

She wanted to be where Hank was when he made his move. That was an easy call. But where would he move . . . the station or the planet? If he rushed the station, he'd control the space above Chance . . . and access to the jump points that lead to all those alien worlds. *Let's not forget that, Short Fork*, she could almost hear Tommy saying. Oh God, she missed him, his easy smile, his way of cutting through her presumptions.

Kris slammed that door shut. Tom was gone.

Hank was here. Now. What was he going to try tomorrow?

Clearly he wanted a riot on the ground. How many Peterwald takeovers started with a barroom brawl—a local disagreement that got out of hand and ended with troops marching in and knocking heads. Everything pointed to Hank leading his troops down to Last Chance, gunning down a few "terrorists and hostage takers," and setting up a pliant government.

Kris snorted. Chance didn't have a planetary government to start with. Things would not go as easy as Hank figured when he declared Last Chance the seat of government for the whole planet . . . and under his thumb. But by then, the fight would be on and Hank would have a plea for help from the Chance "government" and matters would go their usual, bloody way. Grampa Ray was right; Peterwald preferred not to get his planets covered with rubble. But a small planet like Chance wasn't an economic powerhouse. Peterwald wouldn't mind laying it waste to "save" it.

Her best move was to take all her spare weapons, drop down to Last Chance, and keep Ron from becoming suddenly dead.

And if Hank attacked her station while she was gone?

That is the problem, now, isn't it.

Kris rolled over, hunted for sleep on her other side. What were the chances that Hank could take her station if he tried?

The station had the guns. A charge across all that open space on Deck 1 would be bloody and unsuccessful.

So punch a hole in the deck—let out all the air.

Hank had to know that would fail. All the critical areas had their own airtight compartments. His Marines would still be shot down as they covered the distance from their ships to just about anyplace . . . and Kris would let the 6-inchers hack and slash the ships at the same time. Taking down a space station looked easy on the vids. It didn't work all that well in practice. Hopefully, Captain Slovo had educated Hank on that.

Kris shook her head against her pillow. Hank, learn something? That did not sound like a good bet.

If it turns into a fight, where's the best place for me?

As Commander, Naval District 41, there was no question, her place was on her station. That answer took no brains.

Okay, Longknife, where's the best place for you?

Where did she belong? Where would Grampa Trouble or King Ray want her. No, where would their junior-officer selves be? Kris smiled. That was also a no-brainer.

She belonged down on Chance, keeping Hank from rape, pillage, and burning. Maybe there, she could keep the war from starting. And so long as she was down there, Hank would be in a very difficult position. He couldn't start bombing and wildly lasering the people from space.

Besides, I've always wanted to run a guerrilla campaign. On that happy thought, Kris rolled over and went to sleep.

Ramirez's wake-up call didn't come until seven hundred hours. "Steve's on his way up. The shuttle's ahead of schedule. He'll be here in fifteen minutes. Thought you'd like to know."

Kris was showered, in undress whites with ribbons, and just entering the Command Center when Steve arrived. He was clean shaven, hair cut, and in undress whites. "Figured today might be a good one to look Navy," he said, saluting Kris.

She returned his honor and turned to Chief Ramirez, "What's our situation?"

"Not bad, folks. The dregs of that liberty party were a

sorry-looking bunch. We had a few walkers come out around six, but they just looked around, smelled the air, and ducked back in. They did get leafleted by the kids."

"Pull them in," Kris ordered. "If Hank breaches our hull, I want them safe. Get everyone behind airtight bulkheads. Penny, batten down our ships. Have we checked the fire curtains lately?" The station could be divided quickly by curtains that prevented the spread of fire and the loss of air pressure.

"I tested them last week," Ramirez said. "No problems."

"One more thing, we provide waste treatment to the ships. I noticed there are holding tanks in the pier areas. Start storing sewage there. Don't let anything from Hank's ships get to our central treatment plant."

Steve frowned. "I respect the twisted mind that came up with that defense, but I really have to wonder what kind of people would think of attacking a station that way."

Penny swallowed a smile. Jack shook his head ruefully. Kris said, "I'll explain later. Are the lasers powered up?"

"Their capacitors are full," Ramirez said.

"They can be controlled from here," Steve Kovar, Lieutenant, retired, said. "You could get two or three shots off before they need local attention." He grew a big, cat-dining-on-canary grin. "And when we resited them onto the end of the piers, we made sure they could fire at the stern of ships berthed there."

"Very good. Jack, target the stern engines of Hank's ships. Fix it so if you lean on the wrong chunk of your board, Hank's six ships lose a goodly portion of their speed and maneuverability."

Kris thought her grin was big, but Jack's was even wider. "Done, Your Bloodthirsty Highnessness. Grampa Trouble would be proud of your Commandership."

"It remains to be seen if I'm all that proud of him," Kris grumbled at the reminder of Trouble and his . . . trouble. But it was time for Kris to commit to action and no time for inside-the-head arguing with her forebearers. She turned to the former Commander, Naval District 41, and saluted. "I delegate the command and defense of this station to you. I strongly request that you don't let it fall into Peterwald hands."

Lieutenant Kovar returned her salute. "He gets it over my dead body, Commander."

"Let's hope it doesn't come to that, but if it does, you have the right attitude. As of now, you have weapons release for all armament. All of them: lasers, booby traps, auto guns, personal weapons. If you want to use them, they're yours."

The retired lieutenant took the orders with a very bland face. Twenty years of service and it never came to this. Now, in retirement, the hot potato was dropped into his hands.

Jack coughed. "And where does that leave the rest of us?"

"Penny, you stay with the lieutenant. The first shots fired by us should be by a serving Wardhaven officer. That'll assure the fine points of law are observed."

Penny slipped into Jack's chair, but her eyes were on Kris. "What are my orders?"

"My preference is for Hank's forces to fire first. However, I don't expect him to do that until he has everyone exactly where he wants them." Kris shook her head. "You may open fire when, in your opinion, the station is under imminent threat."

"Should we try to make some Peterwald Marine private shoot a bit early and first?" Kovar asked.

"Who would you sacrifice?" Kris said. "Our chain of command is too short to risk one of us. I will not use some old fart or kid. Penny, it's your call to make. Any problems with that?"

"I'm glad we're not sending my kids or the oldsters out to stop a bullet. No, Kris, I have no problem shooting first under these conditions."

"Jack, you're with me," Kris said. "We're heading down to Last Chance with all the personnel and crew-served weapons the Commander here will let us remove from our armory."

"If it hasn't been issued, it's yours," Kovar said. He turned to an oldster on watch. "Reina, you supervise that."

"No problem. Give me five minutes and I'll have another work party ready to load out the armory."

"Go, gal," Steve said, and the gray-haired woman hurried for the door.

"Jack, you're with her. I'll sit it out here for a bit longer, see what develops."

"I may not be able to catch up with her," Jack said, but he was jogging after her before the door closed behind her.

Coming in as Jack left was a none too steady Chief Beni. Showered, shaved, and in a fresh uniform, he still looked fit for nothing more active than his own funeral. "Sorry I'm late."

"When'd you get in?" Kris demanded.

"I rode the three o'clock shuttle up. It was suppose to be the two o'clock, but nothing was right last night."

"And you missed the eleven thirty shuttle because . . . ?" Kris said.

The chief scratched his neck and avoided Kris's eyes. "There were these two friendly locals buying drinks for us. 'Saviors of the planet,' they called us. We must have drunk more last night than . . ." In his present state, the chief couldn't seem to remember when that was. "Anyway, I and the Comm Chief went looking for a cab about eleven—couldn't find one. Maybe we did go back for a few more drinks. Joe, the Chief Engineer and Doc were still putting them away when we left the second time."

Kris didn't want the chief in her Command Center today. "Trot down to the *Resolute*, put your head together with their Comm Chief, hike up their antenna and see if you pick up anything interesting about Hank's ships before the rest of us do."

"Yeah, I can do that. And Beck has great coffee. I could really use some coffee."

Fifteen minutes later, Hank started causing trouble.

First two, then another two walkers left Hank's flagship. Penny drew a bead on the first pair. Then the second.

"Mind if I try something?" Chief Ramirez asked.

"I was wondering why you hadn't left," Steve Kovar said.

"I've been watching these turkeys amble around *my* station, raising my blood pressure, and maybe us having to kill them. I was wondering if there wasn't something I could do."

"What do you have in mind?" Kris asked.

The relief for the folks that had been watching the monitors for half the night trooped in. As the first set of kids and oldsters got up, stretched, the chief said, "You folks good for a bit of fun?"

"Please, let me visit the head first," an old fellow said. "Then I'm yours."

"I'll need a few things out of the armory," Ramirez said.

"I promised most of that stuff to the princess," Steve said.

"She won't need dirtside what I'm gonna borrow."

"Should I ask again what's going on?" Kris asked.

"Just watch," the chief said as she led old farts and pink spiky hair toward the armory. Kris waited for a long ten minutes as the two pairs of walkers became four. At first, they stuck to the forward end of the station, roaming from one pier to the other, but they were edging toward amidships when the elevator opened and six spacesuited figures got out.

"That's what I thought," the old lieutenant chortled. "We talked about some batty ideas in our time. I wondered how this would play out. Penny, you have control of those fire curtains?"

"Yes, sir."

"As soon as those six clear the amidships shops, start closing those forward of midship."

Kris watched as the six came forward, the chief in the lead, the other five in a loose line behind her. In armored space suits there was no way to tell the backup here was old coots and kids. Once the last of them were three meters out from the line of shops, the many segments of gray, airtight fire curtain began to slide closed all around the station. The six didn't look back.

The reaction of the walkers, all dressed for a nice day on the station, was decidedly different. A couple of them might have bolted for the nearest pier if the senior of the pair hadn't demanded they stay right where they were.

The chief and her five walked slowly toward the closest pair. The chief's suit had an external speaker; her words came through loud and clear. "Our commander gave your boss man his marching orders. We don't want you ambling around our station. I suggest you head back before we evacuate the air you're breathing."

"You can't do that."

"Penny," Kovar said, "could you start sucking some of the air out of that section of the station."

"Yes," Penny said, hitting a button.

"There're a lot of things you *think* we can't do. Push us and you may discover to your sorrow just what we *will* do."

The junior of the two suddenly looked around, then nudged his senior's elbow. That one sniffed the air, glancing around, then scowled. "We aren't finished here."

"I think we are," the chief said as all the walkers hurried

away. As they passed to Bay 2 where half the ships were docked, Lieutenant Kovar laid a hand on Penny's shoulder.

"Now close the fire curtains between Bay 3 and Bay 2."

Then the old lieutenant turned to face Kris. "I think we've now arranged that they don't get to rush this station before having to shoot at our fire bay doors. That may not be much of a casus belli; but it's a clear declaration of intent. And it should take a load off this lieutenant's mind."

"Do we pull the air out of Bay 3 once the chief is out?"

As Steve answered, "Yes,"

Nelly said, "Kris you have a call coming in from Commodore Peterwald."

"Put it on a screen," Kris said, and as the nearest one flipped from a security collage to a very red-in-the-face man in a blue uniform she smoothed her face to Navy bland.

"What do you think you're doing, having your people intimidate my crewmen."

"I'm sorry, Hank. The message must have gotten garbled. I'm having trouble maintaining air pressure. We think we have a slow leak somewhere in Bay 3. We're temporarily isolating it while we search." Around Kris, faces reflected high admiration for anyone who could come up with a whopper that big, that fast. On screen, Hank trembled in speechless rage.

Captain Slovo came on screen. "I told the commodore that you might be having that kind of trouble. Your station is quite old and not at all well kept up."

"Sadly, all too true," Kris agreed.

Hank's glare at Kris broke as he glared at his flag captain. "We'll talk more about this when I'm done," Hank snapped. Kris was none too sure if the parting shot was aimed at her or at poor Slovo. Whatever they were paying him, it wasn't enough.

The screen went blank. Kris shook her head. "Slovo told him what he was walking into and he didn't listen."

"He's a commodore," Steve said. "Why listen to a captain?"

"Maybe because Slovo is right more often than his sycophant junior captains," Penny offered.

"That would require Hank to learn something. I don't think he can." Kris went down her threat board and came up with more to worry about. "What if he sends the Marines in light assault craft through another dock or the shuttle bay?"

"Penny will have a misfire with those damn lasers," Kovar said, saluting Kris smartly. "A quick shot aimed at their motors should mess up their day. Then the chief will go out with folks who regularly work in space suits, collect their guns, and push the Marines back ·where they belong. Ma'am, when you've stewed as long as I have about defending this bit of space, you come up with a whole lot of ideas." He looked around the room, a proud father's contented smile on his face. "You go dirtside and ruin Hank's day down there. I've got him covered up here."

Kris ambled aft to the armory. All she saw were gray walls and a few boxes of rocket grenades. As she came in, a kid hauled those out. Their bag of tricks was empty. If they failed, it would not be because they didn't use everything they had. She joined Jack at the shuttle bay, quickly checked the tie-downs on the load of her shuttle, and preflighted it. An hour later, they were on the ground. The shuttle was towed straight to a hanger. There were trucks waiting to take the weapons into town.

Kris rode in the first truck, Jack at her elbow. The drive was long, introduced her to a wide limited-access highway that circled Last Chance, and gave her a better view of how the half million people here lived. Businesses, industrial parks, suburbs were all going concerns, easily the match for the medium cities of Wardhaven. It would be a shame to see all this turned into a free-fire zone for Hank's troops.

The truck took an exit at Southside Industrial Park. It drove by a shopping center, homes, businesses, and then turned onto a winding road that took them through a grassy berm and into an area of light industry, warehouses, and finally, at its south end, a series of low buildings marked Municipal Complex.

"That's where our Safety and Peace Officers get trained," the driver said, pointing at several brick buildings of one and two stories. "That over there is where we train Fire Department Volunteers and Regulars." This time, Kris was directed at a similar cluster of brick buildings. Across an asphalt lot was a seven-story tower, its windows marked with soot. Fighting a fire at the top of a ladder extended that far just might give even an orbital skiff racer acrophobia.

"And there is our Justice Center and jail, busting its seams at the moment." This time the driver pointed at a large, three-story building with only long narrow windows above the first floor. The windows were open this afternoon; Kris thought she got a whiff of the place as the truck drove into the garage of a fire-house and the doors closed behind them.

Ron was there, looking very tired. Somehow he'd managed a change of clothes and a shower. At least the smoke smudge was gone from his face. When he saw her, his eyes lit up. He was smiling as he helped her down, and if he managed a hug for an on-duty Naval officer, it was done with no clear viola-tion of the regulations. He looked like he wanted to kiss her, but stepped back instead. "How much did you bring us?"

"And I thought bringing you all I could spare from my ar-mory was going to surprise you."

"Steve said he'd try to wrangle as much loose as he could." Kris pouted. "So being Mama Claus wasn't my idea."

"It was," Ron assured her as he walked her back to the tail-gate of the truck. "It's just that really great military minds run in the same direction."

"You're laying it on awful thick," Jack muttered.

"Keep it up, I like it," Kris said, enjoying the moment, but business was business. "You have a map of this area?"

"In the office upstairs. Crew!" Ron shouted. "Unload this and get it moving to the other buildings. Keep it covered. The sky has eyes and we want some of this to be a surprise." So the mayor understood the benefit of operational security. Kris fol-lowed him upstairs while weapons, covered with sections of hosing and other fire gear, were run out one door. Another truck came in and started unloading.

Gassy and Pinky were upstairs in a small conference room; long table down the middle, empty chairs around it. A map on it showed the area. Beside the two Kris knew were four others Ron introduced as leaders of two hunting clubs, a sharp-shooting rifle club and the Emergency Search and Rescue Club.

"What are you equipped with?" Kris asked.

"Hunting rifles, competition-quality rifles, those kinds of things," Ron said.

"Anyone know how to handle a crew-served machine gun, a grenade launcher, an assault rifle?"

"Some of our folks have trained with Steve's crew. Few more spent time off planet in the service before they came here. We're not stupid hicks, Princess," the shortest of the four said.

"Good. You want to show me your deployment?" That brought only worried looks from the group.

"That's our problem," Ron said. "We know there's a way to do this, but we don't have any idea what it is. Short of putting some of our folks behind every window and starting shooting when it seems right . . ." He ended with a shrug.

"No one shoots until Ron says to," Kris said. She'd started to say "I give the order," but she caught that social blunder. "The idea is to solve this without a lot of your friends and family ending up suddenly and totally dead. You get my drift?"

"But how?" the tallest of the four asked.

Kris slipped through the men and leaned on the table, eyeing the map. A photo had been overlaid on topo lines, along with representation of sewer, power, and other civic services.

"Ron, can you close down this town. I didn't see a lot of traffic on the road coming in, but I saw more than I wanted. I doubt Hank will march his guys in from the airport. Unless you want to have shuttles shooting up your highway to clear a space in traffic for a runway . . ."

"Gassy, order Black Out and Peaceful Kingdom," Ron said. "For you, Kris, that means everyone has thirty minutes to get home . . . Please . . . and we really don't want people shooting at things. It also means I'm out of a job." Kris glanced at Ron to see if he was joking. He wasn't. "Those orders are in our charter. But any official who invokes them has seventy-two hours to face a committee of city commissioners, explain his reasoning for what he did and why he shouldn't be booted out of office for the next four weeks while he seeks re-election. And anyone who didn't like being bossed like that runs against him."

"Nice system you have here," was all Kris said.

"So, how do you say we fight this guy, now that you've taken control, Longknife," the shorter one said.

"She hasn't taken control, Ernie," Ron told the short one. "I'm asking her, as someone who's been in a firefight or two to offer us some suggestions."

Kris ignored the alpha dog contest and eyed the map. "Is there a runway or major highway south of here?" she said, waving at the empty space on the other side of the table. She missed a battle board she could zoom in and out.

"No," Ron said. "Farmland, some cranberry bogs, then forest until you get to the coast."

"So he has to land on the highway I just drove in on?"

"If he's using the liberty launches, yes."

"And hook a left at the exit sign, then march his troops up the road through all these nice businesses and homes," Jack said, following the path with his finger. "Where do we engage him?"

"We don't," Kris said.

"What do you mean," the short fellow, Ernie, snapped.

"You planning on shooting first?" Kris asked.

"He invades my planet. I'm within my rights to shoot him."

"Is he invading or staging a parade?" Kris said, and told them about the "leak" she suddenly developed. "I've got him isolated to the forward portion of my station. If he does anything, he'll have to blow my fire curtains. That forces him to do something close to an act of war and I can start shooting. At the moment, he can't find a way to get in a good position to take over High Chance, so I suspect he'll come down here and get his guys free from the "terrorists" holding them "hostage.""

"We're not . . ." Ernie started, but the tall one rested a hand on his shoulder.

"If we're under siege by Peterwald's fleet, who's gonna be out there, telling our side of the story. You?" The tall one took his hand off Ernie and offered it to Kris. "I'm Wee Willy to most. I like your station stunt. You got another one in your hip pocket? I hear stories that Longknifes do amazing things."

Ernie muttered something Kris ignored.

"Sometimes we pull rabbits out of our hats. Sometimes the rabbits pull our hats out of our more fundamental parts." That got a chuckle. Kris leaned on the map. "He lands here." She fingered the road. "He's done nothing. He marches through this suburban area. We really don't want to start something. Lot of women and kids." She raised an eyebrow. No one questioned her.

"Hank gets up to this berm. Nice, but not really that good a defensive line. Besides, where do we get him talking to us. No, let him in all the way to the jail's parking lot."

Ron whistled. "That close?"

"But that puts him in a whole lot of fire lanes," Jack said, walking his fingers from the buildings, the tower, the jail. "No reason we couldn't have fire coming from the row of shops behind him. If he does walk right up, he's in one solid kill zone."

"Why would he do that?" Ron asked.

"If you don't get in his way, he doesn't have much of a choice but to keep marching." Kris's smile was all teeth.

Gassy leaned over Kris's shoulder. "So we don't cause him any trouble until he's right where we want him."

"You got it. You'll want to send out some men and women, armed, but with orders to let Hank's men march in. If kids wander out in the street, these folks should get them to safety. If anything looks to get in the way, get it gone."

"You're assuming he doesn't see our preparation from orbit and come in fighting?" Ernie said.

"Have you been too obvious?" Kris asked.

"I don't think so," Ron said slowly.

"What are we likely to face?" Kris asked. "How many of his crew are presently guests in your jail?"

"Four hundred and ninety-six," Gassy said.

Kris whistled. "A third. That must have been some party."

Ron scowled. "We've got three Beergartens wrecked, one burned, along with several houses and our university's admin building. And we never did get a positive ID on the rapists."

"We'll be a long time forgetting last night," Gassy said.

"Let's hope you're not trying to forget this afternoon as well," Kris said. They bent over the map again and divided up the heavy weapons they had among the four sides of the square in front of the jail. "Who gets the tower?" Ernie asked.

"I'd love to have firepower on the first couple of levels of that tower," Kris said. "Some very accurate snipers higher up, but the tower is likely to be the first place they take down."

"I'll put some of my people up there," Ernie said. "That will be my post."

Kris glanced at the short fellow. Just because he didn't like Longknifes didn't mean he was a coward. Come to think of it, it took guts to go up against her family.

Five minutes later they were done. The four left to organize their force. Jack stayed to shake his head. "What do we do if Hank doesn't follow our plan. Can we turn this bunch around?"

"Not a chance," Kris said. "It takes real troops to maneuver under fire. Real leaders. If Hank isn't kind enough to follow our Plan A, we're toast. Plan B is going to be bloody."

"You're betting everything on your knowing how Hank will act," Ron said. "How well do you know this ex-boyfriend."

"He's no ex-boyfriend of mine," Kris snapped. "I spent the longest week of my life cooped up with him on his yacht trying to get him to at least consider that his dad wasn't a god, wasn't perfect, and all he'd heard about my family might not be correct."

"Did it take?" Ron asked, but his phone rang. He listened for a moment, then said, "I'll be as careful as I can, Mom," and hung up. "Twenty launches are headed down."

"Your mom say anything about the light assault craft?"

"Aren't those hard to spot on radar?" Ron said.

"You've been reading up."

"Started as soon as Hank jumped in system."

"Yeah, they're stealthy. I'd like to know if he's bringing the Marines or dropping them all over the place." Kris paused for a second, then her face lit up in a smile. "And, if Hank has really left the ships empty, now might be a great time for Steve to waltz in and take them."

"And who was, just a second ago, telling my best friends that we don't want to start this shoot-out," Ron growled.

"Oops, sometimes I forget myself."

"Only sometimes?" Jack said.

"Do we have any cameras along the highway?" Kris asked.

"Some traffic monitors," Ron said.

"Have someone watch and tell me if they see Marines forming up," Kris said. "Just now, I have another part of my puzzle to put in place for Hank."

"And I'll be checking fire lanes," Jack said. "Making sure these folks know to keep their rears covered just in case Hank does indeed have enough competent Marines to maneuver around even as he marches the swabbies up the center."

16

"**What** are you doing?" Ron asked as they walked to the jail.

"Do you have a list of who's locked up here?" They passed from bright sunlight to shadow; open air to the stink of vomit and sweat.

"Ari should." Ron turned into an office off the foyer.

"Only a partial list. Who you want?" a blond fellow said.

"A Chief Meindl, I believe."

"I think I have all the chiefs listed. Yeah, Meindl, third floor, cell 3A7, Boss. You want to have him hauled down here?"

"No," Kris said. "I'd rather go up for him."

"Suit yourself, Spade, Rori. We're releasing a Chief Meindl from 3A7. You want to take the mayor up there and see that only one of them gets out and the rest don't cause much trouble."

Two men with corporal strips on their green uniforms came out of chairs in the break room across the way and led Kris up two flights of stairs to a cell on the top floor. Iron bars closed off the front, concrete formed its walls. Sized for two prisoners, today, six or eight sat on the lower bed, lay on the

floor, stood at the bars. The eyes that watched Kris looked
feral and angry. This place only needed an excuse to explode.

"Hope those bars are set in there solid," Ron said.

"After last night, I'm real sure they are," Rori told his
mayor. They paused in front of a cell with 3A7 over its door.

"Chief Meindl, are you in there?" Kris asked.

"Yo," came defiantly from the top bunk where one man lay.

"Prisoner, front and center," Rori called. "Someone's here
to see you." The chief rolled lithely from the top bunk to land
in the small space not occupied by one of his juniors. His
glower for the guards ended with a sharp intake of breath as
he spotted Kris. He came to attention. "Sir."

"I would like to have this man released to me," Kris said.

"He's all yours," the guard answered.

The chief reached back onto the bunk for his tie, jacket,
and hat. Kris got her first look at his uniform. His hash marks
and crow were gold; the fruit salad on his chest showed three
good conducts to support that. He also sported the long cruise
ribbon with four stars; hopefully earned on the same cruise as
Slovo. It would be helpful if they knew each other. His sharpshooter badge also had four white lines on it. Maybe Jack was
overly optimistic about the swabbies being out of their ele-
ment in a land bound shoot-out. Now was not the time to
worry about that.

The chief returned himself to proper dress and marched
smartly to the door. Rori eyed the other prisoners, and several
suddenly felt the urge to press themselves up against the back
wall, well clear of the opening door. The chief squared his
corners as he presented himself, hat under his left arm. "Senior Chief Meindl reporting as requested, sir."

"Please walk with me, Chief."

"As you wish, sir," came with full formality. But then, he
was in the hands of his enemy and under the eyes of his
sailors.

Kris said nothing as they retraced their steps. Chief Meindl
spotted a full-length mirror and took a moment to correct the
lay of his collar and hang of his coat. He donned his cover, as
they exited the jail. He breathed easier in the sunlight. Then he
turned to Kris, ignoring Ron. "Do you just want me to walk
with you, or do you want to tell me something, sir."

Kris took a few more steps toward the Fire Training Center, then called. "Ernie, things going fine with those machine guns?" The tower was an obvious target. When the shooting started the race would be on to do as much slaughter as possible before Hank's crew brought it down.

The short man stood in a fourth floor window and waved. "It's in, and I got the snipers in place. Bring 'em on."

"Oh, I wish he hadn't said that," Ron muttered.

Kris said nothing, just eyed the chief, as he swept his gaze slowly over the edge of the parking lot. His nostrils flared and his eyes took on a squint that had nothing to do with the sun.

"Follow me," Kris said, and turned for the row of businesses that would be behind Hank. If the fire from the Municipal Center grew too heavy, this would be their obvious rallying point. Kris caught one glance from Ron. "Are you crazy?" pretty much summed it up. But he didn't say a word. Good man.

"It's good to see you," Wee Willy said from the shaded walkway that covered the entire front of the shops. Kris spotted short jerks of the chief's head as he took in an automatic weapon sandbagged behind a window; a woman with a rocket launcher in a door. Men and women stacked more sandbags behind more windows.

"Step carefully," Kris said to the chief as they entered a shop. "That's a claymore."

"Kris, I've got this area pretty much done. I'm gonna start working on . . ."

"As you were, Lieutenant," Kris said to cut Jack off. "I've got Chief Meindl with me, and while I want him to know something about what his commodore faces, I do want a few surprises."

Jack turned from the map he'd been studying, came to attention, and returned the chief's salute. "I wish I could say it was good to see you again, Chief."

"I wish I could say the same, sir."

"So Princess Kristine is letting you in on the slaughter pen we're setting up for the green kid you've got running your show."

"It appears so, sir," the chief said carefully.

"Well, if you'll excuse me, I have things to do and not

much time to do them in," Jack said, turning his back on them.

"Mr. Mayor, would you take the chief outside a ways."

"No problem, Commander," Ron said.

They watched while the mayor and chief headed back out. "Kris, are you crazy?"

"No more than usual. It doesn't do us a lot of good to win the battle we don't want to fight."

"But we don't want to lose it if we have to fight,"

"Agreed."

"Okay, I'm headed for the buildings close to the berm. See that they're covered if Hank sends his Marines out as flankers."

"That could put us in contact sooner than I want."

"Not if I stay with this screen and see that it collapses ahead of the flankers. But doesn't collapse past about two rows of shops back. We've got to cover Wee Willy's back."

"I kind of wanted you with me," Kris said.

"And that is exactly where I want to be. You know anyone in this lash-up that we can trust to give ground, but not too fast?"

"Be careful Jack."

He snorted at the sentiment. "You do the same." There was a series of sonic booms outside; the shop seemed to take on a permanent tremble as the booms kept coming. "Lots of launches incoming. I better get a move on. Where you headed?"

"I'm going to take the chief up the tower to watch the opening moves, then down to the jail. You?"

"The scouts have set up a command post of sorts just this side of the berm. They've got land line in case things go flaky. I'll stay there for a while. I understand there's a rain sewer under this place that you can move people through. So don't be surprised if I get back to you."

"I'll look for you. Now I got to get moving. Good luck."

"Good luck yourself, Kris. You usually make your own."

Kris rejoined Ron and the chief; they were eyeing the sky. Contrails merged as more and more launches entered the lower atmosphere. "Ron, you might want to go to your Command Center. I'm going up that tower to watch it live. Chief, you're with me unless you think it would be safer in your cell."

"I've had enough of that stinking jail. No thank you."

Kris and the chief climbed up the tower, past a machine gun and two M-6–armed gunners, a rocket launcher, and several sniper teams. "Will you shoot the officers?" Meindl asked.

"Not if they don't shoot at us," Kris answered.

Kris joined Ernie at the top floor of the tower. They had one spectacular view of Last Chance. The sky above them was a liquid blue that seemed to go on forever. Only the contrails of the approaching launches marred it. Ernie had binoculars and called down to a sniper team to loan their glasses to Kris.

She surveyed the highway she'd picked for Hank's landing. Empty, it shimmered in the noon heat. So did the line march into town. Inside the berm, people flitted from one shop row to another. Not a single car or truck was parked anywhere to provide temporary cover to someone caught on the street.

"He'd have to be crazy to march in here," Kris muttered to herself. The chief kept his opinion to himself.

"You holding to name, rank, and serial number?" Kris asked.

"Actually, all they asked me for was my name. They are civilians," he said, scorn for that status flicking his words.

"We'll see who is the dumb one soon enough," Kris said.

"You're going to lose. These situations always go our way. Civilians can't stand up to Greenfeld bayonets." He looked at Ernie. "You don't have the stomach for more than one volley from my sailors. Even this Longknife brat will not make a difference."

"You learned your catechism well," Kris said. "And you may be right, not even a Longknife brat may turn this around. But you sure that Greenfeld sailors can survive the leadership of a Peterwald brat?"

Chief Meindl looked away. He was too honorable of a man to lie to Kris. Yes, he could spiel the official line at her, but make up a lie of his own? No, not this sailor.

"Well, they're landing where you said they would, Your Highness," Ernie said, singing a slightly different tune now.

Kris watched through her borrowed glasses. The landers had their own power because the lead one taxied up and angled to a stop at the overpass that led to the Southern Industrial Park. The next taxied to a stop, nose to the far side of the road, leaving more room. From the first lander, a full color guard marched forth, unfurling their flags as soon as they were on solid ground. Behind them came . . .

"Damn, they brought a marching band," Ernie marveled.

"They are armed," Chief Meindl growled. "You gave me a few obvious freebies. I can give you one or two."

Launch after launch came in, landed, rolled to a stop, then rolled ahead to angle itself right or left. And as soon as the doors opened, shouting sailors ran to form up on the right shoulder. Kris raised the power on her glasses. Yep, there were mortar rolling behind pairs of sailors, extra ammo wheeled along by the next pair. This was a well-practiced ritual.

"The commodore will be in the last lander," Meindl said.

The twentieth launch barely cleared the last overpass, but Hank was down safely and the pilot was breaking hard. The final lander didn't have much spare road to break on, but it came to a halt well clear of the nineteenth. Troops raced to formed ranks outside it. Hank, in blues on a day this hot, strode from the lander last. He received and returned salutes and then . . .

"My God," Kris muttered. "He's going to review his entire force. That's got to be over a half mile to the exit."

"More like a whole mile," Ernie said. "Then he's got close to a four mile walk in here." The man looked at his watch. "Unless he's hired busses, we have a long wait ahead."

Kris eyed Chief Meindl.

"They will march," the chief said, not a shred of doubt in his words. "They are men of Greenfeld. 'Marching is what puts strength in their backs and power in their fists.' "

"And those fists put a couple of my friends in the hospital last night," Ernie snapped.

The chief examined his skinned knuckles. "If *your* people had not so enthusiastically returned blow for blow with *my* people, *you* might not have so many of *my* people in your *hoosegow*."

"Excuse me for being glad we've got them here rather than out there," Kris said.

The chief grunted and muttered something under his breath. Ernie brought his comm unit up to his mouth. "Folks,

we've got an hour or two to nap, get some chow, or so until our
visitors . . ." He frowned at his unit, shook it. Then scowled.

"Nelly," Kris said.

"Halfway through his signal, a jammer cut in, Kris. The local net is off-line, or at least off the air."

"That's not supposed to be possible," Ernie growled. Beside him, the chief smiled happily for the first time.

"Okay, so we go with Plan B," Ernie snapped. "Gale, you
got an extension for that land line you lugged up here."

"I told you you'd need it, Ernie."

"And I'll pay my debt tonight, woman of my life."

A tall, slender woman backed up the stairs, unwinding
cord from the reel in her hand, and gave Ernie a quick kiss and
a phone. "Now what will I have to talk on?"

"You may actually survive a few hours in peace and quiet."

"Oh, you are so wasted when we get home, little man."
They exchanged blown kisses as Ernie punched buttons.
"Tower here. They are down on the road. They have no trans-
port and they've got a two-hour walk ahead of them." He listened for a moment. "Yeah, she's here," he said and gave Kris
the phone.

"Don't you think you ought to come down?" Ron asked.

"He won't touch the tower when he's this far out," Kris told
the mayor. "That would give away his intent and assure he had
a shoot-out on his hands. No, Ron, I'm as safe as you are. Can
you connect me with Jack?"

"I don't know how he stands you doing what you do."

"It's what I do, Ron. It's what a Longknife does."

"You're crazy. Jack, here's that crazy woman of yours."

"What's wrong with him?" Jack asked.

"I think he's discovering that I'm not quite the nice girl he
was thinking it would be fun to fall in love, or at least infatua-
tion, with." Then Kris switched to the business at hand and
briefed Jack on what she could see from the tower.

"You tell me to be careful when I sneak out in front of our
main line of resistance, and then you climb to the top of the
main target in town. No wonder Ron is shaking the dust of
you from his sandals."

"I'll get down before Hank gets too close, which is more
than I can say for Ernie. He's staked the place out for himself

and his favorite mistress. They're plotting sex games for tonight based on who does the craziest thing up here."

Ernie's beaming grin did not disagree with her.

"I got to quit hanging around you, girl. I got to. Okay, I'm
going to keep the watch here. There're a couple of crazy
teenagers who want to help. I've frisked them for switch-
blades, guns, relativity bombs, the basics, and I'm letting
them ride skateboards on the berm. They'll let us know when
Hank's close."

"He has a brass band."

"Hank does? Still, he might let them have a break. And
who knows how long this land line hookup will work."

"Send the kids out. Make sure they know to get gone when
the sailors show up." Kris rang off, picked up her binoculars
and checked. Hank was halfway down the review line of
troops.

"This waiting is going to be the pits," Ernie said. "Maybe
we could send him some busses."

The chief raised his eyebrows in a knowing smile. "Yes,
professionals know that. Keeping your courage for hour after
hour of waiting, that is the hard part. Dancing on adrenaline
for a minute or two. That is easy. That is what we humans have
been doing since we first killed mastodons. But waiting for the
beasty to wander down to the water hole. That is the hard
part."

Kris sat on the shady side of the room; it still smelled of
smoke from its last training run. "You have a family, Chief?"

"Wife, boy, girl," he said. "If you'd let me run down to the
booking room, I'd get my wallet. Pictures." He grinned.

"Nope, you're staying right beside me. And please don't
make me shoot you by trying to escape."

"Ever killed anyone?" the chief asked. Ernie quit studying
the sailors getting ready to march in and glanced at Kris.

"Does Greenfeld add Vs for Valor on campaign ribbons
when they're earned in a fight?" Kris asked.

"No," the chief paused. "No, come to think of it, some
of the recent, ah, antiterror campaigns have had Vs added to
them for those who were involved in combat. Yes, there are
those."

"I don't notice any Vs in the salad on your chest."

"Nope. I'm just a sailorman's sailor."

"Have you checked my collection?"

The chief squinted down at Kris. Then sat down in the shade across from her, careful to stay away from the soot on the walls. "Aren't you rather young to have all those. And that Devolution Service Medal. I was there, swilling beer. Nobody earned a V."

"I guess it's a clerical error."

"I've heard stories about how slipshod things are in the Longknife Navy," he said, but it was clear from the way he studied Kris now that something had changed in him. He was no longer dismissing her as a "girl" or a spoiled brat of the wealthy. "What's that gold trinket?" he said.

"Earth's Order of the Wounded Lion."

He leaned back, lost in thought, not noticing that he was smudging the back of his coat. When he leaned forward, he eyed Kris hard. She gave him steel for steel. "They give you that because you're the Longknife brat?"

"On Greenfeld, do they hand out a lot of fruit salad to Hank because he's Peterwald's brat?"

"And if they did?"

"That's Greenfeld. I earned mine."

He leaned back again, seemed sunk in thought for a long, long time. Finally he roused himself and eyed Kris. "You intent on slaughtering my sailors?"

"Not if I can help it."

"Not like you did those sailors in the pirate battleships that attacked Wardhaven."

There it was again. The canard. Kris let her anger show as she shot back. "First, you're an experienced Senior Chief. You know as well as I do that Magnificent-class battleships don't pop out of empty space. They need bases to build them. They need bases to operate them. I haven't heard of any pirates big enough to operate more than one ship, and a tiny one at that. They get bigger, we come out and take them down hard. At least that's what we do in Longknife space."

"That's what we do in Greenfeld space," the chief said with a frown. He was coming with her. Not happy about where this conversation was going, but he was too honorable a man not to see the truth when his nose was rubbed up against it.

"So where do six humongous battleships come from?" Kris demanded. "And after they've killed my best friends, don't you think I'd want to know the answer to that? Don't you?"

Slowly, the chief nodded. "I would."

"Well so did I. But every last sailor or officer was dead in his pod. Not a few of them, but all of them. Dead men tell no tales. You tell me who got the benefit of that silence."

"The sailors are coming up to the berm," Ernie said.

Kris stood and refocused her glasses. "Yep, there in the lead is your commodore. He must be sweating horribly in blues. Everyone else is in whites. Strange that?"

The chief came to stand beside Kris. "He took a dress-for-success course once, or had a consultation, I don't know. Anyway, he says the camera will always focus on the person in the darker suit over those in lighter ones. He does love his blues."

There was no military value in what the chief said, but it told Kris volumes about what the junior officers and senior NCOs thought in the privacy of their own whispered spaces.

Kris watched as the kids skateboarding on the berm waved at the parade coming up, then did one last rad ride down before taking off for points well out of firing range.

"Good marching," Kris said for the chief. "Better than in most vids. At least everyone is in step. Well, most everyone. I think your commodore is out of step with the music."

"No, ma'am. Everyone is out of step with him."

Kris weighed that and found it interesting. Especially the "ma'am" part.

"What are you going to do with those Marines?" Kris asked, studying the column.

"Is that question directed at me?" Chief Meindl asked.

"No. I don't intend to ask you anything that will cause you trouble when you are returned to Greenfeld control."

The chief frowned. "And the ones in the jail?"

"Unless something goes horribly wrong, all should see Greenfeld again. Remember, I don't shoot prisoners."

"Aren't you worried about a riot when they hear the band?"

Oh, now you have given me something. Was that intentional?

"I kind of expect one, Chief. There are sleepy grenades rigged on both floors. No one should be hurt, but they won't be causing us any trouble, and they won't be in any shape to pick up a rifle and join their liberators in mowing us down, either."

The chief nodded.

Kris refocused the glasses. "Yes, yes, he is doing something smart for a change."

"May I ask what?" the chief said.

"He's deploying his Marines as flankers, sending some of them up the berm to have a look and report back. Ernie, can I borrow your phone." Kris listened for a dial tone, then said, "The forward scouts please."

While she waited to be connected, she turned to Meindl. "Chief, if you cause us any trouble now, I'll have to put you down hard. Should I return you to your cell, or can I have your word that you will not attempt to communicate with your forces?"

"It's my duty to try to escape," he said.

"Gale, love, I need for you to escort someone down the tower," Ernie called out to below.

"But I think my duty to Greenfeld is better served if I observe you and report what I see to intelligence. I will not attempt an escape until shots are fired."

"That's good enough for me, 'cause if this comes out right, there ain't going to be any," Kris said. "Jack, there are observers on the berm."

"We see them. We're falling back from the first line of businesses. How much longer are you going to hang yourself out there for anyone to shoot at? Do I have to come back there and personally drag you down?"

"Not much longer, Jack. Good thing you're out of that first row. Hank just ordered Marines to trot over and look them over. He's covering his flank with Marines."

"Smart, but slow. He's already coming up on the second row if the phone calls we're getting are right. We'll hold the flankers three rows out. I just wish I knew if his own radios were being jammed by this."

"No way to tell. Take care, Jack."

"Now ain't that a joke coming from you. Get down from that tower. Your hair's not nearly long enough to climb."

"Rapunzel is leaving the tower," Kris said and hung up.

"Your boyfriend?" the chief asked as they headed down.

"Why is it that everyone thinks that except him? No, he's the scourge of my life, the head of my security. The one man that can tell me what to do and I have to do it."

Ernie snickered. "Gee, I hadn't noticed him being any more successful than I am with Gale."

"Or Gale is with you," came from below.

"A woman does what a man tells her to do," the chief said.

Kris doubted words could change the chief's mind; with him in the lead, she went down fast and walked quickly to the Fire Training Center. There were lots of trigger pullers looking out the windows; glass was going to fly if bullets did.

"Where's Ron?" Kris asked as they passed a sandbagged machine gun behind the wide glass doors.

"Upstairs."

She found him in the second-floor conference room, dividing his time between the map on the table, a phone, and the window that barely offered him a view down the road.

"He's coming," Ron said as Kris entered.

"He wants to present Chance to his dad on a silver platter."

"Yeah. At college, his dad seemed to come up a lot," Ron said. "I shrugged it off then. I'm rethinking it now. Oh, you still have the chief?" He left the rest of the question hanging.

"Yep, we've been looking at what we've got set up for Hank."

Ron shook his head. "Whatever you want. I guess."

Kris, Ron, and the chief watched the coming parade, the band getting closer and louder. "Chief, is there anyone you could talk to in the jail to cancel the planned riot?"

The chief shook his head. "No one would listen to me."

Kris called the jail. "You have the sleepy grenades?"

"Yes."

"Please use them on your Greenfeld prisoners. They've been ordered to riot when the music gets loud enough."

"Ah, can I talk to the mayor?"

Kris handed Ron the phone. "Yes," he said. "Yes, do it." "Yes, I know it's against our articles, but this whole mess is against it. Do it. I'll be running for reelection next month. You want to run against me?" Ron said, and hung up.

From across the yard came the popping of sleepy grenades. There were shouts, a scream, and quiet very soon. Ron rubbed his forehead. "I'll be doing good to stay out of that jail, Kris."

"It's either prison or a medal," the chief said.

They watched as Hank continued his march. "Good Lord, but that boy cannot get in step," the chief muttered as they watched the flags whip in the slight breeze, the band play, and everyone but Hank march in step.

The phone rang, Ron answered, but quickly passed it to Kris.

"We're falling back slowly. The Marines have a problem," Jack chortled. "We're locking all the doors behind us. Most are old-fashioned key locks. Apparently, the Marine's orders don't allow for just kicking in the doors yet. They had to find a lock pick. I'm going to fall back now to your location."

Kris hung up and went back to the window. Her view really wasn't good enough to command the situation, but she had no communications to command anything anyway. This was almost prehistoric. A bit of poetry came to mind. "The shot heard round the world," she muttered.

"Huh," Ron said. The chief eyed her with a slight smile.

"A shot fired in a situation very much like this at Concord or Lexington. I don't remember which. British Red Coats marched up, formed ranks in the open. Militia formed up across from them, near a bar, I think. No one knows who fired the first shot. By the time the last shot was fired, years later, a new country was born. But that day, the militia got massacred."

"That's what I was taught," Chief Meindl said.

Ron went over to the phone; dialed. "Greta, do a last call around. Remind folks we do not want to fire first. Yes, I know you already did that. Do it again. For me. Thank you."

Ron came back to the window. "Now what do we do?"

"You wait and sweat," the chief said.

"I don't like this," muttered the mayor.

"That is why we win," the chief said.

Five long minutes later, they watched from behind the glass doors at the entrance of the Fire Training Center as Hank marched in; flags flying and band playing. Sailors moved in precise drill as their chiefs wheeled them right and left, to fill up the square. It was a drill designed long ago to show off the skill of the army you faced, to inspire fear and terror.

Kris glanced down at a young man and woman manning a machine gun. They didn't look terrified. No, if Kris read them right, they were determined fighters defending their homes.

Hank, you miscalled this, Kris thought. *The only question left is how many people have to die for your blunder.*

Hank kept eyeing the upper levels of the jail, as if expecting something that wasn't there. He turned to Captain Slovo at his rear often, to talk about something. Kris had a pretty good idea what that was. Beside both of them the squadron's Command Master Chief stood motionless.

Kris did a quick count. There were twelve blocks of sailors not quite a hundred each. Machine gun and mortar teams trailed each. As columns halted, mortar teams unlimbered to the rear, MGs to the flanks. She faced close to a thousand sailors. The ships must be on a minimum watch. It was tempting to call Steve. Kris revised her greeting to Hank.

The music stopped on a signal Kris missed. The Command Master Chief, at a nod from Hank, ordered, "Squadron." That was answered by "Ship," and followed by "Division" in perfect order. "Fix. Bayonets."

The troops answered with a mighty shout as metal scraped on metal. It was a horrible sound. The type of sound that makes the hair on the back of your neck stand up. And your sphincter go weak. The young woman who knelt ready to feed the ammunition belt into the MG whispered, "They do look fearsome."

"They won't look nearly as good a second after I pull this trigger," the gunner beside her said.

Jack joined Kris. He smelled moldy; she was surprised how relieved she was to have her nanny back. "I miss anything?"

"Not yet, but I think Hank's about to raise the curtain."

Hank drew the sword at his side and took a stepped forward. "Ron Torn, you have taken sailors of Greenfeld hostage. I declare you a terrorist, acting outside the law, and demand you release them to me or face intergalactic justice."

"I better go talk to him," Ron said, taking a step.

Kris grabbed his elbow. "You go out there and you are dead. You stay here. I'll go."

Ron glanced back at her. "You think you can settle this, Longknife to Peterwald?"

"Better that she try it first," Jack said.

"And I thought you'd try to lock me in a tower," Kris said.

"Only tower around here is at the top of everyone's target list," Jack said, opening the door for Kris.

"Chief, you're with us," Kris said, leading the way.

"Oh good," Jack muttered. "Three is the charm."

"If you think my presence is going to keep you alive, you're very wrong. We do not negotiate with terrorists," the chief said.

"I am Commander, Naval District 41, Chief. By definition, I can't be a terrorist. Says so in some book I read."

"You sure it wasn't a fairy tale you were reading. One of those cheap fantasy romances?" Jack asked.

"Might have been," Kris agreed.

They were in line now, the chief in the middle, and had naturally fallen into step. He eyed Kris first, then Jack. "Why do I have the sick feeling we are all doomed?"

"You've never been on an operation with the princess, here," Jack said. "You always feel that way at the start of things, and are amazed to be alive at the end."

"Hush, boys, this fairy princess has just one chance to do this right. Hand salute on my order. Hand. Salute." The three brought their right hands up in perfect cadence. Four steps later, Kris was as close as she wanted to be to Hank. "Group. Halt. One," she whispered.

In front of two thousand rifles, loaded with intent, Kris's small detail performed the ancient ritual to perfection.

"Commodore, we need to talk." Hank waved his sword in what might have passed for a salute in some military circles. Kris whispered "two" and her detail dropped their salute.

"I don't have anything to say to you," Hank snapped back. "I demanded that Ron Torn, the hostage taker, come out here. What? Is he hiding behind your skirts?"

"The lawfully elected mayor of Last Chance has asked me to serve as an intermediary between himself and the armed troops that have disturbed, without warning or permission, the quiet of his city. So far, there has been no additional violation of the peace. He would like to keep it that way."

"I want the sailors he's holding hostage released at once."

Hank was firing answers from a playbook he'd probably put

together that morning. *You need a better writer*, Kris thought. *This shindig is way off your script, haven't you noticed?*

Beside Hank, Captain Slovo was studying Kris. This was the first time he'd seen her in uniform, and he eyed her fruit salad with intent. His nostrils flared, his eyes grew wide as he read her service history laid out there for anyone to see.

Except for the Navy-Marine Corps medal, all Kris had were tourist ribbons to show for her service. No Meritorious this, Distinguished that for this girl. But every one of them, even the Navy-Marine Corps ribbon, had a V for having been earned in combat. The sole exception was the Wardhaven Defense Medal.

"Commodore, I think we all want you to have your sailors back," Kris said, reasonably.

"Then why don't I have them?"

"Because I think the local folks will only give them back when you are headed home."

"Greenfeld does not negotiate with terrorists."

Good Lord, doesn't this boy know anything but cant, Kris thought. What she said was very calming. "You are not negotiating with terrorists, Commodore, you are talking with me about a mutual problem we have. I would like to solve your problem, Commodore. Wouldn't you?"

"All they have to do is release my sailors," Hank demanded.

"There is the matter of significant damages done to several buildings here last night by your sailors," Kris pointed out.

"My sailors are gentlemen. Clearly, these damages were done by agent provocateurs hostile to Greenfeld."

For a moment, Kris eyed Hank. *Isn't there anything behind that lovely face, those piercing blue eyes, but second-rate pablum for a brain? Or did you come here for a shoot-out and have no intention of leaving until you've had it?*

"There are witnesses that saw your sailors trashing the Beergartens, tearing down a light post, and smashing its wall."

"They are liars. Paid liars, no doubt."

This was going nowhere. "Commodore, if we don't cooperate to solve this problem, things could quickly get out of control."

Hank opened his mouth to shoot back another one-liner, but the flag captain stepped forward and placed his hand across his mouth. What he said made Hank scowl and curtly shake his head.

"Everything is going exactly the way I intended," the young Peterwald insisted.

"Are you sure, Commodore?" Kris said "From my perspective, it doesn't look that way. I would strongly suggest that you drop this bit of gunboat diplomacy and pull your troops back to their ships."

"And what will you do if I don't. Wipe them out?" Hank snorted at his joke.

Kris said nothing. Beside her, the chief caught the flag captain's attention, then silently guided the officer's eyes to this rifle position, that machine gun nest. Slovo coughed into his hand, and once again leaned next to his master's ear. Hank looked first to one set of weapons, then to another. Then his eyes focused on the tower. "I don't see anything," he snapped.

Oh Lord, Jack and I have done such a great job of getting our shooters to cover that blind Hank can't see them. Kris turned around. "Ernie. Gale, mind letting our visiting friends see what they face." Kris was signing that happy couple's death warrants. Or was if they stood up and countersigned them.

And they did! The crazy pair stood; waved with one hand, held their rifles on their hips with the other. Then they ducked back down into firing positions.

"There's more like them you aren't noticing," Jack said.

For the first time, Hank looked worried. "We can handle those. If need be, we can fall back to those store fronts behind us. My Marines already control them."

Captain Krätz double-timed up from the rear with a Gunny Sergeant beside him. "Commodore, we have a bit of a problem."

The two captains and the commodore put their heads together for a long moment. "Why didn't you tell me about this earlier?" Hank demanded, ending the whispered conference.

"You were at the head of the column, sir," Krätz answered. "The Marines tried to solve the problem on their own, sir."

"And if they bash the doors in," Jack said. "They'll face a hail of fire. I prepared that greeting myself."

"And if you try to fall back on those shops," Chief Meindl

added, "you will be running into claymores. I saw them deployed when the lieutenant here took me for a walk around."

"You go too far, Longknife. And now that you've tipped your hand, we'll smash it," Hank snapped, or tried to. A hard gulp interrupted his words.

"That's what I showed your chief. Did I tip my hand, or just show the tip of an iceberg? You sure you're not facing enough firepower to make this square run knee deep in blood?"

The flag captain looked around the square slowly, taking in carefully what he might have missed before. Kris saw his face harden as he changed his assumptions that he faced amateurs who had no idea how to plan a battle. He glanced at Kris, squinting at the glare off the Wounded Lion in the overhead sun. "That Earth decoration came after de-evolution, didn't it?"

"Maybe," Kris agreed.

Hand again over his mouth, the captain whispered something long and involved to his commodore. Hank's grimace deepened. "I could shoot you down where you stand, Longknife."

"And you'd be dead a second later. What do you say we both live long, nasty lives causing no end of trouble to each other?"

"Not an unreasonable idea," the chief muttered.

"I want my men back," Hank repeated. "I did not come down here just to get sunburned," he said, glancing up. His blue uniform looked summer weight, but Hank had sweated it through.

"I want you to get your men back," Kris said, as she might to a particularly difficult child. "But you have worn out your welcome. There's no beer left on this planet for your men."

"Nobody tells me when to leave," Hank said petulantly.

"I'm not saying that you have to leave, but I am saying that no one wants any of your men in their restaurants, stores, or eateries. You have worn out your welcome," Kris repeated.

Hank frowned at Captain Slovo. He nodded. "Civilians are within their rights to do that, sir. No one can force another person to do business."

A shot rang out as if for emphasis.

Sailors, arms tired from holding their weapons at high port, were slow to react. But they did look around, hunting for the source of the shot. It was as if a great beast held its breath for a moment before it roared.

Kris stepped into that space. "Hold your fire."

For a moment the shock of a woman's voice ordering obedience must have caused the monster pause. Kris raised her arms, spread her hands as if she was personally holding the two sides apart.

"Don't shoot. Hold your fire," she commanded. "Jack, find out who fired."

Jack was already running toward the Police Training Center where Kris thought the shot was from. His automatic was out and raised. He raced to a window where the sun now highlighted a crack running from top to bottom, a hole shining like a star. "You there, put that man under arrest. Now."

Someone must have obeyed, because Jack quit running, scowled at the Police School in general, holstered his weapon, and turned back to his place beside Kris.

"How much longer do we keep this up, Hank? Until one of your men faints and looses rapid fire into your ranks. Me, I got a whole lot of amateurs aiming guns at you with their safeties off. For God's sake, man, let's take it down a few notches so we can talk without some poor dumb schmucks shooting us in the back."

Hank, perfectly sculptured face and all, looked like some kid who had just been told he wasn't getting a Christmas pony. For a moment, he seemed ready to refuse, then he didn't quite stomp his foot, but snarled. "Do what you have to, Captain."

A nod to the Command Master Chief immediately had him shouting, "Squadron." "Ship," echoed, followed by "Divisions." "Order. Arms." Nearly a thousand rifle butts struck the pavement at once. "Parade. Rest." A thousand booted feet stomped down.

Well, at least one side followed orders. Kris turned to her side of the square. "Put those safeties back on," she shouted, "and those rifles down. Don't go away, but for God's sake, let's not have any more accidents."

A low murmur swept the yard. Behind Kris, sailors looked around, measured the level of noise, and frowned worriedly.

"You do have a thousand rifles out there," Captain Slovo whispered behind his hand to Kris.

"Give or take a few hundred."

"I have more machine guns," Hank insisted.

"Maybe," Kris said, conceding nothing.

Captain Slovo turned to the gunny sergeant. "Please advise your commander that we are standing down. Have him withdraw his Marines back a row of businesses and hold himself in readiness."

"Aye aye, sir," the Marine saluted, and double-timed off.

"Now, shall we talk in private?" Kris said.

"I won't enter any terrorist's lair."

"Good. How about walking halfway over to the Fire Training Center. They teach people to fight fires," Kris added drolly.

Ron and Gassy came out the glass doors, giving Hank a good view of a machine gun aimed right at him, as Kris lead them toward the Fire Center.

"I will not be intimidated," Hank said.

"Fine. We're not trying to," Kris said.

They met in the middle. "I want my men back," Hank snarled.

"I want to know who raped our coeds," the mayor snapped.

"My men did no such thing."

"Good, then you won't mind us taking swabs from every mouth."

"I will not have my men's privacy violated."

The two men glared at each other.

"How about the mayor agrees to give you back your sailors and you agree to leave this planet?" Kris said.

"Kris, my police have two fully worked up rape kits. We have the DNA of the men who did this. It doesn't match any in our files. It likely came from off planet. I want justice for my women. Don't you?" That hit Kris in the gut. She'd never been raped. *Not yet.* Her idea of what to do to a rapist started with a rope and ended with him dead. Still. Here? Now?

"So, what do you want to do, Ron, go back to where we were a few minutes ago and see who has the last gunner standing?"

"That's fine with me," Hank snapped. "We will prevail."

"Don't be so sure. I've got grenadiers ready to barbecue your launches. And with all your men dirtside, Lieutenant

Kovar would easily take your ships. Even if you win here, you've lost. This sally was not well planned, Captain Slovo. Very sloppy."

"Some might say so."

Kris turned back to Ron. "How high a price are you willing to pay to get those rapists?"

Ron turned slowly to take in every part of the square; sailors, his riflemen, the machine gunners. He gritted his teeth and turned back to Kris. "Not that high a price. No, I can't."

"Are you willing to give up the sailors in your jail with no further judicial proceedings?" Kris said.

"If they are not identified by their fellow sailors, yes."

"No, I will not leave any of my men behind," Hank shot back.

"You would defend rapists," Ron roared, and moved in on Hank.

Hank whipped his saber out, not expertly, but well enough to almost take Ron's nose off. Made Kris glad for once her breasts weren't any farther out. "I will defend my sailors," he shouted.

Someone must have given Hank the five-second lecture on loyalty up in return for loyalty down. "Ron?" Kris said.

"I never want to see a Greenfeld ship docking at High Chance again. If one comes, we will not let it hitch on. You hear me."

"I'm sorry you feel that way, Ron. I thought we were friends," the commodore said diffidently, sheathing his sword.

Kris pushed Ron back as he lunged for his fellow alumni. "This is settled, Mayor. Let it stay settled."

"Go and don't come back."

"That will take some arranging," Hank said, turning to Kris. "Lieutenant, I assume you will stand pledge for this agreement."

"As Princess Kristine Longknife, I will assure that you get your sailors back, based on the promise given me by Mayor Torn," Kris said, biting out each word.

"Very good. Captain, arrange matters with the good lieutenant. I and the chief are leaving."

"You will have all your shuttles tied up returning these troops to your ships for now, won't you, Captain?"

"Yes," Slovo agreed. Kris noticed that Hank had withdrawn far enough to nod to the Command Master Chief who began marching the men off, but the commodore stayed well within earshot of whatever agreement was being made in his name.

"I would suggest you send ten launches down when you are ready to depart. I believe I can arrange for them to be launched as you are departing from the piers."

"You allow the first launch to take off and I will have the flagship undock," Captain Slovo said.

"With luck, we can have the last launch heading down the runway as your last ship cuts loose from the last tie-down."

The captain looked over his shoulder; the commodore nodded. "Agreed, Your Highness," he said, and saluted Kris. She returned the honor. Chief Meindl stepped over to stand beside Flag Captain Slovo and saluted. They turned and joined their commodore.

The sailors marched off by divisions. Kris watched until they were well on their way, then sent Jack up the tower to keep the watch. A cheer started. "Stow it," Kris commanded. "This isn't over until it's over. Gassy, you might want to visit with your NCOs or whatever you have. Get that message across. This situation isn't over until the last lander is off the ground."

Gassy glanced at his boss. "Do it," Ron said, and the cop trotted off as ordered.

"Sorry, I didn't mean to forget who was in charge here."

"There was no question who commanded here, Kris. I think Gassy was just showing he remembered who signed his paychecks."

"Every time I get into one of these things, it's with a cat-knitted ball of yarn for a chain of command."

Ron stood at the single step up to the Fire Center, watching the last sailors march out of the square. "I'm really going to let the rapist get off scot free," he muttered.

"I didn't agree to that," Kris said.

"Didn't we just agreed to return Hank's sailors?"

"Yes. But we said nothing about their condition at return."

Ron frowned. "What are you up to? You've just stopped a war, Longknife. I know that's unusual for your family. Are you going to start another one now?"

"I doubt it. Are you aware of the gauntlet?"

"A strong glove, maybe fire resistant?"

"But also an ancient form of punishment. You form two rows of nice, kindly folks with clubs, then someone runs between them. I'm surprised one of your commissioners hasn't done one."

"Who are the nice people you're thinking of?"

"The two girls that were raped. Their friends; boys and girls. Who do you think might be interested?"

"Half the planet," Ron sighed.

"I'll head topside as soon as the last launch is off. I'll let you know when the fleet will be leaving. You figure out what you want to do about getting the sailors to the landers."

Ron nodded and walked off. Jack stayed at Kris's elbow. "You hoping the girls flinch. Won't want to club the sailors?"

Kris thought about it for a moment. Things could get dicey if sailors got hurt. Was it better not to? Would she want to beat up the coworkers of someone who raped her and . . .

"I know I'd want to take a lead pipe to anyone who hurt you," Jack said.

Kris looked sideways at Jack. Whichever way it turned out, it was nice to learn that one thing about her nanny. Very nice.

17

Kris watched the *Incredible* cut loose its last tie-down with her station, very mixed emotions riling her gut. Hank was leaving, which was cause for much rejoicing. That Hank was leaving without paying an Earth dollar for the damage his men had done, left a very sour taste in the financial markets dirtside.

That the young women who'd been assaulted chose not to retaliate on the sailors, was no comfort to Kris. Part of her wanted to be down there with a thick leather strap. But there were five hundred sailors and only two rapists. And those rapists might very well have snuck out with the initial release of sailors that first night. Whenever Kris felt the need to pound on a Greenfeld sailor, the mental image that always came to her was Chief Meindl . . . and his wife and two children.

"I'm glad this dirty business is over," Kris muttered. This was part of the Longknife creed she'd never faced before. *We do the least lousy thing when all the other options are worse. Grampa Trouble, are there any more things about being a Longknife that you haven't mentioned?*

The first launch connected with the *Incredible*. There were more on the way, now. Carefully spaced, Hank was rewarded with fifty more sailors every time a ship started to pull out or completed the process. The sensor suites on the *Resolute*, *Wasp*, and even the *Patton* were up. At the first sign of hostility from the ships, Kris would be on the horn to Hank. If she didn't get immediate satisfaction, the station's 6-inch lasers would do their best to fillet and fry those ships. At this range, a 6-inch laser could do horrible things. Of course, return fire wouldn't leave much of the station in one piece.

Matters could still go south in a hurry.

Kris stood the watch, hand never far from the mike. Jack sat at the weapons station, his thumb next to the Weapons Release button. Today, full crews manned the lasers; they were fully charged and tracking. Kris expected a complaint from Captain Slovo, but the commlinks between ships and stations stayed at only those low levels necessary for getting underway details.

The last ship, Max Göckle's *Eager*, trundled down the pier, unlocked its bowline, and angled for the last launch. "Now we're most vulnerable," Kris whispered. "He's got all his crew back. We hold no cards."

"Hank ordered the squadron to form line on the flagship," Steve said from the comm desk. "No hostile sensor reports from our ships." The former and very recent commander of the station was in jeans . . . a chicken farmer once more to all appearances.

"Keep our lasers sighted on his rocket motors," Kris said.

"That's what I'm doing," Jack whispered. Out in space, the cruisers jockeyed into their positions. They were now a battle line. Kris held her breath.

"Message from the flag," Steve reported, the relief in his voice already telling Kris what would follow. "Begin one g deceleration on his mark. His mark is . . . now."

And the squadron broke orbit.

And the bridge broke out in cheers. Decorum regulations were excused long enough for everyone to hug someone . . . or two . . . or three. Well, not quite everyone. Kris stood like a rock at her station, watching as the ships continued their orbital change. Beside her, Jack sat, eyes on his board, looking for any change. Then, as the ships fell further and further away, he said, not looking up at Kris. "Permission to stand down."

Kris took a second to make sure she saw nothing wrong. Nothing changing. Then she sighed and sat down in the chair next to Jack. "Permission granted, Marine."

Jack eyed the people celebrating around them. He reached over and gently stroked Kris's back. She shivered at his touch. And his hand went away after one "pat on the back" that wasn't. "You did it, Kris. You took this planet through a major crisis, stopped a patented Peterwald takedown, and did it without a single person dying. This is better than Turantic."

"I had more support here. Ron was for me. And we did have two rapes. Them and buildings burned."

"Kris, no one gets a perfect score on one of these."

"What are your orders, Your Highness," Steve asked.

"You know you don't have to do that," Kris said. "I don't think Chance will ever recognize Wardhaven nobility."

"No, but I think a lot recognize you. Now, again, I ask what are my orders, or do you want me to salute?"

"Genuflecting should suffice," Jack said.

"And when did a squid ever take advice from a jarhead."

"Gentlemen," Kris said, "I've avoided one war this week. I don't have enough in me for another. Steve, tell your personnel to stand down. They can order whatever they want from the station's restaurants, watch a movie, whatever. The station will pay. I want a minimum staff left on all sensors. Keep the lasers charged. Hold everyone here for the next six hours. I want to make sure Hank's got a solid head of steam up for a jump point . . . and I want to know which one he's headed for."

Now Steve did salute, an informal thing that bore more respect than most in the history of that honor. "Aye, aye, ma'am. Now, if you don't mind me saying so, you look exhausted. You, too, Marine. Why don't the two of you get some sleep. I'll keep the watch. Anything goes wrong, you'll hear real fast."

"I could sleep the clock around," Kris said through a yawn.

"Me, too," Jack agreed, offering her a hand up. Somehow the hand stayed on her back as they left the Command Center. It was good he did; she kind of needed steering toward her stateroom.

Jack opened the door. Kris thought of inviting him in for a drink. But she saw her bed and had just enough energy to fall in that direction. A moment later she felt Jack removing her shoes.

She rolled over. And found herself smiling at Abby as her maid slowly unrolled her from undress khakis. Kris was asleep before her maid was done.

Quite awhile later, Kris awoke to find the clock across the room smiling at her as it told her it was eight o'clock. Having slept six hours solid, Kris hurriedly pulled on a shipsuit and shoes and headed out to look in on the Command Center.

"What're you doing here this early?" Kris asked Ramirez.

"I'm not the one that's early. You're the one that's late. Steve called to ask if I minded taking an extra half watch so he could go back to sleep."

Kris glanced at the duty board. "Oh lord, it's not eight p.m., it's eight a.m.! Where's Hank?"

"Still got his duckies in a row, following the leader right out of my, now quiet, system. Long may we never see him again."

"Which jump?"

"He's going for Alpha. Strange that. I'd have expected him to head home by Beta."

Kris slid into a seat next to the old chief. For a moment she studied the board. Yep, Hank's squadron had done a flip over and now decelerated toward Jump Point Alpha. "That *is* strange. Any idea where he's headed?"

"Nope, and no way am I calling that bunch of hooligans and asking. You want to?"

"No," Kris said. "Anyone else up?"

"We've got a full crew working. I'm powering down the laser capacitors; feeding their charge into the main power grid. We've got the reactor dialed down. They're doing maintenance they put off while that wild bunch was here. We're also policing up all the ammunition we signed out, getting it back under lock and key." Ramirez smiled. "We've got a couple of extra boxes of grenades. I understand they're from your personal reserve?"

"Give them back to Abby, my ofttime maid. Let her see if any are missing."

"Will do. You hungry?"

"Starving."

"Well, someone declared chow free yesterday, and I didn't get my meal. I don't think you did either. And, since, if the budget don't cover all the free food, Tony Chang says you get the bill, you might as well enjoy one." Kris laughed, and followed the chief down to a rather scrumptious breakfast buffet that did its best to make up for the last couple of days.

Stuffed to the gills, Kris did a friendly walk around the station, recognizing jobs well done, hearty efforts and, in general, letting all hands see that the boss was very grateful. Kris also did her own check that stairwells were no longer booby-trapped and auto guns had no belts. She eyeballed all the things that told her the station was back to normal and wouldn't give some unsuspecting kid a 4-millimeter buzz cut when someone leaned on the wrong section of board.

And there were plenty of kids underfoot. The *Patton* was booked solid for the next month with high school and junior high school classes doing sleepovers. The oldsters . . . and the high schoolers that had been working with them . . . put the final touches on everything before putting "their" ship up for viewing. Penny was up to her ears in that.

Kris corralled her for supper that evening.

"You should see what they've done with the old boat," Penny said, ignoring the menu. Kris told her of Captain Slovo's shock at being scanned by a fully commissioned if somewhat long-in-the-tooth light cruiser.

"I've got to tell the crew that. No, Your Highness, *you* have to tell the crew. Coming firsthand from you, they'll be good for another thousand hours of volunteer service."

"Don't they have lives?"

"I thought you were pretty happy with your Navy life?"

"Yes, but it's not like they can join up with Wardhaven or United Sentients. Chance is for Chance."

"Maybe things are changing. I know these folks have helped me change . . . see things . . ." Penny glanced away. "See that there is life after your heart's been ripped out of you."

Penny scanned the menu for a second. "You know that half of the old ladies working on the *Patton* are widows. About half of the old men are widowers. Despite all the hell we were in, two of them got married a couple, three days ago. Life goes on, Kris. It goes on and we might as well go along with it. Cause, kicking and screaming or willingly, we're going. It's either that . . . or get off. Tommy'd kick my butt if I did that."

"Both of ours," Kris said. She put her menu down. "You like these folks. I figured that you'd be concentrating on the *Wasp*, not the *Patton*."

"Oh, I've shanghaied a few folks from the *Patton* to get the *Wasp* good to go. And I've stolen a few hours out of Captain Drago's crew to get both of the other ships up. Fact is, Drago wants to swap me *Resolute* for the *Wasp*."

"I'm the one he has to talk to about that and there is no way I'm trading him even. He'll owe me if he wants *my* hot rod."

And that was the way the dinner went, half banter, half serious, half something far deeper than that. Right up to the time when both women refused the dessert tray and Penny got ready to go. "Oh, wasn't there something you were excited about when you came back from your vacation? You were going to tell me about it, but Hank jumped in."

"Right," Kris said, and leaned back in her chair, checked that they were pretty much alone, and said, "You're a very wealthy woman, or likely to be."

"Not from the last pay stub I looked at."

So Kris told Penny how she'd sworn the crew of the *Resolute* and her team to secrecy and what she was paying them to keep quiet about. "I guess I'm glad you included me in that, whatever it is, but since I don't know what you found, I don't really feel like I deserve being a part of it."

"Penny, if you hadn't been holding the fort back here, there's no way I could have gone off," Kris leaned forward and reduced her voice to a whisper "and found the biggest alien treasure chest since my Grampa Ray stumbled onto Santa Maria."

"Aliens!" Penny said, leaning forward herself and, if anything, getting out an even softer whisper.

Kris nodded. "A planet full of the stuff. Actually, two, but one of them's kind of gone back to nature. The other one is in pristine condition."

"Pristine condition?"

"Too pristine. The defensive gear is still on-line. Almost reduced us to dust. Getting there is just a start. Staying alive while we figure out the stuff will be a huge challenge."

"You've been sitting on this the whole time Hank was here!"

"Not exactly the thing I'd tell him. 'Pardon me while I run back to Wardhaven and give them the greatest news since humans first went into space. Oh, and by the way, don't bother anything here.'" Kris snorted. "No. I sat on it. But as soon as Hank jumps out of this system, the *Resolute* and I are headed back to Wardhaven, fast as we can go. You up to holding the fort again?"

"I'm getting good at that." Penny glanced at her wrist. "About time for Hank to make his jump out. Come watch it from the *Patton*."

So Kris found herself aboard Grampa Trouble's old ship, making nice noises to some very eager high schoolers and older folks. The kids were delighted to show Kris just what they could do with the ship's sensors. She was watching Hank's ships on their main screen as he came up to the jump.

The *Incredible* slowed to a crawl, taking the jump even more carefully than Kris would have, but there was no accounting for just what risks Hank was willing to take.

Then the *Incredible* flipped, goosed itself away from the jump and blew the jump buoy to bits.

"**There** is a call for you at the Command Center," Nelly said.

"No surprise," Kris muttered. Into the murmuring of the bridge, she said loudly, "Let's pipe down folks. We're about to face that gun-happy nut. Let's look professional here."

She stood, knowing her game face was back on. Beside her, Penny eyes had narrowed; her lips were thin. Game time. Kris glanced around the bridge; young faces eyed her, swallowed their shock, and put on the bland, if not deadly, face she showed them.

"They've seen what the *Patton* can do. You worry them. Let them stay worried. Okay, Nelly, tell the Command Center to pipe it through to the bridge of the *Patton*."

And there were Hank's perfect features, bigger than life. He had the camera tight on him, leaving his bridge out of focus behind him. "So, I caught you wasting time with kiddy cruisers. I thought you'd have bigger fans after what you did to me."

"I did nothing to you that you didn't do to yourself."

"Well, I know what you were doing. You may hoodwink that planet, but you can't keep a secret from good Peterwald intel. I know what you found on your little cruise. I know why you were willing to risk massacring all those people on Chance."

"I don't know what you're talking about," Kris said. *At least, not the way you're talking about it.*

"What's the matter, Longknife, don't want to admit you found a fortune in alien goodies even now. Afraid of what they'll do to you now that they know you were playing them for suckers."

"The people of Chance stood up to you because you were a bore and a bully who let rapists hide behind your uniform, Hank. I had little to do with you falling flat on your face."

"Oh, you're good, Longknife. Just like your old man, those old dotards pretending to lord it over the eighty worlds they're tyrannizing. But you screwed up, little girl. You're hanging out with no support. And now that I know your game, I'm going to pluck you like a chicken. This will be Peterwald space."

"Hank, I'm not out here alone. As you've already seen, there's a whole planet of folks that don't much care for you and what you're doing. Now, if you don't mind, I apparently have some unfinished business that needs taking care of."

"I'm coming for you. I'm going to slash your space station to wreckage, and that old wreck you're on, too," Hank was shouting as Kris cut the connection.

She paused for a moment to clear her mind, then said, "Steve, did you copy that message?"

"Kris, I've passed it dirtside. You want to talk to Ron?"

"No, I figure he's got enough problems at the moment," Kris glanced around the bridge of the *Patton*. Eager eyes, some youthful blue, others gray and bespeckled, looked back at her.

One of the old ones stood. "Your Highness, the *Patton* may be old, but she's no wreck. We'll show them. They'll see, right crew!" The shout echoed through the whole ship.

Kris bit her lip. Now was not the time to force these enthusiasts to face reality. That would come later. "Thank you. I have to talk to Commander Kovar. Penny, you're with me."

As Kris fast marched for the *Patton*'s gangway, she told Nelly to raise either Chief Beni or the *Resolute*'s Comm Chief. They both came up together. "We've got a problem," Kris said.

"So we heard," both answered.

"Close down the buoy at Jump Point Beta. No communications in or out and see that it doesn't make any jumps. Also, after you've done that, check its buffers and see if it sent anything from Hank in the last three days."

"We've been monitoring it. Nothing was sent," Beni said.

"Had the destroyed Alpha buoy sent anything from Hank?"

"No. Nothing. Other than playing boats right, boats left with his toys, Hank didn't send any messages."

"Double-check that. There's a lot riding on it."

"And it ain't our bonus for silence," the Comm Chief said.

A fast walk brought Kris to the command deck. There were several watchstanders, some in *Patton* greens. "I'd like to talk to Commander Kovar in private," Kris said, then waited as the rest filed out of the center.

"I, ah, didn't cut the commlink between me and you," Kovar said. "I heard the *Patton* crew offering you their services. I also remember you saying you'd buried enough enthusiastic amateurs after that Wardhaven dust-up."

Kris nodded. She studied the system board. While two ships hovered at the jump, four of Hank's ships were incoming at 2 g's acceleration. He'd be back in a day. Not much time to prepare even Kris's paltry force.

"Commander, I need your help." Kovar nodded.

"As I see it," Kris went on, "the odds against me are two to one, assuming I can get the *Wasp* and *Resolute* both fully crewed and involved in the fight."

"Four cruisers against an armed merchant ship and a corvette look like worse odds than that," Kovar said.

"I won't argue. The station has no ice, and its lasers would be powerless once the cruisers cut the cables to them. We can't fight the station. You'll have to order it abandoned."

Kovar nodded, but said nothing.

Kris turned to Penny. "How far does that contract you and Abby signed Captain Drago to go. Can I count on him in a fight?"

"I don't know. You'll have to ask him. And a few things may have changed since then, if you know what I mean."

"Nelly, find Captain Drago, send him my compliments, and ask him to meet me in my cabin. And where is Jack? I'd have figured him to be locked onto my elbow by now.

"He's in your cabin," Nelly answered. "With Abby."

"Good, that was my next stop. Commander Kovar, can you begin arranging for the evacuation of the station?"

"I think I can arrange things on the station the way you'll need them. What do I do about the *Patton*?"

"That's something I'll take care of myself." Kris glanced at Penny. "Maybe we can use whatever respect they have for my Princessness to keep them from letting their optimism kill them. Now, Penny, let's go see what Jack's doing with my maid."

In Kris's quarters, Abby sat in a high-back chair facing Jack. "When did you tell Hank?" the Marine demanded.

"I didn't tell Hank anything."

"What did you tell him?" shot back in rapid fire.

"I didn't tell him anything."

"Why did you tell him?"

"I didn't tell him anything." Despite the repetition, Abby made each answer come out fresh.

"How much did he pay you?"

"I'd never take money from that self-centered snot."

Jack turned and seemed to notice Kris for the first time. "She's your maid. You try getting something out of her."

Penny, the professional interrogator, sat down on Kris's bed, apparently content to leave this matter domestic. Kris got comfortable in the chair across from Abby, crossed her legs, and said, "Hank's headed back here with lasers charged."

"I heard something to that effect."

"He knows about our alien discoveries."

"Strange that."

"What side agreements do you have with Captain Drago?"

That did catch the maid by surprise. "Penny, here, signed the contract. Why ask me?"

"Because I can't help feeling you and Drago go together, not like salt and pepper. More like nitro and glycerin."

There was a hint of a smile at the edge of the maid's mouth. But she worried her lower lip for a moment before attempting an answer. "I suspect that you'll have to ask him, maybe his whole crew. What they signed for back then, and what they might do just now could maybe be two different things."

Kris nodded. "Not a bad idea. Now, back to what is such a bee in Jack's bonnet. How do you think Hank came to find out about our little secret?"

"I don't know. I do know he didn't get it from me."

"You didn't send him a message, like you sent that message after we jumped into this system on the *St. Pete*?" Jack snapped from over Kris's shoulder.

"I did not."

"Did not send the message to Hank, or the message from the *St. Pete*," Kris fired back.

"I said I sent no message to Hank. Nelly, you haven't cracked the cipher on the message from the *St. Pete*, have you?"

"No, I could not break the code." There was a pause. "Oops, was that a question I was not supposed to answer?"

"Don't worry, Nelly," Abby said. "I paid good money for that cipher. Even you shouldn't be able to crack it."

"And what are you sending in such a muscle-bound code?" Jack demanded.

Abby eyed Kris who raised an eyebrow to reinforce Jack's question. "That the princess, here, arrived safely at Chance."

"Nothing else?" came from both Kris and Jack.

Penny leaned forward from her place on the bed. "So that's how you earn extra money, reporting for the social circuit?"

"I'll never get rich like Kris here, but it does add to my retirement account."

"You're reporting on my movements?"

"Only what you'd read on any social page in a few days," Abby said, evenly.

"Social spy?" Jack didn't quite get it out evenly.

"I'm surprised you didn't spot it sooner," Penny said. "I used to get those reports and, frankly, I'm glad that no one asked me to write them. Saved me time."

"You knew!" Kris said, half out of her seat.

"Kris, servants have been making extra money reporting on their, ah, clients for years. It's part of my basic training to know who to hit on; how to. Not really necessary, now that most of them are working for your standard information providers."

"But if she gave out the wrong thing, it could . . ." Jack sputtered. "Kris could get killed if people knew . . ."

Kris, now standing, looked hard at her maid. Abby seemed intent on studying her hands. She didn't look up when she said. "I have never passed information that I knew or even suspected could lead to my employer's harm."

"But it didn't always work out that way," Kris said.

"No." Abby looked up. "There was one time when what I said, and what a couple of other people said, not all of us in her employ, added up to what someone needed. Yes."

Kris shook her head. "I need time to think about this, absorb it. Abby, consider yourself under house arrest. Don't even try to send out a message, coded or not."

Kris turned to the door. "Kris, I've been there for you," Abby said to her back. "I covered for you. I've never done anything to harm you."

Kris said nothing, but continued out the door. Jack and Penny followed her to collect in the hallway.

"Should I post a guard?" Jack asked.

"We don't have anyone," Kris said, thinking on her maid's words. "And who could stop her. You want to guard her?"

"I'm supposed to be guarding you," Jack said.

"Captain Drago is in the Command Center," Nelly said.

A moment later, Kris found Captain Drago at a workstation playing a complicated game against the computer. He stood when Kris entered. "Steve said you needed to see me."

"You know about Hank's U-turn at the jump point?"

"Rather hard not to."

"What are your plans for the immediate future?"

"I was thinking of heading for Jump Point Beta, until Sulwan showed me where it went. Peterwald. Peterwald, or, ah, Peterwald. Not so good an idea, I decided."

"What are you under contract for?" Kris asked.

"Ah, I signed up to check and restation jump buoys, at least that was what your lieutenant told me. But I've been rereading my contract and find that it's rather vague in key sections. Sections I don't much like at the moment."

"Hank and I are about to have a fight."

A wave of relief flowed over the captain's face. "Oh, much better. You two, pick your weapons, find a nice field down on Chance. Then you and him fight. Man to man, or girl to girl."

"Peterwald to Longknife," Kris said dryly.

"Right. You know what I mean! Just the two of you, cause if you were thinking of fighting it out, his squadron against whatever you can scrounge, and I know you're quite a scrounger, but, senorita, even you couldn't win against those odds. My *Resolute*, that ancient cruiser, and maybe your *Wasp* if you could find a crew for it. No. That is not a fight. It is suicide."

"We won't be using the *Patton*," Kris said.

"Right, good," the captain smiled. Then swallowed his smile. "We. Won't. For what?"

"For the coming fight. Just me on the *Wasp*, you on the *Resolute*," Kris said.

"Senorita!"

"You want the money for keeping the news about the aliens quiet?" Kris said.

"Woman, you drive a hard bargain," Captain Drago said, scowling. "I will talk to my crew."

"And check in with them about who might want to fight the *Wasp* with me," Kris called as he stomped out.

Kris turned to Steve, but he was eyeing his board. "Ron's calling. Want to take it here or in your room?"

"How are things dirtside?"

"Went from dancing in the streets to digging shelters in about two seconds," Ron said. Kris hoped that was hyperbola. "I think I know how Hank found out about your alien find."

"What's your guess?" Kris said.

"No guess. I just finished talking to a barkeep of a small bistro on the south side. A couple of days ago, some of the crew from the *Resolute* took to drinking there with that chief of yours."

"I think I heard about it," Kris said. Jack nodded.

"That last night, while all of us were otherwise occupied, it seems two fellows, decked out like locals but as strange a pair as this barkeep ever saw, were buying drinks for that table.

After your chief and sailor left, the strangers and the last two did some serious drinking. They talked in whispers, got real quiet when he was around, but one word came up several times while he was in earshot. Aliens."

Kris said a very unprincesslike word.

"Yeah, kind of my thoughts, too."

"Well, it takes a lot of pressure off my maid, though I've found out more about her than I really wanted to. How are things really down there?"

"About what I'd expect. Some of our businessmen are making plans to profit from the coming adjustments. Other folks are stocking food and ammunition where they figure to need it. Have you noticed how some of the planets that the Peterwalds take over just drop off the news coverage. I don't think Chance will be getting many tourists if Hank takes over. Much of anything."

"I'll try to do something about that," Kris said.

"That a Longknife promise?"

"Yep."

"Don't promise more than you can deliver."

"Right," Kris said. "Now, I've got to talk to some folks on the *Resolute*, then explain to some optimists that they can't fight a ship as old as the *Patton*, then get ready for a fight. At least this time, we won't have to wait so long. Hank's coming in at two g's."

"Good luck on the *Patton*," Ron said, and hung up.

Kris headed for the door, but paused. "Steve, can you get four shuttles up here to evacuate the *Patton*?"

"I've got six shuttles due in two hours. That enough?"

"Probably," Kris said, and headed for her contract ship. On the *Resolute*, Penny did the interrogation. It quickly became apparent that Chief Beni and the Comm Chief had left the bistro early to catch the midnight shuttle. That left the Engineer and Doc. Both returned late the next morning and claimed to remember little of their talk with their benefactors. Pressed on the point of aliens, they allowed that the topic may have come up but that they had said nothing, or had no memory of it. Really, they had no memory of saying anything.

Captain Drago took Kris aside. "You think my guys spilled the chili peppers?" Kris nodded.

"You're going to fight this Hank fellow."

"Can't let him take this planet down. Folks dirtside are getting ready to form a guerilla resistance. Least I can do is try to hold the space above them."

The captain shook his head, then glanced around his bridge. Sulwan Kann shrugged. Most of the crew looked like they'd rather be boosting out, but . . . "I guess we'll be fighting with you."

"Thanks. Now, if you'll excuse me, I have to rain on some happy optimists' parade."

"You aren't cutting us out of any support, are you?"

"None that would really matter," Kris said, and left the *Resolute* before the captain could raise further debate.

At the *Patton*'s pier, Kris had Penny go aboard and order all hands to form divisions on the pier. Then Kris took position at parade rest, facing the quarterdeck. Slowly at first, then in a flood, the green and blue shipsuits poured out of the cruiser. The kids in green seemed to come at a gallop; the blue suiters came slowly, some hobbling with canes. They formed in divisions across from Kris. Maybe they were a bit ragged at first, but the old hands hadn't forgotten and the new kids were quick learners.

It would have been easier on Kris if it wasn't so. Finally, two lone women, their gray hair in buns marched across the brow as smartly as their wooden canes allowed. They marched through the space between Division 2 and 3 to stand at attention before Kris. The one on the right saluted.

"Ship's crew is formed, Commander. We await your orders."

"Place the crew at ease," Kris ordered, and it was so.

Kris reviewed the speeches she'd made. She'd talked unprepared troops into a firefight . . . once or twice. She'd talked ships into mutiny and battle. Talking willing hands into standing down was something she'd never figured to be a part of.

"You have done a fantastic job of turning a hazard to navigation into a functioning ship. And you did it in an amazingly short time." The ranks rumbled with pride at that.

"You have formed yourself into one of the finest crews that a commander could ask for." That got a roar of approval.

"Four cruisers, however, are heading in, only a day out."

"We can beat'em," someone shouted from the rear ranks. That also got a cheer.

"You are not going to make this easy for me, are you?" Kris said. That brought silence.

"The heart of a warship is steel and gear, lasers and crew. It also is training. And training for a fight is one thing that time has not allowed you. Will not allow you."

The old woman who'd ordered the crew to stand easy frowned into the silence that brought. "A lot of us that fought the Iteeche didn't get much training before we faced those monsters."

"And a terrible lot of you died because of that," Kris shot back. "It makes for heroic vids, but I've seen the look in my great-grandfather's eyes as he remembers the orders he gave. Sees again the faces of those who died on his words."

Kris let her gaze wander over the puzzled faces before her. "I do not want to be seeing your faces for the rest of my life. You will not take this relic into battle."

"But we want to, Your Highness," the older woman said. "You see this ship as just a hulk your great-grampa once sailed in. We know it's better than that. It's good to go, ma'am. We may be gray or green but we're ready to take her out. We can do it."

Kris took a deep breath, and closed her eyes for a second. That was a mistake. She saw the faces of a family that had crewed its system runabout. It had been converted into a missile boat, a decoy for Kris's mosquito boats.

Every system runabout died defending Wardhaven.

"You are correct that you are gray," Kris said, saying her words carefully; slowly. "To stay alive in a fight, the *Patton* must dodge at two or three g's. It must jink at those g's. Do you honestly think that your bones could take that punishment?"

"Yes," the gray head replied.

"I respectfully disagree," Kris snapped back. "All it would take is one person crumbling at a key moment to cost all of you your lives. Just one green sailor's misstep and again, you are dead. Battle is not forgiving. I know. I've been there."

"So have we," the woman said. She turned to look around. "I dare say none of us ever wanted to go there again." Gray or bald heads nodded agreement. "But here we are. Chance needs us. I figured I'd done the bleeding and sweating for my family. I sure as hell didn't want my great-granddaughter to ever go through what I did when I was her age, but she's here, and I know she's training and she says she wants to fight for Chance. Who am I to say she can't? And who are you, Kris Longknife?"

Kris had tried all the logic she had. She hated to be reduced to what was left. "I am Commander, Naval District 41. That ship behind you is in my jurisdiction. The station you stand on is under my command. You are trespassing on Wardhaven Property. I order you off this property."

That caused consternation in the ranks.

"We could refuse your orders," the woman said. "I understand that you've had some experience in that."

"I have," Kris admitted. "If you refuse to go, I will give you no orders. You will be a rogue ship in the middle of a battle. You'll be a danger to yourself and those around you."

"You are a hard, obstinate young woman."

"I'm a Longknife. I do what I have to do. Now, please face your crew left and march them down to the shuttle bay. There will be transportation in fifteen minutes to take you dirtside."

"You already had your mind made up."

"Yes," Kris said. "I've buried all the optimistic amateurs I can bear for one year."

"Maybe you have, but you're making a mistake here." Then the woman did an about face, steadied herself on her cane, and in a voice that belied her years, announced, "Ship's crew. Left. Face. Ship's crew, by divisions. Forward. March." And a moment later. "Incline to the right. Green suits take the stairs. Blue suits, as necessary, fall out and take the escalators. We're heading for the shuttle bay."

"Jack, I saw a couple of kids duck out of ranks and sneak back aboard. You and Penny police up the ship for strays."

"As you wish, Lieutenant," Jack said, his voice brittle.

"What's the matter, you agree with the old lady?"

"I just never figured you to discourage service."

"I'll get better with practice," Kris grumbled.

"I hope you're right to send them away," Penny said. "We are in quite a mess."

Kris had no answer. She turned on her heels and hurried to catch up with the *Patton*'s erstwhile crew. They'd broken ranks to get up from the pier area. At the top of the stairs, Kris found divisions marking time to give the escalator contingent time to rejoin, then they marched off at a slow pace. The scene would give any Gunny Sergeant DI at OCS apoplexy, but—in its own way—it was smart enough.

Kris slow marched with them. Every once in a while, she'd catch a head turned her way. The eyes were puzzled, angry, and stubborn. But they marched. The drop to the shuttle bay meant another stair/escalator exercise. There, the woman tried twice to order the crew into the waiting shuttles, but broke down both times. "I can't do it. You'll have to," she whispered to Kris.

"By divisions into the shuttles," Kris ordered. "Column of files from the right to the left." She paused as file leaders shouted, "Follow me" or "Stand fast." Damn but someone had trained them well. If only she could trust them with lasers.

"Forward March," Kris ordered.

"Belay that order," boomed from Deck 1 above Kris.

As the divisions fell into the confusion of "Order. Counter order. Disorder," Kris whirled to find Lieutenant Steve Kovar standing at the top of the stairs. Before she could get out a demand, he answered her question.

"You can't load a shuttle until it's unloaded, Your Highness, and those shuttles are loaded."

Kris whirled again . . . *this is making me dizzy* . . . to see old chiefs and petty officers in uniform, younger folks in blue shipsuits, and more in green file out of the shuttles. Kris quick marched for the stairs as Steve came down them. She waited until they met in the middle to ask, "What's going on here?"

"The retired staff of Naval District 41, the associated volunteers, their kid brothers, big sisses, dogs, and cats are coming back to roost. We've got a station and three ships to crew and that's going to take quite an effort." He coughed into a hand. "It's not for me to tell you how to crew your district assets, ma'am, but you might want to reconsider sending all these folks home. Some of them, the grayest, the greenest, do need to go dirtside, but all of them?"

Kris felt a flash of anger. "I told you I wasn't going to fight a defenseless station, a museum relic. I won't have people dying for nothing."

"If we lose the high ground, Lieutenant, a lot of my friends are going to die in a hopeless resistance. Kris, Chance was never meant to be occupied; ordered around by someone like Hank. He's called us out. It's personal now. We fight him on the high ground. We fight him on the shuttle landing grounds. We fight him in the streets and in the hills. I read that some-where. Forget who said it, but he could have been talking about us here.

"As I see it," Steve went on, "your job now is to command the force we crew. Hank's inbound at two g's so we don't have a lot of time. Shall we quit wasting what we have?"

"You know we're all crazy," Kris said.

"Better to be crazy than defeated."

Jack and Penny smartly marched up six girls and boys in green shipsuits. He took in the scene and raised an eyebrow. "So, what do I do with this bunch of fire-breathing dragons?"

Kris eyed the shuttle bay. The new arrivals were forming up at their chief's orders, facing the *Patton*'s crew.

"What would you do?" Kris said, not looking at Steve.

"I'd authorize my chiefs and petty officers to comb through the *Patton*'s crew; find the ones they can put to use. Sign up the green suits as trainees, the blue suits as assistants. Then I'd get this station and that cruiser ready for what's coming."

Kris wanted to say "be it on your head," to wash her hands of what she saw coming. But a Naval officer can't do that. In-stead, she stood to attention. "Proceed as you propose."

Steve saluted. "With your permission, Your Highness."

Kris returned his salute. "Carry on. I'll be in the Command Center. Report there when you're done here."

Penny waved the dragons to rejoin their crew. Having heard the officers, they raced to spread the word. Jack and Penny formed on Kris. "So now we fight with everything we can beg, borrow, or steal," he said.

"Again," Kris said. "You'd think just once we could do this with a decently trained and ready bunch of ships and sailors."

"Why send a fleet when a certain princess will make do?" Jack said.

Which almost made Kris miss a step. Was she getting so good at yanking miracles out of hats that someone thought all they had to do was send a hat and her. She very much hoped that wasn't true. Because if they thought Grampa Trouble was a problem, they had no idea what Princess Kris could be.

Assuming she survived this particular hat trick.

"Which ship will you take out?" Penny asked.

"I think Steve wants to fight the station," Kris said slowly. "Drago probably will be best with the *Resolute*. I'm thinking I should take out the *Patton*. It's got the most fire power and ice armor. If it actually can fight, it's our best ship. You've spent time on the *Patton*. Is it good to go?"

"They coated it with a few inches of ice last week. It'll need more. The lasers look fine, but none have been fired. The engines look good, but, again, they haven't actually been run. We need to break her loose and give her a test run. Soon."

Kris nodded. "What do you say we both do that."

"So if you take the *Patton*, who gets the *Wasp*?" Penny said. "You want it?"

"I've studied what you did at Paris debriefing the *Typhoon*'s crew. I was with you at Turantic and Wardhaven. Who do you have here that's better at conning a small combatant? Yes, I know I've been an intel weenie my whole career, but, Kris, you got to know there isn't a JO hatched that doesn't want her own command."

Kris considered the request; there wasn't anyone handy close to her experience and qualifications for the *Wasp*. Should she bounce Penny to the *Resolute* and give Drago the bigger ship? Change this late was never good. No. Penny deserved the *Wasp*.

But was Penny a *good* call? Was a grieving widow the best person to command what might be Kris's best combatant, if the *Patton* went flat? Would she command the ship as well as she said she could . . . or would she go berserker on Kris at a critical moment? Would she follow orders, or lose herself in a killing rage to get Hank, the son of the man who killed her husband?

Neither giving Penny the *Wasp*, nor giving someone else the ship was a good bet, but Kris would have to lay her money down, and now was better than later. "Is the *Wasp* ready for a shoot?"

Penny mulled that over as they came to the escalators down to the *Resolute*. "Materially, she's good to go," Penny said. "I assume we're going to talk Drago into loaning a few hands. Steal some from Steve. But yes, you give the order and the *Wasp* will answer all bells, and be underway with all pulse lasers loaded."

"Then she's your baby. Take good care of her," Kris said with a smile she really felt. "I don't think I've made the last payment on her."

"I'll try not to scrape the paint."

Down the escalator, they headed for the ship. "Shall I call Abby and tell her she's out of hack?" Jack asked.

"Let her stew for a while," Kris said. "I don't like the idea of someone selling news about me. I've never liked the newsies. I don't see any reason I should like it in my maid."

"We might could use her?" Penny pointed out. "She brought twelve steamer trunks this trip. Who knows what's in them?"

"I'll talk to her about that later. Right now, we need to juggle crews."

Captain Drago was not at all happy to have a draft put on his ship to seed the others. Interestingly, he never asked Kris for the *Wasp*. He did ask for Smart Metal. Kris promised him all she had left to coat the *Resolute* and headed back to the Command Center. There, she relented and sent Jack to explain what they now knew and release Abby from house arrest.

"Do I bring her back?" he asked.

"You decide. If she's got some good tricks to share . . . and knows what she sees here isn't shared."

Jack returned with Abby about the same time Steve arrived. "I've got our folks organizing. You going to need any of them for the other ships?" Penny beamed him a list of what she wanted for the *Wasp* and what they'd stolen from the *Resolute*. He glanced down the list. "We can do that. Hilary," he shouted.

A girl in greens ducked in the door; Steve printed out the list Penny had sent. "See that this gets to Chief Ramirez." And the girl was gone like a rabbit.

"I kept some spare troops that didn't make it to permanent party as runners. Let's keep our communications to something Hank can't hack, and let these track stars earn their keep."

"How many did you keep as permanent?" Kris asked.

"A bit over half of *Patton* had bigger brothers or sisters willing to stand for them. If Momma Howe said they knew their job, we took them. Then I added the runners. I'll get them out of here before the shooting starts, okay, Your Highness."

"Momma Howe?"

"Yeah. The woman you were bulldogging when I came up. She's good. A might bit slowed down by the hip replacement, but with that cane, a solid traveler. I'll use her and a lot of the blue suiters on the station. There won't be any high g's here."

"How do you fight a station that just has to sit here?"

"Who told you a station just sits and takes it?"

"Nobody, they just all do. Sit," Kris said. "The 6-inch lasers on Hank's cruisers can reach out sixty thousand klicks and are really effective at twenty thousand. If they can see you, they can shoot you full of holes."

Steve took a seat at a workstation. Leaning back, he put his feet up on it and his hands behind his head. "I spent ten years worrying about what I could do if someone wanted my bit of space. Ten years—with some of the most twisted minds on the Rim—can be quite an education."

Kris settled into a chair, leaned back and got comfortable.

Captain Merv Slovo brought his high g station along-side that of his superior. "Commodore, I believe it would be better for our coming combat if we dropped down to 1 g now."

"And why delay the moment of truth for Longknife?" asked Commodore Henry Smythe-Peterwald the Thirteenth, Hank to some.

"Our men have been confined to their high g carts for most of the last day, sir. They need a hot meal and time to make ready for battle. Equipment needs checking. That is best done at 1 g, Commodore."

Squadron 38's commander turned to look directly at his flag captain. "I was told this squadron is experienced in long cruises. Didn't you practice high g ops on that four-month cruise of yours?"

"We most certainly did, Commodore." Captain Slovo ig-nored the slap . . . with an effort. A well practiced effort. "However, over half of that crew was reassigned to new con-struction or filling out the crews of recommissioning ships. Our present crew is heavily spliced with green sailors fresh off the farm. The last day will have been hard on them. If you want their full effort against Lieutenant Longknife, you will need to make some accommodations to their limits, sir." *Always end with a "sir."*

The young commodore gnawed his lower lip. "That will delay our arrival, give that Longknife girl more time to do things."

"With what, sir? As you pointed out, all she has is a broken-down cruiser, a rented buoy tender, and that other ship of strange antecedents." It was usually good to quote Hank back upon himself. Usually . . . not always.

The young commander looked away. "You can never trust a Longknife. That is the first thing I remember my dad saying. 'Never trust a Longknife. They'll say one thing and do whatever makes money for them.' "

Captain Slovo had found it was usually better to leave references to the senior Peterwald untouched. The younger of the title tended to swing widely in his attitude toward the senior.

"What do you think she'll do when we get there, Merv?"

The question was both unusual and difficult to answer. The captain weighed his options, and spoke. "That is very hard to say, Commodore. Any rational person would take advantage of our arrival to duck behind the planet and bolt for a jump point."

"Longknifes are never rational. She's going to fight me. How will she fight me, Captain? You've studied war for twenty years. I'm supposed to listen to you. Well, talk."

Was the boy getting that nervous, or was this another one of his traps? The flag captain chose to take the risk and do his duty. "That very much depends on what she has to fight with. We know the station has a dozen lasers. However, a station is very vulnerable. We should be able to silence it quickly. The ancient cruiser is a question mark. It has nine 6-inch lasers. How many work? It could be fully iced and armored. Then again, its motors might fail to contain plasma, and it could blow up first time it pulls away from the pier. The *Resolute* has a strange history of late. Let's assume they are hiding at least one, maybe two 12-inch pulse lasers. The *Wasp* is truly an unknown, but why would a Longknife give it a name like *Wasp* if it has no sting. I'd assume another pair of pulse lasers."

The captain shrugged. "Our squadron mounts thirty-six 6-inchers and two dozen 21-inch pulse lasers. If she fights—no matter how—it will be a short fight."

"And a bloody one for her." The commodore seemed to like the sound of that. "A very bloody one for her and those foolish enough to follow her." He clenched his fist. "Wait until my father sees what I've got him. This time it will be all ours. And I made the deal. *I* made the deal."

"Yes, sir." There was nothing more to add to that.

"Slow the fleet, Merv. Tell the navigator to come up with a new course. And tell him to have us go into orbit and then come up on the station, like you suggested. No need to wave our vulnerable sterns even at what little Kris has."

"Aye aye, sir." And Captain Slovo went to do his master's bidding; praying softly that one Longknife would be smart enough to take the time he was offering her, coming up slowly on the orbit of her station, to yank up her skirts and run as fast as she could for Jump Point Adele. The boy wonder here would be greatly disappointed when there was no battle, but even Merv couldn't calculate the disaster for humanity if the Peterwald heir killed a Longknife heir.

Much better that these two don't meet.

Kris tightened the buckle on the command chair of the *Patton* and surveyed her domain. It was good to be in 0g again. Sensors were on-line, crewed by a chief, an old blue, and two young greens. They tracked Hank's squadron on final approach. Good.

Hank was going to make an orbit before approaching the station. Kris had hoped he would. If it was to give her time to run, well, even Hank must know that Longknifes don't run.

The delay *had* given Kris time to finish armoring the *Patton*; the cruiser now sported a meter of ice on her bow, half that elsewhere, beneath a thin coat of aluminum spray for added reflection. The ice was courtesy of Hank. His ships had pulled out without reclaiming the sewage they'd passed to the station. Treated, it now protected Kris.

Chief Ramirez was almost giggling when she reported that they had found two packets of high explosives when they drained the sewage out of the holding tanks. Rigged to explode when they came in contact with methane, they'd been jettisoned. The *Patton* used them for gunnery practice. Seven of the nine lasers had worked the first time. Two were being worked on.

To Kris's great relief, the superconductors in five motors held their plasma. The *Patton* hadn't blown her stern to kingdom come and they were now parked at Pier 7, a tie-down Kris had only learned about when Steve introduced her to it. It put the old cruiser's engines right in the middle of the station's backside. A perfect place for what they had in mind.

Now, Kris waited.

"Bogies are five minutes from sliding behind Chance," Steve reported from the station. "*Resolute*, you cut loose first."

Since the *Resolute* was the most likely ship to run, her undocking shouldn't tell Hank any more than he wanted to hope for. A few minutes later, it was the *Wasp*'s turn. The two ships hung just off the station.

"Station is rebalancing," Steve reported as liquids were pumped from one section of the station to another to perfectly balance her now that no ships hung off the edges.

"Bogies are behind Chance. The station is balanced. Let's rotate." Small station-keeping jets on High Chance, aided by the *Patton*'s maneuvering units, reoriented the station until the *Patton*'s engines were pointed opposite to its orbit.

"Navigator, have you laid in a course?" Kris asked.

Sulwan grinned. "Down to a gnat's eyebrow, ma'am."

"Execute on your mark. Station, prepare to change orbit."

"We're rigged and ready," Steve reported.

"Orbital burn commencing . . . now," Sulwan reported, and Kris was pressed slightly back into her seat as the *Patton* slowed High Chance and started the station into a dive for lower orbit.

This was not something suggested in the station's manual. But High Chance was among the smallest stations built in the last hundred years; that left her with a bit more flexibility than most. And Steve's crew had added reinforcements at certain weak locations. He swore his baby could do it, and just now, she was.

Assuming the *Patton* perfectly balanced the burn from her five working motors. And the station's tie-downs didn't rip out

under the strain. And Pier 7 was still at the exact center of
gravity for the station. And about a dozen other assumptions
that Kris hadn't thought of yet.

They must have all held. High Chance stayed together and
headed down. And at the right moment after High Chance had
swung close by the planet, Kris would interrupt the long
slingshot of that orbit with a burn that parked the station in a
lower orbit.

Kris checked her board. Laser 6 was now taking power.
Laser 7, aft, was still down. Well, she planned to tackle Hank
head on anyway.

"Where is she?" the commodore demanded.

Flag Captain Merv Slovo noted that his young superior
didn't ask where the station was, where the opposing forces
were? No, it was "where is she?" Not for the first time he
tasted the animosity between the young man and the woman.
Letting a fight get personal had never been recommended in
Command and Staff School. Clearly, the boy needed more
book learning.

The captain leaned forward in his command chair. Normally, a flag officer would have his own bridge, own battle
station. Someone high above Slovo had decided that the
commodore and the captain should share their space. *I wonder if they had any idea how much stomach lining this would
cost me?*

"Clearly, neither the station nor the ships are where they
once were. Interesting first move on her part."

"I don't need to be told where she isn't. Where is she?"

"Sensors?"

"We have residue of ionized exhaust. Lots of it."

"Moving a station. Interesting."

"She's headed for the moon. That's what she did
against . . ." The flag captain shot his commodore a withering
glance. *Don't say it . . .* "Ah, the intruders at Wardhaven."

Slovo glanced at his board. It didn't make any sense to
head for Chance's one moon. It was close, and there was no
question the ships could make for it but—moving a station
that far? "I'm not sure about that, Commodore."

"Boost for the moon," Commodore Peterwald ordered. "She's doing to us what she did to—ah—them. You'll see."

"That will involve more deceleration, dropping into a lower orbit. We'll be less able to see what's going on."

"Trust me. I know that woman. She can only think of one thing at a time. And once she's found a good solution to a problem, she'll keep using it. No flexibility."

Why did that sound so much like a description of the young man saying it? Slovo thought, but said, "Navigator, lay in a course for the moon."

"Aye aye, sir. I'm already working on it."

"Get us on that heading for the moon." The young man ordered the older.

"Yes, sir." Who knows, maybe the Longknife girl had headed for the moon. And if she hadn't, the squadron would be safe for the trip. *Maybe I can talk some sense into this young man. Not likely, but maybe.*

The report came in from a ground station when Kris and company were on the other side of Chance. "Four headed for the moon?" Steve said. "They took the bait."

"At Wardhaven, we attacked the invaders after a swing around our moon," Kris said. "I guess he thinks I'm predictable." Big mistake. "Nelly, run me an assumed 1 g trip for Hank to the moon and back. Then calculate an orbit that will put us coming out from behind Chance as he comes back."

"Assuming he comes back headed straight at us," Nelly said, "you need to be in a 149 kilometer high orbit."

"Sulwan, can we do that?"

"Just barely. Starting a burn now," she said and the *Patton* began to push the station into orbit.

"Very good, Sulwan. Nelly. Very good." Assuming she'd judged Captain Slovo right. He struck her as a head-on man, not a long tail-chase kind of guy. A few hours would tell.

Kris leaned back in her chair. On her board, Lasers 2 and 6 were now down. Laser 7 was up. It was that kind of day.

"Sensors, keep an eye on Jump Point Alpha. We haven't sent any communications for a couple of days," Kris said. "Sooner or later, someone's bound to get curious. I know

I would. With luck, they'll send a couple of battleships to ask what's up."

"Yes, ma'am," the old chief said.

"If I knew there was a Longknife on the other side," Jack said from his seat near the helm where he could keep a good eye on everything, "I'd send a whole squadron of battleships."

"Not everyone has such a low opinion of me, Lieutenant."

Jack glanced around the bridge and made a face.

"No fair polling my subordinates," Kris said.

"Ah, we've just been scanned by the Greenfeld squadron, ma'am," the chief reported.

"I wonder how it will go over?" Kris said, and smiled.

"I'll be in my cabin," the commodore said, stamping from the bridge. "Call me when you have something useful to tell me."

Captain Slovo watched him go—and breathed a sigh when he was gone. The entire bridge seemed to relax around him. Then he turned back to his ordered duty. "How do I force this Longknife girl to battle," he muttered. And maybe arrange it so that one or the other of them can realize that they are getting the worst of the fight and run. "Navigator, when we complete this moon trip, I want us in an orbit opposite that station."

"Opposite, sir?"

"Yes. I don't want to have to chase her around and around that damn ball. Let us trade shots at each other twice an orbit and with the range on our lasers, we'll be shooting at her a great deal of the time. She may dodge me some of the time, but she can't do it forever. All it will take is a couple of good hits to end this thing." And every ship in the squadron had an E for gunnery.

"Yes, sir."

18

Kris had the station where they wanted it—way lower than the specs allowed. Kris could almost feel the heat as the *Patton* and station collided with the microatmosphere at this altitude. Low and fast, that should make them harder to see, and harder to hit. Then again, the station was a sitting duck and the duck hunters had very long-range guns.

Unless Kris could talk that hunter out of a duck dinner.

First she needed to unhitch from the station and join her other ships. "Station. Prepare to undock us."

"There's a problem. Didn't you notice a clang awhile ago."

"No."

"Well, we did. The trundles on your tie-downs are off their rollers. Unless we can move them, you can't move."

So maybe they hadn't quite balanced the fire of the five working motors to make up for the two useless ones. "Steve, I don't look like much of a threat to Hank with your station hanging off the snout of my ship."

"We're working on the problem."

"I either roll out of here or I shoot my way out."

"Anyone ever tell you you have quite an attitude."

"Several."

Kris sat back in her command seat and glowered at her board. Now Lasers 7, 8, and 9, her entire stern battery, were down. *This is great. Where I have lasers, there's this station in my way, and where I don't have anything, my butt is hanging out.*

Commanders were supposed to remain calm. Inspire confidence. Kris gnawed the inside of her lip and tried to fake it.

"Ah, Kris, could you try reverse on your maneuvering jets. Just a gentle tap," Steve asked. "Remember, you've got to push this station out of this orbit real soon."

"And fight. Helm, you heard the man. Just a tap." There was a horrible noise forward and the entire ship swayed.

"Thank you. That was a bit more than we wanted," Steve said.

"I couldn't do any less," the helmsman pleaded.

"You did fine. Steve, please fix this."

"Ma'am, they're coming out from behind the moon," the sensor chief said. "It looks like the bogies will come back at Chance in a clockwise orbit to our counterclockwise one."

"Exchange broadsides as we pass." Kris called up a draft plan on her board. Twenty thousand klicks out was when the 6-inch laser started to get accurate, and the pulse lasers on the *Wasp* and *Resolute* began to have any effect. Today, that range was irrelevant. With the planet limiting their line of sight in orbit, they'd be swapping lasers at point-blank range. But then she'd known she was in deep trouble when she took this job.

"Steve, I really need to be on my own way sometime today. Penny, Drago, stretch it out like we planned. I'll join later."

"Roger," came back at Kris. The two ships that had flown in close formation with the station while it did its wandering, now changed orbit. With a bit of luck, they'd confuse Hank.

"We think we've released the attachments that were holding you. Try that back out again. But real careful," Steve said.

"Our helmsman will try."

It didn't work. Worse, Kris felt a wind on her face that stirred ugly memories. She mashed her comm button. "All hands. Look around your area. We may have a small hole in the hull."

"Yes, ma'am, we do," came a tense, if eager young voice. "Laser Bay 1. We're working on it. Didn't want to bother you."

"Bother me. How big is it?"

"Not much, ma'am. Just a split seam where the ice got shoved back. We've got goo on it and are putting a solid patch on top of that. We shouldn't be losing any more air."

Kris did not need the old seams on this tub unzipping from nap to chaps. "Keep on it. Are you folks in suits?"

"No, ma'am."

"Get in them." Kris paused, then switched comm to the station. "Steve, I'm holed and leaking air. I'm not in any position to try to muscle my way out. You've got to cut me loose, or I shoot my way out. You see another option?"

"There is one. Chief Gentle wants to blow the tie-downs."

"Chief Gentle wants to blow me out!"

"Yeah, I always got a kick out of having a demolition expert with that name. Really does fit the man. You game?"

Kris glanced at sensors. Hank was about an hour out. If everyone stayed where they were, they'd have a shooting pass at each other just as he came into orbit. "Let's try the boom."

Then, switching back to ship. "All hands. They're going to try to blow the tie-downs holding us. If you're forward, either get in a space suit or lay aft. I don't want to use our survival pods this early. Let's dog all airtight hatches and pray."

"Steve, give me a ten count before you pop us."

"I'm a minute away from doing that." A very long minute.

"Helm, I want you to give us another boost when he hits zero. If those tie-downs need any extra help, let's give it."

"But what about our seam forward?"

"It's my job to worry about that. You worry about making sure we don't slam into anything hard as we get out of here."

The helm leaned over his board, muttering something about being glad he wasn't a part of that woman's Navy. He liked worrying about what he wanted to worry about. Which reminded Kris she commanded a collection of volunteers, not sworn sailors.

Hold together, she prayed, for both ship and crew.

"Here's your count. Ten. Nine. Eight. Seven. Six. Five. Four."

"Helm stand by."

"Two. One."

"Power!" Kris ordered.

The hull shook and groaned. Then the *Patton* threw them forward as she backed away from the station."

"Damage control reports," Kris demanded. Her board lit up in only one place. Laser Bay 1 had popped its patch. They were working to replace it. The hole was no larger. Here and there, minor things had broken, but she noticed that now Lasers 8 and 9 were taking a charge and Lasers 1 and 6 had joined 7 off-line.

The temptation to boost for Jump Point Alpha flitted across Kris's mind, but she had a promise to keep to Ron. And Longknifes never ran and she wasn't going to start any new traditions. She angled the *Patton* to put it in the lead of the other ships, and made ready to receive Hank's greeting.

"We could come in high and slash the station to ribbons on our first pass," Commodore Peterwald said, studying the flag captain's battle board.

"That would eliminate one of our threats," Captain Slovo agreed. "However, it would let those three ships maneuver up our tail and take slices out of our vulnerable engines. And your father might prefer to get this planet with a working station."

"It won't survive long in that orbit."

"Yes, but just as they moved it down, we can move it up."

"So you suggest we go straight for Longknife and her junk-yard collection. I like that."

That wasn't exactly what Captain Slovo had intended. And he certainly wasn't happy to have his commander disparaging the enemy he faced. Military history was full of too many ragtag-and-bobtail forces that won against the odds. Not a few of those stories had a Longknife in them. "If we use a slightly higher orbit, we'll be moving slower and have targets longer."

"Make it so, Captain," Commodore Peterwald said, preening at the prospects of a quick, overwhelming victory.

Damage control was just getting air back into Laser Bay 1 as Kris boosted the *Patton* into the lead position of her tiny squadron. She wanted to ask the other ships how their guns were doing, but she suspected their communications—a hurried

lash-up—were compromised. Hopefully the others were in better shape than the *Patton*. Kris now had four lasers down.

Worse, the initial reports from observers on the other side
of Chance said that Hank's squadron was coming in low,
maybe making a play for the station. Kris and Steve had bet
that logic, or at least profit motive, would aim Hank at her
warships, not the commercially valuable station. Kris gritted
her teeth and kept her money on her bet. All it would take was
a slight change in course and deceleration and the squadron
would ride right down her throat. *That was what Captain
Slovo would do. Who's calling the shots over there.*

Then the update came in from the other side of Chance and
Kris smiled. "They're coming in high, folks," she announced
on ship net. "Gunnery, if you're ever going to get those lasers
up, now would be very appreciated."

Jack settled into a station close to Kris as she ordered the
Patton to begin defensive rotation. Ice protected the ship, but
lasers burned through ice fast. So big warships spun along
their long axis twenty times a minute, hoping to spin new, un-
damaged ice into a laser hit before it burned into the hull.
Sometimes it worked.

Now, Jack converted the junior sensor station to a general
overview. About the same time, Kris tapped her own board
and turned it from a captain's General Overview to Gunnery
Central. No one on this boat had her experience shooting
other ships. She'd have to wear two hats today. Fortunately,
Jack was willing to share one hat with her. Sulwan would
manage decoys as well as back up the helm. Lots of double
hats.

But Kris had a third hat. She tapped the comm button,
brought it up on guard channel, and said, "Hank, we've got to
talk."

"No we don't," Hank replied. No surprise.

"I really think we do."

"Why? So you can mess with my head?"

That was true, but not what Kris wanted to talk about. "I
don't think us fighting is a very good idea."

"I think this is a great idea, Longknife. I've got you."

"And have you thought through what you've got?"

"I've got you."

"That boy isn't much for thinking, is he?" Jack whispered.

"Okay, Hank, let's follow that thought. Now that you have things the way you want, will you bombard the cities below? You going to enjoy killing me?"

"Don't mess with me, Kris. You've lost. They've lost. They'll have to give up or I will bombard them. And you better run or surrender."

"That's where you need to think, Hank. I've got three ships ready to fight you. Three ships that won't run while there's a shot left in them. Below are folks that will fight you. Stand up fights when they can; snipe at you from behind trees if they have to. You've got us, but we've got you, too. You can't win."

"I've won, damn it, Longknife. I've won. You're supposed to run away. You've lost. Why aren't you running?"

"Because, Hank, this is not a pick-up basketball game; a chess match. Folks don't just resign and walk away. Take you and me. We're on a head-on course. In a few minutes, you'll come over our horizon and we'll be shooting to kill each other. That what you came here for?"

There was a pause at that. "No, no you can't do this to me again. You got me to walk away from that jail. I bet you think you scared me. I know I would have won. I should have done it then. This time, I'll do it. I'm going to blow you out of space, Longknife. This time I know why you did it."

"The alien stuff." Kris sighed.

"Right. You're not going to hog it. Not this time."

"Hank, nobody can hog it. The people on Chance know about it. I know about it. You know about it. Fine. We share it out for everyone."

Hank snorted. "Right. You expect me to believe that?"

"Why not? If you walk through the logic, it holds together better than us killing each other and our families fighting."

"No. You won't talk me in circles this time. You sound like Slovo. If I could, I'd put both of you in the same cell."

Which explained why Kris hadn't heard anything from the flag captain. Only seconds remained before the cruisers came over the horizon and the battle started.

"Hank, this isn't a fight, it's a suicide pact. We're fighting with hand grenades in a broom closet."

"You're wrong, Longknife. I won't let you mess with me. It's not a suicide pact I'm signing, it's your death warrant."

The four cruisers edged over the horizon, their sensor returns still smudged by the atmosphere that lay between.

All four Peterwald cruisers fired everything they had: 6-inch lasers, 21-inch pulse lasers, 4-inch secondaries.

In unpowered orbit, Kris had the *Patton* nose on to Hank's ships and in a soft drift to the right. As Hank's cruisers came over the horizon, Sulwan slammed the *Patton* as hard to the left and as down as the attitudinal jets would take her, while firing off a cloud of decoy chaff in the direction they'd been drifting. The folks on Chance had no rockets, but they did plenty of hunting—now shotgun shells blew ice and iron pellets to distract Hank's gunners. A maelstrom of energy from *Incredible* and *Fury* passed down the *Patton*'s right side, hitting nothing.

Not quite, a pair of 4-inchers raked the meter-thick ice on the *Patton*'s nose.

NELLY, DO YOU HAVE A TRACK ON HANK'S SHIP.

THEY ARE COMING IN ON A STRAIGHT COURSE. DUMB.

FIRE. Forward, the *Patton*'s five working 6-inchers reached out for Hank's flag. Three connected, boiling swirls of angry steam off the ship. WHY'D TWO MISS?

THEY ARE NOT STAYING REGISTERED. THEIR TRUNNIONS ARE OLD. I WILL ATTEMPT TO ADJUST, Nelly said.

"Five-inch battery, engage the second ship in line." And Kris's secondary lasers reached out to rake the *Fury*. Though the difference between 6- and 5-inch lasers seemed small, the main battery hit with over double the energy of the secondary. However, the secondary could fire two or three times while the 6-inch lasers recharged. At this close range, their reach was irrelevant.

"*Wasp*, *Resolute*, engage your opposite number plus one," Kris ordered. The *Wasp* now fired at the third ship, *Dominant*, while the *Resolute* tackled Georg Krätz's *Surprise*. Hopefully, the captain with only daughters would not handle the thin-skinned *Resolute* too badly.

Although the short range of the *Wasp*'s and *Resolute*'s pulse lasers didn't matter today, they were intended as single-shot weapons. It usually took four or five minutes to recharge after firing. Now Penny and Drago used a trick of Nelly's to fire only one-tenth or one-quarter power shots from their pulse lasers. They could worry the Greenfeld skippers longer if they held back, recharged as they went—and waited for them to get closer.

Assuming they dodged death and were alive at close range.

First salvos exchanged, now Kris waited for the lasers to recharge. In a running gun fight, 6-inch lasers usually took ten seconds to do that, 4- or 5-inch secondaries a third as long. But Kris's ships were not under power. No fusion plasma shot from the reactor to the motors and out into space, generating electricity in the superconducting coils of the ship's magnets.

This would not only be a battle in slow motion as the ships followed their orbits, but in slow time as the capacitors struggled to charge up again. Thanks to the expanded racetrack and its trickle charge, Kris had her 6-inchers back on-line in only twenty seconds. She fired. Four hit. More ice boiled off of Hank's ship as it stayed steady in its orbit and on course.

"Sulwan, keep her on a steady course," Kris said through tight lips. "Get ready to execute evasions." Kris watched the seconds click by. Her guess was Hank would need a full half minute to recharge.

When asked how long Hank's ships would take to reload, Nelly had given the equivalent of a computer shrug. "Too many variables, Kris. I will need to observe him for a while."

Kris only had her gut to go on. At thirty seconds from Hank's first salvo, Kris said, "Up and to the right."

"Done," Sulwan said, firing decoys.

"Now left." Kris waited, listening for Nelly's next random move. If only she knew when Hank would be recharged. "Up," Kris said a second later.

And the *Patton* was raked by two 6-inch hits down its right side. Had Hank fired as fast as he could, or waited and out-guessed Kris? No way to tell.

The 4-inch lasers picked at the *Patton*, boiling off a bit of ice here, some more there. Her ship rumbled and shuddered beneath Kris as reaction mass was pumped quickly to rebalance the ship. Otherwise the spin might tear the ship apart, sending ice flying off into space and leaving her ready for Hank's coup de grâce.

"Sulwan, jack up the attitudinal jets. Jink faster."

"These dinky jets weren't meant for heavy lifting." But the woman did. The *Patton* dodged and weaved in its orbit. Every few seconds, Sulwan goosed the main engines, jumping them a bit in their orbit and vacating the space that had gotten too hot. In near-0 g, this was not the mad, punishing dance at 2 and 3 gs that Kris had needed to survive at Wardhaven. Kris doubted the *Patton* could take that. No, they stayed in their orbit and dodged just enough to throw off Hank's gunners.

But the occasional blast of plasma through the five working motors shortened the time Kris needed to reload. She fired her five available lasers as they came up again. Four raked Hank's ship. Only now did it start its own dance. No question Slovo was in the brig. Unfortunately, Hank was learning from Kris how it was done.

Behind Hank, the other ships began the same. And the *Resolute* was taking one, no two, hits.

"Aft gunnery, if you can target the *Surprise*, get a few shots off at them to take the pressure off the *Resolute*." Only two of the stern lasers were up, but when Sulwan put the *Patton* into a left lean, both of then took a nip at the *Surprise*. One hit, boiling a long slash in her ice.

"Bet that surprised them," a gunner chortled on net.

Now Kris's battery was again loaded. She waited for Hank to go from a zig to a zag, let Nelly do the analysis, then sent five lasers his way. Again, she hit. Hank must be trying to do his own dodge pattern. Nelly had developed the one Sulwan and the other ships were using. It wasn't perfect, not at this range, but it was better than Hank making his own calls. "He likes going up and to his right," Nelly noted.

Kris's 5-inchers hammered the *Fury*. The young skipper on that boat was trying for the *Patton*, but rarely connecting.

Which looked good but didn't make Kris feel any better. She was teaching these kids their job—and their slight delay in firing their lasers told Kris something she didn't really want to know. They were recharging their pulse lasers. About the time the fleets were closest, those big hitters would be ready.

Sulwan kept the *Patton*'s teardrop hull pointed at the

Incredible. That put the meter of ice on the nose out where it took most of the hits and the engines out of harm. Kris nipped one of Hank's engines. Penny also got one of the *Dominant*'s. It didn't matter much, since none of the ships were under boost; but now Hank angled his cruisers vulnerable engines away, pointed only his bow weapons at Kris and continued the fight.

They closed at over fifty-five thousand kilometers an hour, dodging and weaving in their orbits, firing as quickly as they could recharge. Steam boiled off the *Patton* to cool into crystalline ice, providing a thin cloak of cover for the ships behind her. That and the residue of decoys gave color to the lasers reaching out to slash ships. It also deflected sensors, making firing solutions less precise. But as the angle of fire approached zero, that mattered less and less.

"Sulwan, get ready to make a major dodge," Kris whispered, firing off a salvo that boiled Hank's ice but did no apparent damage. "He's coming up on closest approach. And he'll have his 21-inch pulse lasers recharged." Kris didn't have to say what the *Patton* would look like if she took five, ten of them at once.

Kris would give her right arm for the four-pulse lasers the *Patton* was supposed to have. Someone had removed them before exiling the boat to the Rim, probably for new construction. Kris hoped they earned their pay wherever that was.

The navigator laid the *Patton* over and boosted; then just as quickly, flipped it, fired decoy, and boosted back. Twice Sulwan did that yo-yo. Sometimes the leg was one second long, another time two. Halfway through the third, the *Patton* shuddered along its length.

Kris's board lit up as the *Patton* shimmied and bumped. Pumps moved reaction mass to rebalance her, but not fast enough.

"Laser Bay 1 is open to space." That was no surprise. "We've got a burn through there." The meter of ice over it, slashed and hacked, had boiled away totally. The *Patton* staggered in its orbit, taking hits as it became predictable. "Sulwan."

"I don't know if the old gal can take this, but here goes." The *Patton*'s engines blasted Kris back in her seat. Kris ignored

the red flashing on Jack's board and aimed for the *Incredible*.
Four lasers answered her order. Hank's ship steamed.

How much longer can I keep this up?

Flag Captain Slovo struggled to make his way back to his
bridge. A man of his age and experience should have known
better than to try to teach a pig to sing. All he'd done was ag-
gravate the pig—and get himself thrown in his own brig.

In his cell, it had done him and his ship no good to shout
orders for battle rotation or evasive maneuvers. The dimming
of the lights told Slovo that the *Incredible* had fired everything
it had at the start of the battle. Only a long minute later did the
ship take on rotation . . . maybe half of what it needed to survive. And then it began to zig and zag in its orbit.

"So that Longknife girl is teaching you how this dance is
done," Slovo muttered as his cell door opened.

"Your presence is requested on the bridge." Maybe Hank
was ready to learn from someone other than that girl.

Against the rotation, allowing for dodges and weaving, and
trying not to let the sudden bursts of power leave him with a
broken leg or cracked skull, Slovo struggled forward.

"I got her. I got her." Hank greeted him as he half stumbled, half swam onto his bridge. The commodore's happy face
turned to him. "I've already won this battle. I didn't need you
after all."

The flag captain locked his face to blank, said "Very good,"
and lurched for his seat. He was just strapping in when all hell
broke loose.

Steve Kovar, Lieutenant, retired, more or less, did not
like what he saw. On the good side, his station remained unen-
gaged by the hostiles. The princess had ordered him not to fire
unless fired upon and the commercial value of the station
seemed to be working as its best defense.

The bad side was that his side was getting the crap beat out
of them. He'd soon face a choice of surrendering or fighting a
hopeless battle. He hadn't joined the Navy to give up without
a fight, so he figured him and his crew for dead.

He went down the list of Kris's ships and didn't like the answer he got. The *Patton* was badly holed by that last salvo. She was still fighting, but didn't look long for the battle.

The *Resolute* had been dancing like mad, but it had taken hit after hit. Its smart armor had to be about gone. One or two more hits and . . . Only the *Wasp* was holding its own.

Steve measured the distance between his station and Hank's flagship. It wouldn't be more than two hundred klicks at closest approach. His station should be able to bring to bear eight boosted 6-inch lasers. "Harriet, jack up the reactor. I'm gonna want all you can give."

"You got it."

Pumping energy into capacitors even as you discharged their lasers was something that had sparked a long series of letters to the Proceedings. Now would be a good time to see if it worked.

"Every gun that can bear, aim for the flag." He paused. "Fire."

"Oh my God," someone prayed on the bridge.

Kris didn't have time; she mashed guard channel. "Hank, you're naked as a plucked chicken. Accept my cease-fire."

"Never. I've got you."

Lasers reached out, lashed the *Patton* as Sulwan dodged.

"Like hell," Kris muttered, and changed channels. "Penny, you still charged?"

"Fully. Where do you want it?"

"Target Hank's engines and power."

"I know just where they are."

"Fire," Kris ordered and did the same with all she still had available.

The *Incredible* steamed, staggered drunkenly, rolled away from Kris, and then went dead in space.

Captain Slovo's board lit up on his command. Then it flashed red and went dead. Around him lights went out but not fast enough to conceal the horror. A huge hole blazed open in the far wall and the entire sensor team vanished in blinding light. Air blasted across his face.

"Life pods," Slovo shouted as he reached for the handle below his seat and pulled it. In a blink, the walls of a pod flashed around him. Transparent, it let him see the destruction of his ship. He saw his commodore, so sure of himself a moment ago, now fighting panic as he also pulled the handle. The survival pod expanded around him. Slovo breathed a sigh of relief.

Then tasted panic; the same that must be swallowing Henry Smythe-Peterwald the Thirteenth. Around Slovo, other pods showed lights as they pumped air, sent emergency signals.

Where Hank sat was deadly dark.

Kris mashed her commlink on guard channel. "Hank, are you there? Hank, have you had enough? Hank, I'm offering you a cease-fire."

Only static came back.

"This is Captain Krätz, Senior Captain present. I accept your offer of a cease-fire."

"You can't do that," one of Hank's captains shot back.

"I can and I am," Krätz snapped. "And I will see that the captain of any ship that violates my agreement is court-marshaled. You want to be the one to tell Papa Peterwald that you didn't render every assistance to his son?" That brought silence.

"This affair is over," Krätz bit out. "Form on the flag and render all assistance possible."

Six hours later, they'd found out how little they could do.

Kris risked the battered nose of the *Patton* to push High Chance into an orbit that would last several months or until someone came along to put it higher. She was just stabilizing it when three ships came through Jump Point Alpha, announced themselves to be from the Helvetica Confederacy and asked what was going on.

Captain Slovo, now commanding the *Fury*, advised that there had been a slight misunderstanding and requested assistance. Kris and Steve seconded the motion in the name of their respective political entities.

The new arrivals listened, took a good look around, and sent one ship back through the jump to make a private call home, then drove for Chance at 2 g's. They docked a day later, just before Slovo brought the three surviving Greenfeld ships carefully alongside, as well.

Thus, Vice Admiral Quang Tu of the Helvetica Confederacy was present with Kris and Steve, when Captain Slovo gingerly brought an unopened survival pod onto the landing of Pier 2.

"I hope that is not what I think it is," Kris said.

"Regretfully, it is," Slovo sighed. "One, very inoperable life pod with one Henry Peterwald the Thirteenth in it." The Greenfeld captain waited until representatives from the other two ships arrived, then ordered one of his own mechs to open of the pod. Jack and Beni were as close as they could get, recorders and sensors out, but there were no surprises today.

Hank Peterwald's very sculptured features were very dead.

"I guess I've finally met someone with more enemies than me," Kris said.

"May I offer assistance?" Admiral Tu asked.

"No," Slovo said. "Regretfully, this situation has become a crime scene and Greenfeld security will handle the investigation from this point." Kris suspected she recognized several of the hard-faced men who stepped forward. One of them had tried to enter the station's reactor. Yep. She'd ID'd them all right.

Captain Slovo nodded to Kris. "If you will order communications through Jump Point Barbie reopened, I will call my headquarters for orders." Kris quickly did.

Vice Admiral Tu, who never explained what a vice admiral was doing commanding a mere division of heavy cruisers or how he happened to wander into the Chance system, let it be known he was in no hurry to leave and might well be expecting additional forces. There were hints of battleships.

Kris took Lieutenant Kovar aside and asked if he'd mind looking after United Sentients interests while she made a quick trip to Wardhaven. Nelly discovered a reg, dating back to the Iteeche Wars, that delegated authority to Naval District Commanders to approve battlefield promotions through Commander. With a grin, Kris promoted Steve to outrank her and gleefully sent the paperwork in to see how much trouble it would cause BuPers.

She was packed when Slovo detached the remnants of Hank's squadron and began a very sedate .5 g acceleration toward Jump Point Barbie.

As Kris marched down with her team to the *Resolute*, Steve went with her. And chuckled as Ron and a half dozen other mayors from Chance waylaid them.

"Kris, I know we can never thank you enough for what you've done," Ron started, "but we've got to at least try. We of Chance have never awarded a medal for valor, but the people who fought with you certainly deserve one." And so Kris was handed the very first Chance Cross of Gallantry with Silver Star. Jack and Penny both rated the Silver Star version. Beni and Abby's award had Bronze Stars in them. Kris heard that those who served beer got palm fronds on theirs. It truly was an award to unite all those who had stood up for Chance in its time of need.

"I told them," Steve said, grinning, "that all your fruit salad was just tourist stuff, been there, done that, got shot at. We made sure this one had a cross and a silver star on it." Kris hugged Steve, then hugged Ron . . . and got kissed.

"Any chance you could, maybe, hang around here long enough for a guy to get to know you? Deserve an entire chapter in that book I want you to write?" Ron asked, his mom at his elbow.

"You know I have to take The Word back to Wardhaven. And now that Hank's dead, I have to tell them why."

Ron was still waving as the *Resolute* undocked.

As soon as they jumped through Alpha, now monitored by a buoy from New Bern, Abby knocked on Kris's cabin door.

"I have a report I need to file with an employer."

"I figured you'd be around soon. It mention aliens?"

"No, I won't give that away. They don't pay me that much."

"Does it have anything in it that might harm me?"

"Other than your reputation, I think you're safe."

"My reputation was lost long ago. Send it," Kris said, then had a second thought. "Pass a copy along to Jack. I may borrow from it if I have to write a report on this."

"You don't want a copy?"

"No, Abby, I trust you."

"No you don't, Kris."

"Yes I do," Kris said, frowning at the bold contradiction.

"You don't trust us any more than any Longknife trusts anyone. Here you dragged us off hunting aliens and you didn't tell us a thing about it beforehand."

"Your steamer trunks had what I needed."

"Yes, but will they always?"

Kris went back to studying alien issues and Abby left. After five minutes, Kris found she was going over the same item for the ninth time. *You don't trust me*, kept coming back.

Well, the maid was selling Kris's life. Why should she trust her? But she hadn't told Jack about the jump points, either. Or Penny. And somebody hadn't told her that Hank was wandering these spaces. *Longknifes don't trust.*

Kris spent much of the voyage home thinking about that.

19

Usually, Kris had to wait for a summons from General McMorrison until her ship docked at High Wardhaven. Not this time. She was just finishing breakfast aboard the *Resolute* with her team when the Comm Chief stepped in with a message flimsy.

"You know anyone named Mac?" Kris averred she might.

"He wants to see you in his office ASAP after we dock. Message is kind of cryptic. You understand it?"

Kris sighed and put down an apple core. "We have these little get togethers every time I come back from off-planet. Mac starts by offering me a completed resignation form to sign. I tear it up and things go downhill from there."

"General McMorrison, the Chief of Wardhaven's General Staff?" Penny asked, a bit unsure that Kris actually was on a nickname basis with someone of that elevated status.

"The same," Jack said. "I cool my heels in the waiting room. Not sure what I'm supposed to do if he decides to threaten bodily harm. Interfere or cheer."

"Well, I'm glad it's just you," Penny said.

"Maybe, maybe not. Jack, you're with me. Penny, you, too."

She looked around the room. Abby was eating her breakfast alone at a corner table. "You, too."

"Me?" the maid said in high theatrical shock.

"Can't tell when I might need a report composed."

"Maybe you can sell the story," Jack said.

"Nobody pays for the obvious," Abby sniffed. "Who's going to take charge of your steamer trunks. I've got to get them back to your suite at Nuu House."

Kris looked around, found Beni munching waffles with Doc. "Chiefs are the backbone of the Navy. I'm sure our good chief can get some trunks to toddle along after him."

"What? How? Why me?"

"The what and how," Jack said. "Ask Abby. Why you? That's too philosophical even for me, but I think proximity to greatness or the near great has something to do with it."

As Kris led her two officers off to change into undress whites, Doc was heard to suggest to Beni that "you really do need to apply to OCS."

At the bottom of the space elevator, Harvey, the family retainer and chauffeur was waiting; he already knew his first stop. His oldest grandkid, a girl who claimed to be old enough to drive and waved a license "with a horrible picture" to prove it, was there with a truck for the luggage.

"There will be a chief down here soon with twelve self-propelled steamer trunks," Kris told her. "No need to be too easy to find, but don't let him get too panicked."

Young granddaughter was delighted that she could be a pain to a grownup and it was an order. "Just remember the point about not being too much of a pain," her grandfather reminded her.

Main Navy was just where Kris left it, a hulking monstrosity of concrete and glass. The lair of the Chairman of the Joint Staff was buried deep in it. Kris didn't know when she was expected, but the secretary just waved her in.

Jack pointed at the two chairs in the waiting room, signaled the women that they were theirs, then found a chunk of wall to hold up. Kris opened the door, ready to march in, again, as usual—and came to a dead stop.

Mac was behind his desk, but seated in his visitor's chair was King Raymond the First to most, Grampa to Kris. On

Mac's other side was Admiral Crossenshield, the head of Wardhaven's black intelligence efforts. Kris eyed them for a moment . . . and they returned the favor. No one broke the silence until Kris shook her head ruefully, took a step back out of the office, and said, "You three, in here with me."

Kris wasn't sure whether the shock and dismay was worse in the general's office or in his waiting room, but under her best Longknife glare, Jack, Penny, and lastly, Abby made their way where she directed them.

Definitely, her team was double-whammied as they walked in the door and found the full extent of this meeting. Jack's nostrils flared. Penny looked panic-struck and ready to flee, but Abby was too close behind her to give the poor woman any running room. Abby took them in, and looked as determined not to disgrace herself as anyone facing a firing squad.

Then again, the consternation across the room was an interesting study as well. King Ray pursed his lips and nodded his head slowly. Mac looked ready to pull out what hair he had left, but kept his hands on the desk at this latest bit of mutiny from his worst subordinate. Only Crossenshield slowly allowed a smile to creep across his face. Why was Kris not surprised.

In the door, Kris's team bunched up, unsure where to go. Kris headed for the chair at the end of the coffee table that put her facing her king and commanders. Seating herself, she said, "Jack," and waved him to the couch on her right, putting him between her and Crossenshield. Probably for the admiral's protection more than hers. She waved Penny and Abby to the couch on the other side, putting them between her and her great-grandfather. Penny got there first and took the end closer to Kris. Abby, her dark complexion strangely pale, looked around for anywhere else to sit. "Abby," Kris said, and pointed. And the maid went where she was told.

The tableaux now set, Kris settled in to wait for whoever had called this meeting to speak up. She was prepared to wait until someone died of dehydration. Grampa Ray broke the long silence. "Did you have to kill the Peterwald boy?"

Kris shot back her prepared answer. "Hank was hell bent on shooting us up. Given a choice of him or me, I chose him. But he'd be alive today if someone hadn't jiggered his survival pod. Any idea who did?" Kris said, locking eyes with Crossenshield.

"As you said. You've finally found someone more people wanted dead than you," he said, misquoting Kris.

"You'd have to have read Abby's report to know I said that."

"Of course I've read her report. We pay enough for it."

And if Crossenshield was one of the recipients of Abby's reports, that might tell Kris a lot about many things. "I want a copy of what you got. Now!" she demanded.

Crossenshield raised an eyebrow at the tenor of Kris's words, or maybe it was the usual reaction of an admiral to getting an order from a lieutenant. He eyed the king who nodded almost imperceptibly, then raised his wrist, and tapped a few keys on his personal unit.

"Jack, you got it?" Kris snapped.

"Yes."

"Check it against what Abby gave me."

"Doing it," Jack said.

"I'm helping," Nelly added.

Abby sat primly, eyes on the ceiling, her face that of every innocent three-year-old caught with her hands in the cookie jar.

"No mention of aliens," Nelly said only a moment later.

"Aliens!" came from those around the desk in perfect three part harmony. Kris ignored them and eyed Jack.

He finally glanced up from his unit. "The words in Crossenshield's version have been randomly modified. The style is more stilted. It reads worse than Abby's original, but it's basically what she gave us."

"I told you," Abby sniffed.

"Any chance I could get your originals from now on?" Crossenshield asked Abby.

"What's this about aliens?" Grampa Ray demanded.

"That's why Hank and I were having that fight," Kris said, and then filled them in on the new jump points Nelly had identified and what they found at the end of three of them.

"Holy Mother of God," Crossenshield whispered.

"I'll tell Alnaba to pack up the Santa Maria Institute and move it to a happier hunting ground," Grampa Ray concluded.

"You better tell her to move carefully," Jack said. "That place is armed and dangerous and almost killed us—twice."

"Maybe I could help you out there," Kris offered.

"Don't you think you've done quite enough to that section of the Rim," Grampa Ray muttered.

"I've got Nelly's chip. It helped us make this find."

"Alnaba and Tru got tired of waiting for you to report on whatever you and Nelly were doing and installed a chip in Tru's computer. They can handle this very well themselves."

No they can't!

Don't say a word, Nelly, Kris quickly thought, before her computer could jump in and start an argument. They'll find out soon enough that they need us.

They sure will, Nelly agreed.

Across from Kris, King Ray, Mac, and Crossenshield seemed to be negotiating in silence the fate of worlds. Mac finally shook his head. "We better bring Chance into your United thing."

King Ray nodded.

Kris slowly shook her head. "Not a good idea. Chance doesn't much care for outsiders telling them what to do. Hank found that out the hard way. Can't we learn from his mistake?"

"We can't leave them out there adrift," Mac said.

"Who says they're alone? I figure them to cut a deal with the Helvetica Confederacy."

"We can't afford to have the gateway to all this new alien technology in Peterwald hands. And after that shoot-out you and Hank had, Harry is going to pull out all the stops pressuring them . . ." Mac said, frowning at the star map on the wall.

"I thought we didn't do things like that. Pressuring people," Kris said, raising an eyebrow to the King.

"Sometimes you have to make exceptions," Grampa Ray muttered, but his eyes stayed locked on hers.

"Will you consider trying something else?" Kris asked.

"What else is there?" Mac asked back.

"Use the assets you have. Naval District 41 isn't much but it's there and Chance recognizes our right to it. It's our ante into this game. What say you put a senior admiral in that billet. One who knows how to negotiate. Conciliate. And give him a decent force. Some ships to cooperate with the Helvetic fleet. Work together to secure their peace. Do we gain anything by working at cross purposes with the locals?"

Kris shrugged. "The last time I checked all we wanted was what the people of Chance and the Confederacy want, for them to live in peace and prosper. Why don't we back them in that, rather than insist they do things our way?"

"The gal's an optimist," Mac growled.

Grampa Ray chuckled. "All things considered, after what we put her through, what else could she be?"

"It might work," Crossenshield offered. "Assuming we don't send a Longknife. There's bound to be someone on our promotion list with a reputation for negotiations and peacemaking."

"Gosh, and I thought that was all I was doing," Kris said.

"Sorry, gal, that's just not our general reputation," King Ray said.

"I still wish she hadn't killed the Peterwald boy," Mac grumbled. "There'll be hell to pay. Either of you two remember a dust-up in the Twentieth called World War I? Started when someone offed the heir apparent to one of the thrones of Europe. Pretty much wrecked the rest of that century."

"I didn't kill him," Kris pointed out. Again.

"He would have lived if his survival pod had worked," Jack put in. "I know. I looked it over when we got it aboard."

"Why didn't it?" King Ray snapped at Jack.

"We couldn't tell from the equipment we had available," Jack said, choosing his words carefully. "And the folks from Greenfeld didn't give us a lot of time to examine the body and the wreckage. The flag captain said he had personally checked the pod before they sailed. It must have been sabotaged during the month or so they were bouncing around Helvetican space. But all that time the bridge was occupied by a watch crew and under observation. How it was done . . . ?" Jack just shrugged.

"Peterwald's security will get to the bottom of that," Ray mutters. "I wouldn't want to be a survivor of that flagship."

Suddenly, Crossenshield sat up straight. He raised a finger to his left ear, drawing Kris's attention to a small device lodged there. "Ray, the survivors of that flagship may have bigger worries at the moment," he said. "Give me a second."

Everyone in the room watched him in silence as he listened intently, eyes locked on the ceiling. Then he began to talk in a whisper, apparently still listening. "The ship bearing Hank's body back to Greenfeld, and the survivors of his flagship, was approaching a jump when its lateral thrusters began firing. It lost all communications and suddenly took off at a high g acceleration. It was in that configuration when it entered the jump. The ships escorting it did not find it on the other side of the jump."

"A bad jump," Grampa Ray whispered.

Mac shook his head slowly. "Harry Peterwald won't have a body to bury. He can't investigate whether this was some palace intrigue or heart-sick relative of someone that died in a survival pod in Wardhaven orbit." The general waved a hand. "Yes, I know their official take is we shot the survivors but there are stories circulating on Greenfeld that the survival pods were death traps, right, Crossie?" The intel man nodded.

"But Harry will damn well know his son died in a fight with us. And with you, young lady."

"I didn't have much choice. Somebody hung me out there with no back up. Nothing but my own two hands and what I and a lot of good folks could come up with to resist Hank. Hank's flag captain, Slovo, kept saying things were mighty strange. He hadn't expected to find me there, had no briefing on me. But I wasn't expecting to see them either. No brief on their trip around at all. Right, Crossenshield?"

"We weren't sure he'd stop by Chance," the spy master said, holding his face blank and unreadable.

"We," Kris spat, and looked hard at Ray.

"We," Ray said. "We're scrambling, Kris. After the attack on Wardhaven, everyone wants a chunk of the fleet. We sent what we could where we could. And Naval District 41 was the bottom of the barrel."

"And I was the scrapings." Kris sighed. "No back-up. Just little old me and a couple of people too dumb to run when a Longknife wanders next to them. No offense intended, crew."

"None taken," Jack said. Penny just looked sad. Abby was trying to look like she wasn't there.

"But we did provide you back-up," Crossenshield said.

"What back-up?"

"The *Resolute*," King Ray said. "If things got too bad, you had the *Resolute* to get you out of there. She could have outrun any of those cruisers. Why didn't you run?"

Jack looked at the king, then at Kris as she struggled to get out a reply. "Excuse me for butting in, but you give this gal a ship named the *Resolute* and expected her to use it to run away from a fight? I was starting to think you maybe understood your great-granddaughter. I guess I was wrong."

"Maybe we should have renamed the ship," Crossenshield said.

The king was looking hard at Kris. "There are times when even a Longknife finds discretion is the better part of valor. I thought Chance might be a hard lesson for you."

Kris snorted. "But when you add aliens to the mix?"

"Yes," Ray agreed. "We did our calculations assuming that only Chance was in the pot we were gambling for. Then you upped the stakes beyond anything imaginable."

Kris let her eyes fall to the floor. "And we had Hank leaving. We'd outplayed him on Chance. Until he found out the size of the pot, we'd won a bloodless victory. Then, suddenly, there was no place to run. He had two cruisers at Jump Point Alpha and Beta led to Greenfeld space."

"I'm sorry, Kris," the king said. "We thought we had it all worked out. An assignment for you that was just your size, and an out for you if it went south."

"Only it went north, east, and west," Kris said.

On that thought, the meeting seemed to wind down to dusty death. After a long moment of silence, Mac looked at Ray, then at Kris. "Consider yourself relieved of command of Naval District 41. I don't have a job for you just now, so hold yourself in readiness for orders."

No doubt, the wait would not be short.

Back on the street, Kris let the traffic roll by for a moment, dappled by the shadows of the leaves in the early morning sun. The air here was city: ripe and full and probably poison even with her father's best efforts. Kris had nothing to do and several million things hanging fire. What she needed was a place to think.

Harvey pulled the car up; she and her team piled in. "Where to?" he asked. "Home?"

"I don't know about you," Kris said, "but I could use a space where I could get my head in some kind of order. Jack, where is that place you took me to awhile back?"

"The Smugglers Roost?"

"Yeah, that place. With Mac and Ray here, we shouldn't have to worry about running into them there."

"I know the place," said Harvey and dialed it into the car.

The Smugglers Roost was in the sunshine this morning, the space elevator casting its shadow the other way. The beat-up industrial area still looked like a prime candidate for one of Father's urban redevelopment projects. Kris thought that would be a shame. Though some of the red bricks were crumbling, and different colored bricks showed where others had been patched, the place looked like it must be two hundred years old, one of the first permanent buildings ever put up on Wardhaven.

Kris led her three companions down the uneven stairs; Harvey had excused himself to run errands for his wife. Kris knew why the old chauffeur had fled the moment she took the last step down. The Roost was almost empty two hours before noon. Almost . . . but not quite. At a back table sat Grampa Trouble. He raised a beer stein in salute as Kris growled, "You owe me."

"And me," Jack added.

"So I'll stand you all for a round. Barkeep, whatever your best is for my easily bamboozled friends here. Hi, Abby, I'm glad to see you're joining us. Is your cover totally blown?"

The maid gave an off-handed shrug, that left you to draw your own conclusion. Kris stowed hers away for later review.

"You knew," Kris said, in full accusation.

"Of course I knew," the old soldier said, unrepentant . . . and proud of it. Then he frowned. "I know a lot, young woman, being as old and evil as I am. But you haven't read any sort of charges against me for a plea. I can confess right now to anything and it won't hold up in any court of law."

Kris sat down, then raised her hand, fist up, one finger out. "You knew if I drafted Jack, that he'd darn near have a hammer lock on my life."

Trouble grinned. "Yep. How's it going young fellow?"

"I'm still alive." Jack sighed. "So is she, despite every effort on her part to the contrary. Tell me, do your offspring ever learn common sense?"

"There's no evidence to support that pipe dream. But then there's little evidence that I have much common sense."

"We can drink to that," Kris said. She looked at her hand and started to raise a second finger.

"Hold your horses, young lady," Grampa Trouble said and put his hand over Kris's, folding her fingers back into a fist. "Barkeep, what's keeping you?"

"I'm hard of hearing. Comes from being yelled at," muttered a fellow maybe half of Grampa Trouble's hundred plus years as he hurried across the floor. He produced a cloth to wipe down the table. "I hear you want my finest. Which finest?"

"Pilsner," Trouble said, "but not for me just now. How about the rest of you. Kris, can I talk you into a beer?"

"Grampa, even when I was drinking myself to sleep at night, I hated the taste of the stuff. I don't think I ever got drunk enough to enjoy it. No, what I'd kill for is a milkshake. Nice, thick, creamy. And fresh made, not one of those thin ice creams trying to fake it."

"I should warn you," Jack told the barkeep, "from her, the idea of killing for it might not be just a turn of phrase."

"Then I think the little lady came to the right place," the gray-haired fellow said. "The Smugglers Roost prides itself on the best milkshakes this side of Guernsey Island on old Earth. Only the finest of ingredients. What will you have?

"Chocolate," Kris said. "No, double chocolate."

"I suspect I could handle a shake, too," Abby said. "You make strawberry shakes, with fresh strawberries?"

"They're in season," the barkeep assured them.

"I'll have one like Kris," Penny said. "Double chocolate."

Jack took in a worried breath. "Only the best ingredients, you say. Sounds pricey. Don't know if a mere First Lieutenant can afford such frippery. You paying, General?"

"I may have gotten you drafted into your ill-paying job, son, and I may have offered to stand you to a good, healthy beer, but even I tremble at the potential cost of where these women of ill repute are leading you."

The waiter pointed them at a menu. Jack scanned it, then whistled. "You could pay for a round of beers for one of these."

"I'm paying for Jack's," Kris said. "What flavor, oh chief of my security. After all, you kept me alive."

"Banana," he answered quickly.

"Hold it, I've helped keep you from ending up very quickly dead," Abby said. "Why aren't you paying for my milkshake. I am just a poor working girl."

Kris waived the barkeep away. "And speaking of which, just how many people do you work for?"

Abby grew very interested in a fly buzzing the next table.

"Let me count the cost centers if I can," Kris said, her fingers once more coming up. "And you, oh troublesome grampa are not off the hook yet. But right now, let's look at you, my maid of many surprises. Mother pays you."

"A mere pittance. Hardly keeps body and soul together."

Kris didn't argue that, but went on, raising a second finger. "Then there is some information broker who's soaking Crossenshield and who knows how many others for the privilege of reading the idle rumors passing through your head."

Abby gave the group one of her patented sniffs. "And not passing nearly enough of his vast profits on my labors along to me. What with me taking all the risks to life and limb keeping my distance from your targeted person."

"Which brings us to the steamer trunks," Kris said, raising her third finger.

"I was waiting for that," Jack said, grin wide, all teeth.

Kris continued. "While I'm sure your reports are fun reads to many people from Crossie to even Henry Peterwald the perverted twelfth himself, I don't think information brokers usually invest in keeping the subjects of their purulent interest alive. Course, I don't watch that much media."

"Not an Earth dime," Jack said.

"Certainly. Each messy death is a separate fortune. And there's always another hot item coming along. Who cares about yesterday's big name?" Penny said.

"So Abby, who's buying all those lifesaving goodies in the steamer trunks," Kris demanded.

"I don't know," Abby said. Then, in the face of four incredulous faces . . . no, three, Grampa Trouble was scrupulously studying the bubbles in his beer . . . Abby went on. "Really, I don't know. Someone contacted me when I was on my way to take this job. Someone that said my broker had referred his client to me, and asked if I'd be willing to provide some extra services to this Kris Longknife kid I was going to primp and pamper. I asked what he had in mind, me not being interested in anything dangerous, and you know the rest."

"No," Kris said, "but I doubt you'll be more forthcoming."

Abby locked eyes with Kris and did not blink. Kris chose not to see who would break first, suspecting any victory would be pyrrhic. "Do you have any hunch who is behind this contract?"

Abby shook her head. "Ain't something I need to know. What I can tell you is that it's my largest source of income and its first clause is that I don't ever do anything that could cause you any kind of harm." The maid shrugged. "Kind of crimps my style on the other two contracts. When you brought home those tar-filthy hands, I couldn't do half of what I wanted to."

Kris waved her hands to shake off the recollected pain of that manicure. Grampa Trouble had a twinkle in his eye as he said. "That's something I want to hear about."

"What, it wasn't in any of her reports?"

"I don't read the scandal sheets on my great-granddaughter. She deserves some privacy."

"Painfully little."

"I hope the second clause in that contract," Jack said, "is to protect Kris."

"So long as it doesn't put my sensitive skin at risk."

"But you don't have any idea who?" Kris repeated.

"I might have suspicions as to how many," Abby admitted under Kris's intense gaze. "I got a raise awhile back, just after we got back from Turantic. Pay went up 50 percent."

"As if a new interest had joined a two-party consortium. Or two had joined a four," Penny said, quickly doing the numbers.

"You were only hired a bit before the Turantic dustup," Jack pointed out.

"Let's assume there are now three groups that want me to keep breathing," Kris said slowly. "Who?"

"You're father?" Jack said.

"He's doing all he can legally, under Wardhaven law, by tying you down here," Kris said, glancing at her protective service agent/Marine guard. "If he wanted more . . ."

"He'd have to have Crossie pay it out of black funds," Penny said. "If it ever got into the papers, it would . . ."

Kris eyed Grampa Trouble. Again, he seemed fascinated by the pattern the bubbles were making in the dark brew before him. Just how much did her Grampas Ray and Trouble talk about her? Worry about her?

"Crossie tried to get me to work for him just before Turantic," Kris said. "Maybe he figured that would make it legal for him to spend money on me if I was one of his lost souls . . ." Kris weighed that and labeled it Kris's Protection 1.

"What about your Grampa Al?" Jack asked.

"He might be slipping a bit of cash that way. God knows he's got enough money. Though after Turantic was when I slapped him up for being a slumlord."

"Yeah, that sounds more like the time he'd cut you loose," Penny agreed.

"You came from Earth," Kris said slowly to Abby.

"That's where I was when your mom hired me."

"Could someone there be interested in keeping you alive?" Jack said.

"We know we're in a mess because we offed Hank," Penny whispered. "Could someone there have looked at the enmity between the Longknifes and the Peterwalds and be investing a few bucks to keep the heat at a low boil, below what it might get to if you ended up suddenly dead."

"All good guesses," Kris agreed. "And I suspect we'll have to settle for guesses," she said, eyeing Grampa Trouble. He refused to meet her gaze, but kept on studying bubbles. *No wonder I don't trust my best friends. How much do I trust you, you old war horse? Is there any reason not to?*

And the milkshakes arrived.

The barkeep hung around until all of them had sampled his offering and praised it highly, then retreated at a nod from Grampa Trouble. Kris slowly relished the creamy chocolate shake while reviewing in her head what she knew . . . not much . . . and what she suspected . . . a lot more.

Clearly, Grampa Trouble knew more than he was telling. *Do I trust him with my life?* He'd brought her back from the walking dead, too drunk to live. No question she owed him her life. But would Grampa feel obliged to correct them if their guesses were wrong, but not deadly wrong at this moment? Mentally, Kris shook her head. She had guesses and nothing that couldn't be denied if it showed up in the noon news.

Life is like that for a Longknife. Get used to it.

"If Kris has all these big bucks out to keep her safe," Jack said around the straw in his mouth, "I'm starting to feel redundant, if not puny."

Kris measured Jack's words, compared them with the deep lines around his eyes, and tasted fear. Not Jack's. Her own.

Unless she badly misread Jack, he was facing his own doubts. Why should he follow her through fire and hell? Why should he keep placing his life in her hands so she could do what she did, relying totally on him to keep her alive?

Kris swallowed hard and pushed the shake away.

"You really feel that way?"

"Hey, Boss, Abby's the one with the magic hat. She's the one that pulls all the stuff out that we need just about the time that we're desperate for it." He shrugged and took a long pull on his shake. "I'm just here to lug around all that hardware. I'm paid for a mule and I do a mule's job."

"You really are feeling down in your beer, son," Grampa Trouble said. But he didn't say more.

"Would it help if you got the same pay as Abby?" Penny said.

"No, damn it. I'm not talking about pay. I'm talking about my job. About knowing where I'm going and that I'll have the gear I need to do my job. About being involved in deciding what we take on these wild quests Kris goes charging off on, even if I don't get to veto what rabbit hole she dives into."

Kris didn't discount the pay issue so quickly, but she did respect the professional pride it must cost Jack every time he had to turn to a maid for armor or an armory . . . or for medical gear or . . . The list went on. "Jack," Kris said, "have you noticed that when we're in trouble, Abby is rarely to be seen."

"Very rarely," Penny said.

"Not that rare," Abby insisted.

"Jack, you remember what you told me. 'I take your bullet.' You will take the bullet aimed for me. For Abby, this is just a job. For you, it's a mission. A sacred trust. That engineer on the *Wasp*, faced with meeting the clause in his contract about blowing up the ship. What did he say? 'They hadn't paid him enough.' " Kris raised an eyebrow. Jack made a wry face.

Kris went on. "I know money is not why you're here. I think you know better than I what makes you stay. I hope you do. I don't know what'll become of me if you ever forget. I can't believe I'll ever look around and not find you covering my back."

Jack's breath went out of him in a snort. "Not unless they got me with the first shot. But, damn it, Kris. This isn't a joke anymore. It was funny, at first. I could laugh with you, about how Abby seemed to always have what we need. Not now. I want to know what's in the trunks, Abby. You're either part of our team, or . . ."

Kris cut him off. "You don't have to finish that sentence, Jack. As of today, things are going to change."

"Now hold it, baby ducks. There ain't no amount of money you can pay me to take your bullet."

"Nothing I can do to change that," Kris said. "But we can make sure you understand that Jack is number one when it comes to my safety. You're at best number two. You will keep him in the loop. I expect Jack to know what you're packing in those trunks, and I expect him to approve everything." Abby's face was a storm ready to break as her glower bounced between Jack and Kris.

"And if you can't agree with what he says, you bring your disagreement to me and I'll ask Grampa Trouble for advice on what will look after me the best," she said, turning quickly to take the old soldier in.

"Hold it. I'm no part of this," he started, but Kris had his eyes hostage. This time, she didn't look away . . . and he couldn't. "Okay, you can count on me for logistical quibbles."

"And what if I want something that's too expensive?" Jack said. "That's not funded by Abby's employer?"

Abby was shaking her head. "It ain't nearly as easy as you think, baby ducks."

"Then we'll just take it up with Grampa here."

"Can't see why you'd do that," Grampa Trouble said mildly, but he left it at that, and Kris went back to sucking on her melting milkshake.

Kris waited until she was nearing the bottom of the glass,

before she spoke again. "I sure wish we hadn't killed Hank.
I don't think they're gonna let me anywhere near Chance
space for a long, long time, and I do want to work on those
alien things."

"Me, too," Nelly said dolefully.

"Given enough time, any place will cool off," Grampa
Trouble said. "But as far as that spoiled brat, I don't feel at all
sorry." Kris snapped around to eye her great-grandfather. He
of all people knew the unknown problems that lay ahead because of Hank's death.

"Yes, I know. Human space can't afford the death of that
poor kid. I've heard it all, and I'll do my bit, stuffing my finger
into any dike Ray asks," Grampa Trouble said, taking a pull
on his beer. "But what Hank did was plain dumb. You can't
loose the hounds of war and expect to know the tree those
puppies are gonna bark up. That's why any smart man does
his best to keep those sons ah bitches on a leash."

Which was a rather blunt way of putting it, but Kris didn't
doubt Grampa Trouble's assessment. She and the others finished their milkshakes in silence. Done, Kris took in a deep
breath and let it out slowly. "So now Henry Peterwald has no
heir and the guy who's been trying to kill me for the last couple of years really has it in for me."

"I can't disagree with your assessment, Kris, except,"
Trouble smiled enigmatically, "Peterwald still has an heir."

Kris blinked four times before she could wrestle her
thoughts to ground and say, "Hank was an only child. At least
he always left me with that impression."

"Don't doubt, considering Greenfeld attitude toward girls."

"He has a sister?" came from everyone.

"Twin, of sorts," Grampa Trouble said, sharing one of his
wicked grins with them. "Seems that the womb they installed
the thoroughly engineered and refined Hank in either had or
was about to get a totally natural rider as well. Big surprise.
Lots of recriminations. Bigger surprise was that the natural
survived. Usually, they don't, but that baby girl was feisty
from the start. So, nine months later, out comes Hank. And a
few minutes later, Vicky makes her appearance as well."

"Vicky?" Kris said.

"Mother's joke. She named her Victoria."

Everyone needed time to let that sink in, take root and have any chance of being considered reality.

"What do we know about Victoria?" Kris asked.

"Not a lot. She kind of disappeared into some kind of harem on Greenfeld. Hank did a lot of traveling, part of his education. Vicky's pretty much a mystery. But she can't be too much of a problem," Grampa said, looking sideways at Kris. "After all, she's just a Greenfeld girl."

Kris snorted. "Yeah, right. And I was just supposed to be Brother's campaign manager." Two years ago, given a choice, who would have considered her the deadlier of the two siblings.

A beep came from Trouble's pocket. He pulled out a reader, scanned it, and shook his head. "Don't these folks know that you don't cause Trouble trouble unless you want big trouble."

"Trouble?" Kris asked.

"Seems they've settled on a job for you and they're too cowardly to say it to your face . . . so they've deputized me for the job. They're going to pay for that."

"Where to now?" Kris asked, keeping her expectations low.

"You like shopping?"

That was *not* one Kris expected. "I hate shopping."

"You'll love this. They've got a job for you about as far from the Rim as they can go. Your next assignment is to the Wardhaven Naval Purchasing detachment on New Eden."

"The first colony ever!" Jack frowned at Kris.

"The very same. With all it's industry, gun control laws, police, and, oh, decadence and wild parties."

"I'll be buying laser cannons and electronic gizmos?" Kris said, insisting that hope spring eternal.

Grampa shook his head. "Nope, paperclips, general office supplies, that sort of stuff."

Kris pushed back from the table. "They're joking."

"Nope. Jack, you go along as her personal liaison with embassy security and the local cops. Penny, you're tagged to work with intel. I'll let you guess where all of you fit into keeping Kris safe from Peterwald's vengeance."

Kris pulled herself back up to the table and picked up her glass. It was truly empty; she watched the last drip roll around in the bottom. They had her. Trapped and worthless as the dregs of this shake. Or maybe not. "Tell them I'll go if they throw in Chief Beni for product quality control."

"For paper clips?" Penny asked, giving Kris a raised eyebrow that says volumes without a word.

"Or whatever," Kris said, wrapping herself in all the injured innocence she could find handy. It wasn't much.

"You folks have fun," Abby said. "New Eden is one place I have been and one place in human space I am not going back to."

"Oh," said Kris. "But you are. You have a new employer. One you can't refuse. Salary to be negotiated, but you are most definitely working for me now, lady. You've shown that you have a price. You're mine for as much of you as money will buy."

"This I want to see," said Jack.

About the Author

Mike Shepherd grew up Navy. It taught him early about change and the chain of command. He's worked as a bartender and cab driver, personnel advisor and labor negotiator. Now retired from building databases about the endangered critters of the Pacific Northwest, he's looking forward to some serious writing.

Mike lives in Vancouver, Washington, with his wife, Ellen, and her mother. He enjoys reading, writing, watching grandchildren for story ideas, and upgrading his computer—all are never ending.

Oh, and working on Kris's next book, *Kris Longknife*: *Audacious*.

You may reach him at Mike_Shepherd@comcast.net.

THE ULTIMATE IN
SCIENCE FICTION AND FANTASY!

From magical tales of distant worlds to stories of
technological advances beyond the grasp of man, Penguin has
everything you need to stretch your imagination to its limits.

penguin.com

ACE
Get the latest information on favorites like
William Gibson, T.A. Barron, Brian Jacques,
Ursula Le Guin, Sharon Shinn, and Charlaine Harris,
as well as updates on the best new authors.

Roc
Escape with Harry Turtledove, Anne Bishop,
S.M. Stirling, Simon Green, Chris Bunch, Jim Butcher,
E.E. Knight, and many others—plus news on the
latest and hottest in science fiction and fantasy.

DAW
Mercedes Lackey, Kristen Britain, Tanya Huff,
Tad Williams, C.J. Cherryh, and many more—
DAW has something to satisfy the cravings of any
science fiction and fantasy lover.
Also visit dawbooks.com.

*Get the best of science fiction and fantasy
at your fingertips!*